Raves for *Sanctuary*:

"In Lackey's well-crafted third Dragon Jousters book, wing-leader Kiron, the former serf known as Vetch, and a disparate group of refugees from the countries of Alta and Tia flee to the desert, to a hidden refuge that the gods have uncovered and named Sanctuary. Spot-on dialogue and just the right amount of exposition mark this rip-roaring adventure as superior fantasy fare." —*Publishers Weekly*

"The tension is palpable throught as Lackey wraps up the trilogy begun by *Joust* in fine style, remaining true to the characters and their world." —*Booklist*

"Fans of dragon-powered fantasy sagas will thoroughly enjoy how Lackey delves into the legendary creatures and their relationship with their human riders." —*The Barnes & Noble Review*

"One of Lackey's trademarks is her sympathetic characters, and she doesn't disappoint here. Fans will enjoy this satisfying conclusion to the 'Dragon Jousters' series." —*Romantic Times*

SANCTUARY

NOVELS BY **MERCEDES LACKEY**
available from DAW Books:

THE HERALDS OF VALDEMAR
ARROWS OF THE QUEEN
ARROW'S FLIGHT
ARROW'S FALL

THE LAST HERALD-MAGE
MAGIC'S PAWN
MAGIC'S PROMISE
MAGIC'S PRICE

THE MAGE WINDS
WINDS OF FATE
WINDS OF CHANGE
WINDS OF FURY

THE MAGE STORMS
STORM WARNING
STORM RISING
STORM BREAKING

VOWS AND HONOR
THE OATHBOUND
OATHBREAKERS
OATHBLOOD

BY THE SWORD
BRIGHTLY BURNING
TAKE A THIEF
EXILE'S HONOR
EXILE'S VALOR

VALDEMAR ANTHOLOGIES:
SWORD OF ICE
SUN IN GLORY
CROSSROADS

Written with **LARRY DIXON:**

THE MAGE WARS
THE BLACK GRYPHON
THE WHITE GRYPHON
THE SILVER GRYPHON

DARIAN'S TALE
OWLFLIGHT
OWLSIGHT
OWLKNIGHT

OTHER NOVELS:

THE BLACK SWAN

THE DRAGON JOUSTERS
JOUST
ALTA
SANCTUARY

THE ELEMENTAL MASTERS
THE SERPENT'S SHADOW
THE GATES OF SLEEP
PHOENIX AND ASHES
THE WIZARD OF LONDON

And don't miss:
THE VALDEMAR COMPANION
Edited by John Helfers and Denise Little

SANCTUARY

SANCTUARY

Book Three of *The Dragon Jousters*

MERCEDES LACKEY

DAW BOOKS, INC.

DONALD A. WOLLHEIM, FOUNDER

375 Hudson Street, New York, NY 10014

ELIZABETH R. WOLLHEIM
SHEILA E. GILBERT
PUBLISHERS

http://www.dawbooks.com

First Paperback Printing, May 2006

1 2 3 4 5 6 7 8 9

DAW TRADEMARK REGISTERED
U.S. PAT. OFF. AND FOREIGN COUNTRIES
—MARCA REGISTRADA
HECHO EN U.S.A.

PRINTED IN THE U.S.A.

Dedicated to the Lunatics.
You know who you are.

 ONE

IT was the silent, blue time before dawn. The air
hung cool and still above the pale sand, not a hint,
not a breath of breeze, so still one could hear the tick of
grain against grain as a thin trickle at the crest of a
dune. The desert stretched out all around Sanctuary, as
if beneath the calming hand of a god. Or a goddess,
perhaps; Nofet, whom the Altans called Nefer-et, the
Goddess of Night, had not yet withdrawn the hem of
her robe from the land. Re-Haket, the sun, still lingered in the Summerland beyond the Star Bridge.

It would not be cool for much longer, nor still.

Kiron stood on the roof of one of the four buildings
that surrounded a courtyard that had been given over
for use as the dragons' sand wallow and leaned on the

parapet to watch the dawn come in over the desert. Not difficult; at this point, although there were still refugees finding their way here all the time with the help of the Bedu (also called the Veiled Ones), there was no structure in the entire city that was more than three buildings away from the open sand.

He was, given a choice, not usually awake at this time. But in a little while, the dragons would, slowly, begin to rouse from their slumber, and they would be hungry. Here in Sanctuary, unlike in Alta and Tia, there was no butchery from which to feed them, no Temple sacrifices to provide the carcasses. If the dragons wished to eat, they must hunt like their wild brethren. Hunts were always more successful when the Jouster and dragon hunted as a team. So if the dragons wished to eat, their riders must waken and go out with them.

Kiron might be the first one awake and out today, but by now, the others of his wing were stirring at the very least. He generally didn't beat the rest by very much. Besides, the terrible heat of the desert at midday in the middle of the Dry meant that their schedules were much changed from Alta. Here, they flew at dawn and dusk, and spent the hottest part of the day well away from the burning rays of the sun.

The sun: Altan Re-Haket was not the kindly Solar Disk, the bringer of life here—oh, no—not "beautiful with banners." He was not even the Re-Haket that the Tians knew. Here in the desert, he wore the harsher

visage of Se-ahketh, the Tester, the Scourge of Fire, he
who had no mercy, only an unwinking Eye that tested
to destruction. Even the dragons sheltered beneath a
canopy from His Eye at midday. Sometimes Kiron wondered—was this where the Magi of Alta had gotten the
idea for *their* unwinking Eye, *their* scourge of fire?

Kiron preferred to greet Avatre with a clear head
and unclouded eyes, this morning especially, because
it was all the more needful on this day that each
dragon of the wing fly to the hunt and return with
prey before the sun reached its zenith. Because today,
they had another reason besides the sun's implacable
hammer to be well in shelter. There would be a great
sandstorm today, so said Kaleth, and Kiron saw no
reason to disbelieve him.

And when Kaleth meant a "great" sandstorm, he
was not speaking of a quarter day of wind and blowing sand. Kiron and the others had not yet weathered
a "great" sandstorm, but the Veiled Ones had, and so
had Kaleth; the Midnight *kamiseen*, the storm without
rain that brought the darkness of night at midday. The
Bedu spoke feelingly of a sky black at midday, of wind
too strong to stand against, of air so thick with dust
and grit you could not breathe—

—of a storm full of sand like millions of miniscule
knives that flayed clothing from the body, and flesh
from bone, and packed every open orifice with wind-
driven dirt. Get in the shelter of a rock or a dune, and
you *might* survive, if you could get a clear space for

your face, breathe through cloth, and manage to keep from being buried alive.

There was no sign of such a storm. The thin, clear light and the cloudless sky held nothing but peace.

Kiron did not trust the promise of such "peace." He trusted Kaleth.

Kaleth was, without a doubt, god-touched. Had he not led them all here, to the once-buried city of legend they now called Sanctuary? If he said such a storm would blow up, Kiron would believe him. Certainly the Veiled Ones did. Those within the area of the storm had either taken themselves out of its path, or moved into the city, little though they liked living within walls even for a single day.

Kiron nodded to himself, as he looked out over a city that seemed very strange to the eyes of one accustomed to the straight, clean lines of the buildings of Alta and Tia. Once, Kaleth (then *Prince* Kaleth) had been nothing more than the quiet, studious twin brother of the more charismatic Prince Toreth. True, he, with Toreth, was one of the four designated heirs to the Thrones of Alta, but until Toreth had been murdered, he had been something of a cipher to most.

Well, he certainly wasn't a cipher now. A Winged One of Alta, in truth, *and* a Priest of Haras of Tia, he spoke for the gods of both peoples.

Gods, which were, Kiron was coming to understand, one and the same. Or at least, there was so little difference it mattered not at all.

Kaleth was accepted by the Veiled Ones, the Wanderers of the desert, the Blue People, as a Seer, a Hand of the gods and a Mouth of the People as well. And if Kiron only had an imperfect understanding of what *that* meant, well, he knew it was a position of great respect, and that was enough for him.

As the city slumbered under the clear, predawn sky, Sanctuary hardly looked like a city at all, more like a collection of squared-off mounds, very like wind-sculpted, sand-polished mastabas, nearly the same color as the sand around them. Hardly surprising no one had found it until Kaleth led the Veiled Ones to it; even if it had not been buried beneath the dunes, when Kiron thought of a city, he thought—well, he thought of nothing at all like this. To his mind, the word "city" called up the image of the tall, angular sandstone or granite edifices of Mefis, the capital of Tia, carved and painted with images of the gods and Great Kings, reaching five, six, ten times the height of a man. Or the "city" of his slave days, the mud-brick, two-storied, mathematically laid out buildings along the narrow streets where ordinary folk dwelled. Or, possibly, the white-columned, long, low buildings of Alta, reflected in the shining surfaces of her seven ring-shaped canals. He did not think of buildings the color of sand, with rounded corners and edges, walls as thick as a man's arm was long, and scarcely an opening to be seen anywhere.

But that was because the buildings of Sanctuary

were armored against the blistering desert heat by the thickness of their stone walls, and against the sand-storm by their curves. Not even the dragons, much as they reveled in heat, spent more time in the sun than they could help, once the great disk had reached past the point of midmorning. Some of the buildings, in fact, were mere antechambers into a labyrinth of rooms carved out of the rock bed beneath the sand, a network of man-made caves which all connected eventually to that most precious of desert treasures, the water source that lay at the heart of Sanctuary itself.

Water. Water was the reason for anything made by man in the desert. Men sought for it, fought over it, bartered what was most precious to them for it, killed and died for it and for lack of it. And yet here, through long years gone, and until the gods permitted it to be found again, was a kingdom's ransom of the precious stuff.

Beneath the sand, beneath the rock that lay beneath the sand, there flowed a river of the purest water, a quiet, steady stream, clear and cool, that widened here into a channel as wide as Great Mother River, and deep enough that it took an effort to touch the bottom, before narrowing again and flowing onward toward the Altan delta. Kiron supposed it must come to the surface at some point, but no one had yet been able to pinpoint that spot, not even the wise desert dwellers, the Veiled Ones, who themselves had (until now) not even guessed that here was the life-giver that fed a great many of their oases. Here was the reason for Sanctuary existing at all, the reason it had been built in the far past. Here was the reason why Sanctuary was able to prosper now. Even the Veiled Ones required water, and in this part of the desert that they called the Furnace and the Anvil of the Gods, they deemed it more valuable than the caches of gold that the new owners of Sanctuary were still discovering when wind freed another building from the grip of the sand.

Which might happen today, actually. Kaleth had hinted as much, calling the storm the instrument of the gods, and saying that in the past, it had given what was needed when it was needed. And, certainly, Sanctuary was still surrounded on all sides by dunes and hard-packed sand. There was no telling what might lie beneath some of those mounds.

A voice behind him interrupted his thoughts. "What do you think the sandstorm will show us when it passes?"

"Sometimes, I wonder if it isn't only the dragons' thoughts you can read, Aket-ten," Kiron laughed, turning to wrinkle his nose at the only female Jouster—to his knowledge—ever to fly a dragon.

Aket-ten, sister to his good friend Orest, dimpled at him, as awake and alert as if this was midday. Well, she always had been a lover of the morning, already up and doing while he and Orest were still shaking the sleep from their eyes. It was a small fault, that. She was in all other ways, to his mind anyway, anything that anyone could ask for in a companion.

Not perfect, but who wanted perfection? It would be far too tiring to have to live up to the perfection of another. A companion who had flaws, now, that meant that you could have an affectionate rivalry without feeling as if there was no chance that you could ever come up to the standards set by your friend.

She was not too tall, but Kiron himself was by no means overly tall. Besides, the best Jousters were light and lean, for the less of a burden they were to their mounts, the better. Light and lean, Aket-ten certainly was, reed-slim and shorter than he, and he was no giant. Her lively black eyes met his with a look of acceptance and candor, and her ready smile warmed them further with good humor. If she did not have the finely chiseled and perfectly regular features of one of the images of the goddesses, she had a face that was full of personality. Since coming to Sanctuary she had chosen to forsake wigs and wear her own blue-black hair cut in the short helmet style favored by the rest of the wing, which made her look superficially like one of them, but the gentle curves under her simple linen tunic made it clear with only a second glance that this was no boy.

She wasn't beautiful, but truth to tell, Kiron found himself somewhat intimidated by beauty. The elegance of court ladies made him flush and feel tongue-tied, and *that* was when they had ignored him. When they had spoken to him or glanced at him or—worst of all—smiled, he found himself looking for someone to hide behind. But when Aket-ten smiled, which was far more often here than she had back in Alta, she always made him smile in return. What more could anyone ask?

Once one of the Fledglings of the Altan Temple of the Twins, one of her strongest Gifts was that of Silent Speech with animals. While in the past she had sometimes disparaged herself for having such a "minor" Gift, it had been worth more even than being god-touched on that black day when Kaleth's twin brother, Toreth, had been murdered by the Magi, and his dragon had nearly thrown herself (and every other dragon in the compound) into suicidal hysterics with grief.

Until first Ari, the Tian Jouster, then Kiron, and then the eight other Altan boys had raised dragons themselves, from the egg, it had been unthinkable that a dragon should actually have a bond of affection with its Jouster. Dragons were, at best, controllable, and only when drugged with the dust made from a dried desert berry called *tala*. No one had ever thought that a bonded dragon, if it lost its Jouster, would choose to give its loyalty to another.

But that was exactly what had happened when Toreth died, and his midnight-blue-and-shaded-silver dragon Re-eth-katen had nearly died of her grief and loss. When Aket-ten "spoke" to Re-eth-katen and comforted her, that dragon had bonded again to the Fledgling Priestess, and had become *her* dragon, renamed Re-eth-ke, thus making Aket-ten the first ever female in the Jousters' Compound as anything other than servant or couch companion. Just as well, since it had only been possible for her to hide from the increasingly imperious demands of the Magi in that one place in all of Alta. The dragons did not like the Magi, and not all the *tala* in the world could stop them from making that dislike evident.

The feeling of animosity was mutual, and the Magi had made it their business to remove the Jousters—heroes of the war—by steady attrition.

"Well, if you're thinking that we're better off *here*, no matter how hard life is, than *there*, well, I agree with you," Aket-ten said. "I'd rather starve and bathe in sand than stay in Alta one moment longer. Not," she added with a shiver, "that I think I'd be aware of where I was by now if I *had* stayed there."

Kiron nodded and grimaced. Aket-ten was clever (if, perhaps, sometimes a little too inclined to flaunt that cleverness), brave (if a bit rash and headstrong), loyal (if stubborn), kind (if a little sharp-tongued), and the best sort of friend.

And she was right. If she'd stayed—well, if any of them had stayed—they'd probably be half dead from injuries and overwork, or entirely dead. Except for Aket-ten, who would be locked up in the Magi's Tower of Wisdom with the rest of the Winged Ones, somehow being drained to give the Magi the strength for their magic.

But—thanks mainly to Kaleth—they'd escaped. They were safe in Sanctuary, and if the future was shrouded in uncertainty, it was at least a future that held freedom. As for Aket-ten, it was Kiron's hope she was inclining toward becoming more than just a "friend" of late, though he was not pushing too hard. Aket-ten could also be very stubborn if pushed, and hated with a great passion the least hint that she was being pressured into doing anything.

He probably had the Magi to thank for that. Still, his position could be much worse. He'd once thought that she harbored a secret passion for Toreth, and that had turned out to be false. The last thing he wanted to do was to give her even the faintest of impressions that he was putting pressure on her. Aket-ten was not a desert antelope to be swooped down upon, knocked over, and devoured. Rather, she was like her own blue-black dragon Re-eth-ke, to be courted with circumspection, tact, and delicacy, so that when she made up her own mind, it was with the impression that *she* had been the one who'd had the idea in the first place.

She came up beside him to lean on the parapet and look down into the sand pit where the dragons were just beginning to stir. All the dragons shared a sand wallow, rather than each having their own as they had back in Alta. There hadn't been much of a choice in that; the Jousters' Compound had been tended by a small army of servants, builders, and slaves. There were no slaves here in Sanctuary, and precious few servants, and none to spare for building something like the complex of quarters and sand wallows the dragons were used to. Fortunately, they were all, with the exceptions of Avatre, and Ari's huge gold-emerald-and-blue dragon Kashet, out of the same batch of eggs. All but Kashet had romped together as nestlings and fledglings, and had trained together, under the guidance of Kiron and Avatre, from the beginning of their lives. There was no serious quarreling, much less the fighting that happened among unrelated wild-caught Jousting dragons, and though there might be the occasional squabble, it was soon sorted out without much worse than a swat or a nip or two. For her part, although the lovely scarlet Avatre reacted to being forced to share her sand with the "infants" with a pained disdain that was sometimes quite funny to see, she never bullied them.

As for Kashet, who might have been expected to react poorly to the herd of youngsters, the eldest of the dragons actually took to the half-grown dragonets with great tolerance and even some show of occasional pleasure.

"I wouldn't even try to get inside your thoughts," Aket-ten teased. "I'd find myself listening to echoes."

"Hah," was all he replied. "You only think that because you've spent so much time around your brother, all boys have heads as empty as last-year's *latas* pod."

"Last year's *latas* pod isn't empty!" her brother Orest exclaimed, coming up the stairs to flank Kiron on his right. "It is *full* of the seeds of wisdom, I will have you know! Ah, they're starting to stir."

He leaned over and made kissing noises at his own beetle-blue dragon, who rewarded his attention by slowly raising his bright blue head from the sand wallow and turning to gaze at Orest with sleep-glazed ruby-colored eyes.

Orest's face was full of such infatuation that Kiron smiled. Not that he was under any illusions that *he* didn't look like that around Avatre. It was quite clear to anyone with eyes that Orest and Aket-ten were brother and sister; in fact, at first glance, they might look like brother and brother. Both were slim, with broad cheekbones but delicate chins, making their faces the same almond shape, and both had the same merry eyes.

"Come on, little prince, it is time to greet the sun with sharp eyes and a clear head," Orest cooed down at his dragon, coaxingly. "You need to wake up, precious jewel. We need to be in the air quickly this morning." He turned to his sister. "You *did* remember to tell them all about the sandstorm, didn't you?"

"Last night before they went to sleep," she promised, with a hint of reproach. "You don't think I'd have forgotten *that!* They know. I was careful not to confuse them either. When I told them, I took care to show them images of what they know—a black storm, wicked wind, and evil air currents. That was enough. He's just sleepy from the heat of the sand; he'll remember it for himself in a moment and he'll be more impatient than you to get hunting."

Without waiting to hear what her brother had to say, she turned and skipped down the staircase on the inside wall of the pit, to trot along the ledge surrounding the neck-deep sand until she came to where her own dragon was just now waking.

"Don't tease her, you know how she feels about her responsibilities," Kiron told his friend. "Look, see! Your *little prince* has just remembered that if he doesn't get up in the sky soon, he might not eat today."

And indeed, the young male had raised his head to look to his rider with sense and a bit of urgency in his gaze. The dragon snorted at Orest with impatience, and began to pull himself up out of his wallow, golden sand cascading from a blue back, without another word of coaxing from the young Jouster.

A familiar whine from just beyond Orest's dragon caught Kiron's attention, especially when it was paired with an equally familiar snort. He followed Aket-ten down into the pit, to make his way in the opposite direction from the one she'd taken.

Kashet and Avatre had taken to sleeping near to each other; not precisely curled up together, but they did seem to appreciate one another's company. Perhaps Avatre remembered Kashet from her earliest days in the Tian Jousters' Compound, when Kashet had been in the next pen over, before she and Kiron (then called Vetch) had escaped and fled northward to Alta with Ari's help. Certainly Kashet remembered her.

He remembered Kiron, too, and with *quite* evident affection. The huge dragon snorted again when Kiron came near, and craned his emerald-and-blue neck over Avatre to blow his hot breath into Kiron's hair.

Whereupon Avatre bristled with jealousy and shoved his head aside, claiming *her* rider for herself. Kiron had to laugh as she tried to puff herself up and interpose herself between him and her rival for his affections. Kashet could bowl her over without even taking thought for it, even now. She had a hot temper to match her fiery colors when she was irritated.

Fortunately, Kashet was a good-natured soul, and— well, it was possible that there was some instinctive behavior involved, too. Most male animals would put up with things from females that they would never tolerate in another male.

"Peace, little one!" he told her, as she shoved him a little off balance and tried to look up at him in adoration with one eye while she glared at Kashet out of the other. "You are first in my heart, always—and Ari will be here any moment and Kashet will cease to remember that I live."

"Ari is here now," called a voice from above, and Kashet reared up to his full height at the sound of that voice, which put his head well above the level of the roof. Ari looked down over the parapet of the building next to the one that Kiron, Orest, and the other members of Kiron's wing (except Aket-ten) shared, waved to his protégé, then reached up to scratch the bony eye ridges of his own dragon as Kashet rested his chin on the parapet and sighed gustily. As Kiron had predicted, Kashet was now quite oblivious to the fact that the younger man even existed, which made Avatre perfectly pleased.

Ari alone stood out from among the Altan inhabitants of Sanctuary as noticeably different. He was much darker, to begin with; here in the desert, he had tanned to the color of old leather, while the Altans had gone the same golden brown as a properly baked loaf of barley bread. His face was broader than the Altan "type," his chin stronger, his eyes a shade of brown that was very near to black.

Kiron would have liked to remain there, giving Avatre the caresses and affection she lived for, but there was no leisure for that this morning. The cramped quarters of the sand pit made it necessary for almost everyone to leave in order to get saddled, which would mean another delay in taking to the air, and this was a day when no one could afford much in the way of a delay.

Kashet was the first to get out—by virtue of his size and strength, he simply hooked his front talons into the parapet and *climbed* out over the roof. The first time he'd done that, Kiron hadn't been the only one who'd gasped and shrunk back, expecting the wall to come down. But either they were all very lucky, or Kashet was a shrewd judge of construction; he hadn't left more than a scratch or two on the top of the wall. Kiron still didn't know *what* the walls of Sanctuary were made of. It looked like hard-packed sand, or sandstone, but it wasn't, and it was tougher and stronger than anything Kiron had ever seen before. The walls weren't made of stone blocks either; the entire city could have been carved from single pieces of stone. There were no signs of seams or block lines, and although the corners and edges were all rounded as if scoured that way, at a guess Kiron would have said that they had been carved or sculpted that way on purpose from the beginning, given that nothing much seemed to mark them. Whatever material those walls were made of, it was something that stood up to the abuse of dragons climbing all over them.

Nor could Kiron have put an original purpose to this courtyard that now served as the dragons' sand wallow. When the wing had come to Sanctuary, the space had been filled with sand still, left that way on purpose for the dragons' use, and the doors and windows that had once looked into the yard had been blocked up at Kaleth's orders. It was about the size of the landing courtyard at the Jousters' Compound in Tia, which made it just about big enough for ten dragons. Now—if somehow, there should be more dragons one day—

I will leave that in the hands of the gods, Kiron told himself. The gods had provided for these ten; he would have faith that they would provide in the future. Or else he and Ari would come up with some clever plan to create more wallows and shelters somehow.

Though the sands were not heated, as were the sands of the pens back in the Compounds, they didn't yet need to be. The stone of the buildings and the sand itself stored enough heat over the course of the day to keep the dragons comfortable all night. And as for heating the sands in the winter— Well, the eccentric Akkadian Healer and Magus Heklatis had some ideas on that score, and Kiron was content to leave it at that. Certainly the wild dragons managed; theirs could, too. At least there would be no cold rains to contend with.

"Time to go, my son," Ari told his dragon. "No one else can move until you do." With a grunt, Kashet heaved himself up; first getting his forequarters up to the parapet, then carefully planting hindclaws in the blocked-up window-slits and slithering the rest of himself over the edge.

Avatre uttered what sounded like a sigh of relief. She was still small enough that she could use the open staircase as a climbing aid, and that was what she did, leaving the rest of the dragonets the room to shake themselves free of the sand and follow her lead. She and Kashet shared the roof of Ari's building as their harnessing stop; six of the eight dragonets made use of the other three roofs, two apiece, leaving the pit to Reeth-ke and Orest's striking blue Wastet.

Harnessing these days was a far cry from the complicated affair it had been back when the dragons were part of Alta's (and Tia's) fighting forces. The saddles were the same, but there was no armor, no helmets, and no Jousting lances.

Not that they were unarmed. Especially not when hunting. Aristocratic Gan had trained his gentle green dragonet Khaleph to tolerate a light hunting spear flying past his head, so his saddle had a quiver of javelins attached to it. Orest, Ari, Pe-atep, and Aket-ten could get their mounts to put up with arrows. The rest of them used slings and stones—not much good at bringing down game of the size a dragon needed, but good enough to distract, irritate, or with luck, stun, and that was all the opening a dragon could ask for.

No making formations for this task; dragons needed a big hunting territory, and each of them had his (or her) preferred ground. By common consent, Aket-ten and Re-eth-ke got what was nearest Sanctuary, and the rest of them simply let their dragons define the hunting ranges as they saw fit.

They were up and into the air as soon as they were strapped into their saddles, scattering to the four directions. Much as Kiron would have liked to hunt alongside Aket-ten, the plain fact was that it was impossible. Neither dragon would have tolerated another in her hunting grounds.

So he and Avatre launched themselves into the soft blue eye of the cloudless morning sky, and headed for their allotment without a backward glance at Aket-ten and Re-eth-he. Later, perhaps, if they both got in well ahead of the storm, they could fly together. First things first.

Kiron was minded to chase wild ass this morning; they hadn't preyed on those herds in a while, and if they were going to have anything left to bring back for Avatre's evening meal after Avatre ate her fill, it would have to be a substantial kill. That meant flying to the farthest extent of Avatre's hunting range, where the sand gave way to scrubby hills and wadis, but she was fresh and strong, and the wind was in their favor. Provided that they made a kill quickly, they would beat the storm back in plenty of time.

So with a quick prayer to Besh, the pot-bellied, bandy-legged luck god, Kiron began to scan the horizon and, pragmatically, made sure he had a heavy stone for his sling.

 **TWO**

THE sun was only halfway above the horizon as Kiron gave Avatre signals with hand and legs that she was to gain height. She pumped her wide red wings as hard as she could, valiantly answering his direction. The only problem with flying this early was that there were no thermals to ride, and every wingbeat a dragon took came with heavy labor. A dragon's preferred method of flight was to glide from thermal to thermal, spiraling up on the rising current of air, and gliding down to the next thermal, with as few wingbeats in between as possible. Such a flying style saved energy, and the one thing that a flying dragon needed a lot of was energy. It was Kiron's preferred method too; riding dragonback was hard work, though you'd never know that from the serene wall paintings of Jousters in the sky in both Tia and Alta. With every downward stroke, he was flung back against the cantle of his saddle as Avatre surged forward, and with every upward sweep he hung weightless for just an unnerving moment, then fell forward against the pommel. Jousters learned to cope with this, of course; he felt what she was going to do with his legs and he had learned to shift his weight to make himself less of a burden, but it was hard work for both of them, and he always felt guilty about putting her to the extra effort of carrying him when she had to work this hard to get in the air.

Below them, Sanctuary dwindled to a child's play village made of sand, in the midst of a sea of sand, with the other dragons scattering in all directions, the only spots of color against the pale sweeps of the dunes. He sometimes wondered how the dragons felt about this new life; were they angry because food no longer was delivered to them? Or did they prefer to make kills on their own? He didn't detect any new grumpiness in Avatre's mood; the contrary, actually. He thought that she liked hunting, and he knew for certain that this dry, hot desert suited her. Even at sun's zenith, when the dragons moved out of the direct rays, they didn't stay out of the heat for too very long.

Avatre knew "her" territory now, and headed for it without prompting. He squinted against the light of the rising sun, and sighted in on their goal, the far-off hills and wadis where the wild ass herd roamed. It was cold up here in the morning, but he shrugged off the chill; already the sun on his skin was warming him, and before very long he knew that it would stop being pleasant and start being uncomfortable, and he would be glad of the coolness of the upper air. By the time they headed back, he would be wishing for just a breath of the chill of early morning.

He kept an eye on the ground beneath them, because it was always possible—not likely, but possible—that he would spot something worth chasing even before they got to the wadis.

Besides, every flight was different. You never knew what you were going to see. A desert horned lark singing his heart out as he soared into the blue bowl of the heavens, a viper sinuously leaving "s" marks in the sand of a dune below—or a wild dragon. There were more of those about than he would have thought. He wondered how many of them had been Tian Jousting dragons. Once Heklatis had discovered the way to neutralize *tala* and render it ineffective at drugging dragons into submission, there was no way, short of love alone, that a dragon could be induced to remain with a Jouster. And the dragons that had escaped from Tian Jousters would probably not have gone back to their old territories. They would have been wary even if they *had* been inclined to fly all that way back; after all, that was where they had been captured as fledglings.

Avatre reached a height she found comfortable—somehow, he had not been able yet to understand how—dragons could "read" the invisible currents of the sky—and knew by that where their flight would come with the least effort. She settled into the longer, slower wingbeats that moved her forward rather than upward, and he leaned down over her shoulder to make himself less of a drag on her progress.

The sands seemed empty of life this morning, but with Kaleth's prediction of a sandstorm, it could be that the wildlife sensed its approach, and had taken to shelter early.

Only when they reached the wadis, and the landscape beneath them turned from undulating waves to the hard earth and rock, cut by the occasional dry wash, and punctuated with wind-eroded mastabas, did he start to see signs of life. Birds flitted from one bit of scrub to another; he saw a desert hare loping away as fast as its legs could take it, and finally, in the distance—the only cloud he'd seen today, a cloud of dust.

The sort of dust raised by a herd or a group of animals.

Avatre spotted it at the same time that he did, and reacted to it sooner, changing her course and heading as straight as the flight of an arrow for the sign of game on the horizon. If Aket-ten was right, the dragons understood a fair amount of what she tried to tell them, and Avatre would know that something bad was coming and there would be no afternoon hunt.

Or, if her instincts were as good as those of the wild animals, she would feel the urge to get under cover warring with her hunger, and that should also add to her eagerness. Now, as long as she didn't get *too* eager. . . .

He noticed after a moment that she was angling slightly upward again, which meant she was going to try for an attack from high above, which would add to her speed. Good for a quick kill, but not so good for him! He would have to get his stone off at the last moment, and wouldn't be able to make another cast. Then, if he missed, and she missed, and the herd stood at bay or got into a wadi, there might not be a second chance.

He freed one hand from the saddle, felt for the biggest stone in his ammunition pouch, and, with his eyes still on the approaching dust cloud, slipped it one-handed into the sling in his lap. He wouldn't drop the sling into the ready position until he was almost onto the target, otherwise he risked losing the stone before he could throw it.

Avatre's eyes were better than his; he felt her putting more effort into her wingbeats. She must have seen the animals in the dust cloud. Beneath his legs and the hand on her shoulder, her skin was hot as a kiln, a sign that she was excited. Even if she could not yet see the prey, she knew where it was.

The amount of dust being kicked up increased; the herd was in a canter now. They must have been seen. The creatures of this part of the desert had not known an aerial predator before the dragons came, but they surely knew one when they saw it now.

A pity, that. No more easy hunts.

Three hard wingbeats that bucked Kiron back against the cantle of the saddle, and they were directly above of the herd. He looked down on the brown backs, through a haze of dust as they ran, weaving back and forth to elude the shape above them. He smelled them; hot dust, animal sweat, even as far above them as Avatre was. Three wingbeats more, and they were pulling ahead of the lead ass. And that was when Avatre stalled, giving him just enough warning to brace himself, and did a wingover, plunging down toward the herd of asses with wings folded and Kiron pressed tightly against her neck.

She plummeted for a point well ahead and to one side of them of them, and did a quick turn, still halfway above them and still diving, to face them without losing any significant speed. With frantic brays, the ass herd broke right down the middle as she pulled up out of her dive with a snap of opening wings and raced straight at them, head outstretched. Roughly half went left, the other half right, but as there always is, there was one individual who couldn't make up her mind to go in either direction. Kiron pulled the sling out of his lap in a practiced movement as Avatre made straight for the indecisive one, whirled it, and let the stone fly as Avatre pulled up, skimming just above the tops of the mare's ears.

The stone struck her full in the forehead, and she went down. Kiron crouched down in the saddle again and held on for dear life.

As the straps holding him in cut into his flesh, Avatre did a second wingover and plunged back down, all four sets of talons extended. Even as the ass was trying to struggle to its feet, Avatre struck it from above and behind, killing it instantly with a jolt that sent Kiron into the pommel of the saddle again.

The rush of wind stopped; dust began to settle around them. The only sounds were of Avatre settling herself and the hoofbeats and braying of the retreating asses.

She mantled her sunrise-colored wings over her prey and began tearing into it before the dust had even settled. The rest of the herd, sensing that the chosen victim had fallen, stopped dead and turned their heads to look. The air was full of the smell of hot sweat, dust, and blood.

Sometimes Kiron felt sorry for the prey, but today had been a quick, clean kill. And he was used to seeing Avatre killing and eating now; it was with no sense of revulsion that he slid down out of her saddle and left her to her feeding. No, his thought was just to make sure that the mare they'd taken down hadn't had a foal at heel. Such indecisiveness sometimes meant the prey was guarding a little one.

There was no sign of a loose or abandoned foal in the herd. In a way, that was a pity; he would have caught it and brought it back alive, to be tamed and added to the Sanctuary animals. So far, all they had was a few donkeys, goats, and camels. Granted, keeping them fed was a chore. Sand did not make good pasturage for anything.

Still, the original inhabitants must have managed in some way. They just needed to find out how. And there was no doubt that having working animals made life easier for the humans. If they had enough asses or donkeys for instance, they could operate a water wheel to bring water to the surface to irrigate small gardens.

Another day, perhaps. As the ass herd formed up again and sped off to the shelter of the wadis, Kiron eyed the sun. The sun-disk of Re-Haket had not yet approached the point that marked "danger," but it was time to get on with his part of the work.

With the edge taken off Avatre's hunger, it was possible to approach her and work side by side with her on her kill without her bristling or even snapping at him. She might love him past all understanding, and he, her in return, but love does not trump a growling stomach for a dragon. She'd already cleaned out the viscera, which was actually helpful, as it made the butchering go easier and a lot cleaner.

He butchered the hindquarters for packing up, while she tore into the front. By this time she had eaten the head, so it wasn't so bad . . . there was nothing quite as unnerving as watching a dragon take apart a skull, unless it was to have the reproachful (albeit dead) gaze of the prey seemingly focused on you. That was one problem the butchers at the Jousters' Courts of both Alta and Tia had never been forced to deal with.

He had sacks that he tried to make of equal weight when she had finally eaten her fill. He wasn't going to leave anything behind; this was a little more than Avatre would eat right now, since her growth had stalled out and she wouldn't be flying this afternoon, but one of the others might not be as lucky in the hunt as he and Avatre had been. As it was, with the burden of four bags of animal parts and himself, when Avatre lumbered into the air again, it was a good thing that the sands had heated up enough to give them some thermal lift. She labored hard the entire way home, and by the time they reached the city, she was as tired as if she had flown a full patrol with a fight at the end of it.

The flight back to Sanctuary was unexceptional; Avatre was soon back in the pen, ready for a buffing and oiling, waiting patiently for Kiron to haul the sacks of meat into temporary storage. They were the first back, despite having taken the longest flight out (or so he guessed), but he had just begun scouring Avatre's ruby-scaled hide with sand when Ari and Kashet came in to land on the rooftop above. Kashet's landing was, as ever, a thing of precision. There was no better flier than Ari's big blue.

"How went the hunt?" he called up, since he couldn't see anything of Kashet but the dragon's head from his vantage point below.

"Three gazelles. Kashet had one, and I brought the other two back, one for Kashet later and one in case someone didn't do so well," Ari replied, and grunted with the effort of taking sacks from his dragon. "You won't hear me say this often, but days like this make me wish for the old times in the Jousters' Compound and the butchery. I don't mind not having a dragon boy, but being my own servant and my own hunter to boot is a bit of a hardship."

Kiron grimaced. Not that he didn't sympathize in principle, but he'd never really gotten used to servants—having been a serf and as such, less than a slave, most of his life. For him, life in Sanctuary just meant going back to old patterns of hard work.

For Ari and some of the others, however, it was a new and unpleasant experience. But there were no serfs, no slaves, and precious few servants here. There just weren't enough people to spare for anyone to devote his time to waiting on someone else. The only servants that Kiron knew of were the two that served Kaleth and the other escaped Healers and priests, and they were more in the nature of being acolytes than servants.

In fact, the very nature of the city meant that there

were several classes that were entirely missing. No serfs, no slaves, no servants—and no farmers. All foodstuffs had to be brought in from across the desert or hunted on dragonback.

Avatre squirmed and twisted to help him reach every inch of her hide, and grunted with pleasure when he got a particularly itchy spot. While he was working, Orest and Wastet came in with a flash of ruby and sapphire, followed by Aket-ten and Re-eth-ke, like a silver-edged shadow. Both were laden, so that was four in with good kills. Aket-ten and Re-eth-ke joined him in the sand pit, while Orest stayed up on the roof with Ari. A moment later, Oset-re and copper-colored Apetma landed next to them.

"Orest." Aket-ten shook her head and made a faint sound of disapproval.

"What about him?" Kiron replied, rubbing oil into Avatre's wing webs.

"Hadn't you noticed? You're no longer Orest's hero. Ari is." She shook her head again. "Not that he'd ever disobey you, but he's transferred all that hero worship he used to have for you over to Ari."

Kiron thought about that for a moment. "Huh!" he said. "I think you're right!" He pondered the altered state of things for a little more. "Well, good."

" 'Well, good'?" Aket-ten replied incredulously. "Is that all?"

"Actually, it's *very* good." The more he thought about it, the better he liked it. He had to be wingleader

for right now, but with more people, and more dragons, eventually Orest would be a wingleader in his
own right. There was only just so much of a leadership
role that Kiron was comfortable with. Let Ari be the
Commander of Dragons; he was suited to such things.

"*Very* good." Aket-ten threw up her hands in exas-
peration. "I would have thought you might feel
strongly about losing Orest's allegiance."

"I'm still his wingleader. He's still my friend, and
besides, Ari's older and a lot better leader than I am."
He looked under Avatre's neck at her. "Aket-ten, let's
not bring the game of nation and politics from Alta to
Sanctuary. It's a good thing that the others are looking
to Ari for guidance. He has more experience with a
hand-raised dragon than anyone, he's older and a better fighter than I am, and he's a good man. So what if
he's Tian? If the Magi really are moving into Tia, I bet
we'll start getting more Tians here in Sanctuary before
long. You'll just have to learn to live with them, Aket-
ten."

She hunched her shoulders; he couldn't see her face,
but he imagined from her posture that she was frowning. "All my life, they've been the enemy," she said.
"And *everyone* knew about the rider of the big blue
dragon that was so devastating to our side. Now
everybody seems to be fussing over Ari as if he'd
never killed any of our people!"

"Probably fewer than you think," Kiron said slowly,
thinking about all those times that Ari had returned

from a patrol to brood unhappily all alone. "And he regrets every single one. You know how people exaggerate; I doubt he's done a quarter as much as rumor would have it." Her shoulders were still hunched stubbornly, and he gave up. "Look, if you can't be nice to him, just don't be rude."

"I am never rude," came the untruthful reply, but he had the feeling that was all he was going to get out of it.

Why is it that my friends just can't all get along?

He supposed he could thank the Magi for that as well.

Possibly she was irritated because it wasn't just Orest that was accepting Ari without question—it was most of the others in the wing, and Nofret and Marit and Kaleth.

You'd think that if Kaleth has no issues. . . .

Well, perhaps she was feeling neglected.

Certainly, ever since they'd come here, it had been nothing but nonstop work for everyone. And Aket-ten was another of those who was not at all used to doing her own work.

"When the storm comes and shuts us all in, do you want to try and teach me to play hounds and hares again?" he asked.

She turned around, looking rather surprised. "Yes!" she said. "I would! It'll probably be too dark for mending."

"It will be very dark," was all Kiron could say. "I

only went through one midnight *kamiseen* in Tia and the ones in the desert proper are supposed to be a lot worse. I think most people are planning on going all the way down to the river cave for as long as the storm lasts."

"But we can't take the dragons down there," Aketten observed. "It will be too cold for them."

He nodded. "We'll move them in there—the winter quarters." He pointed at the end building of their court, which might have been a stable, or something of the sort. They'd decided that would be the winter "cave" once things got too cold. Heklatis had not yet worked out how the Ghed priests transferred heat into the Tian dragon pens, although he was certain that between them, he and Ari could puzzle the magic out. At least the dragons would actually fit into this building, and it could probably be heated conventionally.

"I don't want to leave Re-eth-ke," she replied after a moment.

"I don't think any of us plan on leaving our dragons," he said truthfully. "They'll probably be all right, but you never know. So it won't be as comfortable as being down by the river, and we might have our hands full if they get restive or frightened."

"I can think of too many bad things that could happen if we leave them alone," she told him.

At just that moment, the rest of the wing started to straggle in. Pe-atep and scarlet-and-sand Deoth were the first of the lot, with Deoth looking more nervous than usual. "I think he senses something," Pe-atep called in his booming voice as Deoth landed on the sand, and immediately went to a sheltered corner. Kiron nodded; having been a keeper of hunting cats, even lions, before becoming a Jouster, tall Pe-atep was perhaps the most sensitive of any of them to his dragon's moods except, perhaps, the former falcon trainer Kalen.

"Kaleth's prediction is holding true, then." Kiron did not even bother to voice the question of whether the scarlet-and-sand dragon was picking up his nerves from his rider. Pe-atep was not only more sensitive to his dragon's moods, he was outstanding at dealing with them. He knew better than anyone in the wing except perhaps Kalen how to keep his own nerves from being communicated to his dragon.

"I think he knows it's something he's never seen, too," Pe-atep dismounted, but didn't bother to take off Deoth's burdens. The dragon craned his neck around, showing the sand-colored throat. "I'm going to take him straight into the shelter; no point in letting his nerves get any more worked up."

"I'll come with you," Aket-ten said instantly. "It'll leave more room in the court for the others, and Reeth-ke's starting to fidget, too."

"So're Wastet and Apetma," Orest called down from above.

Ari leaned over the edge. "The only two dragons that aren't fussing are Kashet and Avatre—and they've both lived in the desert. I expect all of your Altan-born dragons that have never seen a real sandstorm, much less a midnight *kamiseen*, are going to be restless and on edge; they sense something coming, their instincts tell them that it's dangerous, but they don't know what it is. Getting them into the shelter now is a good idea."

Aket-ten made a little face, but said nothing, she only led Re-eth-ke behind Deoth as they took the staircase to the building roof. On the other side would be a matching stair to bring them to the street side of the shelter. Orest led Wastet out of sight, presumably to take the dragon down to the street as well. Ari raised an eyebrow at Kiron, who shrugged.

"She's seen everything but a midnight *kamiseen*, so she probably is thinking it's just another sandstorm. I think she's more interested in getting groomed, so I'll finish oiling her before I take her in." Kiron looked up, as Gan and his green dragon Khaleph winged in to a landing.

Gan threw his leg over the saddle and slid down from Khaleph's back with a flourish. But then, Gan did everything with a flourish. "I saw the others going inside as we came down; Khaleph isn't too bad, but I might as well take him below anyway. He'll help the others calm down." Gan was the oldest of Kiron's wing; despite his theatrical nature, he'd be something of a calming influence himself. And if that wasn't enough, his exceedingly sharp wit would have them laughing.

Huras and the heart-stoppingly beautiful Tathulan swooped in, a blue-purple-and-scarlet blur coming to a dead stop in the pit by using the sand itself as a brake. "It's coming," said Huras shortly. His eyes were wide and it was clear from his expression that he was alarmed. But even though he was "only" a baker's son and had never even been off his ring in Alta before becoming a Jouster, he was intelligent and steady, as steady by nature as his big dragon, the largest of the hatch. She trusted him, and he trusted in Ari and Kiron's knowledge of the desert; they wouldn't panic unless it was clear that panic was called for. "We were at the edge of our range, and saw it when we got height. She caught breakfast, but has anyone got a spare for her second meal?"

"I do," Ari volunteered, as Kalen and brown-and-gold Se-atmen and Menet-ka and indigo-purple Bethlan landed on opposite buildings at almost the same moment. "Huras saw it coming!" he called, as they dismounted. "Don't bother to unharness, just get into the shelter!"

By the time Kiron and Avatre got up to the rooftop themselves, it was clear that everyone else in Sanctuary was under cover and probably had been as soon as morning chores were done. The very few windows were already covered with wooden shutters, and the city might as well have been as empty as when they had arrived.

Avatre seemed perfectly calm, even now, but when Kiron looked to the east, he saw a brownish haze just at the horizon that made him hurry his steps. Ari was right behind him, with Kashet on his heels.

When the double doors of the stable were shut and barred behind them both, Kiron turned to look the situation over.

This was not the most ideal place for the dragons. The largest of them had to crouch to keep from knocking their heads on the ceiling. In the bars of light that filtered in through the closed shutters, it was barely possible to see, and the air seemed a bit stuffy.

It was also quite crowded. Mealtime for the dragons was going to be interesting.

Outside, there was a sound—

—a high-pitched whine at first, then a deep rumble, like the sound of hundreds of chariots approaching and then—

Then the light vanished, and the walls and shutters shook as the midnight *kamiseen* struck Sanctuary.

The wind—the wind did not howl. It roared, it thundered, it tore angrily at the walls and shutters. It made the walls vibrate. It filled the air with a dust as fine as flour. In that moment when the light was gone, Kiron felt himself groping for Avatre's comforting presence.

This storm felt like a living thing, like a great beast—

like a lion, that roared defiance of all the world, that seized entire buildings in its jaws and shook them until their contents rattled like seeds in a dry *latas* pod. Yet there was nothing inimical in this fury. It didn't care if the building was empty or full of people and dragons. There was nothing malicious there—not like the storms the Magi had created.

That didn't stop Kiron from feeling like a mouse sitting in a hole with a hawk in the air above him—but at least he knew that the hawk had no plans to torture him if it caught him.

Thanks to Kaleth's warning, they had planned ahead; no sooner had the light gone, than someone near the back held up a lit oil lamp. The flame wavered and flickered in the conflicting air currents. Whoever it was quickly sheltered the flame with his hand, and a moment later, others clustered around him with lamps of their own.

It wasn't stuffy anymore; wind whined through all the cracks in the shutters and around the door that a moment ago had let in light. Wind wasn't the only thing coming in. So was the sand. It was some measure of the force of the wind that the sand was spraying in through cracks hardly wider than a hair.

All the dragons, Avatre and Kashet included, inched toward the back wall until they were huddled together. Their pupils were as wide as they could go, making their eyes look like black plates rimmed with ruby or gold, and every time an especially fierce blast shook one or another of the shutters, all their heads swiveled as one to face the source of the noise.

"I doubt they're going to panic," Ari said over the scream of the wind. "And if we all settle down and act normally, they'll relax."

Gan cleared his throat, then tossed his head as if dismissing the storm as a trivial inconvenience. "These walls and shutters have withstood centuries of storms, and *this* one has nothing of magic in it. I doubt they're going to fail now. So, who's for a game of hounds and hares?"

They had made the stable ready long before the storm arrived, and at Gan's prompting, the others unpacked game boards, jackstones and dice. Kiron arranged a couple of flat cushions next to Avatre and Aket-ten brought over her gameboard. They settled in, Kiron to learn the game and Aket-ten to teach it, within the circle of light cast by an alabaster oil lamp found here in the ruins. Shaped like *latas* buds, one of its three cups was broken, but the other two cast a fine light, sheltered from the weird breezes whipping through the stable. Gradually, as nothing worse happened than drifts of sand forming at the windows and door, and the howls of the wind shaking the shutters, the dragons relaxed. Eventually, they put their heads down on their forelegs, or draped head and neck over a neighbor's back. They still showed no signs of relaxing their vigilance enough to nap, but they weren't ready to bolt at the first alarm anymore.

There was no way to gauge the passage of time, but the Altans had known that would be the case. The artificial darkness was a lot like the darkness cast by the storms the Magi conjured in order to drive the Tian Jousters out of the sky, and they were as used to such conditions as anyone could be.

However. . . .

"I think we should feed the dragons at the first sign of hunger," Kiron said, looking up from a game at which he was (predictably) losing. "If we wait until they get really hungry, there might be fights."

"I can keep track of that," said Aket-ten. He nodded; with her Gift of Silent Speech with animals, she should have plenty of warning when they began to complain.

When the first dragons began getting hunger pangs, she alerted their riders. As the meat was distributed, there was some minor squabbling, but not much, and quickly sorted out before it escalated beyond a nip and a hiss. This could never have been done with the wild-caught dragons; there would have been bloody fights over the food in no time, and woe betide any human who got in the way.

The storm continued to howl long after sunset, only dying around the middle of the night. By that time, as the oil lamps burned out one by one, everyone had gone to sleep; Kiron only woke because a beam of moonlight penetrated the shutter and shone directly into his eyes.

He got up and opened the door. He expected a flood

of sand to pour into the room, but instead, it appeared that the storm had scoured the street clean. There was no real sign that such fury had lately raged out here; the air was still, cold, and calm, and the streets peaceful. He wondered what the storm had buried—or revealed.

But that would have to wait until morning.

 # THREE

THE dragons woke early that morning, and wanted *out!* They jostled each other and whined with impatience, once they were fully awake, and if it had seemed crowded before, with the dragons fussing, it was like being in the middle of a cattle pen that had been crammed too full. No one could sleep with the fidgeting, impatient snapping, and noise. It was obvious that it was time to go. As soon as the stable doors were opened wide, they crowded through, shoving and squabbling, in a hurry to get to their saddling stations. It was time to fly, time to eat, and most of all, time to be outside of walls.

Whatever those walls were made of, it was remarkable stuff. There was not so much as a gouge or a scratch on them after half a day of being abraded by wind-blasted sand.

But a cracked water jar that had been left carelessly beside the door was now little more than a sand-smoothed lump of baked clay.

Laden with saddle and guiding reins, Kiron climbed the stairs to get to the rooftop; too impatient to climb, Avatre spread her wings and flew up. He had to smile at that. She was not only maturing, she was showing more initiative. He'd begun teaching her to come at his whistle some time ago, thinking it would be a useful trick if they were parted; now she obeyed him as eagerly as any dog, and the others had begun teaching their dragons to do the same.

Aket-ten and some of the others were already up there, staring out to the west. When he joined them, it was clear what they were staring at. The sandstorm had uncovered more of the city beneath the dunes; this time there was a temple-sized building, and a vast complex a great deal like a Great Lord's house. These were a mix of the familiar structures of the sort they all lived in now, and a carefully laid-out area of roofless courts divided by walls next to the temple that bore a striking resemblance to the dragon pens.

"We could use that temple for the dragons, instead of this building," said Pe-atep speculatively as he tapped a toe on the roof of the stable they had just used, then glanced down at Aket-ten from his superior height, and added, "if the gods allow."

"I shouldn't think they'd mind," she replied, rubbing her ear. "But I'm not the one to ask."

"I think," called a cheerful voice from below, "that they will not mind at all, seeing as that building has the sign of Haras upon it."

Kiron looked down at Kaleth, who grinned up at him, teeth very white in the tanned skin of his face. His spotlessly white headcloth nearly matched them. Kaleth had been thriving out here, and anyone who was under the impression that someone serving as the literal spokesperson for the gods would be frail and ascetic would have a great shock when confronted with the lean, hard, athletic Kaleth. He was one of the few who had adopted the Tian custom of shaving the head out here in the heat, and generally appeared in public in headcloths, as Ari did. His appearance was a curious mixture of Tian and Altan dress, and Kiron was quite certain that this was a deliberate decision on his part.

"You look like you've been up for ages," Aket-ten called down.

"I have. I've been inspecting," he replied, his mild eyes sparkling. "The gods provide, you see. We'll be getting another caravan of Altan refugees soon, and we'd have been a bit crowded without some help."

Another caravan of refugees? Well, if anyone would know, it would be Kaleth, god-touched, Winged One of the Far-Seeing Eye. If anyone had asked Kiron long ago what he thought a god-touched person would look like, he probably would not have described someone like Kaleth. Except when the gods spoke through him, there was nothing about him at first glance that was uncanny; he could have been one of Kiron's wing. Stronger, browner, and more vigorous than he had been when he was merely Toreth's scholarly twin, and with him, the heir to the Twin Thrones, the power of a Winged One sat lightly on him. But it was there—oh, yes—those with the eyes to see it knew very well that the gods had set their mark on him. It was in his eyes, the straightness of his back, and the very way he moved, as if always conscious of the lingering presence of something greater than himself at every moment.

"While you were inspecting, I don't suppose you came across a cache of enchanted, sleeping wenches, did you?" asked Gan wistfully. "They wouldn't have to be princesses or anything of the sort, just old enough to have cut their child locks and young enough to still have all their teeth." Kiron bit his lip to keep from laughing, though he knew that half of what Gan said was for effect. If anyone was to have taken a vote as to which of the Jousters was the best looking, Gan would have swept the tally boards, and while he certainly was (understandably) vain to a certain degree, and took full advantage of the effect of his beautiful body and features on women, he also enjoyed mocking himself and the teasing of his friends.

Kaleth laughed. "Ah, poor Gan, you have certainly

suffered more than any of us here, with no one to admire your handsome face except Heklatis!"

Gan grimaced. "Believe me, I tell you in all sincerity that by now even that scrawny old Healer is beginning to have his charms!"

Oset-re feigned alarm and edged away from him. The rest laughed, and Kaleth spread his hands wide. "Well, the gods have heeded your suffering. Cheer up! That problem will be taken care of before very long, I promise you!"

Imperious Bethlan whined and shoved Menet-ka with her indigo-blue nose. She didn't give a toss about new buildings or newcomers. *She* was hungry, and right now! Avatre wasn't as demanding, but she made it known with little anxious bobbings of her head as Kiron glanced at her that she was uncomfortably empty herself.

"I've already allotted the big building and its courts to you!" Kaleth told them. "It's much more suited to the dragons than this makeshift arrangement anyway."

"We'll come look when we get back!" Kiron promised, and turned to saddling Avatre so they could get out of there. As they leaped into the air, the pattern of the newly uncovered buildings came clear. There were two distinct sections. One looked exactly like a Great Lord's city manor, with the Great House and all the attendant outbuildings. The other was that very large building, in seemingly excellent preservation with a

ring of roofless, walled courtyards all around three
sides of it, looking for all the world exactly like dragon
pens. . . .

Well, even if that wasn't what they were, if they
could be made to work as pens, he and the others
would be taking them over. And, he reflected, as Avatre banked away from the city, this meant he and the
others could build in their own separate rooms within
those pens, exactly as they'd enjoyed in Alta. It would
be a relief to have separate quarters again.

It wasn't that he minded sharing his living space
with the others, it was mostly that there never seemed
to be any place to be private. For all that he had been a
serf, Kiron had been accustomed, most of his life, to
being alone, for his lowly status had meant that not
even Khefti-the-Fat's slaves had been willing to share
a room with him. Even when he had been Ari's dragon
boy, that status had made it necessary to accommodate him in Kashet's pen rather than the quarters of
the rest of the Tian dragon boys. But now, crowded up
into a single house with all of the riders but Aket-ten,
he had been very aware of the presence of others
around him and it had felt exceedingly uncomfortable. Sometimes it was only sheer exhaustion that allowed him to sleep.

"So, it looks as if we'll be alone again, at last!" he
said cheerfully to the back of Avatre's head. She was
listening, he could tell by the way she glanced back at
him, but she wasn't giving him a lot of attention. She

was colder than usual in the morning, and that made her hungry; her concentration was on the hunt.

She'd get her fill of it today. With no sandstorm coming, and with yesterday's storm confining the human hunters within walls, today would be one of those days when he and Avatre would be doing the new work of a Jouster—helping to keep the people of Sanctuary fed. Hunting was not just for the dragons. Hunting was for the people, too. He slapped her shoulder. "The sooner we get game, the sooner I can see what we can make of this gift from the gods! Let's try that watering hole where the thorn trees are. After that storm, I bet a lot of the game is thirsty."

A pity there had been no one to take that bet. When they returned, with two small gazelles, and Avatre full and ready to sleep the afternoon away, he found that they were the last to make it back. As they flew in above the roofs of Sanctuary, he could see figures prowling the newly uncovered buildings, and recognized Ari (by his striped headcloth) and Aket-ten among them. He unharnessed Avatre, and as he was putting her saddle up, Hurok-eb, the Provisioner, approached him. The Provisioner, a solemn-faced old fellow with a sturdy, compact body who was naturally bald without needing to shave his head, had been appointed by Kaleth to take charge of the common treasury and to make sure everyone got a fair share of the food that came in. Eventually, Kiron supposed, this would stop. Sooner or later people would be, if not raising their own food, certainly finding ways to make money to buy it, rather than depending on what was brought in, paid for by the treasures that were turning up in the city. Or, at some point, those treasures would stop turning up, and only what was brought in by the dragons would be available to distribute. At that point, things would be as they were in every other city.

But that was for another day, and hardly Kiron's concern. The Provisioner was certainly happy with the morning's catch; he made his usual point of thanking both Kiron and Avatre for their work before he carried off the bounty.

Kiron gave Avatre a quick sand buffing, but she didn't seem to want an oiling and definitely *did* want to nap, so he left her to doze in the hot sand of the pen while he went out to join the rest of the wing in exploring what the storm had uncovered.

Of course, the first place he went was that big building with the surrounding penlike structures. It naturally drew the eye and their attention, since the tall building loomed over the surrounding structures by a full story. He followed the sound of voices when he got there, straight to one of the "pens," where all the rest had gathered.

". . . workshops," Ari was saying judiciously, as he kicked through bits of rubble embedded in the sand.

Kaleth nodded. "I would guess the same," he said. "As we have been looking through the ruins, I've found broken tools, half-finished projects. I agree that these were all temple workshops, and you know what that means. This was a great temple at one time, one that had many workshops making statues of the gods, and offerings. These workshops must have had roofs of palm-leaf thatch, so when the sand overwhelmed this place, what little was left of the roofs crumbled away to nothing."

Kiron joined them, noting that Ari's prodding toe had turned up a half-finished statue of the god Haras in his falcon form. It seemed Kaleth's guess was correct.

"Which suggests to me that at one point there was a palm oasis here, too," Ari replied, stooping to pick up the statue and turn it over in his strong hands. "What was here once, we can build again. And meanwhile, if you are sure the god Haras will not begrudge us living room—"

"Very sure," Kaleth replied, with a nod. "As sure as I have ever been of anything. These workshops can be made into pens, as you have been suggesting, and that big enclosure that was probably a corral for sacrificial cattle can be made into a nursery for little ones."

"Little ones?" Kiron felt it was time to make his presence known.

Kaleth favored Kiron with a half smile, though the smile didn't reach his eyes this time. "You don't think the Magi are going to leave us alone forever, do you? One day, we will need Jousters to fly to defend Sanctuary, I fear."

As a matter of fact, he had hoped for something of the sort, but it appeared that his hopes were in vain.

"As he told us this morning, Kaleth says that we are soon to see our population increase," Ari said. "And then—well, he has a plan, and I will let him explain it to everyone when the time is right."

"But part of that is that we're going to have dragonets again, and new Jousters to train, is that it? And this will be soon?" Kiron persisted.

"Absolutely," Kaleth replied. He looked so sure of himself that any doubts Kiron might have had faded away.

"But we haven't any dragons other than Kashet who are of breeding age," he pointed out. "If we're going to be hatching our own and raising them from the egg—"

"It is safe to transport an egg when it is first laid, before it has begun true incubation," Ari observed. "I wouldn't do it by cart, or transport it for more than half a day, but in a sling between two camels—it would probably be fine."

"By the time the wild dragons are laying their eggs, Heklatis will have perfected the magic that makes the sands hot, and we will be able to incubate the eggs," Kaleth said, with his eyes looking off into the distance. "After that you will train new wings and—" he broke off what he was saying. "One step at a time. We will make these workshops into new pens, the old temple into a place where dragons can wait out a storm or shelter from the cold, and the cattle pen into a nursery for eggs and dragonets. And meanwhile, other things will be happening. And for that, we need a council and official leaders."

Well, that was new. "A council?" Kiron asked. "Leaders? But—"

"All in good time," Ari cautioned. "But it is best to have the plan in place before you need it."

"Does Lord—" Kiron began.

"Lord Khumun knows and approves," said Kaleth, and that seemed to be that. After all, if Lord Khumun, who had been the de facto leader of the refugees since they had all arrived here, had no difficulty with these plans, who was Kiron to object?

"Oh, yes," Heklatis said, when Kiron came to talk to him. "A good deal of what your priests did to bring heat to the sands was mummery. Mind, it is a good thing to have the blessing of the gods when you decide to work a bit of magic! But there was no need for all the chanting and incense and pretty priestesses in mist linen." He chuckled. "Except, of course, that the old priests probably liked looking at pretty priestesses in mist linen." He raised an eyebrow at Kiron. "Mind, mist linen is a very good choice for adorning a fine body, don't you think?"

The Akkadian Healer—who was also a Magus, according to his own people's way of magic—was a short, bandy-legged fellow with a knowing eye and a head of curly, silver-streaked hair. Wiry and agile rather than slim and graceful like the Altans, he stood out among the refugees physically for more than just his Akkadian tunics and his wild halo of hair.

He also was not in the least interested in *priestesses* in mist linen. Which Kiron knew very well.

Kiron felt his ears growing hot, and gave himself a moment to think by looking around Heklatis' quarters—which did not differ substantially from the ones he had in the Jousters' Compound in Alta. Everything he remembered from there was here; the Akkadian statues of gods, the mix of Akkadian and Altan furnishings, the case of scrolls, the odd metal lamps that Heklatis favored.

Then again, Heklatis had been able to take virtually everything he owned with him. Unlike the Jousters, he hadn't had to abandon anything, because he and Lord Khumun had smuggled themselves out disguised as an aged husband and wife leaving for the country. A wagon full of belongings made a useful foil.

"But—" he began, deciding to quickly change the subject, "Kaleth seems to think we're going to be needing everything the *kamiseen* uncovered and more! I thought Sanctuary was pretty much just for the Jousters and people that the Magi were determined to do away with! Just how many people are going to be turning up here?"

Heklatis turned sober. "More than either of us think, I suspect," he replied. "I have the feeling that things are not going at all well back in Alta. Kaleth has been

very close-mouthed about what he has Seen. I believe
he is waiting for this next lot to arrive to confirm with
their own words what he knows, rather than risk our
incredulity—because I think he knows that the skep-
tics among us will take it all more seriously with eyewitnesses."

Kiron felt his heart sinking. "It won't be good," he
replied, shaking his head. "I didn't want to think
about it as long as we were all right, but . . . well, he
won't have to have eyewitnesses to convince me."

"Nor me," Heklatis sighed, scratching his head absently.

The Magi had certainly begun their covert takeover
of Alta long before Kiron had arrived, but shortly after
he had joined the Jousters of Alta, they had moved
from covert to overt. Once, they had relied only on
their own strength, like the priest-mages of Tia, and
their magic had been used to defend Alta. Now, however, their power was stolen from others, and their
magic was used to help them in a bid for control of the
people and the land. Kiron had discovered that they
were stealing whatever it was that enabled the Winged
Ones to see into the future and predict earthshakes,
and to see at a distance to predict the movements of
Tian troops—leaving Alta vulnerable. Worse, they
were draining enough of it that the Winged Ones were
dying of it. And they had begun moving to drain the
same resource from those with other abilities.

Like the Healers.

Once, the Eye they had created was a potent weapon that lashed the earth with fire and had been Alta's last-ditch defense. Now it was used to keep the people of Alta in fear, lashing out whenever anyone challenged the authority of the Magi, incinerating the very people and places it was supposed to protect.

Whoever, whatever, had started the war between Tia and Alta was lost in the past and a hundred thousand recriminations. But now (so Kiron and others believed) the war was being prolonged because death, and all the magic inherent in the years that might have been lived, gave the Magi the power they could no longer live without and could not raise for themselves without harm to others. They had used up as much of their own power as they were willing to part with, they were using up the Winged Ones, and there was every indication—or had been, when the Jousters had fled—that the Magi had learned how to profit from the sacrifice of others.

And now that they had found this new source of power, he and Heklatis and the few others who suspected it had no doubt that they would exploit it as ruthlessly as they had every other source. It gave them stolen youth, it gave them the power to control the Eye, and Kiron could not even begin to guess what else they had planned.

One thing he did know; it had given them supreme secular power, or at least, it had put the Twin Thrones of Alta within their grasp.

Of course, in order to get access to the Twin Thrones, and to set themselves up as the heirs apparent, they had needed to be rid of the then-current heirs. The murder of one, the disgrace of the other—the fabrication of a twin-bloodline—and the deed was done.

The murdered heir had been Toreth, a Jouster, and Kaleth's twin. He was not, by any means, the only one they had killed, but this was the death that had shown the Jousters, all of them, just what the Magi had become. And subsequent subtle persecution of the Jousters had proved to them that the Magi were determined to be rid of the one group that resisted their takeover.

When Kiron and the rest had fled Alta, it had been with the knowledge that the Magi were going to destroy the Jousters as the last obstacle that stood between them and their control of the entire country. The trouble was that the Jousters of Alta were all that stood between the people of Alta and the depredations of the Jousters of Tia, who were responsible for some true horrors.

Kiron and the others decided they could not make their own escape until they had nullified that threat, so they had done their best to even the stakes between Alta and Tia by destroying what had kept the wild-caught dragons under control, the drug called *tala*. The Jousters of Tia had been overwhelming in their number and the strength of their larger desert-born dragons. But with the *tala* gone and the wild-born dragons no longer controllable, at least the conflict came down to equal numbers and equal armies.

The only dragons left under human control now were those that had been raised from the egg by their Jousters—the eight dragons born in Alta and raised by Kiron's wing, and the two born in Tia and raised by Kiron and Ari.

These were now the dragons and Jousters of Sanctuary, who served and protected those who were pledged to end the war, though they had no idea yet how they could do that. There was only one thing that any of them knew for certain. Ending the war began with ending the power of the Magi, because the Magi were the ones prolonging the conflict, and the only ones who benefited from it.

So now the question in Kiron's mind was, how badly had things deteriorated in Alta since Kiron and the rest had fled the city? He could not imagine that they would have improved.

"Have you heard anything from the Healers?" he asked Heklatis. The Akkadian shook his head.

"Not that I expected to," Heklatis added. "I think that whatever information comes to us will come in with these newcomers that we are expecting."

"How much do you think Kaleth already knows?" Kiron asked, with a growing sense of unease that was not directed at their enemies—but at the one who was supposed to be guiding them. It was one thing for Kaleth to be the mere mouthpiece for the gods, but another entirely for him to be withholding vital information if he had it. Was Kaleth already keeping secrets—as the Magi had?

"Not nearly as much as you think he does," Heklatis said immediately, as if he were able to read Kiron's thoughts, and he gave Kiron a reassuring nod. "The Magi are able to block *my* scrying and the attempts by the Bedu to overlook the city. I think they can probably even cloud whatever ability the gods gave Kaleth as well. My bet would be that Kaleth knows just enough to make him sure he hasn't got sufficient information to give good advice, much less base decisions on."

Kiron shook his head, for that made no sense at all. "How can *men* block the power of the gods?" he protested.

Heklatis gave an exasperated snort. "Oh, do think, will you? There are gods of the light, and are there also not gods of darkness? Oh, yes, I know, among you Altans and Tians every god has some aspects of both—but are there not gods that are *mostly* of the darkness, as Haras and Iris and Siris are *mostly* of the light?"

"Well," Kiron admitted, slowly, "Ye-es."

"And did those gods of light and darkness not go to war against each other in the distant and legended past?" Heklatis persisted.

"Not *war*, precisely, but—"

"And do you not think that the Magi of Alta are, even now, giving those dark gods what they most crave? And in return, for those gifts, those dark gods are preventing the servants of the light from seeing what they do?" Heklatis looked at him as if he were a particularly dense apprentice.

Kiron shivered. It was bad enough, thinking that the Magi alone were working against them—but to think that gods might be getting into it—

How could they ever hope to prevail against gods?

"The good thing is that gods seldom intervene directly," Heklatis went on, with an arched brow as he noted Kiron's shivering. "Probably because, having warred with each other in the long past, they are loath to begin such a war again. I do not believe we need fear divine *or* infernal retribution. Interference, perhaps—but that, my young friend, can go both ways. Do not grant the darkness more power than it already has by giving in to your fears. And remember that if this is the case, and they have allies, well, so do we."

Anything else that the Healer might have added had to be left unsaid, for their conversation was interrupted by Huras, who diffidently rapped at the doorpost of Heklatis' dwelling. Heklatis almost never closed his door except during a *kamiseen*, saying that a Healer must *always* be available to those who needed him.

"Kiron, Healer, I wouldn't interrupt you," the stocky young man said, as Kiron saw immediately by the excitement in his eyes that he must have some news. "But one of the Bedu guides has just come in with word. The people Kaleth has been expecting are not more than half a day behind him, and you will be most glad to hear who they are!"

The weary caravan of refugees arrived at Sanctuary in the last gleam of twilight, as the full moon rose over the desert. Weary they might have been, but they arrived in good order; which was only to be expected, since their leader was Lord Ya-tiren—the father of Orest and Aket-ten.

And with him was his entire household. Wife, sons, servants, and every other relative and *their* households that wished to escape. Every bit of movable property, every scrap of food they could buy or harvest, every animal that could take the desert trek; all of it. They formed an irregular blot against the pale desert sand as they approached, a blot that brought its own dust cloud and heralded its approach by the bleating and calling of the animals with them.

Small wonder that Kaleth had said that without the sandstorm uncovering the new parts of the city, they would be crowded.

There were others with Lord Ya-tiren as well, but no other Great Houses intact and entire. Some Healers, most notably those who had the special gift of Healing by touch, and a few—a very, very few—of the priestly caste.

Aket-ten and Orest were beside themselves with relief and joy, and could not wait until the caravan arrived; they flew out to meet it on their dragons, and arrived back leading the refugees from the air, so Kiron did not witness how they greeted their father. Not that he needed to; he knew that the greeting would have been full of tears and pleasure, and he also knew that while he was very happy that his best friends had their mother and father safely with them, there would have been a small part of him eaten up with envy. *His* father, after all, was dead beyond a shadow of a doubt; his mother and his sisters, if they weren't also dead, were worse off than slaves. He couldn't begrudge Aket-ten and Orest this meeting, but he was glad he didn't have to see it.

Instead, he was able to wait by the side of Kaleth and Lord Khumun with all the rest of the Jousters to welcome the refugees to their new home. He would not even have put himself forward as the Lord was greeted by Khumun as an equal, and himself gave Kaleth the bow of deep respect—but Lord Ya-tiren caught sight of him and greeted *him* with an enthusiasm he hadn't expected.

"And there you are!" Lord Ya-tiren exclaimed, embracing him as he might have one of his own sons. Kiron felt himself flushing with a mingling of embarrassment, pleasure, and affection. He had not realized just how much he liked Lord Ya-tiren until that moment. He had known how much he respected the man, but not that he had come to think of the Lord and his family as a kind of second family of his own. "Kiron, it is *good* to see you again!"

"My lord, I am happy beyond telling that you have come safely here," Kiron managed to say, with only a little stammer of confusion. "And with your entire household!"

"We should have been here sooner, but he would not leave anyone behind," said Iris-aten, Aket-ten's mother, with a warm smile for her husband. She didn't look much like Aket-ten; where her daughter was flexible and tough, she was willowy and gracile. If Aket-ten was a bit like a cheetah, Iris-aten was a pampered temple cat. Nevertheless, she had made the trek, and evidently without a word of complaint. "Not that I didn't agree with him; I will leave nothing for those wretches to seize in their greed. Not the least servant, nor the youngest goat!"

"I would leave nothing for those monsters in their Tower to use against us either," Lord Ya-tiren said, his face darkening; his wife put a comforting hand on his arm. "Nor would I leave anything or anyone behind to suffer their wrath."

"Not that we believe the Magi have so much as a clue that we have fled," added a young man who looked very like Orest, but who was wearing what looked to Kiron like the robes of some sort of priest. "We left behind a great deal of misdirection. They should think that we left for the remote estates, well past the bounds of the city, and they should believe that it is because we fear the earthshakes."

This must be the brother that's a Te-oth priest. Kiron had not had the chance to meet all of the brothers—or even Aket-ten's mother, except in passing. He tried not to feel too overwhelmed by this sudden avalanche of brothers, but he couldn't help but wonder if they were eying him.

Were they looking at him and wondering how he felt about Aket-ten? Did they wonder how she felt about him?

But there were eight other young Jousters, and if they didn't know—

He resolved to put the worry out of his mind for the moment. "How did you manage that?" he asked.

"A great deal of carefully placed gossip," said yet another brother; this one *must* be the eldest, the one who had been Lord Ya-tiren's steward; he looked like an older and taller version of Orest. "We have been dropping hints, acting terribly worried about the earthshakes, for—well, ever since Father let us know that we might need to take ourselves out of reach of the Magi. We aren't the only ones either. There are those who really *are* making for property as far away from Alta as possible."

"The Akkadians are leaving," said yet another brother, somberly.

"Am I properly holding back my shock?" asked Heklatis, dryly. "Greetings, my Lord. I am exceedingly pleased to see all of you."

"And I am exceedingly pleased to see you, Healer," Lord Ya-tiren said. "We have more of your colleagues with us, though not as many as we would have liked. And we are, to be frank, very weary."

"My old friend, we anticipated that." Lord Khumun eased his way into the group, and he and Lord Ya-Tiren clasped forearms in greeting. "Our friends the Bedu have been helping us prepare temporary places for you; they will do until you can shape what the desert uncovered for your use to your own liking. Now come, and we will show you."

With a sigh of relief, Kiron eased out of the way and let Lord Khumun take over the shepherding of the entire group. It was with a feeling of shock that he realized that this one group was going to more than double the population of Sanctuary.

As soon as we move out of our quarters, I suspect some of those that are not of Lord Ya-tiren's household will move into them!

It was just as well that it wouldn't take much to turn those empty workshops into the combination of pen and living quarters that they all had enjoyed in Alta.

We have a lot to do. And so did everyone else. *Well, one step at a time. Tonight—*

Tonight he would let Aket-ten and Orest enjoy being with their family again. Tonight was for celebration. Leave the work for tomorrow.

 **FOUR**

"**M**Y heart is glad for Aket-ten and Orest," Menet-ka said, quietly joining Kiron as the latter slipped off to go back to the Jousters' quarters, taking advantage of the crowd and the deepening darkness. "But I have no stomach for much celebration."

Kiron glanced aside at him and they locked eyes for a moment The moon just coming up and the last of the twilight showed Menet-ka's melancholy expression with painful clarity. "My own family is still in Alta, and not likely to escape any time soon," Menet-ka elaborated quietly.

Kiron winced. Poor Menet-ka! Though the young Jouster had come a long way from the shy fellow who scarcely raised his voice above a polite murmur, he was still so good at concealing his feelings that Kiron hadn't quite realized until this moment that Menet-ka was at least as lonely and concerned about his family as the more vocal Aket-ten and Orest. And here Kiron had been feeling sorry for himself, when everyone else in the wing with the exception of Ari was virtually in the same position as Menet-ka. Not everyone had the resources that Lord Ya-tiren had. How would Huras' family manage to get enough money together to get the beasts they would need to bring them across the desert? Everything they had was tied up in their bakery, and if they tried to sell that, even if they could find a buyer, it would raise suspicions. The rest were scarcely in a better case, even those who had wealthy or noble families. First, how to persuade them that the son they likely thought had been killed when the dragons shook off the last effects of the *tala* was actually still alive? Then, how to convince them that it made more sense to flee into the desert and the unknown than remain under the heel of the Magi? The choice seemed very simple out here; back there, it meant leaving everything one had ever known, sometimes leaving a home that had been in the family for generations, leaving friends, a business, fortune, status . . . disposing of things that might have been in the family for generations, paring everything down to what could be carried away and going off into a completely unknown future. No matter how bad things got in Alta, at least you were home. For most people, abandoning everything they had or had fought to gain was not worth the possibilities on the other side of escape.

Huras eeled his way through the crowd to join them, then Gan, Pe-atep, and Kalen let the crowd follow Lord Ya-tiren and his caravan of refugees, and separated themselves by the simple expedient of standing still while the crowd moved off.

"Hu!" Gan said, scratching his head and looking after them. "I knew my lord was ranked, and highly so, but I never knew that household was so cursed big." But his kohl-rimmed eyes were bright with interest as two of Lord Ya-tiren's pretty servants looked back over their shoulders at him, whispered something to each other, and giggled. He didn't see Oset-re behind him, making doe eyes at both of them.

"There's more of it than he brought with him if you count all the people on all the estates he owns," Menetka observed wistfully. "He just brought the people he couldn't leave on his most remote estates, I suspect, and those the Magi would think to use as hostages."

Kiron tried, for a moment, to think like one of the Magi, then like Lord Ya-tiren, to work out what the Lord might himself have done. "The Magi wouldn't look at anyone without rank," he said, after a moment. "So anyone like servants or slaves—less than an Overseer, say—is probably safe enough, even if they're in my Lord's household and kinship line. *They* don't trust their servants or underlings with anything, so they wouldn't think Lord Ya-tiren would either."

"Speaking from personal experience, to those of a certain mind, anyone less than an Overseer is invisible," Gan observed. "Simply not worth troubling your mind about."

Oset-re nodded. "Scarcely more than a living *abshati*, if it comes down to it."

Gan shrugged. "And if I were Lord Ya-tiren, I'd feel safe enough in leaving some of those behind so long as I got them out of Alta City. Out of sight, and out of immediate reach, is pretty much out of mind."

"Something about the Magi is worth thinking about," Menet-ka added after a moment. "They don't travel outside the Third Ring. *Ever.* I'm not sure the remote estates really exist to them, except as an abstract concept. So . . . if we needed to, we might be able to use those estates to help funnel people out of the city, or to hide people on, because the Magi might not think to look there."

They walked on in silence under a sky blossoming with stars. And something else odd occurred to Kiron in that moment. In Alta and in Mefis, both, people had been afraid of the night, afraid of the hungry ghosts that haunted it, the spirits of those who could not cross the Star Bridge into the afterlife. Sanctuary of all places should have been awash with haunts.

So why was it that no one feared to walk in the night here?

He was thinking about this so hard that when a voice came out of the dark, he nearly leaped out of his skin.

"It seems I am not the only one who is looking for a little peace."

Gan recovered first. "Kaleth?" he said incredulously, peering into the shadows in the lee of their building.

"The same." A long, lean shadow detached itself from the rest, and moved toward them, resolving into Kaleth. "It seems that there will be a celebration, and I dislike being the skeleton at the feast." Kaleth approached them, slapping Kiron lightly on the back and Gan on the arm. "I thought I would come spend some time with my friends who I have seen far too little of lately. Besides, there is a slight difficulty in being the one who speaks for the gods. When people are sober, they look at you out of the corners of their eyes and are afraid to speak to you. And when the date wine has flowed too much, they suddenly wish you to trot out your trick, like a prize flute girl who can play while bent over backward."

"Well, that's one trick I can do without," Gan said fervently. "Unless the gods are telling you how we are to feed all these new mouths."

"Ah! I don't need the gods for that. Come up on the roof and we'll catch the evening wind, and I'll tell you." Kaleth sounded a lot more cheerful, and Kiron felt some of his own melancholy melting. They all went up onto the roof as he had suggested, and sprawled on the warm stone with him. Baked in the sun all day, though the temperature of the wind off the desert was dropping, the stone under them—and the sands of the dragon pen below—radiated heat, and would for the rest of the night. Down below, the sounds of the dragons dozing recalled nights that seemed a thousand years in the past, when they had gathered in one or another of the pens while the dragonets slept.

"We have water, which is the main thing," Kaleth said, after a long silence. "Some of those folk that Yatiren brought with him are growers, and not the usual sorts of Altan swamp farmers either. These are the fellows that cultivated his city manor gardens. They know how to grow things in containers, with a trickle of irrigation. And in all that maze that the storm just uncovered is a manor where things were grown in just that way. But we won't be growing food."

"We won't?" asked Gan.

Kiron found a wind-smoothed curve of stone that just fit his back, and tucked himself into it. Kaleth sounded more like his old self tonight than he had in a very long time.

"No. We'll be growing things worth more than food—yes, even here, in the desert. Spices. Medicines."

Oset-re laughed. "Ha! Now I know why Lord Yatiren was cosseting trees across the desert! Incense!"

"Exactly so," Kaleth replied. "Incense, which is far

more valuable than gold or turquoise. There are young incense-trees and seeds for spices and herbs in the packs Ya-tiren brought with him." Kiron glanced over at Kaleth and saw that he was nodding. "There is no reason to try to grow what doesn't suit this place, when with care, we can grow what does, *and* is worth so much that traders will bring us whole caravans of foodstuffs in exchange for what a single camel can carry away."

"But that won't be for another growing season, surely," Huras protested mildly.

"True enough. But the gods do provide. And until we have that precious crop, they have provided." Kiron could hear the smile in his voice. "The sand-storm also uncovered another treasure trove. It's enough to feed us all for some time, even with our population doubled."

"Well, that's a relief. I was afraid we'd be out hunt-ing from dawn to dusk." Gan shook his head. "As it is, if we aren't going to overhunt our territories, I think we'd better start ranging out a bit farther."

"Ah, that brings up another thing. Who ranges to the east the farthest?" Kaleth asked.

"I do, I suppose," Kiron volunteered. "Ari goes far-thest to the south; we have the two oldest and biggest dragons, after all."

"Then I want you to range farther than you already have, into the wadi country. There's another aban-doned city there that used to be allied with this one, and we'll want to colonize it for the dragons and Jousters eventually." Kiron didn't ask how Kaleth knew that; after all, Kaleth had been the one who'd found Sanctuary.

"Well, what am I looking for?" he asked. "And can you give me some direction?"

"Only that you should follow the game into the wadis, and you'll find it." Kaleth sighed, and tilted his head back against the stone of the parapet that supported his back. "This business of being Winged is not as clear as any of us would like. In many ways, it is as if someone handed me a box of shards from several shattered jars. I can see a face I recognize here, the curve of an arm or a bit of a duck or a *latas* flower, and sometimes I can make out what the shape of the vase—that is, what the shape of the future will be, but unless one of the gods actually chooses to speak through me, or a moment that I have foreseen comes to pass and I can say something pertinent, often it is just images that I can put no real meaning to. Until, of course, something actually happens, but by then it's a bit too late to do anything about it."

No one seemed to have any good answer to that, so there was, for a moment, an uncomfortable silence. Kaleth himself broke it again.

"I would very much like to be able to see things afar, as others in the Temple of the Twins could, but that is not within my power either," he admitted. "So I cannot do as I very much wish to, and see what is toward with any of your families. What I See—well, when it isn't like a pile of shards, it is like looking at the Great Mother River at Flood, when she is full of silt and what she has swept away. Anything could be hidden beneath the surface; I can only see what the direction will be, what floats to the surface, and sometimes those things that influence the direction."

Menet-ka let out his breath in a huge sigh. "Well. *That* is somewhat less than useful for us mere mortals! Next time you talk to the gods, tell them I am severely disappointed in their performance and planning!"

It was a moderately feeble joke, but good enough that they all laughed, which lightened the mood considerably.

And Kiron reflected after a moment that the fact that Kaleth had *not* "seen" anyone's relations might actually be a good sign, because it meant that they were going to be quiet enough that they made no impact on the course of the future. Right now, where the Magi were concerned, it was best to be unnoticed.

A burst of laughter from the other side of Sanctuary made them all look up. "I am glad they are weary," Kaleth said feelingly. "Dawn comes too soon, and an all-night celebration is not what I wish to be next to when it's time to sleep."

"Yes," agreed Huras. "And I am glad that I will not be there when they realize life here is not as it was in Alta. There will be much wailing, I warrant. And bitter complaining."

At least we all knew how to work, Kiron thought. Those who had come to Sanctuary first had no illusions about what the conditions were. In fact, their expectations had been lower than reality. No one had anticipated water in such abundance, which made a great deal of life much easier than it would otherwise have been. He closed his eyes and let the warmth of the stone bake into his back.

"At least Lord Ya-tiren brought servants with him," Gan observed. "I cannot imagine the amount of complaining if some of the household learned they were to haul their own water and wash their own linen because there was no one here to do it for them."

"I think that Lord Ya-tiren has sufficiently warned them," Menet-ka countered. "It isn't as if Lord Khu-mun hasn't been able to get *some* information to him.

Kiron sighed and opened his eyes again. "It is hard to imagine what is going to come of all this," he said, quietly. "With lives being upended. Those used to being served having to fend for themselves."

"Well, Lord Ya-tiren will not need to be worried about that," Gan pointed out. "He has brought enough people with him to ensure that his inner household will not be cooking their own food and washing their own linen—"

"Ah, and he did bring something else with him that you lot should be grateful for," Kaleth replied slyly. "Females. Young women. Two thirds of his household is female, most are young, none are children, and half are unmarried."

"And we are no longer in the army, to be subject to soldiers' rules, and Gan cannot possibly monopolize all of them," added Kiron. "So you may pursue young women to your hearts' content. Or at least, as I am your wingleader, I should say that you may pursue them in the time you are not spending in hunting and caring for your dragon!"

Even as he said that, he wondered how much time he would be able to get with Aket-ten, now that her family was here and she was no longer needing to hide from the Magi. Surely she would want to spend most of her own free time with them.

Why was it that nothing in his life could ever be simple?

"Gan!" said Kalen instantly. "If you cause *all* of them to become enchanted with your handsome face, I will be very put out!"

Kiron glanced over at Kalen to see if he was joking, but couldn't make out anything but a shadow among the shadows.

"By At-thera's horns, aye, leave some for the rest of us!" exclaimed Pe-atep.

"He *does* have competition, you know," Oset-re reminded them.

"Perhaps we ought to prevent him from venturing anywhere near until we have our chance," Kalen suggested, in a tone that sounded as if he was entirely serious.

Surely not.

Quite taken aback, Gan evidently decided to put a gracious face on the matter. "I," he announced, with a dignity that bordered on the ponderous, "have no intention of frittering my time away in pursuit of women. Or at least, no more than one or two women. We have a new home to create! That temple that was uncovered—it is to be our winter quarters, and what had been workshops are to become our dragon pens, and that will take much work. As you yourselves pointed out, we have no one to do it but ourselves. There is too much to do to waste our precious time on such nonsense."

"Ehu!" cried Huras in mock alarm. "He's demon possessed!"

"Or else the Magi stole him and left a changeling!" Kalen said with a shudder. "For surely that is not Gan!"

"Perhaps I should exorcise him," Kaleth said slyly. "A long fast, and an ordeal might do the trick, or perhaps there is a more expedient solution. It is said that neither changelings nor demons can survive immersion in running water."

"Attempt to duck me in the spring, and you *will* regret it," Gan growled. "That, I do pledge you!"

"And you the one who cannot get enough bathing!" Pe-atep chuckled. "What is the difference between a cold bath and a ducking, I ask you?"

"A world of difference, I thank you." Gan's face was quite visible in the moonlight, and he was glowering.

No one made any move to get up, but they teased him unmercifully, at least until it looked as if the jests were about to get more irritating than amusing.

Kiron refrained from joining in, and for the most part, so did Kaleth. After all this time together, they all had a fairly good sense of how far they could go with each other, and a distinct aversion to stepping over that line, though they could, and would (and tonight, did) go right up to the very brink of it.

The great irony of it all was that in this case, the others were far more likely of success than Gan was. Most of the young women that Lord Ya-tiren had brought with his household would be common-born, servants and laborers and the like, and with them, Gan's noble blood and handsome face were likely to count against him. It had been Kiron's experience—limited though it might be—that young women who were not born into wealth and privilege tended to be suspicious of men who were. And when wealth and high birth were combined with good looks, that only made them doubly suspicious that, whatever the man in question *said,* what he actually *intended* was to have his joy and wander on to the next conquest. Whereas for someone nearer in rank, philandering came with attendant high costs . . . and not just social costs, for if the girl in question had brothers, those costs could swiftly become both physical and painful.

In fact, those few young women who were of anything approximating Gan's social rank probably already knew him, knew of his reputation of old, and might well be as uninterested in him as their lesser-born sisters.

No, in fact, Pe-atep, Huras, and Kalen were all more likely to have success among Lord Ya-tiren's household than Gan, and Menet-ka be more likely to succeed with young ladies of rank. As for Oset-re—he might well prove Gan's equal now.

But Gan probably hadn't realized this, and it was pretty certain that it wouldn't occur to the others either. Kiron didn't intend to point it out. For one thing, it wasn't too likely that any of them would believe him, and for another, it was pretty amusing to see Gan stew a little.

"Peace, enough," Gan said finally. "Women and cats will do as they please, and there is no predicting either of them. Except that *I* would advise any of you who wish success to sacrifice to Pashet on the morrow, and leave me be. *She* is like to contribute more to your benefit than anything I could do."

Since Pashet was both the goddess of cats and of love, it was generally agreed that Gan was right. And a sacrifice to that goddess was a light one, anyway—a bit of a tribute to one of the temple cats would serve. Kaleth had lured a few wild *mau*-cats out of the desert, and their first litters of kittens had grown up tame. They had taken up residence in the temple he and

Heklatis had set up. And to make doubly sure, a little incense burned at Pashet's image would do the trick. Pashet was the sort of deity that preferred admiration to worship, and a practical tribute to one of her chosen creatures to an expensive or elaborate sacrifice.

Kiron yawned hugely. "Sacrifice to Pashet or not, as you will. I agree with Gan in this; there is a great deal to do, and I very much wish Avatre to have a pen all to herself soon. With these new people about, the sooner I can give her privacy, the better."

"There is . . . something you should know," Kaleth said, and the hesitation in his voice caught the attention of all of them instantly. "There is another group of people coming. And on the one hand, you will be pleased because of what it will mean for your dragons. But on the other hand . . . I do not know what you will think."

There was such a long silence following that astonishing statement that finally Kalen burst out with, "*Well?* You cannot just say something like this and leave us hanging! Out with the rest of it!"

Kaleth sighed. "The new group will be here in two days, three at the most. You will be pleased because they will give you heated sands for your dragons. But you may not be pleased because—because they are priests from several temples. From Tia."

 FIVE

THE entire population of Sanctuary was waiting, when the travel-worn and weary caravan of Tians arrived with a light escort of Bedu. There was no doubt that they were priests—their shaved and wig-less heads marked them. But these were not the sleek, polished, and gold-bedecked priests and priestesses Kiron remembered.

They wore the simplest of garments, nothing more than linen kilts for the men, simple sheath gowns for the women and mantles for both to shelter them from the worst of the direct rays of the sun. The kohl about their eyes was smeared, and it did not look as if they had renewed it since they left the borders of Tian lands. They were not laden with gold and faience jewelry either; the most any of them had were common amulets on leather thongs to mark which god they served. The little priestesses were in the saddest condition, nearly fainting with weariness, thin and parched looking, so much so that it would have taken someone with a much harder heart than anyone here possessed to turn them away.

But it was Kaleth who stepped forward first, to extend his hand to the priest in the lead of the group, as the Bedu who had guided them here dropped discreetly back.

The leading priest drew himself up with weary dignity. "We have come to fling ourselves at your mercy, Altan," he said, his voice hoarse, the Tian accent and pronunciation sounding strange in Kiron's ears after all this time away from it. "We are no longer safe in our own land." Not only did he look weary, he looked bleak, as if he had no real hope of anything other than being turned away.

"This is why we called this city *Sanctuary*, my friend," said Kaleth, his hand still extended. The priest looked at it for a moment, as if he could not quite believe it—then he stretched out his own hand, and the two clasped arms, hands to wrists. "Welcome, brother," Kaleth added softly.

One of the little priestesses burst into tears of relief, and as her sisters clustered around her, the rest of the women of Sanctuary, Aket-ten among them, hurried up to them, enveloped them, and carried them off before the priests could say a word.

The priest smiled wanly. "Trust the women to cut through all the nonsense we men put up as barriers. I am Baket-ke-aput."

Kaleth's smile was broader. "I am Kaleth, and you all are weary, hungry, and, most especially, thirsty. Come. You can tell us the rest after you have remedied all these ills, and when you are not standing in the desert sun."

But the priest held up his hand. "There are some others with us. I would know if they, too, are welcome."

Some of the priests stepped slightly aside, and from the back of the group came forward—a set of faces that Kiron had never expected to see again. Especially the tall, blocky, bald-pated, white-kilted man in the front of the group of much younger men and boys.

Nor, it seemed, had Ari.

"Haraket?" they exclaimed simultaneously in disbelief.

Haraket, once the Overseer of the Tian Dragon Courts, squinted in equal disbelief, looked briefly stunned, and then stumbled forward. "Ari? *Ari?* By Nofet's breasts—you miserable cur! You're alive! You're *alive!*"

They fell on each other, embracing like long-lost brothers. "Sobek's teeth, I should have known you were too evil to die!" Haraket rasped out. "You jackal!

You dog! How did you come here? Did the Bedu bring you? Tell me you have not lost Kashet—"

"I have not lost him; it would take a god to part us, I think. But there is more—" Ari said, pushing Haraket a little away and gesturing behind him. And as Haraket's eyes fell on Kiron, he saw them widen yet again with disbelief. When he and Ari parted completely, he continued to stare at Kiron and finally said, "Is that—that can't be—but you're dead!"

"No more than Ari," Kiron said, flushing a little. "And I'm afraid you have Ari to blame for the deception." Then he raised his head, with pardonable pride. "I did not steal that little red dragon, Haraket. I raised her from the egg, as Ari raised Kashet, but in secret; and in truth, you could say that she stole me." And with that, he whistled.

Avatre might have been waiting for his call; she shot up out of the pen to the complaints of the others, whose rest she had disturbed. It was too crowded there for her to fly straight up from the sand, but as the Tians exclaimed and pointed, she half leaped, and half flew from the rooftop she jumped up onto, hovered for just a moment to pick out a clear space, and landed in a backwash of wing-made wind and airborne sand. In the next moment she was butting Kiron with her head, and looking curiously at the newcomers, while Ari beamed.

"Hu!" exclaimed someone from behind Haraket. "She's a beauty, by Haras!"

"You think she's a beauty, wait until you see Tathulan and Re-eth-ke," Kiron replied, rubbing the sensitive skin under Avatre's chin.

"You have more?" said another, raw envy in his voice.

Haraket shook his head, and passed his hand over his shaved head. "I am—I am at a loss. Vetch—I suppose you have another name now?"

"Kiron, son of Kiron." He looked up at Haraket, and realized that he did not have nearly so far up to look now . . . "Which is my right and proper name."

"A man's name, and you are growing into it." Haraket managed a smile. "You look so unlike the boy Vetch, I do not think I will have difficulty remembering what to name you." He looked back to Ari. "In truth, I do not know what to think or say, so I shall say nothing and allow you to do my thinking for me, Ari. Are we welcome? I have with me all the dragon boys trained by Baken, aye, and Baken himself. We could not stay, Ari, not when— But the priests will tell you."

"The priests will tell us all, when you are all rested and calmer," Kaleth told him firmly. "And yes, you are welcome, too. This is, after all, *Sanctuary*, and it would be a poor sort of sanctuary that did not offer shelter to anyone who needed it."

In the end, not *everyone* in Sanctuary came to hear the tale the Tians told that night, when they were fed and rested, but most people elected to. Some came out of curiosity, some out of concern, and some, sad to say, to gloat over the sad state of the former enemy.

They gathered in an open square, beneath the stars, the only place big enough to hold them all. At the center were the Tians that seemed to have been given the authority to speak for the rest; Haraket and several of the senior priests. So, too, were the most-senior in Sanctuary; Kaleth of course, and Heklatis and Lord Khumun, Lord Ya-tiren, his wife Iris-aten, and their eldest son, and Ari—

—and somewhat to his own surprise, Kiron, drawn firmly out of the crowd by Lord Khumun and Kaleth. The rest—with the exception of some of the Tians who were still deep in the sleep of exhaustion—arrayed themselves around the court, or on the roofs of the nearby buildings. The court had the acoustic advantage that anyone speaking at the center of it could be easily heard by everyone in and around it. Rugs were spread for the group at the center to sit on; anyone else sat or stood as he or she wished. Most stood, the better to see the proceedings. It was a calm and windless night, still warm enough to be comfortable, though by midnight anyone under the stars would need a mantle.

The Tians began to explain what had brought them across the desert to seek a haven here, and the sense that Kiron had at first was that his fellow Altans were prepared to enjoy their tale of woe.

But it did not take long until they were all united in

shock and a certain sick feeling of *déjà vu*. The tale was all too familiar.

"When the dragons revolted, we didn't really have a good idea of what had happened," said Haraket. "We knew the dragons had been getting restive and hard to control, but you know, none of us ever really thought that there was anything wrong with the *tala;* not even Baken or me. My guess was that your sea witches were to blame somehow, but it never really occurred to any of us, I don't think, that we'd actually lose the dragons until it happened."

"No one knew the dragons actually had been lost for days," one of the priests put in. "It wasn't until messengers came back from the battlefield with the report that we knew why no Jousters had returned from the battle."

"And until then," Haraket continued, "we actually thought your sea witches had found some way to make lightning strike them out of the air—or something. About half the riders came back afoot, though most of the ones that didn't were not actually killed by their dragons or by falls. Or so I'm told. They generally managed to get their dragons to land, but it was the soldiers on the ground that got them."

Kiron nodded. There was some relief in that. Not that he had any great love for most of the Tian Jousters, but—well, he wouldn't wish the kind of terror and death (or the terrible life-in-death of a paralyzing injury) that came from plummeting out of a dragon's saddle on anyone. Well, anyone except, perhaps, the Magi. . . .

"So, without dragons, and with no means to control captured dragonets, there was no need for the Courts of the Jousters," Haraket said glumly. "It wasn't long before orders came that took most of the servants and slaves away; only a few of the dragon boys, me, and a couple of slaves remained. The Jousters that survived generally went into the King's army, and most of the dragon boys dispersed as did most of the servants. Baken decided he'd try either to pay one or more of the trappers to try to get an unfledged young dragonet right out of the nest, or else he'd get one himself, but right about the time I was going to attempt to persuade the Great King's advisers that this was worth trying, the Great King—got new advisers."

He looked over at Baket-ke-aput, who took up the thread of the story. The priest looked much better now; shaved and bathed, and with a proper headcloth and a bead collar that might have come from one of the ancient city treasure troves. That was Kaleth's touch, Kiron had no doubt. Kaleth knew that to have respect, oft-times one had to look, as well as be, impressive. The man was dressed in a fashion that clearly marked him as a priest, yet he no longer had the distinctive look of a Tian priest about him. The priest's eyes remained on Lord Khumun and Lord Ya-tiren as he spoke, but Kiron had the sense that he was very aware of everyone else whose face he could see in the torchlight. "The first we knew of these new advisers was when the Great King's previous advisers were suddenly called up, thanked, and dismissed. Sent back to their estates, if you please! And in their place, as if conjured from air, there were strangers who remained with the Highest at all times, and that was when the trouble started." He shook his head. "Small things, at first. The temple tribute was reduced; not by a great deal, but it was reduced in order to support these new advisers, who had no land, and seemingly no family. Then there were—accusations. People who objected to the presence of the advisers, or even voiced any questions about where they had come from and who they were, why the Great One had chosen them, were sent out to the provinces."

"That was if they were of wealth or birth," growled another priest. "If they were neither—they tended to disappear. And it wasn't wise to ask after them either."

Baket-ke-aput sighed. "Then—came the orders that certain young people in each temple should come to serve the Highest at the Palace. It took some while, though, and the god-touched were summoned from each temple separately, by name." He paused a moment, rubbing the back of his right hand with his left. "Perhaps I should explain that in our land, those who are god-touched with special powers are spread about all of the Temples of the Gods, rather than being concentrated in a single temple as, so I understand, you Altans manage things—"

Baket-ke-aput cast an inquiring glance at Kaleth, who nodded. "We call them Winged Ones," he said. "The priests are Winged, those who are not yet trained are Nestlings or Fledglings, and they all serve and are trained together in the Temple of the Twins. Well, except for the Healers, who have their own temple, in which all gods are honored, including those we Altans know not."

"That," said Heklatis briskly, "is because *all* Healers, whether they Heal by the knife, by the leaf, the flower, and the root, or by the touch of a hand, must learn every aspect of Healing, and all gods favor the Healer. It is so in Akkadia as well."

"I suppose being scattered thinly through every temple in Mefis and outside it was the reason why it took these so-called Advisers so long to find our equivalent of Nestlings and Fledglings, which we call acolytes," Baket-ke-aput said with a grimace. "And because they were spread about the temples, and the summons came, not all at once, but over days and weeks, it took *us* longer to realize that these so-called 'advisers' were making off with *every* child and adolescent that was god-touched."

"Nothing like this had ever happened before?" Kaleth asked, in tones that suggested he knew that it hadn't.

Baket-ke-aput shook his head. "Never. What need had the Great King of those who were untrained or half-trained? I know that I asked why they were being taken, and I was told that since there were no more Jousters, the untrained were going to be learning to act in concert, as the Altan sea witches could. This was meant to give Tia a weapon equal in magic to what Alta had. And since Haras priests *do* use magic—when they have it—in combat, I thought no more about it."

Lord Ya-tiren pursed his lips. "Even though these were the youngest, and untrained, and not the experienced and trained?"

Baket-ke-aput closed his eyes, as if in pain. "To my shame and sorrow, if I thought at all, I was simply glad that the ones called were those whose untrained or half-trained abilities we could afford to do without. And to be honest, we didn't, any of us, think that there was anything wrong. After all, these were the Great King's *advisers* who had issued the orders! Why would they do anything to harm Tians, especially consecrated youngsters?"

"We soon found out differently," said another priest, bitterly. "We did not see the young ones at all after a time. Some parents began to make diffident inquiries. Still, there was no sign of them, no rumors, and no one within the Palace would talk about where they had been taken.

"And then, one terrible dawn, the bodies began to turn up—thrown by night into Great Mother River!" Baket-ke-aput looked sick. "That was when we realized how wrong we were."

"*What?*" Ari exclaimed, turning white.

"Bodies," said Baket-ke-aput succinctly. "The bodies of the god-touched that we had allowed the minions of those advisers to take. Something in the Palace, or wherever those demons are working their evil magic, was killing them—the youngest and weakest first."

Kiron felt sick. Kaleth only shook his head.

"This is what I feared," he said quietly. "When I stopped being able to See what lay within Tian lands, I feared there were Magi there now, and that somehow they had wormed their way into the Tian King's good graces."

Another priest, considerably younger than Baket-ke-aput, who wore the amulet of Thet about his neck, leaned forward. "We should never have known, had they not been so greedy about draining so many of the children of their power until they died," he said bitterly. "There were too many for the crocodiles to take them all, and so we found some of them. That was when I made to approach the Great King, and as soon as I was given audience, I knew that I should say nothing. Not only was there a shadow upon him, but he looked to be as he had been in the full flower of young manhood. And so did the three advisers."

"That has a familiar taste to it," Lord Khumun said, with controlled anger in his voice. For some time now, Kiron had been a little concerned about the older man. Being forced to flee his own land had taken something out of him. But now—now the old warrior was back. And Kiron was relieved to see it. "So did the Magi of

Alta, and our rulers, when our Winged Ones began to be taken."

The Thet priest looked angry, and resolute, and just as much a warrior as Lord Khumun. "*I* know the forbidden spells that can give one a second youth, though I am sworn never to use them; it is the business of those of Thet to be upon the watch for shadow magic and the powers of darkness. We know these spells so that we may combat them; I knew the signs of what was happening. Those children had been killed so that their power might be absorbed and their years might be stolen and given to the Great King and his advisers."

Every time those words were spoken, Kiron felt colder. Bad enough to be profiting magically from the deaths of fighters in combat, but to murder children . . . !

"You said nothing," Heklatis said shrewdly. "Else you would not be here. And do not feel guilt; if you had confronted them, I think none of you would be sitting here now."

The Thet priest Pta-hetop nodded. "I made some excuse, some trivial request, and fled the abomination, before they realized that I knew them for what they were."

"And Pta-hetop, here, wisely began by telling his own priests what was happening, then they in turn spread out by ones and twos to the rest of us," Baket-ke-aput continued. "It was the gods' own will that he went softly and secretly, rather than trumpeting the abomination to the world and being cut down for it."

Pta-hetop shook his head, and his expression, al-

ready mournful, saddened further. "It was cunning—
and perhaps the gods gave me warning. I knew there
were no Thet priests strong enough to take those jackals of darkness in their own lair. When you cannot
fight, you must flee, for you cannot fight on another
day if you are dead."

Baket-ke-aput nodded—and so did Lord Khumun,
Lord Ya-tiren, and Kaleth. "It took us but a single night
and day to organize our flight. And since Pta-hetop
was the good childhood friend of Hokat-ta-karen, the
remaining Haras priest for what was left in the
Jousters' Court, and knew he could trust Haraket, he
told Haraket and the dragon boys with him also, and
asked if they could aid us in any way."

"There was nothing left for us in Mefis—and priests
are not accustomed to defending themselves,"
Haraket pointed out. "We are. So—" He shrugged.

"I had some few acquaintances among the Bedu, as
does Haraket, and we managed to gain their aid,"
Baket-ke-aput concluded. "They told us of Sanctuary,
but warned that we might not be well received here.
We said we would take our chance that you would accept us. That is the whole of the sorry tale."

That was not the whole of it, Kiron was sure. How
they had smuggled themselves out, the long and terrible crossing of the desert, even with the help of the
Bedu—that would fill a hundred scrolls, he was sure.
But it was not, at the moment, as important as what
had been imparted.

"But the god-touched children—" someone said from the darkness. "Why—"

"Why did we not rescue them?" Baket-ke-aput asked, savagely, his eyes flashing anger. "Because by the time we had organized ourselves, and knew what the advisers were about, we had found the last of the bodies. The eldest of the children. There are no more. We failed them, we failed in our duty to them, and we might just as well have set a knife to their throats ourselves. Now, shall I pound the ground and weep and strew ashes on my head, or will knowing that *I* know my guilt and know that I can never expiate it satisfy you?"

It had been a very long time since Kiron had heard that level of bitterness in anyone's voice . . . and the last time, it had been Ari, crying out, *I do not make war on children!*

"We will build a shrine for them," Kaleth said into the heavy silence. "You will give us their names, and we will build a shrine to them in the river cave, where the sand cannot etch the names away, nor time erode them. They will have in the afterlife all that they should have enjoyed among us. They will not haunt this side of the Great Sky River as hungry ghosts for much longer."

Baket-ke-aput let out his breath in a sigh. "I will carve those names with my own hands," he said heavily. "I would do so with my fingernails, if that was the only tool I had. Thank you."

"They are not the first to die at the hands of the Magi," Kaleth told him, and the restrained anger in his voice penetrated even Baket-ke-aput's rage and grief. "Nor will they be the last. Listen now to who these abominations are, and what they have wrought in Alta."

He rose to his feet, and stood, as if he was about to officiate over a ceremony. Kiron thought that he had never seen Kaleth look so full of authority; this young man who was not a great deal older than Kiron himself was standing among men much his senior in age and authority, and yet they were listening to him with as much deference as if he had Lord Khumun's years and experience. As the torchlight flickered, the shadows moved across his face, and the larger shadow he cast behind him stretched up the wall like a kind of guardian spirit. Briefly, and succinctly, Kaleth told the Tians what the Magi of Alta were, the weapons they had created, how they had consolidated their power for decades, and how they had finally moved to take Alta into their hands. "It is the Winged—the god-touched—who give them the most power, but power, and years, can be stolen from any living human, we think."

The Thet priest nodded. "So we have been told, in the scrolls of the forbidden magics. Though it takes the deaths of many to equal the power of a single god-touched victim."

"So, as they exhaust those with the holy powers,

they turn to the common man," Kaleth continued, and raised his eyebrow. "Do you see now why they should be so very interested in this war, and the indefinite prolonging of it?"

Baket-ke-aput closed his eyes, while some of the others behind him exclaimed, as if thunderstruck that they had not thought of this before. "To my shame," said Pta-hetop, "That had not occurred to me. I thought only to take the rest of us out of their reach—"

"*Wisely*," Lord Khumun put in with emphasis, speaking for the first time since they had all sat down. "You could not do any good by allowing yourselves to be taken! You have removed one arrow from their quiver. That was well done."

"And the trek across the desert is not well-suited to taking thought for anything but the journey," said Lord Ya-tiren with sympathy. "As we who lately took that trek know too well."

"That is why we meddled with the *tala*, we young Jousters and Heklatis," Kiron put in. "We knew we could not hope to stop the war, but we thought we could at least put it on the footing of soldier against soldier, without the dragons adding to the slaughter. But—" he added, feeling sick again, "—I never thought that the Magi would take themselves to Tia and infect it with their evil."

"Well, we can all play the *I never thought* game until we are so bowed down with grief and guilt that we cannot move," Heklatis said sharply, cutting through

an atmosphere that was increasingly loaded with just
that. "Now we know. Kaleth has the guidance of the
gods themselves, as well as the Eye that sees into the
futures. We have dragons. Kaleth tells us that we will
have more flocking to our banner, and we have the
best minds in both Kingdoms to deal with this. We
have traded what we know, found it appalling, and
have joined forces. And this is enough for one night,
don't you think?"

Words so blunt they were the equivalent of clubs left
everyone sitting in stunned silence.

Then, after a long—a very long—moment, in which
Kiron fully expected *someone* among the Tians to take
offense at the Akkadian's rudeness—the silence was
broken.

By laughter.

It was laughter with an edge of bitterness and grief
to it, but it was laughter all the same. And it was coming from Baket-ke-aput, who bowed his head as his
shoulders shook, and finally sat straight up again and
wiped his eyes with the back of his hand.

"By the gods, Akkadian, your tongue alone is
sharper than twenty swords," he said, and Kiron
thought there was just a touch of admiration in his
voice. "If ever I need a goad, I will come to you, direct.
I wonder that you are still alive; in Tia, you'd have
been challenged a hundred times by now."

Heklatis shrugged, looking smug. "In Akkadia, I
was. Why do you think I am here? But in Alta-that-

was, a man who cannot fight with his wits has no right to challenge one who can to a battle with swords. Especially when that one is in the right. And you know that I am."

"I do. I do. Just keep that tongue of yours to a goad, and do not turn it to a flayer's whip to take the hide off those you would help. You are right. There is nothing we can do this moment—but simply by exchanging these words, we have done much already." Baket-ke-aput looked back over his shoulder, and seeing no disagreement among his own folk, looked each of those in the circle in the face. "If you will have us, have our skills, have us at your side—we are your brothers, from this day."

Lord Khumun stood up, as did Baket-ke-aput, and the two men clasped arms as equals; Kaleth put his hand over both of theirs. "Welcome to Sanctuary, brothers," Khumun said fiercely, then softened the ferocity with a smile. "And as your brother—I advise you to rest. Tomorrow begins the real work. Tonight—may the gods give you dreams of a future we can be proud to build."

 SIX

KIRON went to sleep feeling as if he had just been through an earthshake, and woke up in much the same mood. And he had thought that he would have some time to get used to the situation before anyone rang in new changes on him.

He was, however, mistaken.

He had not been back from the morning hunt longer than it took to unharness Avatre and give her a sand buffing and oiling, when Menet-ka came looking for him.

"Ho! Kiron!" he called from above the pen. Kiron looked up, but before he could ask anything, Menet-ka answered his questioning look. "You're wanted," he said shortly. "In that little temple of Kaleth's. Kaleth sent me to get you."

Avatre was ill-pleased by the interruption, and she snorted at Menet-ka, her golden eyes flashing her displeasure. Kiron patted her shoulder, where the scales shone like armor made of rubies. "For what?" he asked. "I was going to go work on the new pens—"

Menet-ka shrugged. "They didn't tell me, but I expect they want you *as* the wingleader. Anyone who's like to be in charge of anything is there right now. I suppose they're forming that council Kaleth was talking about, and they want you for something having to do with it."

Well, he could see why they would be doing that now—while people were still in shock and feeling sympathetic to the Tians, it was best to make them a fundamental part of Sanctuary. Especially if more Tians were likely to be coming.

Only the priests of the temples at Mefis had reached here so far, though according to what Kiron had heard rumored this morning, warning was spreading out to the farthest-flung temples like the ripples after a rock has been thrown into a still pool. Soon every priest in every temple in Tia would know what had happened in Mefis, and if they had any sense at all, they would realize it was only a matter of time before the hands of those "advisers" stretched out for *them*. Or at least, any of them that had extraordinary powers.

After that, anyone Winged (or "god-touched" as the Tians put it) who had any measure of common sense and self-preservation would be fleeing. Some might choose other directions than into the desert, but some would follow the priests of Mefis. And many who were not god-touched might also choose to escape.

Then the rumors would begin to fly as priests and some of their servants and slaves vanished, the story about the dead children would eventually surface and although it might be embellished or changed out of all recognition, fingers would begin pointing in the right direction. The Magi in Tia did not have an Eye, the terrible means of enforcing their will and controlling the populace at large that the Magi of Alta did. The King's soldiers could punish and arrest, but they could not strike from the sky—ordinary Tians might begin to look askance at the Great King's new advisers, wonder if the rumors were true, and think about a retreat across the desert themselves.

Perhaps. There was the same difficulty there as there was in persuading Altans to flee; it was hard to leave everything you had built and sweated for, and go off into the unknown. Especially when what you had sweated for was very little. When you did not own much, every bit of what you did have was precious. A bit of land—well, it might be no more than a few rods of soil, but how could you leave it and go somewhere else where you owned nothing? A small house—but if it had been where your father, and your father's father grew up, the very dust was precious. And without the double threat of the Eye and the earthshakes to threaten them, it would be difficult to persuade Tians to flee.

Not all, not even most would make the journey. Most would remain where they were, reluctant to leave their only homes and possessions. Many of those who initially left would turn back after the first few hardships. But there were a great many Tians and Altans, and Sanctuary until now had been very small. The population of Sanctuary was about to be increased from both sides of this conflict, and Kiron could easily see that there had better be something in place to rule over them and adjudicate the inevitable differences *before* the influx became too great.

Though why he should be involved—

Well, only one way to find out. He gave Avatre a final caress, and left her basking in the heat while he sought the building Kaleth called the "House of All Gods."

There had been too few priests and too few resources when they first came to Sanctuary to have a temple for each god. Kaleth had simply solved the problem himself by setting up the same sort of temple that the Healers and the Winged Ones had, in a great building that had surely once been a temple itself, with small shrines to every God the Altans knew around the walls of the chief room. As more buildings were uncovered and explored, little statues turned up that more or less resembled different Altan deities. Whenever that happened, he or Heklatis modified them to suit and put them at the appropriate shrine. There were several small rooms—looking exactly like the rooms where priests lived in the temples that Kiron knew. Kaleth and Marit lived there now.

The door to the House of All Gods stood open, and the Tian acolytes were busying themselves with various tasks as Kiron approached. It appeared that Kaleth had taken in the Tian priests as his guests. This would probably serve, but—

But we'd better get another sandstorm soon, Kiron thought, as he entered the door, moved to one side out of the way of traffic, and surveyed the crowded central hall.

As they had last night, those most closely involved with what Kiron was beginning to decide *was* going to become the council were seated in a rough circle, with other interested parties behind them. Fewer now than last night, but still . . . there were a lot of them in this audience. Interesting; once again, it was a mix of Tians and Altans, but now, instead of being completely separated into two groups, the Tians and Altans were at least sitting close to one another and if not yet talking, were at least trading cautious glances.

Kaleth, who was seated next to Lord Khumun and beside the chief Tian priest, glanced over at the doorway from time to time. When he finally spotted Kiron, he lifted his head and gestured to him to come in. "Kiron!" Kaleth called, when he made no move to enter the room. "Come sit beside Ari. You are to speak for the Jousters."

His own head came up; to say he was startled was

an understatement. How could he possibly speak for the Jousters? "But Ari—" he began. "Ari is older than I and, besides, Ari is more experienced—"

"Not in the sort of things we will be asking you new, young Jousters to do," Lord Khumun pointed out, as Kiron made his way through the crowd to sit uneasily next to Ari on a flat cushion that one of the Tian acolytes handed to him. "His expertise dates to the days before, when no one had a tame dragon but himself, and even he will have to learn what you already know. And besides that—we have another purpose for Ari."

Ari stirred, looking a little apprehensive at that pronouncement. But before he could say anything, Lord Ya-tiren stood up, and any murmuring sank into silence.

Lord Ya-tiren had never been the sort to have any patience with ostentation in his dress, so the plain kilt he wore and the simple collar, sash, and wig with it, would not have been out of place among any gathering of moderately prosperous men. It was not his physique that commanded the room either; like most Altans, especially compared with Tians, he was slender, and although he was in excellent condition, his was the build of a scholar or scribe, not a warrior.

It was something else entirely that set him apart; the feeling of completely unconscious authority, as if, all his life, men had listened to him and obeyed when he gave an order.

Which, of course, they had.

"I make bold to call this meeting into order. We are here because things have come to the point that we need a council of peers to govern us," he said, in such reasonable tones that there was nodding all the way around. "I think we are all agreed on that, even our new—allies. And we were fairly agreed some time ago on who should sit on this council. But after last night, it is clear to me, and perhaps it has *always* been clear to Kaleth, that Sanctuary is not going to be the retreat for Altans alone that we once thought. It will be bigger, holding far more people, and a council alone will not suffice to govern it."

He paused, but there was no sound of disagreement. "We are used to being ruled by Kings and Queens, both Altans and Tians alike. I believe most folk will be uneasy without such rulers. Perhaps a council might have served if Sanctuary was only to be home to a handful of Jousters, a few renegade Great Houses, and a gaggle of priests. But it is not. The common people of the Two Lands will be coming here, and we need a single figure—or perhaps, I should say, a pair—to serve as leaders. Our peoples are used to bringing their troubles to a single source of remedy, not a council. And there should be one deciding voice to cut through dissent and say, '*this* shall be' when there is no clear agreement."

There was murmuring, but it was the murmur of agreement rather than dissent. No one was going to argue . . . yet.

"You, my lord," Ari began, but Lord Ya-tiren shook his head.

"I will not be accepted by Tians," he pointed out, before any of the Tian priests could even think to object. "I would not even truly be accepted by Altans. By our laws, the ruler *must* be out of the royal bloodlines. Kaleth and Marit are already out of the succession, by reason that he is claimed by the gods and she is claimed by him. So aside from them, there is only one person here who matches that requirement."

And he looked across the circle to where Nofret was sitting beside Ari, on the side opposite to Kiron. She looked up at him, eyes as wide as a startled gazelle.

"But!" she began, "I do not—I am not—" but Lord Khumun and Lord Ya-tiren together shook their heads.

"You must," said Lord Ya-tiren. "We are all—all!—taking duties we feel we are ill-suited to. This must be yours. Besides, Nofret, you and your sister were trained to sit on the Twin Thrones. You may not have the experience, but you have the knowledge of how to lead, and you certainly have the example before you of how *not* to lead."

"But Tians will never accept an Altan leader," began Baket-ke-aput, his brow clouding. "There have been only two Queens who ruled in all of our history, and even then they ruled as Regents for their infant sons!"

Kaleth held up his hand. "We did not say she was to rule alone. In Alta, that would be unthinkable anyway.

We are no longer to be ruled by the Sacred Twins, I think, but—" And now he looked at Ari, "—there is a logical partner for Nofret who would be accepted by the Altans. And that is you, Ari."

Ari started visibly. He had not been expecting *this!* But then, by the murmurs, neither had anyone else. "I cannot see why—" Ari began.

"Only because you are far too modest. If I recall correctly, it is you, Ari, who more often than most, has the best ideas." Kaleth lifted his right shoulder in a kind of shrug. "Ask anyone, and they will tell you. It is you who is the likeliest to devise solutions to problems quickly. But most important of all, you are a peace-maker. It is you who most often can take people who are quarreling and bring them to work together."

"Oh, no—" Ari objected, shaking his head. "It is *you*, Kaleth, who does all that and more!"

"But only when under the hand of the gods! When I am myself, I am no better at it than—than Gan!" Kaleth replied, causing those who knew Gan well to laugh. Then his expression darkened, and grew serious. "Besides, no man can serve at two tables. The gods demand my time, and our history tells ill tales about those who thought to hold power over men while the gods demanded their own kind of service."

"It says worse of those who styled themselves as Priest-Kings," Heklatis put in dryly. "Or those who claimed to rule in the name of the gods. The temptation is to say that what you want and what the gods want is one and the same, and it is difficult for ordinary folk to prove otherwise."

"As always, your tongue delivers wisdom as well as
stings, Healer," Kaleth said, nodding. "To be brief,
then: I will not deny the gods what they will of me."

Marit placed a hand on his shoulder; she said nothing, but her expression spoke as loudly as any words.
No more shall I.

"I," said Lord Ya-tiren, "would not be accepted by
Tians, nor, more importantly, by Nofret. And, most importantly of all, the First Lady of my house would strip
my skin from my flesh with her words if I were to try
so foolish a thing."

That brought another bit of laughter from those who
knew the lady in question. Sweet-natured as Lord Ya-
tiren's wife was, she also had a dangerous tongue
when she was angered. And there was little doubt
how she would react to the notion of her husband attempting to take a wife young enough to be his daughter, she who had never permitted a Second Wife to
enter the household. "I am pleased and happy to handle administrative tasks," he finished, "but I know
where my abilities best lie."

"And I," said Lord Khumun, "am, and always will
be, a soldier. Ask me strategy, tell me that tactics are
needed, and you will have all you desire. But outside
that—" He shrugged. "And even less am I, a soldier of
the Altans, like to be accepted by Tians."

"I do not know how much you know of the ways of

our people and their rulers," Lord Ya-tiren said to the Tian priests. "In our tradition, the male twins of royal blood who marry the female twins of royal blood can be made Kings. And unless I am very much mistaken, in the Tian tradition, the man of the appropriate bloodline who marries the royal daughter can be made King. Is this correct?"

Baket-ke-aput nodded. "Entirely. And—" he added, with a lifted brow, "—there is a saying among our people that the man who *least* wishes to be King, is the man who is like to be the best suited. Still—"

"Then by all qualifications, Ari is the only choice for all of us," Kaleth replied, "since he is Tian and will be accepted by Tians and I will not divorce my Marit to free her for some other husband." Marit still had her hand on Kaleth's shoulder, and he covered it with one of his own. "My beloved, who has the secrets of her sister's heart poured daily into her ear, tells me that Nofret does not find Ari distasteful."

"Ah, but Ari is a commoner," Ari objected—

Except that when he said those words, he did not sound at all certain. In fact, he sounded like a man who was telling a lie. And Kiron's ears pricked up at that.

Kaleth drew himself up and stared at Ari, putting on that invisible mantle of dignity that transformed him into someone Kiron felt impelled to bow to. The back of his neck prickled a little. Kaleth *knew* something. And it had not come from the mouths of men. Furthermore, he was about to say something—or perhaps it was more appropriate to say, Someone was about to speak through him.

"I believe, Ari-en-anethet," said Kaleth, in a voice that seemed to echo in the overcrowded room, "that it is time and more than time that you told the truth about your birth."

The reaction of the Tian priests to that voice was altogether satisfactory from an Altan point of view. They looked very much as if they were going to throw themselves on their faces, and only the fact that no one else was doing so kept them still seated. At the back of the room, the few acolytes who were still here *had* thrown themselves prostrate.

So these Tians do recognize the Voice of the Gods when they hear it. That made Kiron feel a good bit better. It meant that the priests *knew* now what Power was holding the reins here, however lightly those reins were being held. And when their fellow countrymen showed up, the priests would take care of whatever "enforcement" of the laws and ways of Sanctuary needed to be done. It was one thing to claim to speak for the gods, but when you could demonstrate the fact, well, that was another bundle of reeds altogether.

But others here had paid more attention to the words than the tone or the way in which the words were delivered. "Your birth?" Haraket looked from Kaleth to Ari, his face screwed up in puzzlement. "What about his birth? He's the son of a scribe—"

"He is the *nephew* of a scribe," Kaleth corrected, in a voice that no longer echoed. "His mother was a Temple of Senet handmaiden. Which was where his father came upon her and came to love her."

Sharp glances among the Tian priests, and some whispers among the oldest. So. There was something about this that was calling to mind things that they knew.

"My father was a simple soldier," Ari said stubbornly.

Kaleth laughed. "Your father was a soldier, yes, but hardly 'simple,' and well you know it. Ari, the gods have shown me your life laid out as an open scroll. Let your tongue at last tell the truth. It is the answer to how to unite our people, and though it is not the only answer to that conundrum, it is the best one."

Ari looked as stressed as Kiron had ever seen him, as if he both loathed what he was about to say, and had longed to say it aloud all his life. "It is—it is nothing I wished anyone to know. *Ever!*" he managed. "It is an accident of birth! It is not meritorious and not ignoble either, but it is no recommendation to be made a leader! Kings should be made of more than bloodlines! This is—"

"Vital," Kaleth said firmly. "To the common man, it is the hand of the gods. Perhaps blood does not make a king, but having a noble bloodline does not make him less of one. You have the skills. Now tell."

Ari hung his head. "My father," he said, to the

hands lying clenched in his lap, "Was—is—the King's brother, the Royal Commander of the Armies of Tia."

Baket-ke-aput looked absolutely thunderstruck. So, in fact, did every other Tian. It was Baket-ke-aput who recovered first and said, falteringly, "Then Ari-en-anethet, Jouster of Tia and Sanctuary, would be—acceptable to the priesthood and the people of Tia as a coruler with the Noble Maiden Nofret. If he is accept-able to the Noble Maiden."

Nofret's expression was sober, but her voice was firm. "He is acceptable."

"Just one moment." Ari stood up. Kiron had never seen him so tense in all the time he had known the sen-ior Jouster. He practically vibrated. *It's a good thing that Kashet isn't here, or Ari's nerves would have that poor dragon looking for something or someone to attack.* "Nofret, no matter what these people want, I will not take a wife who is coming to me out of a sense of duty!"

Nofret regarded him gravely. "Jouster Ari," she said, with great dignity. "All my life I have known that I must wed out of duty. To have a husband who is pleas-ant, kind, and a—" she hesitated, "—a friend, a very dear friend, is more than I expected."

Ari shook his head, stubbornly. "Maybe *you* have been trained to think that is the right and proper way to do things, but I have not. Thank you for saying that I am pleasant and kind and a friend, but I—I require more."

He turned to Kaleth. "The Lady Nofret has no other kin here but you and her sister, Mouth of the Gods," he said with great formality, before anyone, even Nofret, could respond. "Therefore, I beg your leave to court her and win her love as well as her regard."

Baket-ke-aput was dumbstruck. Nofret looked first shocked, then puzzled, then, slowly, her eyes glowed with warmth and pleasure.

Kaleth did not so much as lift a corner of his mouth, even though Ari was almost old enough to be his father. "You have my leave," he said gravely.

"And mine," said Marit, just as gravely, though the twinkle in her eye and the furtive flush on Nofret's cheeks suggested that Ari already was well on the way to having that love. Assuming he didn't have it already. Maybe Kiron wasn't very old, but there was one thing he did know, and that was that there was no telling what a female would think.

"And you will not pressure her into a decision!" Ari continued. He sounded desperate, but Kiron didn't think he was looking for an excuse not to wed Nofret. On the contrary. He wanted her desperately. He meant exactly what he said; he didn't want a co-ruler, he wanted a wife and a partner.

Kiron took another glance at Nofret. If he was any good at reading expressions, she didn't think Ari was looking for any excuses either.

"By no means," said Kaleth, before anyone else could speak. "After all, there is time yet before so many people come to Sanctuary that we will *need* a King and Queen. Take whatever time you need. Unless Nofret objects?" he raised an eyebrow in her direction.

Nofret blushed a deeper crimson, but smiled. "What lady ever objects to being courted? Any who would must be mad."

Baket-ke-aput looked as astonished as if a camel had spoken to him—but then, in Tia, while women were held in high regard, *young* women were accustomed to obeying fathers and elder brothers until the day they had a household of their own.

Baket-ke-aput might as well get used to this change in "the way things were." Kiron knew very well what would happen when Tian girls saw how much freedom Altan girls enjoyed.

"Until then, however," Kaleth continued. "You must needs be on this council. That, *I* require. I want your skills and your knowledge of your fellow countrymen. Sit, please, Ari."

Ari did.

People obey him as if he were as old as Lord Ya-tiren. Kaleth, it seemed, was acquiring a little something in the way of personal authority each time the gods spoke through him, and it wasn't the sort of thing that wore off. "And now—let me beg of you all a little time."

Kiron sensed an abrupt change in subject—and he wasn't mistaken.

"Time," Kaleth repeated, "and attention. I wish to

spread before you the lines of the possible futures we face, as I have seen them."

Kiron leaned forward at the words. That Kaleth had seen a future for this place—more than one, actually—was without a doubt. But he had not yet shared that vision with anyone.

Kaleth drew a deep breath and turned to the Tians. "Forgive me, Priests of Tia, if I repeat what you already know. Among our people, the ways of those who are Winged are not well known, and I must begin with an explanation."

Baket-ke-aput nodded gravely. "Even among us, the Eye that sees ahead in time is rare. Please go on as you will."

"The future is like Great Mother River entering the delta," Kaleth said gravely, looking into the eyes of each of them in turn. "It is not a single straight path. It bends and curves, breaks into daughters, and each of the daughters wanders on. Some merge again, some fade to nothing. And I—I am a dragon flying above at dawn, and have only glimpses of what is below as the morning mist chooses to part, or clings stubbornly to land and water. The nearer we are in time to what I see, the clearer it is—but the nearer we are, the more difficult it is to find ways to change what I can See."

"I have heard something similar from the priestesses who tend the Mirror of At-thera," said Baket-ke-aput. "Save only that they have never, in my lifetime, Seen far enough ahead in time to do more than give warning." He looked at Kaleth with increased respect.

Kaleth acknowledged the admiration with a nod. "We have come to a point where that branching begins, and I cannot always tell what decision will put us on a beneficial path—nor can I always control what will put us there. And I have seen many endings to our story." His face darkened. "Some, I will not speak of. But there is one ending that I greatly desire, and in it, the Two Lands are—not one, but bound, as husband and wife are bound, partners in all respects. In that future, the King and Queen rule from a new city on the river, equally distant from Mefis and what you call Bato, and we call Alta City. Sanctuary is become the city of the Gods of Alta and Tia together in harmony, the symbol of the joining of the Two Lands, and the Jousters are its protectors. It serves also as the way point for a rich caravan route, bringing wealth to the gods from trade, and not from taking it out of the hands of the people. No longer at odds with one another, the task of Altan and Tian Jousters alike is to guard those who dwell in Sanctuary, to make the caravan route across the desert safe to travel, and to watch the borders." Kaleth's eyes shone with enthusiasm, and the reflection of his dream. "In that vision, all Priests of Alta and Tia come to Sanctuary to be trained, and the aged and most wise come here to impart their wisdom. Sanctuary is a place of peace, where enemies learn to become friends, and ways are found to heal old wounds and make new dreams grow."

Kiron caught his breath at that vision, and he was not the only one. What a dream! If only it could come to pass. . . .

"That is the vision I desire you to hold in your hearts, and give to the people as a goal," Kaleth went on. "Would I could tell you how it is that we will come to that place, but that is the end I hope you will strive for." Now he looked deeply into Baket-ke-aput's eyes.

This is the one he has to win over. The Senior Priest, perhaps the High Priest. He's had power in his hands. When Tians come here, he'll have it again. Will he barter some of that power to Kaleth for a piece of Kaleth's vision?

"You have us, Mouth of the Gods," Baket-ke-aput said, slowly, and then to Kiron's complete astonishment, the priest bowed. Not the bow of equal to equal; he abased himself, as he would have at the altar of a god. The only thing he did not do was to lift up Kaleth's foot and place it on his own head in token of complete abasement, and Kiron had the feeling he had actually considered doing even that. After a moment of shock, so did every single one of his followers bow, down to the acolytes who stopped hovering at the edges of things, trying to pretend they were busy so they could listen. They, too, dropped what they were doing to throw themselves on the ground.

Kaleth rose, paced slowly to where Baket-ke-aput was stretched out, and touched his shoulder. "I do not need minions, holy one of Tia," he said quietly. "I need—*Sanctuary* needs—partners. Friends who share the work and the dream."

Baket-ke-aput rose also, and once again, he and Kaleth clasped arms. "Those, you have. I swear it. For myself, and for these."

"Then that is all I can ask." With a radiant smile, Kaleth went back to his seat. "Now," he continued, looking around again, "There is the little matter of where we are to put all of you. . . ."

 SEVEN

THE acolytes of the various Tian gods were surprisingly willing to help with the work on the new dragon pens. Not that acolytes of any sort weren't used to working hard, but they were generally not accustomed to the kinds of labor that might be termed "common." Nevertheless, they turned their hands to it, fitting stones into place, making cement to hold them together, although the task of trimming them to fit was left to Lord Ya-tiren's experienced stonemason. But perhaps that was because the four buildings surrounding the original pen were destined to become temple quarters for them all once the Jousters moved; at the moment, the priests and acolytes of the entire Tian party were all crowded very closely together in

Kaleth's Temple to All Gods, sleeping with scarcely a place to put a foot between them, and it could not be comfortable for any of them. At any rate, with their help, and the help of some of Lord Ya-tiren's people, the conversion occurred within a few days. The original doors—which fortunately had no lintels anymore, if they ever had possessed such a thing—were bricked halfway up, and the walls raised, so that a real sand wallow could be made deep enough for a dragon to dig him- or herself in.

Then, before the sand was brought in, a walkway was constructed around the periphery of each pen, just as the pens in Alta and Tia had been constructed, with a wider platform at the rear. Last of all, copying the pens in Alta so that the riders could live with their dragons, a single-roomed shelter was built on that platform at the back of the pen, and a water trough where a dragon could drink.

Since Kiron had been put in charge of the new Jousters, there was one thing he had made very clear. Everyone, including Ari, had agreed with him.

No Jouster would ever live apart from his dragon again.

Jousters were going to change; it was time for that change to begin. They would no longer live as lesser nobles, not that they'd be able to under the current conditions anyway! They would be housed in conditions no better, and no worse, than any officer in the Tian or Altan armies.

Jousters would still be like no one else, and part of that difference would be signaled by other ways in which they lived besides the bare fact of their housing.

It was no longer possible, with the bonded dragons, to treat a dragon like an inanimate thing, the chariot that one drove, the sword in one's hand. It was no longer possible to shrug, walk away, and get another if one's dragon was ill or injured, or worse, died. Not that anyone with a bonded dragon would be able to do anything like *that*. Look at the way every Jouster in Kiron's wing fussed over their darlings, fretting over a bit of scuff on a scale, seeing that their dragons were fed, watered, and comfortable before they even considered their own needs!

They hadn't much cared for having walls between them and their beloveds, but now that the new quarters were built, that would end. The new Jousters were partners with their dragons, and like the faithful hound that slept at the foot of his master's bed and followed at his heels, the dragon would spend as much time as possible with his own Jouster. Which was, after all, the way that both dragon and Jouster wanted things. Kiron had not really slept easily without being able to wake in the night and hear Avatre's breathing. . . .

Perhaps one day, when there were more resources, the quarters could be enlarged. For now, they were comfortable enough, and at least when the temperature dropped, as Kiron very well knew, they would be better than most.

The one thing they didn't have to worry about out here was rain; any rain that fell in the desert was sporadic and wouldn't turn a pen into sand soup the way it did in both Tia and Alta, so no awnings were going to be needed over the pits. A sturdy roof on the Jouster's shelter to keep out the sun, however, was a must. Otherwise in summer, the heat would be a punishing thing, even for a dragon.

Once the construction was done, the biggest job, other than raising the walls and making the walkways, was in filling the pens with sand. Kiron had a hope that perhaps the gods would oblige with another sandstorm, but in the end, it was done by the simple, if more back-breaking means of having every single able-bodied person in Sanctuary get together to spend a single day helping to carry and dump sand into the waiting pens.

Then the Thet priests, with Heklatis watching closely, invoked their spell. It was the same magic used in Tia and Alta both that kept the sand in the pens at a temperature comfortable for the dragons. Without the need to impress, as Heklatis had shrewdly guessed, it was a much simpler affair than Kiron had observed when he spied on the ritual. What Heklatis had *not* realized, however, was that the little priestesses *were* actually needed and were not merely decorative.

In fact, in many ways, they were crucial.

Theirs, it seemed, was a passive power; Kiron suspected that if the Magi had guessed what it was they did for the priests, their names would have been first on that list of those who had been called to "serve" the advisers, and their status as priestesses would not have saved them.

They amplified the power of the spell, giving it, not merely strength, but reach, sending it far beyond the area in which it would normally operate. So the Thet priests were able to "steal" heat from somewhere far outside the walls of Sanctuary, and sink it into the sands. But they also created, at long last, one of the "cold" rooms where meat could be stored for days at a time at need, channeling the heat from that space into the pens as well. In the times when there was more game caught than the dragons could eat that day, it could be stored against greater need. The Thet priests were adept from long practice at finding good ways to channel the heat, but it was clever Heklatis who suggested one change that had never occurred to them—to move the heat through time as well as distance, taking heat from Sanctuary during the day to be used at night, keeping the buildings cool by day, as the Palace at Mefis was.

The mere concept made Kiron's head spin, but apparently they worked out how to do that. It seemed so impossible that he finally decided to just pretend he hadn't heard any such thing.

When they brought the dragons to the new Compound, there was not a moment of hesitation out of them on seeing their new quarters. The dragons had never been so happy since they had left Alta. They lofted over the walls and plunged into the hot sands with little squeals of glee, and every one of them, even Kashet, immediately buried him- or herself to the shoulders in the sand, leaving only the wide, leathery wings spread out across the hot surface.

The Thet priests, who back in Mefis had never actually stayed around long enough to see what the dragons made of their pens when the heating spells were renewed, watched them with spreading grins on their faces. By this time, they had all made the acquaintance of one or more of the dragons and had, predictably, been charmed by them. It was hard not to be charmed by indigo-colored Bethlan with her assumption that everyone she met was a friend, and by the gentle green Khaleph, and beautiful tricolored Tathulan who could excite admiration in the dullest of observers, but each of the others had their little coterie of admirers. All of the dragons liked people, even shy scarlet-and-sand Deoth. And why not? People had never hurt them, and people were the source of satisfying attention and even more satisfying scratches on the sensitive skin under the chin and around the eye ridges and the join of head to neck. In Tia, everyone had heard of Kashet, but few had seen him up close; dragons were to be admired from afar, but were dangerous, even deadly, up close. And of course, all that had once been true of the wild-caught, *tala*-controlled dragons. Although a dragon that killed a man would be put down, nevertheless, it was possible to be seriously hurt by one that was clever enough to know he could harm his handlers.

But these—these creatures were as clever as temple cats, as keen and beautiful as falcons, as personable as a high-bred and intelligent horse, and as eager for admiration and affection as a hand-raised cheetah. It was quite clear the moment you approached one that he (or she) liked being in your company, and would no more harm you than your favorite hound would.

Every one of the newcomers had a favorite among the dragons; that had begun from the moment the Jousters had come to Sanctuary, and those who had just arrived had simply carried it one step further—for they began wearing little tokens in the dragon's colors to denote that partiality.

Now that the pens were complete and the priests had done their magic, they all lingered, congregating around the pens of their particular favorites, talking with great enjoyment about new ideas for improving the dragons' living conditions, while the humans of the wing moved their belongings, at long last, into their shelters. There was a great deal more to move than Kiron would have thought. Somehow, all of them had managed to accumulate enough personal comforts to make life reasonably close to the one they had once enjoyed.

"Perhaps," said one young priest to another as Kiron hauled in a load of flat cushions, "we ought to build a hatching pen? It would be better to have it before we need it."

"These dragons aren't old enough to breed yet," objected the one he was talking to, chasing away a fly with a whisk, though not the pretty, bleached-horsehair-and-gilded thing he would have had back in Tia, but an improvised switch made of frayed palm fiber. "I don't think any of them except Kashet is. What would you hatch?" Still, he looked interested. And this was very new, this interest in dragons in general, as well as partiality to particular ones.

"Wild eggs," said a third decisively—this one bearing the hawk pectoral of a Haras priest. "It'll be nesting time soon, and if you get an egg before the mother starts incubating them, you can move it safely. Steal them the way my mother stole wild goose eggs, and bring them here to hatch. Sling it between two camels or something, so you don't addle it while moving it."

Ari was passing by at that moment with his bedding, and laughed. His dark eyes crinkled at the corners with amusement. "You've never seen a nesting she-dragon, have you? Even if she isn't incubating, she's guarding, and it'd be worth your—"

Then he stopped, and Haraket, who was carrying another load just behind him, nearly ran into him. He had a most peculiar look on his face, and Kiron tossed what he was carrying into his shelter hastily and went to join the discussion.

"What are you thinking?" he demanded of Ari, before Haraket could ask what was wrong. "I know that look! You've thought of something!"

"That we've got forty or fifty inexperienced she-dragons out there right now," said Ari, staring off into the hard blue sky as if he could conjure a dragon out of it. "That instinct will tell them how to mate, but not what to do afterward. Remember how you got Avatre's egg so easily away from her mother? I don't know that the she-dragons out there will be much different. So I'm thinking that we'll have dragons laying eggs in the wrong places, or in more than one nest, or just laying them and going off without knowing they have to incubate or guard. And *some* of those eggs will be laid near enough to Sanctuary to retrieve them. I can't see a reason to let good, fertile eggs go to waste."

"And we have eight or ten dragon boys right now who would give their privates for a dragon of their own," said Haraket, nodding. "Tell 'em they've got to go retrieve an egg a couple days away from here? That's nothing! They'll bring it back on their own backs if they have to!"

"I'd go back to Mefis for a dragon egg," said Baken, coming into the conversation, his voice raw with longing. "I'd do it barefoot and in a loincloth."

"You shouldn't have to go that far," Kiron replied, and when the others looked him, he grinned. Oh, he'd seen the envious looks from the Tian dragon boys, every one of them thinking: "If I'd only had an egg, I could have an Avatre now." They'd seen enough of

Kashet, and worked enough with the young ones that were about as "tame" as a wild-caught falcon to have gotten the fever for themselves. "Look, when the *tala* ran out, you had all those dragons loose on the border of Alta, and I do think that most of them didn't go back to the hills beyond Mefis. For one thing, the pickings in the swamps are better, though they would only hunt there, not den up. For another, if they tried to go back, the other dragons would drive them out. The wild ones have established groups and territories, and the Tian dragons would have been nothing more than clumsy interlopers."

Ari nodded his approval of Kiron's assessment. "Oh, a few of them would get accepted, but the rest would be driven out—and of course, some of them wouldn't have bothered to try and go back since there would be good hunting here, and none of them are afraid of humans. That means they're forming wild wings of their own, and making new territories all over this desert. In fact, I think I've been seeing some of them in the distance. I just didn't think about it, because as long as they didn't bother me, they didn't really matter."

"I believe I have, too," Ari replied thoughtfully. "But I've been so busy hunting I hadn't paid a lot of attention to the wild dragons in the distance."

"I know *I* have," said Menet-ka, quietly, from behind Kiron. "There's a natural hot spring in my hunting area, and there's a whole—flock? herd?—a group of them, anyway, that I see there most mornings. They sleep around it at night. I *know* they're Jousting dragons, because they let me get pretty close before they fly off."

Baken's eyes lit up. "Females?" he asked eagerly.

"At least four. And they're all breeding age." Menetka chuckled. "They left us alone, I don't know whether it's because I'm with Bethlan, or because Bethlan is too young to be considered a rival."

"I think I know where there's at least one or two," Kiron said slowly. "I think I'll go look; I have to go there anyway to hunt tomorrow. It's where the mountains meet the desert."

"Then I think *we* should construct a hatching pen," said the young priest firmly. "We haven't the need to hurry, the way we did to work on these pens so we could all move to better quarters, and it won't take all that long to do a single pen."

"We'll help!" replied Baken. Then he hesitated, and looked at Kiron. "That is, if—"

A memory flashed through Kiron's mind, of how Baken had made friendly overtures to him despite being given very unfriendly treatment on Kiron's part. How Baken had inadvertently been the one who had taught *him* what he needed to know to train Avatre. Without Baken, he probably would never have escaped successfully with her.

"Baken, we've done without dragon boys this long, why start spoiling us?" he said with a laugh. "No, this

is important. Kaleth has said we must have more dragons, and until ours are old enough to breed, this is the
only way we'll get them. You build the hatching pen,
and as many more new pens as you can. We'll see if we
can spot any groups of the old Jousting dragons about,
and when we find them, we'll start watching them, or
asking the Bedu to, and—trust to luck and to Haras."

"Haras will favor us," said the young priest firmly.
"He must. If he fails to do so—he may well find himself with no one to worship him but those the advisers
deem too unimportant or ineffectual to repress."

Kiron winced. But after what he had seen in Alta, he
couldn't find it in him to disagree.

***

He slept better that night, with Avatre literally
within reach (she had elected to rest her head on the
platform, with her nose just inside his shelter!) than he
had since the first days of utter exhaustion following
their arrival in Sanctuary. It was good to be with his
beloved again, good to have her scent of hot stone and
spice in his nostrils, good to know that if anything disturbed her in the night he would be right there to
soothe her.

Not that anything did. She slept as soundly as he;
perhaps she was as comforted by his presence as he
was by hers. They were both up and awake without
needing outside prodding as soon as the sky lost its
stars, and she was truly awake and ready to move immediately, with none of the sluggishness of having

spent a cold night. It was just light enough to make out the shadows of things against the lighter stone and sand; the rack for the harness and saddle, the stone trough that had been moved here with much grunting and labor for Avatre's water. She stood waiting for her harness, as good and obedient as anyone could have asked. It was a distinct pleasure to be able to saddle her without jockeying for space with the others. He had done this so many times that he really didn't need to see the worn-familiar straps and buckles to get her harnessed up. And as for Avatre, she kept looking upward and making little contented snorts, not the grumbling that had been her usual accompaniment to this chore. It seemed that everyone else in the wing was having a similar experience with their dragons this morning, because he didn't even hear whining from Deoth, Pe-atep's scarlet-and-sand male. And although he and Avatre were the first in the air, it wasn't by much. Aket-ten took off right after he did, and before he had gotten too high, Pe-atep and Ari were a wingbeat behind her.

Mindful of his promise to range farther today, he took Avatre up high. She followed his signals and his encouraging hands, rising upward in as close to a vertical climb as a dragon could manage. He was glad of the saddle straps today, leaning over her neck and feeling the thrust of her muscles under his legs with each upward surge of her wings, each wingbeat a flash of glowing scarlet in his peripheral vision, and when they could see the distant mountains, he signaled her to level off and head in that direction. By moving her up as high as he could safely take her while she was still fresh, she had the height to take some glides, saving her some laboring in the thin, cool, morning air.

Cool? It was more than cool, it was cursed cold—but that was the way of things in the desert. He glanced down; at this point, a wild ox would look smaller than an ant, but the only thing he saw was a single Bedu on a camel down below, and the only reason he knew there *was* a Bedu on the back of the camel was by the barely visible flapping of his robes. It was probably one of the outriders, bringing back waterskins full of precious water from the spring below Sanctuary to his clan or family group.

They flew on as the sky lightened, going from deep, velvety blue to gray, as the eastern horizon brightened, and at last, the very edge of the great disk showed at the world's edge. The sun gilded the tops of those distant mountains at their halfway point, though the land beneath them was still in shadow. He held himself back from asking her to fly faster, even though he feared that if there *were* dragons in there, he would miss the sight of them taking off for their morning's hunts. She needed to save her strength for her own hunting.

But he kept his eyes strained toward those low, rough crests, rather than looking for game as he usually did—and so luck was with him, and he did catch sight of them as they powered up out of the canyons cut into the rock. The sun struck them as they came out of the darkness, flashing on their scales, and making them look like distant, iridescent gems being flung into the sky by a careless child.

Ten of them, altogether: ruby-red, deepest maroon, two sky-colored blues, a blue-green like a beetle's wings, a green-gold the color of sunfish scales, a red-gold like an enameled pendant, an indigo, and a coppery brown. They scattered to every direction in order to avoid each other as they hunted, though they spread mostly to the north, but there was no doubt in his mind that they were using that canyon as their den. He marked it in the map in his mind, and with a feeling of relief, turned to the important task of helping Avatre with her hunt. He could scout the canyon later; she was hungry *now*. He could feel her impatience in the way she kept scanning the desert below, and the sudden way in which she changed direction when she thought she spotted something.

And a good thing, too, for the hunt was singularly frustrating.

They spent most of the morning gaining height, searching for prey, gliding down and having to labor for height again. All the while, she was getting hungrier and more impatient—and, in fact, losing her temper. Finally, just as the thermals were starting to help, he spotted something, a dust cloud, in the direction he had least expected it, the mountains where he had seen the dragons taking off from their canyon.

If they're living there—then they're used to avoiding dragons. This isn't going to be easy. . . .

Avatre saw it, too, and by now, she was so hungry she didn't wait for his signal to pursue that distant clue, she tilted sideways and slipped around in a tight turn that sent her straight for the sign. She wasn't wasting any time either; with grim determination, she clawed for height in a stomach-lurching series of powerful wingbeats before flattening out into a racing flight. She had seen those dragons, too—and she was not going to let one of them get "her" prey.

When this kind of mood was on her, the only thing Kiron could do was duck down over her neck and hang on. Woe betide anything that got between her and her meal. . . .

With a feeling of great pride, he realized after a while that she was a lot faster, and a great deal stronger, than she had been just a few moons ago. She hadn't put on a burst of speed like this in a very long time, and there was no doubt in his mind that the ground was speeding past down below them much faster than it had before.

But triumph—and breakfast—was not going to come easily today.

As he had expected, these oryx—he had just enough time to identify them before they threw their heads up· and bolted—knew what dragons were. They probably knew every single step of their territory and the best places to hide. And they knew that dragons were more dangerous than lions.

They also knew how to escape them.

Instead of scattering in all directions, they bunched up as they ran, churning up a huge cloud of choking, obscuring dust, and making it impossible to single out one for an attack from above. And they were heading right for a crack or canyon cut into the mountains, a narrow slot where dragons would have a hard time following. Avatre put on another surge of wingbeats as his heart began to race, and he felt one-handed for his sling and stones.

Kiron cursed under his breath, but also gritted his teeth on a savage grin; his blood was up, just like Avatre's and Avatre had an advantage that wild dragons didn't.

She had him.

Avatre saw where they were heading, and put on a last burst of speed to try and cut them off before they reached their shelter, but it was too late; they made it into the crack as she dove desperately through the dust at what she thought was the last of them.

Her reaching talons came up empty, and she had just enough room to end in a controlled landing before she smacked into the rock face. She skidded to a halt in the fine dust that passed for sand in this part of the desert, tucking her haunches under her and back-winging as Kiron clutched the saddle and waited for her to stop.

The sudden quiet as she shook herself and hissed at the rock told him that the oryx herd had done exactly what he expected them to do. They hadn't run on wildly through what was probably a maze of passages—the passage they had ducked into wasn't all that wide, and they had probably slowed to a walk the moment they knew that they were safe from Avatre. And now they had stopped, somewhere inside that canyon, where Avatre could still sense or scent them. She knew they were there, and she was angry. And there they would stay until Avatre went away, safe, where she couldn't reach them.

But he could.

He slid off her back, and got his sling and stones ready, and smiled to himself as he realized what a good team the two of them made. She would not go hungry or frustrated for much longer. And those oryx were about to get a big surprise.

He wouldn't have tried this with a herd of wild oxen, but the oryx wouldn't charge him the way oxen would.

Avatre was still hissing and tearing at the ground with her talons to vent her frustration and anger at missing her kill; he pounded her shoulder to get her attention, and was rewarded with a snort and an astonished look as she craned her neck around to peer at him. Her golden eyes flashed as the pupils pinned, then dilated, in her excitement.

"They haven't beaten us yet, my love. Up!" he said, suiting the gesture to the word. "High up, my girl! Fly!"

She gave him a long and level look—but this wasn't the first time he'd hunted on the ground while she waited in the air and her frustration vanished as she realized what it was he meant to do. She pushed herself off, the dust blowing up in a huge cloud that made him cough and cover his mouth and nose, as he headed into the narrow crack of a canyon.

The transition from light into shadow was startling; the dust didn't follow him for more than a pace or two, the temperature dropped, and he had to pause a moment for his eyes to adjust. He found himself in a passage just big enough that he couldn't quite touch the walls when he spread his arms wide, with a worn path running right down the center of it. Rough stone walls towered high above his head, showing mostly the effect of wind erosion to smooth them out. When the wind whipped down through this place, it must howl like a jackal.

The crack was one of those twisting and turning affairs, and he went around a couple of corners before he found the oryx that Avatre had scented. In fact, he practically blundered into them. The crack had begun to widen at that point, and they were milling about restlessly; his sudden appearance took them entirely by surprise, as their startled snorts proved.

For a moment, they just stood and stared at him out of astonished eyes, then a couple of them danced sideways, as if trying to make up their minds whether to run or stand their ground.

A stone from his sling against the leader's flank and a wild shout decided them.

Within moments, the herd was off and running again, this time concentrating on him, and not on whatever was above. Which was exactly what he wanted, of course. He had no intention of trying to bring any of them down with his sling; he was going to drive them ahead of him until they burst out into some place where Avatre could get to them.

Whooping at the top of his lungs and swinging his sling, he urged them on, his voice echoing above the pounding of their hooves as they charged away from him. At some point this crack would widen out enough that Avatre could dive in from above, and by now she had already found just such a place. She was probably perched on the edge of the cliff above, waiting to plunge down as soon as the herd galloped into ambush. He and she had played this game before. The thunder of hooves echoed back to him, along with squeals and grunts—and then, a scream.

He put on a burst of speed of his own. The crack did widen out, rather abruptly, turning from a passage to a sun-drenched dry valley, and as he ran out into the sunlight, it was to see the last of the oryx vanishing into another canyon, and Avatre in the middle of the space with her talons on not one, but *two* dead oryx, feeding on one with a savagery born out of frustration as much as hunger.

But that wasn't what stopped him dead in his tracks.

Avatre was devouring her prey in the middle of a deserted, and heretofore hidden, city.

 EIGHT

AVATRE was oblivious; she had an oryx in front of her, another beside her, she was ravenous, and all she was interested in was getting herself on the outside of that beast. Kiron, however, stared in astonishment, and it wasn't until his mouth began to dry that he realized it was hanging open and shut it quickly.

Kaleth had told him he would find a city. The thing was, Kaleth had not told him what kind of a city he would find. He had expected something like Sanctuary, newly uncovered in the sand, perhaps with the rounded lines of Sanctuary's buildings. And truth be told, he had expected something more derelict even than Sanctuary, with roofs gone, walls caved in. Even if it was made of that strange stuff Sanctuary had been built of, the legends all said Sanctuary had been buried (and preserved) in a single day. He calculated the new city to have been abandoned over the course of years.

This was a city hidden in canyons, and it had not been built of the hard stuff of Sanctuary. It had not been built at all. It was carved out of the living rock of the cliff face. It didn't look abandoned at all—well, except for the fact that there were no doors, and no shutters for the windows. Otherwise, he would not have been at all surprised to see people come hurrying out of those doors to see what the noise was about.

There was—so he had been told—a temple like this in Mefis, the funerary temple for one of the many Great Kings buried across the river in the City of the Dead. As he stared at building after building, turning slowly in place, he could see resemblance to the buildings of Alta and those of Tia, but not as if this was a blending of the two styles. The style of carving here was older, simpler—more as if this was the father of both styles, and each had gone its own separate way.

The amount of work here made him shake his head a little in disbelief. Every bit of cliff face was carved, in clean, simple, geometric lines. And these buildings were not single-storied, either, which made a vast difference from both Altan and Tian styles. Two and three sets of windows looked down into the canyon from each site.

There must have been thirty separate "buildings" —or at least, building facades—in this canyon alone.

Each one was subtly different from the one next to it. That might reflect the tastes of the original owners, or it might reflect the passage of time—each building having been carved later or earlier than the one next to it. The pale gold of the sandstone of these cliffs made the whole city look as if it had been made of that precious metal.

He had to know what these buildings looked like inside! Were they just caves, or were they as elaborately carved inside as out? Could people actually live in them?

We could carve the doors wider on the bottom floors to let our dragons in; make a sand pit there if the ceilings are high enough. . . .

It looked as if the bottom floors had been made with dragons in mind; twice as tall at least as the ones above. But the only way to find out, was to look.

He headed for the nearest, after another glance at Avatre to be sure she was all right, but she was nose-deep in her prey, and oblivious to anything else. He crossed the threshold—noting as he did so that there were places for hinges and, presumably, doors which were long gone—and paused inside for his eyes to adjust to the darkness.

For dark it was, despite the windows cut into the façade. Kiron could see, however, this was a man-altered cave. And yes, the ceiling here was as tall as in the Temple of Haras in the Court of the Jousters in Mefis, a place where Kashet had walked comfortably. A dragon could live here.

The interior was simple: a box of a room, with thick square pillars holding up the ceiling, the spaces between fully wide enough for two dragons to pass. It was a big box, though, and that high ceiling gave it a cavernous feeling. After his first feeling of vague disappointment, he realized that the simplicity was the opposite of crude. Floor, ceiling, and walls, all were polished so smooth that when he touched the wall, and then the floor and the pillars, they felt like sueded leather under the hand.

And at the rear of the room, climbing up toward the ceiling, was a stone staircase. So there were more stories above this.

He moved toward the back, hearing his footsteps echo in the emptiness, feeling the room growing cooler and cooler as he got closer to the rear and away from the windows. This could be very good. With magic heating the dragon's sand, the bulk of the stone would keep living quarters more than tolerable, they'd be comfortable.

And this was where the Jousters would eventually live?

Could there be any more perfect place for them to live?

He found himself smiling, then grinning with glee. How could anything be better? There was more rain here, as evidenced by the signs of flash floods and the bits of green here and there. But you wouldn't have to worry about rain when your dragon's pen was sheltered by all this rock. And there were midnight *kamiseens,* but when you were behind this sort of wall, who cared? The worst that would happen would be that you had a bit more sand to sweep downstairs into the pen. And if this became a city for Jousters and their helpers—

There might be problems in supplying all those dragons with food if there were no temple sacrifices to feed them, unless—

Sanctuary is going to be a city of temples. No law says we have to feed the dragons in their pens. That had been a necessity with the wild-caught, *tala*-controlled dragons; put two together while feeding and you'd have fighting. Not the current lot. So long as everyone had enough food, they ate peaceably side by side. And they had all learned that although a dragon wanted a nap when she was full, she didn't have to have one. They flew perfectly well on a full stomach. They had to, after all, a wild dragon didn't laze about after making a kill, and neither could the tame ones. So there might not be any issue here; you could fly to Sanctuary for the morning feed, go out on patrol from there, come back for the midday feed, go out on the second patrol, return for the evening feed, then come back home. The dragons would complain at first, but only until they realized that breakfast came at Sanctuary without having to hunt for it.

He looked around as his head came up through the floor of the next story; it was identical in every way to the room below it, except, of course, for the view from the windows and the height of the ceiling. He took a walk around the room, trying it on for size. It was comfortable; very comfortable. A brazier near the windows would keep it warm—or you could go down and spend the night with your dragon in the sand. The one thing it lacked was a place to bathe—well, there was nothing of the sort in Sanctuary either. No point in getting beforehand with things.

There was another story above this one—this time the room was a little smaller, but not by much. The view was amazing. Short of being on the back of a dragon, there was no view like this anywhere. Beneath him, the white-gold sand of the canyon stretched like a fat snake between the carved walls—and from here, looking down at how regular the floor of the canyon was, he had the feeling that it, too, had been smoothed by stonemasons.

How long had it taken to build this city? And why? Sanctuary supposedly had been a stop for caravans crossing the desert, but what had this place been? There were no legends telling about it.

And why had it been abandoned?

Perhaps because the caravans stopped coming?

Perhaps there had been something here worth mining, and when it ran out, so did the prosperity of this city, and gradually, people left it to the oryx and the lizards.

Across from him, stood a building façade with false

pillars framing a mathematically precise doorway and windows with beautiful simplicity. Each façade reflected a different personality; some very rigid and formal, some less so, some so pure in their simplicity that they made him think of some of the temples in Alta. Some had false urns carved into the rock, or the stylized forms of gods that looked familiar, yet strange, reduced from the realistic, if rigid forms he knew to the kind of sketched-in shape that an artist would rough out before carving the details. Yet, he could tell by the elegant curves and carefully smoothed surfaces, these images *were* in their finished forms.

Yes, there was Thet, or something like Thet—the curve of an ibis-bill thrusting out of the otherwise featureless head, but as smooth as a bone fishhook. And there was Pashet, in her feline form; two of her, in fact, flanking a door, with the barest curves for brow ridges, and no sign of eyes or nose, and yet more the essence of *cat* than anything but a real, living feline.

After he had studied them, he began to have the feeling that he would never quite look at the images of the gods in the same way again. These seemed so much more powerful, purer.

From here, he could see four more canyons branching off from this one, and in at least two of them, there were more buildings. How many Jousters and dragons and their helpers and families could be accommodated here? Fifty? A hundred? More?

He felt dazzled by the idea. A city, an army of

Jousters, whose duty was to guard the borders, and the priests of Sanctuary, and protect the caravans coming across the desert. Jousters who could actually have families—perhaps raising sons and daughters to ride dragons themselves? Dragons flying to mate, and new dragonets being raised from the egg by the children of Jousters. The vision was nothing less than intoxicating. Could that possibly come to pass?

I'm getting ahead of myself again. Far ahead. We've a long way to go before we're safe from the Magi, and that has to be taken care of first. He shook his head. All that was for the future; for right now, he needed to keep his eye on the immediate needs.

Still, he ought at least to investigate this place and get some idea of how big it was, and whether it was all in as good a repair as this building was. Kaleth would want a report, and so would the others. Even if they weren't going to be able to move here in the immediate future, they would still want to know everything about the place.

He trotted back down the stairs and out into the canyon. Avatre had finished her first oryx and was beginning, in a much more leisurely manner, on her second. She looked up as he neared and made a little noise of inquiry.

"Eat, sweetheart," he said, and passed on to the next building.

All the ones in this first canyon proved to be in excellent repair, although despite the uniform appearance of the facades, only a third of them were actually three stories tall once he looked inside. It was clear why; in some, the rock had flaws that would have made cutting a third floor dangerous, and in others, it appeared that work had stopped before a third floor could be put in. He wondered about that, but cutting so much rock was difficult and dangerous, and perhaps these places had all begun with single stories, then as the owners acquired wealth, second and third levels had been added.

He couldn't imagine how a family would cope with the noise of having someone cutting away at the rock above them until the room was completed, though.

Maybe they'd moved elsewhere until the work was finished. Aket-ten would probably be full of theories about these people, but unless they ever found, say, wall paintings showing how they had lived, her hundreds of questions would go unanswered.

When he'd finished taking inventory, he found that a third of the structures were limited to two stories, and a third were only a single story inside. The rock itself told the tale for the most part; there weren't too many of these places where the carvers had simply stopped without a good reason.

He moved into the first side canyon, and here, he met with his first disappointment.

This canyon, much narrower than the first, was nothing like as grand. The facades were simple blocks of stone, where the rough face had been sheared off in a flat plane, and the windows and doors were just geo-metric holes in the rock. Many of the facades had fallen, choking the entrances; it looked as if they were victims of earthshakes. The carving here was inferior, too, with nothing like the fine finish in the first canyon.

So, in this city, too, there were the wealthy and the not-so-wealthy. It was quite possible, actually, that far-ther down this canyon—or others—he would come to a place where the living spaces were nothing more than caves crudely recut.

The second side canyon was similar, and a third was completely blocked by fallen stone.

As in Sanctuary, however, there was no sign that people had ever shared their city with dragons, not even the wild, *tala*-controlled kind. That was disap-pointing, though he was sure that the buildings could be fitted with the sort of things the dragons needed.

And there was no obvious water source, which was more worrying. Given the evidence of earthshakes, he had to wonder if the reason that the place had been abandoned was because a tremor had cut off the water source and it had failed.

In the fourth side canyon, however, which was al-most as wide as the main canyon, the buildings were virtually intact—and had a sense about them that they were not private dwellings, but public places. Tem-ples, perhaps, and schools, libraries, records houses, courts—he couldn't have told why he felt this way, there was just something about the facades that seemed impersonal, yet open. Certainly they were all more uniform than the ones in the first canyon, even though the carving was just as high a quality.

As he approached the largest he caught a whiff of—water!

He sniffed eagerly; yes, there was no doubt of it, he smelled water! There was another scent along with the moisture; a hint of sulfur, that suggested that this might be a hot, rather than a cold spring. That was all right; they could make do. They could build catchments and cisterns for rainwater, so long as there was a water source that wouldn't run dry.

Thinking now of nothing but the water, he broke into a trot, noting that for the first time he'd found a building that already had an enormous front entrance. Quite large enough for a dragon, actually—

Without thinking, he hurried toward that entrance, and the increasing dampness to the air as he neared made him move faster. From the scent, there was a *lot* of water there! Maybe as much as flowed beneath Sanctuary!

Then an angry hiss from the darkness made him stop for a moment, while his feet refused to move.

The hiss came again. And it wasn't the hissing of steam escaping from a vent in the rock.

Slowly, never taking his eyes off that black rectangle of a door, he started to back away. His heart had started again, but now it was pounding, and he felt very much like a mouse that had inadvertently walked up to a cobra's den. There was something moving in there, back in the deeper shadows. Something big. And he had a pretty good idea what it was—

Move slowly. Don't run, or you tell it that you're prey. Keep your eyes on it, and hope that it doesn't decide you're prey anyway.

It would be the height of irony if he had come through all he'd weathered so far, to be eaten by a wild dragon through his own inattention and carelessness.

If I get out of this one, I don't think I'll be telling the rest just how I discovered there were dragons living here.

He had managed to get about halfway back up the valley when the wild dragon inside that building made up its mind to charge him. Maybe it decided that it wasn't going to let him get away. Maybe it thought he was going to bring back other humans—if it was a former Jousting dragon, it wouldn't want to be caught again.

For whatever reason, he glanced back for a moment to see how far he was from the main canyon, and when he looked back, a thing that seemed to be all teeth and talons and three times the size of Avatre was bearing down on him.

Despite that he had thought he was ready to face an attack, he wasn't.

All he could see was death with teeth as long as his arm, and eyes that held nothing but rage.

He couldn't help himself; he screamed with fright, the sound was driven out of him, and his heart, which had been racing, now pounded like a madman's drum. He ran backward as fast as he could go, still not daring to take his eyes off the beast. Bad decision; he tripped and fell and landed sprawling, and the dragon kept coming.

He scrambled in the fine sand, desperately trying to get to his feet without taking his eyes off the beast. "Get away!" he yelled shrilly, knowing the creature would never obey him, yet madly hoping for a miracle. "Get back! Back!"

It kept coming. He scrambled up, but he knew he could never get into cover quickly enough, and as the beast came close enough to rear back for a strike, he screamed, unashamedly—

Then felt himself shouldered aside as Avatre counter-charged.

He fell down, but this time he didn't try to get up. She got within talon range of the wild dragon, swiveled to put her whole body between him and the other dragon, and put her head down, hissing defiance.

With a snort of astonishment, the other dragon, a green, skidded to a halt. He was much bigger than Avatre, but she caught *him* by surprise, and as she stood between him and Kiron, tearing at the sand with her talons, neck outstretched and hissing furiously, he backed up a pace, his neck stretching upward, eyes wide and shocked.

This was a strange dragon in his territory. A strange,

young dragon, who should have given way to him. But she was defending the creature he had thought to make a meal of!

Kiron watched the wild dragon blinking at her as surprise turned to bewilderment. Wild—or now-wild, for although he didn't recognize the beast, he thought that it probably was one of the Tian Jousting dragons. Most wild dragons avoided humans; they fought back with particularly nasty weapons, they didn't taste as good as oryx or wild ass or ox, and there wasn't as much meat on them. Wild dragons mostly didn't see humans as worth the bother.

But a Jousting dragon would know the difference between an armed and an unarmed human, and a Jousting dragon wasn't as good a hunter as a wild dragon. He'd settle for anything he could catch.

Poor thing, he was caught now in a war with his own instincts. Avatre was a youngster, and his instincts said she was off-limits to fighting. She was female, and that, too, cooled his aggression. But she was protecting the enemy—and standing between him and his next meal.

Kiron got to his feet again, and moved slowly, very slowly toward Avatre. This was not the time to startle her. She might turn around and lash out at him without knowing who she was striking at.

She glanced back at him briefly, and when the green male made no further move to attack, raised her head a little and turned it so she could watch both of them at the same time, though she was still hissing like a steam vent and kept most of her attention on the other dragon.

Kiron moved up beside her and put his hand on her shoulder. He'd never felt her so hot! She almost scorched his hand. He had the feeling that in this case he was going to be a lot safer on her back than on the ground. But he didn't want her to crouch; that might give the other dragon a chance to attack. "Avatre," he said quietly. "Leg."

Without taking her eyes off the green male, Avatre slowly backed up a pace, then extended her foreleg for him to use as a step to vault up into her saddle. The moment he was in place, she straightened her neck, and still keeping her eyes on the other dragon, began to back up.

The male remained where he was, still looking thoroughly bewildered. Kiron, meanwhile, was losing no time in fishing for his restraining straps; he wanted to be buckled into place and quickly.

He hadn't quite realized how frightened he'd been—and was!—until he tried to get the straps buckled and discovered that his hands were shaking so much he was having a hard time with that relatively simple task. He fought with the metal and leather, and it felt as if someone had glued all of his fingers together. They just wouldn't work right—

Come on! he told himself, fiercely, feeling his heart pounding so hard he had to swallow around the pulse in his throat. *If she has to fly for it—*

But the straps were not cooperating, and neither were his hands. As Avatre reached the mouth of the side canyon, the green male suddenly made up his mind to charge again. And this time, instead of charging back, Avatre leaped for the sky.

And he only had one strap fastened.

With a yell, he grabbed for the front of the saddle and hung on for dear life, wedging his feet into the chest straps and clamping his legs hard against her sides. Forget the reins! She sideslipped and turned in the air with a lurch that sent his stomach where his heart had been, and put his heart in his throat. Fear ran through him like a bolt of lightning as he nearly came out of her saddle.

With tremendous wing surges, she threw herself upward. He clung like a flea on the nose of a racing camel, while she clawed for height. Height was her only hope if this green decided to challenge her after all. The only way that a smaller dragon could win against a larger was to have the height advantage.

But as he dared a glance down—in between trying to wedge himself more firmly into the saddle and trying *not* to be sick—he saw the green claw the ground, snort, and stare upward at them.

He wasn't going to follow. Either he wasn't that hungry, or he didn't want to have to work that hard for his meal.

A couple of wingbeats later, Kiron saw him retire back into the building where he was making his den.

So if he wasn't going to pursue—time to get Avatre down before he fell out of her saddle!

And Avatre responded to his frantic directions to land on the top of the cliff. It wasn't the best place in the world to pause, but as his heartbeat sounded in his own ears like the pounding of war drums, he managed to get the saddle straps fastened securely around him and tightened down, and gave her the signal to take to the air again.

This time she made his heart race for an entirely different reason.

Instead of leaping up and using her powerful wings to send her higher in surging jolts, she looked down into the canyon, seemed to make up her mind about something—and pushed off from the cliff.

And fell—

—and fell—fell almost three stories, then at the last moment before she hit the canyon floor, snapped her wings open just as it seemed as if she was going to hit the sand. If this hadn't been exactly the kind of maneuver they had practiced to run against the Tian Jousters, he'd have probably dropped dead out of fear. As it was, he found himself yelling involuntarily and once again hanging onto the saddle for dear life just before she turned the drop into a climb.

By the time she was flying high, drifting sedately from one thermal to another on the way back to Sanctuary, he was dripping with sweat, the waistband of his kilt and the roots of his hair absolutely saturated.

If I never have to go through that again, I will be very, very grateful.

He could have been killed. Avatre could have been hurt. It could all have gone horribly, horribly wrong.

Yet as the fear wore off, the exhilaration of what he had just discovered replaced it. Not only had he found Kaleth's mysterious hidden city, but he had found wild dragons *and* they had a place where they could incubate any eggs that were laid!

Avatre was still agitated, but not seriously so. She seemed more concerned about him, turning her head to look back at him from time to time as if to reassure herself that he hadn't come to any harm.

Well, with all that yelling, she had probably thought he'd gotten hurt. He leaned over her shoulder and patted her neck, telling her what a fine, brave lady she had been, and how proud he was of her. After he'd done that for the third time, she finally heaved a great sigh, her sides inflating and deflating under his legs. Then he felt her relaxing, stretching out, lengthening as her muscles let go. She stopped looking back over her shoulder at him, concentrating on the far-off smudge on the horizon that was Sanctuary.

He half expected her to try to land, as usual, in the old communal pen, but to his pleased surprise she spiraled in on her new pen and dropped down lightly and under complete control precisely where she belonged.

He was off her in a moment; and within the space of

time that it took to unsaddle her, he realized that except for her emotional agitation, which was mostly fading, she was by no means as tired by her exertions as he had thought she would be. She had just spent an overlong hunt, had faced down an older dragon, and made a fear-charged escape flight, and she wasn't really breathing heavily. All this hunting for themselves was putting the dragons of Sanctuary into better physical shape than any of the Jousting dragons had ever been.

Which meant—could they actually face down wild dragons on a regular basis? If they *could*, then two or three could go out when nests were discovered, and hold off the mother if she turned up before an egg was successfully taken.

"Kiron!" Pe-atep called from the door to his pen. "Any luck?"

"The best!" he replied, "Come on, you'll all want to hear about what we found today!"

 **NINE**

THERE were eight fertile eggs in the hatching pen, claimed by six Altan and two Tian dragon boys, one of whom was Baken. At last, the slave who taught all of them the best way of training young dragons to be ridden had won not only his freedom but his own dragon. Kiron was both amused and bemused to see how the acquisition of his very own egg had changed him. He had gone from a young man who was all business about the beasts he was training, to one just as egg-obsessed as anyone else who had ever been granted the chance to hatch out a tame dragon of his own.

Those eggs came from four different clutches; only half of the eggs had proved to be fertile, and all four clutches had been abandoned before the female in question began incubation. To Kiron's mind, and to Ari's, this meant that the females must be former Jousting dragons, who were too inexperienced to know what to do, and whose mothering instincts had not yet fully awakened. Which, in turn, meant that their theories were right. At least some of the Tian Jousting dragons had not gone back to the desert and the hills near Mefis when they fought free of the last of the *tala*. Two Tian boys were with some curious Bedu their own age watching two more dragons to see if they'd abandon their clutches, too. There were six more would-be Jousters waiting besides those two if all of those eggs proved worth incubating.

Quietly, Kiron took Kalen and Pe-atep aside when they knew that at least some of the eggs were going to hatch. He intercepted both of them after their dragons were bedded down for the night, before they went looking for something to eat for themselves. Lord Ya-tiren had issued a standing invitation to the Jousters to come to his kitchen whenever they needed to be fed, and they had jumped at the offer. Anything other than have to eat their own cooking. . . .

But Kiron wanted to talk to these two alone, and had asked Aket-ten to bring food for four to Avatre's pen. She had been so curious about the odd request that she hadn't even registered a weak protest.

She was waiting with the plain fare that all of them subsisted on these days; flatbread, vegetables, herbs, and whatever the Jousters scavenged from their dragons' kills. Kiron had decided a long time ago that meat was meat, and it was better to wrestle with a bit of tough wild ass in freedom than the sweetest cut of young calf with one eye out for the Magi. Since he didn't hear any complaints from the others—except, perhaps, the sort of complaining one always heard in situations like this one—he thought it reasonable to suppose the rest felt about the same.

"I suppose you have a reason for this little party," Kalen said, blunt as ever. "And from the look on her face, you didn't tell Aket-ten what it is."

The interesting thing about Kalen was that although he was small, thin, and almost as dark as a Tian, he was nothing like the falcons he had once tended. He was more like one of the small brown owls, always watching, silent and still—and when he moved, moving so quietly you were unaware that he had until he was gone.

"We have eight fertile eggs, and more coming, I expect," Kiron replied. "That's eight new Jousters. They'll have to be trained—we'll have to train them, once they get into the air. And then?"

"I don't think we should have a wing any larger than eight," Kalen said, after a moment of struggle with his strip of meat. "Eight's more than enough to muck up coordination. More would be impossible to keep track of."

"Exactly my thought," Kiron agreed. "And now we

get to the reason why I had you all choose colors in the first place. Eventually, each of you will have a wing, and each of your fliers will wear one of your colors, so we can tell who the wingleader is because he has two."

"Oho!" Pe-atep said, raising his eyebrows. "Now it makes sense!"

"You two are the two steadiest, and you've come from lives where you were used to being in charge of something other than servants," Kiron continued, as Aket-ten nodded sagely. "I want you to take the first two new wings as wingleaders. But if you don't feel equal to it, I want to know now, please, so I can take my third or fourth choice."

"Oh," Pe-atep said, with a glance at Kalen, modulating his deep voice into a more conversational tone. "I think we can manage. These dragon boys aren't really boys at all. They've been training young wild dragons with that Baken fellow. And they're the faithful, the ones that stuck after the *tala* wore off and the dragons escaped. The Altans are our own dragon boys from home, so they should be all right, too." He smiled, then frowned. "The only question is, how are we going to feed all those growing dragonets?"

"Kaleth says he's arranging something with the Bedu." Kiron replied. "That's all I know."

But Kalen, the former falconer who shared that passion with the nomadic desert dwellers, snickered. "What he's arranging is cattle raids in Tia. The priests have told the Bedu where the sacrificial herds are, how they're guarded, and how to frighten off the herders. The Bedu either don't believe in our night-walking ghosts, or don't care. They're going to come in by night, convince the herders that they're demons, and ride off with the herds."

Kiron stared at him for a moment, and then began to laugh. Pe-atep looked at his friend with something akin to affrontery.

"What?" Kalen demanded.

"But those cattle are meant for the gods!" Pe-atep protested.

"If the gods put this idea in Kaleth's mind, I suspect they don't care," said Kalen carelessly. "And besides, the priests can sacrifice them *here* just as well as *there*."

"Well," Pe-atep said, with some reluctance. "Ye-es."

"And if people begin to get the idea that the actions of the advisers have so displeased the gods that their priests have abandoned the temples and night demons are stealing the sacred herds, that's good for us." Kiron remembered only too well his former master's fear of the night demons and hungry ghosts, and Khefti-the-Fat was by no means the only Tian to fear those supernatural creatures so profoundly that *any* misfortune that befell after dark was immediately laid to their influence. So if *actual* (as opposed to imagined) catastrophes befell the gods' own property—there would be no doubt in anyone's mind that if the gods had not yet abandoned Tia, they were certainly angry.

"Ah, now that's a stone that can strike a rock and rebound to hit the caster in the head," said Kaleth, strolling in at the end of that sentence. "There is always a problem, you see, with making people afraid of you. Ari and I were just discussing this. I trust we are welcome to this discussion?"

"It started with me asking Pe-atep and Kalen to be the wingleaders for the new wings," Kiron replied, as Ari joined Kaleth in the doorway. "Ari, I—"

"I don't need to be wingleader of anything," Ari replied, with a mournful, harried expression. "I have enough to concern me. When I am in the air, unless it is hunting, I want someone else to be in charge for a change. It will be a relief not to have to think a hundred moves in advance."

Kiron sighed. He felt a little sorry for Ari—but only a little. The responsibility might be a burden, but everyone else was carrying burdens of their own these days.

"Explain to me how striking fear into the hearts of the Tians is bad for us!" Kalen demanded.

"Because fear is a sword with no hilt," Ari replied. "It is as like to be turned against you as against the right target." He sat down on the edge of the platform. Avatre opened one eye, saw who it was, and wriggled her way around so she could plant her head on the stone beside him, silently demanding a head scratch. Ari absently obliged. "Here is how it goes. The priests vanish. The Great King will surely not say they have run away! No, the advisers will concoct some wild tale of how they were abducted by Altan Magi, and the proof of it is the very bodies of the acolytes that proved to the Tian priests that their own lives were in danger."

"But nobody will believe that," said Pe-atep, then added doubtfully, "will they?"

"There are, and always will be, people who are so loyal to their leader that they will believe no evil of him, even if he were to commit the murder of an innocent before their faces," Kaleth replied with a heavy sigh. "They would say that the victim was a threat, or that the leader was mistaken, or worst of all, convince themselves that the victim somehow deserved it and brought the punishment on himself. So, yes, there will be a solid core of those who will be convinced that the Altans somehow made away with the priests and murdered the acolytes, even though they *know* the acolytes were summoned to the Great King's palace and were never seen alive again. In fact, I have no doubt that such tales are being bruited about as truth even now."

"So, we have the vanished priests, who might have been done away with by evil Altan sea witches," Ari continued. "And to this, you add the cattle raids and the night demons. Well, who could have sent those evil creatures but the Altans again!"

"And then, the last piece falls into place," Kaleth said sadly. "I have seen this. I wish I had not. When the fear and hatred are built up, then comes the next edict. The gods have turned their faces away, not because they disapprove of what the Great King and his advisers decree, but because they grow weary of softness, and to bring them back, it is time to worship their harsher faces. It is time to purge the nation of those who do not support the Great King in all he says and does. It is time to rid the country of those who believe the time has come to speak of peace."

Kiron winced. It was true enough that the gods always had two faces—a kind and gentle aspect, and a darker side. Even the Altan goddess of Healing was also the Dark Lady, the bringer of the sleep that ends in death. But the Tian gods took this to an extreme—the god of justice was also the god of revenge. The goddess of love was also the goddess who devoured men, heart and soul. Even the great sun-disk who brought life and light was also the Scorcher of Earth, who withered all before him.

Pe-atep took on a stubborn look. "The people will not abide it," he said. "Look what was happening in Alta before we fled! They will grow weary, worn down by fear until they are accustomed to it—and *then* they will see the truth! When they realize they have little left to lose, the veil will fall from their faces and they will rise up and—"

"And that will be long in coming," said Ari dully. "The truth is, the less people have, the more fiercely they cling to it. And the less likely they are to risk losing what little they have. Not all slaves are like Baken, striving to be freed. Most think only of the next day, the next round of bread and jar of beer, and no further than that."

"Left to itself, it would be long in coming," Kaleth agreed. "But it will not be left to itself. There is Sanctuary; we will not sit idle while the Magi have it all their own way."

Ari roused at that and shrugged. "True. And even though it may be turned against us, we must have those cattle. There will be hungry mouths to feed, and no way to feed them, else. The Bedu have secret canyons in which to hide them, bringing over only what is needed, for we surely have no way to feed so many beasts here. Are you two going to take Kiron's offer?"

Pe-atep looked at Kalen, who grinned. "I suppose we must," said Kalen. "If only to show him how a true wingleader handles his men!"

Cautious exploration of the new city had proved that there were two water sources—or, rather, that the hot spring fed into an underground cistern that also collected rainwater from all over the city, mingling the two sources. The constant addition of springwater kept the cistern fresh, and by the time the sulfurous water from the spring was diluted by the rainwater, it was as drinkable as the source beneath Sanctuary. A wing of wild dragons was using the city to den-up in, but the mere presence of the Jousters and their dragons was making them uneasy, and Kiron suspected that they might well choose to move on without being harassed or driven out.

And refugees from both Alta and Tia continued to trickle in—by ones and twos and small family groups now, rather than entire Great Houses or temples full of priests. Kaleth and the priests of both nations had managed to establish escape organizations for those who were desperate enough to try hunting for a myth rather than endure another day in lands in which the Magi were growing ever more powerful. There were still Tian temples—those in which there was not, and never had been, a tradition of magic—where the priests still remained in place. The Temple of At-thera, for instance, the goddess who, in one of her aspects, was the Divine Cow, the Holy Nursemaid who nurtured the rest of the gods as children with her sweet milk. She was a minor deity, and her priests and priestesses often came from rural and modest backgrounds. There was no great prestige in serving her, so no great families ever offered their children to her service. But there were small temples to her scattered across the countryside, and it was easy to move escapees from one to the other, as humble pilgrims looking for the blessing of children, unnoticed, until one moved out of Tia altogether.

Most of these new refugees were Healers, the sort who, like Heklatis, used magic in their Healing, and to say that they arrived in Sanctuary profoundly divided in their emotions was something of an understatement. Healers had a sense of duty so powerful it bordered on the suicidal, and it took a great deal to persuade them to abandon their patients and their duty. But many of these men and women also reported disturbing encounters with Magi, encounters that were disturbing because afterward, they could neither remember what had happened, nor exercise their magic for a time. A typical example—a call would come concerning a brain-storm, the sort of thing that only a Healer who used magic could cope with. He or she would follow the servant ostensibly sent to fetch him; the servant would lead him to a veritable wreck of a house that looked utterly abandoned—

But of course, many homes in Alta looked like wrecks these days, what with all the earthshakes. Plenty of people went on living in the ruins—where else could they go? So the Healer would go in, and find he had been called to the bedside of a Magus and—

—and he would come to himself back at the Temple of All Gods with no recollection of how he had gotten there. He would find, if he tried to use his Healing magic, that it was as if there was a well within him that had been drained dry. Within a few days, he would be able to Heal again, but this experience would be nothing like the sort when a Healer simply overexerted himself. It was—so one reported—actually painful to work Healing magic for a time, as if something had been ruthlessly torn out within him, with no regard for what was damaged when it was stolen. And that was more than enough to send most of them looking for an escape.

Not all of them came to Sanctuary. Plenty went to Akkadia, which had a fine school of Healing, and where Healers of every nation, even nations at war with Akkadia, were considered sacred and always welcome. Some took ship with the tin traders, for Healers were always welcome on such long and uncertain voyages, and some in Tia went south, into the lands called the Kingdom of Saambalah, ruled by the Lion Folk, strong and skillful warriors with blue-black skin who sometimes came north into Tia to serve as fighters for hire. There, Healers were so eagerly sought after that they were considered royalty of a kind, and commanded the highest wages—wages which were necessary, since there was no temple to support them. Five and six villages would pool their resources in order to attract a Tian Healer and keep him in comfort and even luxury.

There was a long tradition of alliance and mutual cooperation between the Lion Folk and Tia. Once every few generations, one of the Lion Kings would even send a daughter to the Great King of Tia as a wife, to renew the bonds of alliance between the two lands.

"And what will happen when the Lion Folk learn of what the Great King's advisers have done to the acolytes they took, do you think?" asked Lord Khumun of the latest arrival, a Healer with the blue-black skin of the southern race, the child of one of those well-paid warriors and his wife, who had elected to settle in Tia rather than return home when his fortune was made. The Healer was a very old man, his head of curly hair as white as clouds was a startling contrast to his dark skin.

"I cannot speak for a king, nor even claim to have some way of knowing how the great and powerful may think," the old man said carefully. "You must know that though I have letters from time to time from my far kindred, I was raised in Tia, and am a Tian at heart. But what I can say is that if I were the King of Saambalah, I would watch my borders very carefully and look to my warriors. It may be that the Tians, whose hunger increases with each season, will hunger for more land. It may be that they will hunger for the other precious things in the south, the gold and ivory, incense and spices. It may be that they look upon the strong men and handsome women, and desire a new kind of slave, and to have at no cost that which they now must hire. For now, they have their war with Alta to pursue, but when that war is over, what then? There will still be an army. And the Great King may turn his eyes elsewhere to employ it. If he cares not that these Magi prey upon his own people, even to letting them eat the power of his Healers, he will care even less that they prey upon outsiders."

Lord Khumun thanked the old man, then looked at the rest of the council. "Another Altan Healer arrived this morning, and says that he has disturbing news. It was disturbing enough, evidently, that when the Bedu heard it, they put him on racing camels to get him here."

Kiron thought that Kaleth already knew what the disturbing news was. After all, he had seen a great deal in those visions of his, and something this disturbing was something Kaleth would *surely* have gotten a glimpse of.

Oddly enough, though Kaleth did not look surprised, he did not look as if he actually knew anything either. It was more as if he had expected bad news, known it was coming, but didn't know what the shape of it was.

Kaleth nodded agreement when Ari said, "Then we should see him now, if he is not collapsing of exhaustion."

The messenger might not have been on the verge of collapse, but he was showing the effects of his journey far more than any refugees they had yet seen thus far. His long hair, left long in the Altan fashion with two small braids at each temple, was still tangled from the journey; his skin was sunburned and red, and he was clearly unsteady on his feet, but his voice was strong enough when he spoke, if a bit harsh.

And he recognized Lord Ya-tiren and Lord Khumun, who flanked Ari and Nofret. By design, something like an audience chamber had been set up where the council met, and where urgent messages were

heard. Ari and Nofret sat side by side on slightly taller
stools than the two Lords who sat on either side of
them. It was an arrangement meant to show who the
real authority was.

The messenger looked at them all in exhausted confusion, then must have decided that they were the
closest thing he recognized to a King and Queen and
their advisers.

"My Lords. And Lady," he said, his voice hoarse and
rasping. "I was sent by the Healers of the Temple of All
Gods, for there is grave news from Alta City that you
must hear. There are two new faces on the Twin
Thrones. The old Great Kings are dead. And it is whispered that their deaths came neither by accident, nor
illness, but by the hands of men."

Lord Ya-tiren winced; Lord Khumun only looked
angry. Ari remained as unreadable as a statue, but
Nofret—

Nofret nodded with resignation, as if this was news
she had long expected to hear. She was not surprised,
this only confirmed her deepest fears.

As the rest of the people in the room buzzed and
murmured, Kiron stole a glance at Kaleth. He expected
that Kaleth would look smug or, at least, unsurprised.

He didn't. He didn't look *surprised* either, but it
wasn't as if he had somehow foreseen this happening,
at this moment.

That—was interesting.

The messenger held up his hand for silence. "The

Great Ladies were wed to the Twin Heirs, even before the Days of Mourning were begun, much less completed," he continued, and the disgust and affront in his tone told how most, if not all, of the citizens of Alta must have felt at the news. "The mortuary priests had not even come for the bodies before they were wed to the men who are now the Great Kings. Magus Pte-an-hatep and Magus Rames-re-bet now sit in the Great Hall and reign. Before the death of the old Kings could be proclaimed, their earlier betrothal to the young princesses was dissolved and they were wed to the Twin Queens, all in a single afternoon."

"I cannot imagine how this could have surprised anyone," Nofret said aloud, her head up, as she surveyed the murmuring crowd. Her dark eyes shone with some of the anger and hatred she must have been holding back all this time after Kaleth's twin brother, Prince Toreth, was murdered. "Especially not in the court. The Great Kings set their seal upon their own death sentence the moment they allowed those men to be adopted into the Royal Houses and declared twins. Surely none of you actually believed they would *wait* for little Che-at-al and Weset-re to grow up and wed them to take the Twin Thrones and become the Kings? It was an excuse. And anyone who does *not* believe that the death of the Kings was anything other than murder is a fool!"

"I do not think you will find anyone in Alta to naysay you, Gracious Lady," the messenger rasped.

"The Magi now rule in Alta virtually unchallenged and alone; the Great Ladies are seldom seen, and never on the Twin Thrones. When they *are* seen, they are silent, and move like those who walk when sleeping. That is the sum of what I came to tell you." He paused a moment, then added in a very subdued voice, "May I remain? I do not wish to return to a place so altered and so near to madness."

It was Ari who got to his feet and said, in a voice pitched to carry beyond the room, "Never will we turn *anyone* away from Sanctuary, be he Altan or Tian, or half-crazed Akkadian—" the latter with a glance at Heklatis, who kept his indignation down to a poisonous glance.

Aket-ten nudged Kiron in the ribs. "That's important!" she whispered.

"That it was Ari who said that to an Altan?" He nodded. He was starting to see how this business of being in charge of people worked. Well, more people than just a single wing of young Jousters. There were things you had to do, ways you had to deal with people. Ari might say he was unprepared for all of this, but really, he was much better at it than he thought, and he was improving with every day.

The messenger was taken off, and Ari and the rest of the council settled in to discuss what they'd learned. It was fundamentally obvious, though, that there wasn't much that Kiron could contribute, so he excused himself, and Aket-ten followed him out.

"Are you as depressed as I am?" she asked him, in a voice full of resignation.

"Probably." He sighed, then felt his spirits lift, just a little, when she slipped her hand into his. "I suppose I've been expecting it, but still. . . . I keep hoping someone back in Alta will manage to poison all those scorpions, or that they'll turn on each other and stab each other to death—"

"That might be just what happened in a way," she replied. "You know how Marit and Nofret told us that the Magi were always at each other's throats. Those three so-called Advisers that turned up in Mefis just might be Altan Magi who lost some sort of confrontation."

He groaned. "If anything, that makes it worse. They'll *never* give up the war! Why should they? The longer it lasts, the greater their power!"

"And I don't want to think about it anymore," she said, cutting him off. "Or at least, not right now. I want to see this city of yours, and there is absolutely nothing that we need to be doing right now. If we leave now, before either Re-eth-ke or Avatre are really hungry, we can find out if dragons *can* hunt together when there's no urgency to the hunt. And then you can show me the city."

Kiron controlled his expression with an effort. He had been trying to get Aket-ten alone ever since they all arrived here in Sanctuary, but one thing and another had always interfered with his plans. But it seemed that she had some plans of her own—

"Let me just leave word—" he said, because the one rule he had imposed on *all* of them, himself included, was to never fly off dragonback without first telling someone where you were going. If he or Avatre or both had been hurt by that wild green dragon back when he'd first found the new city, at least someone would have known the general direction to go looking.

That done, he hurried for the pens, to discover that Aket-ten was already in the saddle and waiting, with Re-eth-ke perched on the wall, fanning her silver-edged blue wings while Avatre watched them both with no sign of hostility. His breath caught as Aket-ten turned her head a little; she and her dragon made a wonderful pair. Re-eth-ke's scales shone the same blue-black as Aket-ten's hair; Aket-ten's lithe body moved so easily with Re-eth-ke's that the two of them might have been a single creature, like the human-horses in Akkadia that Heklatis told tales about. The linen tunic she wore was exactly the same as the boys all wore, but it certainly looked better on her than on any of *them*. . . .

She turned toward him at that moment, saw him, and grinned and waved. He felt his heart pound a little faster. His feet certainly started to move as if his whole body was suddenly lighter.

And his hands, when he saddled Avatre, seemed to have eyes at the ends of his fingers.

The mere thought of being far away from Sanctuary with only Aket-ten made him feel almost deliriously happy.

"Got your sling?" she called when he was in the saddle at last, and Avatre shuffled her feet impatiently, waiting for him to give her the signal to take to the air.

He nodded, and held up the sling for Aket-ten to see. He didn't have to ask if she had her bow, it was there, with her arrows, in the quiver at her hip.

But she waited, as a good Jouster should, for *him* to go up first. He was the wingleader, after all, even if today the wing consisted of two.

Re-eth-ke fell in slightly behind, a position that seemed to take less effort to hold, for the dragon who wasn't in the lead didn't have to cut through the air. All he could figure was that air acted like thin water, and the lead dragon cut a wake that the ones behind could ride. He decided that since there were two of them, he would try for a more challenging prey today: wild ox. Ordinarily, he wouldn't go after one. They were tough, and even Kashet found them a challenge. As a consequence, they hadn't been hunted much in his territory, so they were plentiful and unafraid. This might be the time to take down one or more. The dragons weren't hungry yet and could probably be persuaded to cooperate in a joint hunt—

Especially since one of them was being flown by Aket-ten.

"Wild ox!" he shouted to her, over the flapping of the dragon's wings and the wind in his ears.

She nodded. Her main Gift as a Winged One was that she could speak to animals. She—and to tell the truth, the priests and priestesses in charge of the Fledglings—had thought that a lesser Gift. But if it had not been for her ability, she would never have been able to save Re-eth-ke from mourning to death after the murder of Toreth, whose dragon she had been.

And, thanks to Aket-ten's abilities, the training of the entire wing had been swift and smooth; much smoother than it would have been had she not been able to explain to the dragons exactly what their riders wanted.

He had a good idea that she was "speaking" to both dragons once he told her the quarry he planned to hunt, and when Avatre looked back over her shoulder at Aket-ten several times, he was sure of it.

"Stooping runs?" she called forward, over the steady *whump, whump* sound of the dragons' wings. He nodded. That meant that he would dive in first, trying to stun the quarry with a stone, but not allowing Avatre to close and bind. Aket-ten and Re-eth-ke would follow, with Aket-ten using her bow. Then he would come in again, and this time, if they'd managed to do enough damage, he'd let fly with a second stone and allow Avatre to attack and bind. Meanwhile Aket-ten would be ready to come to his rescue if the ox turned on them.

It was a maneuver they had worked out to use against chariots. They'd never actually had to use it in that manner, but they'd practiced it enough that it should work.

The burning air coming up from the baking desert smelled of dry grass, furnace-hot earth, and a faint hint of animal musk. A herd of oryx saw them and went to shelter under a grove of thorn trees. They only got a glimpse of camels from a distance, as wild goats scattered and fled away into the hills, and a herd of wild asses ducked into a canyon too narrow for dragons to get into. Not that any of those ploys would work against a dragon partnered with a human, but it showed they were used to being hunted from the air now. Which might mean more wild dragons were somewhere about.

Finally, he spotted what he was looking for—a herd of six or seven wild oxen grazing on the tough, sparse grasses in the lee of a hill.

Clamping his legs on Avatre's saddle, he got a rock in his sling, and sent her into a long, flat dive, with the oxen at the end of it. Just before she reached them, and their heads came up to stare belligerently at him, he whirled the sling and let fly, striking the nearest right between the horns. It staggered and went to its knees, as Avatre pitched up and began working her wings, trading speed for height.

In the end, the kills were a little anticlimactic. With two dragons attacking, rather than one, even a tough wild ox didn't have much of a chance. The hardest part was pulling Avatre off her kill to help Re-eth-ke with another, and that was the moment where it helped to be hunting while neither of them was hungry. The pull of the chase and the kill combined with Aket-ten's persuasion overrode the need to eat.

But when both were finally down on their respective kills, Kiron deemed it wise to allow both dragons to stuff themselves. Even so, they could hardly eat more than half of the kill, and he and Aket-ten got the unpleasant but necessary chore of dividing up the remains so that neither dragon was unbalanced nor overburdened with the extra meat.

His original intention had been to leave it in the back of one of the bigger houses while he and Aket-ten got a chance to spend a little time alone together.

But that was before they reached the city.

They came in on an odd tangent that took them over a part of the city where midnight *kamiseens* had dumped a great deal of sand, half-burying the entrance to the houses, and filling the canyon to a depth that a dragon would find comfortable—

And, in fact, to a depth a dragon *was* finding comfortable.

The sprawl of scarlet on the pale sand was startling, but not nearly so startling as the four mounds uncovered when she looked up at them and moved her wing. Eggs! There was a nesting dragon here—

As if Aket-ten really did have the Gift of hearing human thought as well as animal, both dragons tilted over and soared back so they could all get a second look.

Since the female didn't seem at all disturbed by them, Kiron sent Avatre in a little lower this time. He

didn't like what he saw. The female's ribs were starting to show, and her movements were slower than he
liked. She wasn't in good shape, and when she
crouched over her eggs and mantled her wings over
them, Aket-ten called out, "She won't leave them—
and her mate's not bringing her food!"

As the words left Aket-ten's mouth, *he* was already
sending Avatre back for a third pass, and sawing at the
cords holding the ox quarters to Avatre's back. Luck
and timing were both with him; the first quarter
landed nearly under the scarlet female's nose, and the
second within easy reach.

As he looked back over his shoulder, he saw Aket-
ten doing the same—and the nesting female devouring the gift as if she hadn't seen food in a week. Which
she probably hadn't, actually. She wasn't wasting a
scrap; she might be eating quickly, but she was eating
neatly.

He sent Avatre up to land on the cliff above the nesting female, and a moment later, Aket-ten landed beside him. "Are you thinking what I'm thinking?" she
called, as Re-eth-ke backwinged to land.

"If you're thinking we need to keep feeding her,
yes," he said, watching the wild dragon make short
work of the first quarter, and leap on the second, with
one eye on them and the other on her food. "Mothering instincts like that need to be fostered, not allowed
to die out. But I'm wondering. Because that dragon
looks—familiar—"

"Wondering what?" she asked, sliding out of Re-eth-ke's saddle, and coming over to stand at his knee, still watching the wild dragon eat.

"I'm wondering if she isn't Coresan," he said slowly, peering at her and trying to match up what he saw with a memory. "Avatre's mother. . . ."

 TEN

"SO I think it's Coresan," Kiron finished. "And—look at her! She doesn't even react to us being here now!"

They both took a look down into the floor of the ravine, where the dragon was giving her entire attention to the food and not even looking up at them.

"I think she can hear my voice from here, and I'm sure she recognizes me, or she'd be watching us," Kiron continued, thinking aloud. "She's the only wild-caught dragon in either Alta or Tia that spent a significant amount of time on half-rations of *tala* while also being tended by humans. And *I* was the human who made sure she was properly fed and tended during that period. I think she knows exactly who I am, I think she pairs good things with me, and I think she might trust me, at least at a distance."

"It would be awfully good if we could get one of her eggs," Aket-ten said, wistfully, gazing down at the dragon with one hand shading her eyes. "But I know we'd never get her away, given how she's protecting them. But she's such a good mother and Avatre is magnificent—"

Kiron sucked on his lower lip. "But if we bring the food in a little closer to her each day, we might be able to get her to let us close enough that the dragonets take humans for granted. If they see us feeding her, when they fledge, they might come to us for food."

"Maybe—closer," Aket-ten mused. "If *I* can get close enough to her to talk to her, she might let us quite near, and when I can talk to the dragonets, I can make sure they know humans are all right. Especially if I get a chance to touch them. That won't happen right away, but—but given time, if she starts leaving them to hunt, I think I can get right to them."

He looked at her askance, trying not to let her see how horrified that idea made him. It was one thing to approach a *tala*-drugged wild-caught dragon in a pen. It was quite another to approach an *undrugged* dragon tending eggs or youngsters. "Are you sure it's worth even trying?" he asked cautiously. Cautiously, because he knew exactly how Aket-ten would react to being told she shouldn't do this.

Poorly.

"Oh, this is probably one of the least-clever things I've ever considered doing," she admitted cheerfully. "But it's still something I think I can do and, more importantly, get away with."

Re-eth-ke snorted anxiously, and Aket-ten patted her shoulder. "I feel the same as Re-eth-ke does about you getting close to Coresan," Kiron admitted. "I'd rather you didn't try at all. I didn't actually think about trying to get as close to Coresan as I did when she was in the pens."

Aket-ten shrugged, and then put her hand on his bare knee, and the touch made him feel very—odd. Good! Oh, yes. But—odd. Like all his skin was doubly alive. Aket-ten seemed oblivious to the effect she had on him. "That's all I'm going to do, really. I don't *have* to get close enough to touch her to talk to her."

He looked down at her. "I don't like it. But I won't tell you not to. You're the Winged One. The gods might not speak to you as directly as they do to Kaleth, but maybe they're the ones saying you should do this." He laughed ruefully. "And to think I was planning to have you all to myself for part of the afternoon! Trust a dragon to interfere with that!"

She blinked at him, then, unexpectedly, blushed. "I like you, Kiron," she said, quite out of nowhere. And that would have been fantastic, except it was the sort of statement that was usually followed by "as a friend" or "you're my best friend" with the implication it shouldn't go any further.

He felt his heart sinking. "But?"

Then she shook her head, blushing harder, and his heart rose again. "No buts. I like you—rather a lot. I'd rather spend time with you than anyone else I know. And it's not because you keep making a habit of rescuing me either."

His heart rose further, and he tried desperately to think of something clever to say. Unfortunately, he couldn't manage to come up with anything. Awkwardly, he put his hand over hers. "I just—think you should stay *you*," he said, and cursed his thick tongue for not managing anything more eloquent.

"Well, that's good, because it would be very difficult being someone else!" she laughed, her eyes twinkling. But he got the feeling she understood what he was trying to say. That he didn't want her to change, didn't want her to stop taking risks just because *he* was terrified she'd be hurt. Maybe someone else wouldn't have felt the same, but he had been a serf, and he knew what it felt like to have chains, visible or invisible, binding you. He wouldn't do that to anyone else, but especially not her.

And she didn't say, as he half-expected her to, "Well, we should be getting back." Instead, she stood there at his knee while they both watched Coresan finish the meal they'd brought her and settle herself around her precious eggs, then fall asleep.

"Do you think she's starting to trust us already?" Aket-ten asked.

"Maybe. I don't know." He sighed. "We need to get back."

"Yes, we do." But she sounded reluctant. Nevertheless, she mounted Re-eth-ke and looked to him for direction. He gave it, sending Avatre up with powerful wingbeats, rather than letting her take her preferred path of diving down into the ravine and then trading speed for height at the last minute. He guided her away from Coresan's valley at an angle. Re-eth-ke followed; Coresan did not even raise her head to watch them, which made him think that Aket-ten might be right, she might have already decided they weren't going to hurt her or interfere with her or her eggs.

They caught good thermals all the way back, which speeded up their return journey considerably. Most of the wing was waiting for them at the pens; for a moment he was afraid, as Avatre spiraled in to land, that something had gone wrong. But as they got nearer the ground, their expressions, of varying degrees of mischief, made him think otherwise. No, they were there to tease him—or tease both of them.

Not if I give them something to distract them first.

"Ari!" he called, as soon as Avatre folded her wings. "Coresan is nesting in the New City, and she recognized me!"

All right, maybe saying that it *was* Coresan and that she recognized him was an exaggeration, but it got their attention, even though no one but Ari could know who, or what, Coresan was.

As he slid off Avatre's shoulder, and began unharnessing her, he gave them a detailed account of what had happened. Ari's eyes glittered with excitement as he asked further questions; all of them were excited, really, once they understood the implications. "—and Aket-ten is going to try to 'talk' to Coresan," he finished, and had to hold a flash of anger when Ari, rather than expressing concern over such a dangerous idea, overflowed with enthusiasm for it.

"That would be ideal!" Ari said, "With Aket-ten there, once we get her close enough she can communicate with them, I'm sure Coresan will let us help with her dragonets. After all, the males help to feed and tend the nest, and we're the closest thing she has to a mate right now. Her instincts must be telling her she needs the help, and if she was as starved as you say, between the food and what her instincts are telling her, we can probably get Aket-ten as close as she let a dragon boy in no time."

He could picture that all too easily. What's more, he remembered Coresan snapping those formidable jaws right over *his* head, and it was even easier to picture her making that show of aggression into a real attack on Aket-ten. And he very nearly started trouble over such a cavalier attitude, when Ari suddenly got a taste of what the bitter brew of anxiety tasted like.

Because— "*I* want to help tend these dragons," said Nofret, stepping forward from behind Menet-ka, her head up and her expression firm with determination.

It occurred to Kiron at that moment that she looked very much the Queen.

Ari's face was a study in dismay. "But—" he began.

Nofret cut off his objections with an imperious wave of her hand. "I want a dragon, too, Ari. If we're to be co-consorts, as the Altan tradition demands, we must be equals in all things. How can we appear before your people or mine in that state of equality if I am riding behind you, like—like a piece of baggage? Besides, it is not fair to Kashet to keep asking him to carry double. I want a dragon of my own."

By the sun-boat! She's come a long way from the woman who clutched me like death and didn't dare look down! He couldn't help but think this was all to the good. And if she was willing and ready to do the work needed to get a dragon, all the better.

That was not how Ari felt, though, if his expression was any guide. "I absolutely—" he began.

Just in time, Kiron managed to kick Ari surreptitiously in the shin, while simultaneously saying, with innocent enthusiasm, "I think that's a good plan, Nofret. We already know that Coresan throws intelligent and steady babies. If Aket-ten can get her to accept us, the dragonets will do the same, and if you start tending and feeding the babies alongside their mother, you'll have the best of both worlds, a dragonet that's tame, but knows she's a dragon. It's going to take time, a lot of work, and concentration, though, I hope you realize that."

Ari opened his mouth again to protest, and Kiron kicked him in the shin again. He shut his mouth with a snap, and Nofret smiled at both of them. "Thank you for being reasonable about this," she said and excused herself. "I'll go talk to Heklatis and Lord Ya-tiren about shifting audiences and meetings to after sundown when the time comes." She laughed a little, and winked at Kiron. "At least I can sleep in my own bed! You can leave me with them when you go to hunt, and get me at sundown, and that should serve very well."

Bethlan and Khaleph stuck their indigo and green noses over the wall to Avatre's pen and whined; they were hungry and wanted to go out to hunt. Since it didn't look as though there was going to be any more excitement, the rest of the wing went off to saddle their dragons to take them out to hunt the last meal of the day.

The rest of the wing—except Ari, who turned on Kiron.

"Why did you *kick* me?" he demanded, with a face full of wrath.

"I was saving you from doing something stupid," Kiron retorted. "Didn't you pay any attention to Nofret's expression? One word about forbidding her to do *anything*, and you'd be arguing about it for moons. That's assuming she even talked to you at all after being told you were forbidding her to try! Ari, she was the Queen-in-waiting! She's not used to being told she's forbidden to do something that's perfectly reasonable."

She's not asking to do anything worse than Aket-ten is planning on doing. And you thought that was an excellent idea!

"Reasonable?" Ari yelped. "She wants to spend time with a wild dragon! What's reasonable about that?"

"Aket-ten is going to do the same thing, and you were all for that. And Nofret not only wants a dragon of her own, I think she needs one," Kiron replied. "The eggs we've got have already been spoken for—and besides, I don't think that she's up to the challenge of raising one from the egg; she doesn't have the time, for one thing. I don't think her idea of the partnership is the kind of tight bond that the rest of us have with our dragons. I think she's looking for something of the kind you'd get from a tame cheetah or a lion. She's a very—" he groped for a word, "—*self-contained* person. Marit is the more dependent of the twins. Nofret never wanted pet dogs, for instance, but she loves cats. I think that doing the double-rearing, if it can be done, will give us a much more independent-minded dragonet."

Ari looked off in the direction Nofret had taken. "You kicked me because if I'd said that I forbade her to do this, she'd never have forgiven me, and I would have undone all the courting I've done with her."

Kiron coughed. "I don't know about *never....*"

He left the sentence hanging in the air, though, because he did want Ari to think about it, and think about it hard.

Ari looked away from him for a moment, and cursed. "This is why I *never* wanted to have anything to do with noblewomen!" he said under his breath. "With a paid flower, you know where you are—"

Now Kiron was right out of his depth. All he could do was shrug. Ari looked over at him, and his expression turned wry. "As if *you'd* know anything more about women than I do."

"I know they don't like to be treated as if you have a right to order them about," Kiron said carefully. "No more than you do!"

Ari sighed, and closed his eyes for a moment, then shook his head. "At least you kept me from a mistake that was likely to cause trouble. Kashet is probably starving; I'd better get into the air."

Kiron snorted, and turned his attention back to making Avatre comfortable. She hadn't had a sand scrub today, and when she saw him getting out the buffing cloths and the oil, she was nearly beside herself with happiness. Making her happy soothed his nerves, and his nerves definitely needed soothing. He was out of his depth. . . .

What am I doing? I'm the son of a farmer, I used to be a serf—

"Can I help?" asked Nofret from the doorway. "If I'm going to have a dragon, I need to learn how to care for them."

And this is a daughter of the Royal Lines and the nearest thing we have to a queen. And I'm going to be taking her to a wild dragon and somehow making it possible for her to bond with a dragonet. And Ari, who was my master and is her betrothed and is going to be our King, just asked me for advice on how he should treat her. Haras help me, is she going to ask me for the same? And I don't even know what to say to Aket-ten. This is insane.

He nodded, and she made her way along the walkway to stand beside him. He showed her how to use the sand to buff Avatre's scales, how to gently scrub away flaking skin, and how to oil the exposed skin afterward. "I hope you don't think I want a dragon for the—the look of prestige," Nofret said, after they had worked together for a while. "It's not just that; it isn't even most of the reason. I didn't really see that much of Toreth to understand what having a tame dragon was like. I've spent so much time in Ari and Kashet's company that I couldn't help but see how he has such an amazing bond with Kashet, and—and I wanted my own dragon, when I saw how close they were. Mind, I do think that to be taken as seriously, and as his equal, I must appear in every way to be his equal—"

Kiron nodded. "From what I know of the Tians, I think you are right. They have no Great Queen—only the Great Royal Wife, which is not at all the same."

"So I need a dragon." She carefully buffed a patch of dull scales. "But now that I've gotten used to flying, and I've seen Ari and Kashet just being together— Kiron, I am just as eaten with dragon envy as any of those boys out there with their eggs in the hatching pen, and if I could spare the time to tend an egg, I would go looking for one myself! Mind, if this works, I hope my dragon has a slightly different personality. Kashet is more like a dog, and I think I would get along better with a dragon like Re-eth-ke, who is more like a cat."

Kiron had to laugh at that. "Aket-ten said the same thing. My father used to tell my mother that women liked cats better than dogs, because they recognize that they are like cats themselves!"

Nofret laughed herself, making Avatre crane her neck around to look at her. "There's some truth to that," she admitted. "I don't like slavish dependence. Do you think that I'm mad for wanting a dragon, too?"

"I don't think anyone is mad for wanting a dragon." They were just about finished with Avatre, and when Kiron stepped back, the scarlet dragon picked her way daintily to the center of her pit, then spread herself out luxuriantly over the top of the hot sand to bask.

"You're frightening Ari, though," he continued, picking up the cloths and oil flask. "It will be dangerous. Not as much for you as for Aket-ten, but Coresan won't be drugged, and her reactions will be sharp. I honestly don't know what her behavior is going to be like, or even if it will be consistent from day to day."

Nofret spread her hands wide. "Shouldn't we be able to learn that by watching her while we approach her?" she asked, reasonably. "I promise, if she looks as if she's going to be dangerous, I'll give up the idea. It's going to take enough time as it is. But I do have my reasons, and a great many of them, and I think they're all good ones."

He looked at her soberly, wondering if she really understood what she was letting herself in for. How much the bond with her dragon would affect her.

Then he decided that it didn't matter whether she understood now. When it happened, she *would*. And when it happened, well, she wouldn't regret whatever sacrifices she had to make.

"She's *beautiful*," Nofret said, in tones of awe.

"She's a bit scrawny still," Aket-ten countered. "but she's rounding out again."

It had taken less time than Kiron had thought to get Coresan—and there was no doubt now, it *was* Coresan—to allow both Kiron and Aket-ten quite close, and on foot, on the ground. Her hunger, combined with her need to stay with her eggs, and her recognition of the dragon boy who had tended her so well (despite how much he had changed), made her much more cooperative than Kiron had expected. Her behavior was nothing near as erratic as it had been when she had been drugged either. Before too terribly long, Coresan was stretching out her neck and gazing longingly at the bucket of sand and the buffing cloths and oil Kiron had brought with him. By the time they were thinking about bringing Nofret along, she let him give her a sand bath; by the day after that, it was Aket-ten doing the honors, and of course, once Aket-ten could *touch* the dragon, things became much simpler. At first Coresan reacted to Aket-ten's power with startlement—and it must have been odd for her, having that contact inside her mind. It took her most of a day to get used to it and calm down. But once she accepted it, and knew that not only could she communicate with Aket-ten, but Aket-ten could "talk" to her in the same way, she seemed to realize this was an excellent state of affairs.

At that point, it was time to introduce Nofret to the dragon.

Avatre was still significantly larger than Re-eth-ke, so Nofret rode behind Kiron. The difference between this ride and the one they had taken to get Marit and Nofret to Sanctuary initially was amazing. Then, Nofret had hidden her face and clutched at Kiron, and once, when she had realized how high they were, she'd shrieked loud enough to startle Avatre. Now she watched everything avidly, her grip on his waist and the back of his saddle just enough to keep her steady and balanced, and when he looked back at her, she was smiling, and her kohl-lined eyes were wide and bright.

According to Aket-ten, Nofret had said that Ari was still trying to persuade her, more or less delicately, to give up on the idea of having a dragon. This was why she hadn't told him she was coming along today.

The moment they had landed, she had slipped down Avatre's side to stand facing Coresan, as Kiron untied the butchered goats the Bedu had brought—the first fruits of their raids on the Tian Sacred Herds. Coresan, of course, knew what was coming, and though still standing vigilant guard over her precious eggs, was swaying side to side with eagerness and hunger. She did look immensely better than she had when they had first found her. Her scales were shiny and clean, and although she was lean, she no longer had bones showing. Her golden eyes were bright, and the membranes of her wings supple, smooth, and a healthy copper-orange in color. Kiron privately thought that Avatre was much more beautiful—he liked Avatre's deep scarlet, and didn't much care for the lighter, more coppery shade of her mother. But there was no doubt that Coresan was impressive.

Aket-ten had landed before Kiron had, and was about to drag a goat quarter over to the eager and visibly hungry dragon. "Should I take that?" Nofret asked eagerly, as she stepped forward.

Well, that's a good sign! She's not afraid at all!

"Not just yet. We want her to get the edge off her hunger first," he cautioned. "Let Aket-ten introduce you to her; she'll have to get quite close before she can use her magic."

Though visibly disappointed, Nofret nodded, and once about half of Aket-ten's load was inside Coresan, Aket-ten motioned that Nofret should come take the next quarter over.

Kiron and Aket-ten were quite used to hauling large

chunks of meat about, but poor Nofret staggered for a moment under the unexpectedly heavy burden. Once again, though, she gamely rose to the challenge, and pulled the haunch to the waiting dragon.

Coresan eyed the newcomer carefully. Nofret didn't look anything like Aket-ten; she was taller, willow-slim, and even her hair was different—since Lord Ya-tiren and his servants had arrived, she had been able to wear her long hair in the noble style of thousands of plaits ending in beads, so that every time she moved her head, she rattled pleasantly, like a systrum. Nofret made no sudden moves, only looked the dragon squarely in the eyes as she'd been told to, and waited for Coresan to take the meat.

The dragon looked extremely reluctant to take a step nearer the stranger, despite what Aket-ten "said" to her. Instead, she stretched out her neck as far as it would go, and with the very tips of her jaws, snagged the skin of the haunch in her teeth and dragged it to herself, keeping one eye on Nofret at all times.

Interesting. No snapping, no testing. Coresan hadn't been whipping her tail around either. She'd become much more predictable and even-tempered since she'd been flying free. Perhaps some of her irritability had been because she had been chafing to be gone, even under the influence of *tala*.

With every piece of meat Nofret brought, Coresan allowed her to get closer. And when she had finished, and was ready to curl around her eggs for a nap, Coresan actually allowed Nofret to put a hand under her chin for a brief moment.

When Nofret turned back to them, she was practically afire with excitement, and Kiron hid a smile. When he thought about how aloof she had been back in Alta, scarcely noticing the dragonets, and compared how she had been then to what she was like now, it was clear that being around Kashet and Ari had caused a fundamental change in her attitude.

"This is amazing!" she exclaimed in a whisper, as Coresan sighed and slipped into the deep breathing of slumber. "I've watched Ari feed Kashet, of course, and even helped myself, but this is a *wild* dragon! And she's letting me touch her!"

"You don't have to whisper around her, in fact, it's better not to," Aket-ten said in a conversational tone. "When you try to be quiet, you tell her that something's sneaking around, and she'll wake up."

"Well, she's not exactly a wild dragon, but she's as close as we're going to get," Kiron acknowledged. "She was born wild, and she remembers being trapped, which is likely to make her even warier of humans than a fully wild dragon. So, are you determined to stay here until we go on the afternoon hunt?"

Nofret nodded firmly. "I brought my sling," she said. "I might be able to kill some desert-hares or pigeons that I can give her as tidbits, and if not, I can at least practice my aim. I know this is going to be hard—"

"Mostly, it's going to be boring," Aket-ten advised. "She's sleeping a lot, since we've been feeding her. That's just as well, since she doesn't dare leave the eggs until they hatch."

Nofret shrugged. "It can't be any worse than some meetings," she replied. "It *certainly* will be more entertaining than standing attendant to the Great Queens. Much though I would have enjoyed doing so, I wasn't allowed to hurl stones at anything while I was a lady-in-waiting."

Aket-ten grinned, and Kiron had to chuckle. "Then here's your waterskin—if you need to refill it, the cistern is over there, inside that building with the *latas* columns—" He pointed at one of the false fronts carved into the wall of the ravine across from them, and Nofret nodded. "If you see wild dragons, either stay close to Coresan, or go inside a building with doors too small for them to get through."

"Should I give her a sand bath?" Nofret asked anxiously.

Aket-ten shook her head. "Not yet. She'll tell you when she's ready for you to touch her. She doesn't wallow in caresses like Re-eth-ke does, but she does like being scratched under the jaw, and when she solicits you to do that, she'll be ready to take a sand buffing from you."

"We'll be back in the afternoon," Kiron said, and tried not to feel too anxious. Nofret was no wilting *latas;* she had hunted river horse and crocodile, and even lions. She had been living in extremely primitive conditions in Sanctuary long before the rest of them arrived. Still—when Ari found out—

"I think we ought to do some hunting for the city," he said aloud. "As long as you don't have anything else to do, Aket-ten."

She raised an eyebrow at him but didn't object. And this way they could do flyovers to make sure Nofret was all right—

—and avoid Ari—

"We could bring Nofret smaller game that way," Aket-ten agreed. "That's more how a mate would feed Coresan anyway."

So that was exactly what they did; they went back to Sanctuary just long enough to leave a message as to their intentions, then flew out again. Hunting in tandem, they managed to bring down several of the smaller gazelles over the course of the morning and afternoon, more than enough to not only keep Coresan fed, but to bring back to Sanctuary, where they would certainly be put to good use. Every time they did a flyover, it looked as if Nofret was getting on quite well. She was erring on the side of caution, staying out of what Kiron calculated was Coresan's threat-perimeter, but staying well within sight. And Coresan must have been eating, because most of the time when they did a flyover, she was asleep with a distinct bulge in her lean middle.

Finally, in the late afternoon, he and Aket-ten made

their own hunts and kills, took up what was left over, and brought it along when they came to pick up Nofret. She was in very good spirits, and Coresan had lost some of that wary watchfulness. This was definitely another good sign.

Which was just as well, because as Kiron knew, when they finally returned—they would all have some explaining to do to Ari . . . and that was something he was not at all looking forward to.

Nofret gave Coresan one last feeding and climbed up behind Kiron. As Coresan watched with interest, but no alarm, they headed home.

 **ELEVEN**

ARI was waiting for them.

As they banked in at a steep angle necessitated by the stiff breeze over Sanctuary, it was easy to spot the lone figure waiting in Avatre's pen, and just as easy to recognize it as Ari. He was the only one likely to be wearing a Tian-style kilt rather than an Altan-style tunic who was also likely to be waiting for them.

This was not good. At least, not as far as Kiron was concerned. Glancing over at his partner in this particular escapade as she sideslipped toward Re-eth-ke's pen, it looked to him as if Aket-ten didn't think she needed to worry—

—well, *she* probably didn't. Ari wouldn't blame *her*, he'd blame Kiron.

Fortunately, Ari was the only one waiting in the pen. It would have been painful to be verbally flayed in the presence of the rest of the wing, even if he didn't deserve it. After all, Ari had, in theory, agreed to this. And it wasn't as if Nofret wasn't her own woman, and perfectly capable of making up her own mind about what she wanted to do and how she wanted to do it. But Ari would still blame *him*.

As Avatre lined herself up on her target, Aket-ten and Re-eth-ke touched down inside her own pen, and Avatre backwinged, preparing to drop down onto the sand. Kiron braced himself for the assault.

And it came as soon as Avatre furled her wings. "Kiron!" Ari called, his chin set. "I—"

"You'll take up your grievance with me, not Kiron, Royal Husband," Nofret said, swinging her leg over and sliding down Avatre's back. She staggered a little as she landed, then made her way around the walkway to confront her betrothed, arms crossed over her chest in a way that should have warned Ari that no matter what he thought, he was going to lose this particular argument. "I am the one who organized this expedition to be introduced to Coresan. Not Kiron. I have the right to command him. There was no danger, as Aket-ten introduced me, and Coresan accepted me within the time of her first morning feeding."

Ari's mouth opened and closed, without anything coming out. Kiron decided that he would just pretend nothing was happening, and untie the hide full of leftovers that Coresan hadn't eaten. Nofret continued to stare at Ari with her arms crossed, her chin held high, her black eyes narrowed. She looked uncommonly like one of the statues of the Great Tian Kings, lacking only the crook and flail in her hands to finish the appearance. Ari could hardly have missed the resemblance.

For his part, Kiron was wondering which was going to be extended this time—the crook—or the flail.

After a moment she softened. So, it would be the crook. "Ari, I *must* do this. I don't know why, but something within me says that I need to share the parenting with Coresan, that the work has to be done by me, personally. Perhaps it is nothing more than my need to prove that I am as worthy of a dragon as any of you who raised your own from the egg; I don't know. I only know that it is important, and that I can't take an egg from someone who already has one, or has one promised to him. So don't place any blame on Kiron. If he and Aket-ten had not agreed to help me, I would have found another way to go out there. And they kept very careful track of me the entire time."

Kiron thought about verifying that, then thought better of it. This was shaping up to be a lovers' quarrel, or at least, almost a lovers' quarrel, and he knew better than to put himself in the middle of something like that.

Neither side would welcome his interference, and both might turn on him. He'd seen that before.

So he shouldered his burden of green hide and meat

and walked around the walkway on the other side of the pen, trying to look as if he wasn't even aware the two of them were there. Either the ploy worked, or else they elected to ignore him the same way he was ignoring them, because neither of them looked at him as he edged sideways through the entrance. Avatre, of course, could not care less who was in her pen as long as she was left alone to flop down onto the hot sand and bask before the sun went down. She was full, quite happy, and all was right with *her* world. If two humans, neither of whom was her rider, wished to make mouth sounds at each other, so long as they got out of the way when she rolled over, they could do so wherever they wished.

Kiron breathed a sigh of relief as he got out of sight. He might not be out of danger yet, but at least Ari was going to have to deal with Nofret first before the older man came down on Kiron.

He never did learn what Nofret said to Ari, nor what Ari said to Nofret. Whatever it was, when Ari caught up with him, later—much later—that evening, it wasn't to give Kiron a dressing-down.

Kiron was looking forward to joining the wing in Lord Ya-tiren's kitchen, which was where he and the others were all taking their evening meals these days. After delivering his load to Gan, whose green dragon Khaleph had not had a particularly successful hunt, he had gone checking on all of the new boys with their new eggs, making sure they had been turning the eggs properly, and listening at each one for signs that all was right within. Satisfied that everything was going along exactly as it should, he joined the rest for the evening meal with Lord Ya-tiren's household. Normally, he and the rest ate with the servants rather than the family; it seemed enough of an imposition to have Lord Ya-tiren's servants preparing their food without also inflicting themselves on the family as well. Besides, Kiron had the feeling that falconer Kalen, cat keeper Pe-atep, and baker's son Huras, all commonborn, would feel very uncomfortable at the table of a nobleman—and never mind that they were all, from highest to lowest, actually eating the same diet. He had set the standard by insisting on eating at the kitchen, and the others had simply followed his lead— even Orest and Aket-ten, even though it was their father's kitchen they were eating in. "It's all politics with Father," Orest explained after the first few evenings. "It's generally him and Ari, Nofret and Marit, and Lord Khumun and Kaleth, and sometimes the priests from Tia, all politicking and planning. Look, I just want them to tell me what they want me to do, and I'll do it. Just don't make me sit there until my head aches, listening to them!"

Kiron didn't blame him, and Aket-ten must have felt the same, since she joined all of them as well almost every night. It was a particularly jovial evening; even with the possibility of Ari's wrath descending on him,

Kiron enjoyed it. The extra hunting that he and Aket-ten had done had made it possible for the household to have meat this evening, and it had been very pleas-ant to enjoy the sort of meal he'd gotten used to in the Jousters' Compounds of both Tia and Alta.

And when Ari joined them after the torches were lit, which was at the point that they were just about fin-ished with their meal, though he looked worried and a little unsettled, he didn't immediately seize Kiron and haul him away. Instead, he sat down with them, got a jar of beer and a bit of honeyed bread from the cook, and glumly started eating, only to stop after the first few mouthfuls.

"Nofret will be going out to stay with Coresan and her eggs—and later her dragonets—from now on until she bonds with one herself," he said abruptly. "Since that's in Kiron's territory, I expect him to keep an eye on her, but I'd like the rest of you to try to do the same in turn. I know it will be difficult, but it's the season of the rains, so it should be a bit cooler here in the desert, and I hope not so hard to stay out all day."

Orest blinked. "Ah—" he began. "You're going to keep watch also, aren't you?"

"I . . . I will," Ari said, with exaggerated care. "But I don't want to give her the impression that I am being—over-protective."

Kiron braced himself, expecting *one* of them—prob-ably Orest, who had all the tact of a charging river horse—to say something disastrous. But instead, Gan gave Ari an understanding look, poked Orest in the ribs with an elbow just as Orest was opening his mouth, and said smoothly, "Nofret's determined to have a dragon; that's not a bad idea. Among our people, the two Queens rule as equals with the Kings, or at least, they have until this last sorry lot. I could have thought of easier ways to get her one, but women and cats will do as they please, Ari, and men and hounds just have to endure it. Why don't you and I go join Heklatis as soon as we've finished eating? He may have some ideas to help keep her safe out there."

Orest gave him an indignant look, opened his mouth again, and on his other side, Oset-re stepped hard on his foot, smiling as he did so.

Ari looked up at that with faint frown—then smiled. "You know, that might not be a bad idea."

Kiron heaved a sigh of relief that he hoped he managed to hide. Let Gan—who had had so many affairs with girls that they were practically stumbling over each other on their way to and from his bed—and Heklatis, who although he was *not* minded to women, still had a very great deal of sexual experience, romantic and otherwise—sort Ari out. *He* was still trying to figure out how to tell if Aket-ten thought of him as a friend, a kind of surrogate brother, or something else entirely. She was never less than friendly, but—well, serfs weren't encouraged to think of girls, even if he'd been old enough to be interested while he lived in Tia. And afterward—well, in Alta, he'd been frantically busy, and anyway, Aket-ten hadn't spent any great amount of time with him until the Magi took an interest in her. And at that point, he was concentrating on how to keep her safe, rather than how he felt about her, or she about him.

He hoped she had begun to look upon him as a great deal more than a friend and surrogate brother, but she was not exactly forthcoming about how she felt, and while she was very good at reading animals' minds, she was curiously blind to the reactions of people around her.

Or at least, she didn't act as if she knew what he was thinking.

Yes, he reminded himself, as he got up from the table and headed back to Avatre's pen in the darkness. *But I don't know what I'm thinking, so I shouldn't expect her to, now, should I?*

All he knew for certain was that he would rather be in Aket-ten's company than out of it. That when he was around her, his skin felt as if it had a life of his own. And that he would often lie at night under the stars, looking up at them, and feeling ridiculously happy to know she was probably gazing at the same stars.

But he had no idea if she felt the same, if she would react poorly if she knew how he felt, or, perhaps most importantly, how her father would react. He was only a farmer's son; she was a noble's daughter. And while the present circumstances had made them *more* equal, they were not *actually* equal, and it was impossible, for him at least, to forget that.

He wandered back to the pens through the quiet streets of Sanctuary, keeping an eye out for the scorpions that liked to come out at night. Not that there were many of them anymore. The dragons thought scorpions were extremely tasty, small as they were, and they never lost an opportunity to snatch one up, like greedy children licking up a bit of honey from a scale insect or the end of a blossom. Scorpions evidently knew this, and had mostly deserted the city.

As he was passing Re-eth-ke's pen, he heard a soft whistle from the doorway, and stopped. "Are you particularly sleepy?" Aket-ten called from the darkness.

"Not yet," he answered truthfully. "Why?"

"Because one of the Bedu said there's something remarkable going to happen tonight, and for the next couple more nights, and I thought you might want to come with me and see if they're right." He couldn't see her face, but there was a smile in her voice. "They tell me it's a good thing that there's no moon, because we'll be able to see it much better."

His curiosity now piqued, Kiron nodded. "Why not?" he replied.

"Excellent. Come on, then." She emerged from the shadows with something heavy draped over her arm and took his hand. "You can see better than I do in the dark anyway. We need to get up on a roof. Preferably one where someone isn't already sleeping, and one not near where anyone is going to be burning oil lamps or torches."

Fortunately he knew a roof that fit that very description. "I know just the place," he replied, and led her through the maze of pens, feeling his way as he went. It wasn't that he could actually see better in the dark than the rest of them; it was more that he was able to sense where walls were without actually running into them. No one ever gave a serf or a slave a lantern to see by; he'd just learned to do without them as a boy, and the sense had stuck with him.

Beyond the pens, in the labyrinth behind the temple that the Jousters had been *intending* to take over, and now no longer needed to since the Thet priests of Tia had solved the problem of keeping the dragons warm in winter, there were several half-ruined and empty buildings in the process of being renovated. None of them were done yet, since the construction of dragon pens had taken precedence. Like all the buildings in Sanctuary, they had flat roofs that had external stairs leading up to them—and probably, like the buildings in Tia, those had been meant for the people who lived in those buildings to use as sleeping places in good weather. Right now, though, they weren't being used at all—perhaps because they were at the very edge of the city, and people were understandably nervous about sleeping in a part of the city where jackals were known to prowl at night. Where jackals went, sometimes, so did lions, and the prospect of waking up to a lion's hot breath in your face was one that did not appeal. Kiron didn't really think that lions would dare an area where dragons were, but you never knew. Peatep, who knew better than any of them what cats thought, said the same, but added that old, hungry, desperate lions might dare to go anywhere that they thought there was easy prey, and nothing was easier than a sleeping human. So until there were so many people here that a really effective wall could be built and a full night guard could be posted, it was probably better to err on the side of caution.

That was more than enough to keep people inside at night to sleep, with the doors closed and the shutters barred.

So as he led Aket-ten up the narrow stair, it was with the certainty that the rooftop would be just as unoccupied as she had wanted.

"Oh, this is perfect!" she said with enthusiasm when they reached the top. "Here—"

She took that draped something off her arm—in the darkness it was hard to tell just what she was doing— but he heard the sound of heavy cloth being shaken out, and a moment later she was tugging his arm downward as she sat down on the roof. He put out his hand as he went to sit beside her, and felt the rug she had spread out on the stone. "Lie down on your back," she said, "and look up at the Seven Dancers."

The Dancers were a cluster of seven stars well known by that name to both Tians and Altans. He did as she asked, and no sooner had he begun to relax and wonder just what this marvelous thing was he was supposed to be looking for, when—

—a brilliant streak of light flashed from the third Dancer to the tip of the star formation called the Dragon's Tail.

"A falling star!" he exclaimed, with surprise and delight, and as more streaks appeared against the blackness, pointed upward. "Look—another—and there—and there—"

"The Bedu say that tonight the Goddess of Night weeps for her dead lover," Aket-ten replied. "The Mouth told Heklatis and the Thet priest about it, and I overheard them talking about it. They didn't seem to mind my listening. Heklatis says his people say it's the sparks from their smith god's forge as he's making arrowheads for the Huntress Goddess, and the Thet priest says it's the lost ghosts who've had someone to make them a shrine rushing across the Rainbow Bridge to the Summer Country, but that usually you can't see this in Tia because it's the middle of the season of rains. Which is why we Altans never see it either, I suppose. There are other star-falls over the course of the year, but nothing like this one."

Kiron blinked, and tried to remember if *he* had ever seen such a thing—but as a serf, he'd always been so tired he fell asleep as soon as he was prone, and as a dragon boy he had paid more attention to first Kashet, then Avatre, than to the goings-on in the sky. There was no set season for lost spirits to go to the Summer Country so far as Altans were concerned. When your family built your shrine, you just *went*.

He certainly didn't remember ever seeing anything like this. There were so many bright streaks across the sky that it seemed as if all the stars should have vanished by now. But they were still there, so maybe it *was* the tears of a goddess—or the sparks from a heavenly forge—or something else that no one had even thought of yet. They were all coming out of the area of the Dancers, so maybe it was star petals that the Dancers were throwing.

Whatever it was causing this—it was beautiful. And as he lay on his back, he felt Aket-ten's hand close over his, and hold it.

"I think you did a good thing for Nofret by helping her, and letting her go out to Coresan," Aket-ten said softly. "She needs to prove herself to Ari. She told me that she thinks he's seen too many spoiled noblewomen with nothing but idle time on their hands; that he thinks she was a lot more pampered than she was. She wants to prove to him that she *can* do things, that she can be his full partner in just about everything."

"She doesn't intend to fight, I hope," Kiron replied, staring up at the falling stars with a sinking heart. "If it comes to that, I don't think that's a good idea. I know that being on a dragon evens things out a lot, but—"

"If she has to, she'll fight, just like everyone else here. If Ari fights, I know she intends to be there. And it's because she can't bear the thought of something happening to him, and her not being right there to do whatever she can if it does. It's horrible, being left behind, not knowing what's happening. It's worse than going out to fight in the first place. When you care about someone, it's unbearable." A pause. "I feel the same way about you."

His heart stopped sinking, and with a jolt, seemed to leap into his throat. "Uh—you do?" he managed, sounding stupid even in his own ears.

"Of course I do! It would be horrible to watch you fly off and not know if you were coming back!" She sounded indignant. "I care more about you than—than anyone. Even Orest. Even my father. There isn't anyone I would rather be with, for the rest of my life." She squeezed his hand. "I don't know if it's right, making promises before we know if we're all going to get through this without being killed, but I told my father he might as well not bother making any betrothals for me, because if I couldn't marry *you*, I wouldn't marry anyone."

"Aket-ten!" he exclaimed, with trepidation, delight, and a touch of horror. "You didn't! When?"

"When he first got here, of course." She laughed into the darkness. "I told him that night we all had our welcome dinner together. I didn't want to take the chance that he'd get all worried about what was going to happen and decide that he wanted to see me safely married. And he said he wouldn't dare make any betrothals after such a declaration, because I'd probably tell Re-eth-ke to eat him if he tried."

"I—" he tried to think of something gallant to say, but his heart was racing with elation, and he could only manage a single fumbling sentence. "I'd fight even your father to be with you—except that I'd be afraid that would break your heart, seeing the two of us fighting. I'd throw myself off a cliff rather than break your heart."

"Then it's a good thing you don't have to fight him, because he likes you, and said we can consider it settled between us." She giggled. "And Mother likes you even better. She told Father that if he dared reject you as a suitor, he'd be sleeping on the floor in the kitchen from now on. Orest doesn't know about it yet, of course," she added thoughtfully. "Neither Father nor I told him because he'd be an idiot about it. He'd either decide you weren't worthy or else he'd go completely the other way and want the whole thing settled immediately, and we can't have that until everything is—well, normal again. Or at least, until you don't have to be wingleader and fight. Or until he figures it out for himself, which he might, since he isn't *quite* as stupid as he used to be."

"Or—" Kiron said thoughtfully, feeling a slow smile spreading over his face, "until I make him think it is all *his* idea. If I do that, he won't rest until he's got your father's consent. Besides, it will give him the chance to act important, as if you couldn't possibly consider me unless he suggested it."

"That's brilliant! And that's why I love you!" Aket-ten exclaimed, and she rolled over on her side just as he did the same. But they both misjudged how close they were to each other and somehow, as they turned toward each other, they managed to find themselves kissing and—

—and it was like falling into a scalding spring, except that it was good, it was wonderful, and he didn't want it to stop—

—and Aket-ten broke it off first, but not until they were both hot and breathless.

She said she loves me—

We don't dare complicate things. His thoughts were all tangled up in possible consequences, even while his body wanted him to go right back to what it had been doing, and reminded him of all the times he'd seen lovers entwined by accident, since no one ever paid any attention to serfs. And that ache in his groin demanded that he do something *now*, and if he didn't—

He flushed all over and willed himself not to move.

"Not—" he said, feeling as if it took every ounce of willpower he had to say the word. "—now. Aket-ten I want to, more than anything, but not now."

"No—" she agreed. "We can't." She sounded as breathless as he felt. Well, small wonder. His body wanted one thing and wanted it very badly, and his mind knew it would be a very bad idea. There were already enough complications in their lives. They didn't need more. "We haven't the right, we have to think of the things we have to do. We can't be lovers yet. Not until things are—better. There might be babies, and we need every dragon and rider we have. I can't take the time for a baby right now."

"But—" he managed.

"Yes," she sighed, and brushed his hair off his forehead in a way that made him shiver. Then she pushed him away a little. "But the *moment* we're free—you'd better find a quiet place big enough for both of us!"

Somehow, a completely unspoken agreement had passed between them. Maybe that ability of talking to animals *did* extend to humans sometimes.

Whatever it was—he was content. For now anyway. Maybe not forever—probably not forever—probably not even for too many moons. But for now.

And all he had to do was to convince his body of that. . . .

 TWELVE

THE next morning, and for every morning after that, Nofret was waiting to be taken out to Coresan without anyone having to fetch her. Aket-ten told Kiron that Nofret had arranged all of her audiences and meetings for the evening, after she came back. And she was brought back, every evening, if not by Kiron, by one or another of the other Jousters because no one was going to allow her to remain in that deserted city, unprotected, after darkness fell. No one knew what might prowl there, anything from cheetah to other dragons. There would certainly be poisonous snakes and scorpions. There might be ghosts or other evil spirits.

And Ari fretted, though he said nothing, and he was

very careful to fetch Nofret home no more often than any of the others. In a way, Kiron couldn't blame him for being anxious about Nofret's welfare. If it had been Aket-ten out there alone, he'd have fretted, too—and as far as he or anyone else knew, unlike Aket-ten, Nofret didn't have any special powers to protect her or help her. He'd have trusted to her good sense, but he couldn't help but wonder—did anyone who would insist on spending time with a semiwild, nesting dragon in a deserted city crawling with unknown hazards really have good sense?

There were other ways of getting a dragon. She *could* even wait until next year. . . . What did she have to prove? She was already given all the deference anyone could ask for from the Altans in Sanctuary, and if the Tians didn't quite understand yet that she was due the respect of a coconsort, they would soon work it out.

All he could guess at this point was that the person she was trying hardest to prove something to was— herself.

Still, she was clever, and if Coresan wasn't exactly *taming*, she had come to accept Nofret's presence and food without a sign of nerves or suspicion. Nofret still couldn't touch her unless Aket-ten was around, and she still kept her body between Nofret and her eggs, but then, Coresan had watched while Kiron himself stole one of her last clutch, so he couldn't blame the dragon for being cautious. No matter how many times Aket-ten "talked" to Coresan to reassure her, surely the first thing in her mind when she saw Nofret's eyes going toward the eggs was that the human was going to take one. It did make him wonder, though, just how much Coresan was able to think—and if she was somehow able to recognize Avatre as her own off-spring. And if so, was that making a difference in how she treated the humans who were with Avatre?

The days stretched on, much the same except that they slowly got a little longer every day as the time for the rains arrived and passed. Or what would have been rains, if much rain actually fell out here. There were brief cloudbursts, followed by an explosion of flowers and greenery, but nothing like what was happening in Tia, and to a lesser extent, in Alta.

More refugees arrived, still trickling in by ones and twos, or at most, a family group. The Tians reported that the demonically ferocious storms that had hammered Tia consistently for the last several years had not appeared this season—only the "normal" storms, the ones to be expected, followed by the general rise of Great Mother River for the annual inundation. The Great King's new advisers were taking credit for this, claiming to have found a way for all Tian priests to work as one. And also claiming that this was why only the lesser priests were still in their temples.

Kiron had wondered how they would explain the absence of so many priests. He'd been hoping that they wouldn't be able to.

The Altan refugees reported with shudders that fear

was the byword. Boys barely into their teens were being conscripted for the army, and the Magi were reputed to be examining and taking select children as young as six. They *claimed* these children were going to serve in the Palace. But no one ever saw them there, and who would want a child *that* young serving them?

But no one complained because there were always terrible things happening: murders, poisoned wells, other acts of sabotage, all blamed on Tian agents within the city. You couldn't even trust your own neighbors, said the refugees. You never knew if they were Tian agents—or if they would denounce *you* as a Tian agent.

At least, for the moment, the earthshakes had stopped, and the Magi were not lashing the earth with the Eye, burning out nests of so-called traitors and the hidden strongholds of agents within the city (or so they said). So even though rain saturated the city every day, people were trying to rebuild their houses. Some of them were anyway. Some who had nowhere to go in the Altan countryside, like the ones who made their way across the desert with the help of the Bedu, had decided that terrible as the Tians must be, it was better to face them than huddle in terror in a wrecked house in Alta.

Kiron knew, or thought he knew, why the Magi weren't using the Eye at the moment. He thought it rather likely that they simply couldn't. The burning lance of the Eye used sunlight, somehow concentrating it into a weapon, and with the sky overcast constantly during the rains, there was no sunlight for it to use. And although earthshakes were perfectly normal occurrences in Alta, he had also noticed that every time they used the Eye, there was an earthshake, as if using it somehow disturbed the earth as well—which would be why the shakes had stopped.

And as he watched the faces of Aket-ten, Kaleth, and the Tian priests, he knew that *they* knew why those young children were being taken. These were the youngsters that would have been Nestlings, had there been anyone in Alta to train them. Those with arcane powers who had not fled were mostly comatose from being repeatedly drained to serve the uses of the Magi. So the Magi needed a new source of power— just as the "advisers" in Tia had needed a source of power.

It made him feel sick; sicker still that there was nothing, realistically speaking, that he could do about it.

Meanwhile, the Tian priests had found a way to call and direct the rare rains *kamiseen*, to enable it to uncover still more of Sanctuary. It didn't look as if they would be running out of buildings any time soon. Or—so Kaleth confided to him—treasure. There was enough to pay the Bedu, enough to put some glory into the shrines of the gods and give the priests something in the way of regalia again. The gods were providing still, it seemed.

So the days lengthened, and the nights shortened,

and the refugees came in, and what passed for the rains here in the desert ended.

And then, at long last—the hatches started.

The eggs in the hatching pen began cracking first, and that triggered the need to contact the Bedu to start raiding the Tian Sacred Herds. There was no way that Sanctuary could feed the growing population and the hungry dragonets on hunting alone. They needed meat, and a great deal of it.

By this point, the Herds themselves had been moved to make those raids possible without penetrating too far into Tian lands. Those priests that had not fled to Sanctuary were colluding with those who had, and had brought the herds to grazing grounds seldom used, right on the edge of the desert. The excuse was that the herds were looking thin and sickly, a bad omen, and something that could be easily remedied by taking them to fresh pastures. And why should the advisers care what happened to the herds? They played no part in the sacrifices, cared nothing for omens or portents or other priestly matters, and probably thought that they had more important things to worry about. With the few novices that they had managed to get their hands on used up and dead, they were forced to turn their attention to other sources of power. Rumors had come via the priestly caste that one of the advisers himself was making a tour of temples; only now, forewarned, the priests were making very sure he

didn't find the source of power he was looking for—
those few priests that had not left their posts who were
god-touched. They were moving one step ahead of
him, from temple to temple.

And there were too few of those advisers to make a
search among the Tian children for those who had not
yet fully shown the hand of the gods on them. Kiron
had a notion that the Tians, unlike the Altans, would
not take tamely to having their children taken—not
after those novices were found dead.

Then again, the Tians were not living in the shadow
of the Eye either—nor under the baleful gaze of several hundred Magi.

Now that the season of rains and floods were over,
the assault on the Altan border, however, had been renewed. Once again, there was a steady flow of casual-
ties on both sides, to feed that unspeakable appetite for
the magic and power of lost life.

It was maddening to know that there was nothing
those in Sanctuary could do. . . .

The first of the sacred sacrificial animals began ar-
riving in Sanctuary about the time that the little dragonets came into their full and voracious appetites.

These *were* beasts sacred to the gods, however, and it
was Nofret who suggested that the Tian priests actually undertake the full ritual sacrifices they would ordinarily have done, rather than simply butcher the
beasts or allow them to be butchered.

"I can't see any reason why not," she said, at the

evening meeting after the first lot of cattle and goats was driven into the pens waiting for them, a meeting which Kiron was attending in his capacity of wing-leader and strongly interested party. "And I can see every reason why you should. We *have* a much larger temple now—the one the Jousters were going to take and don't need. It has an inner shrine and a proper sacrificial table. And I think it is a very bad idea to cheat the gods of what is, after all, rightfully theirs."

"But—" The Thet priest looked at her askance. "They are not your gods, Lady."

"Pah. Who was worshiped there before? It looked enough like Lord Haras as to make no difference, but it was probably called by a different name. And in a thousand years, the Falcon-headed One will probably have yet a third name. I do not think the gods care what names we use, so long as we do good and not evil. They are the gods of both Altans and Tians at this point, and it doesn't matter a hair what name you call them by," she replied instantly. "You have never consulted a woman about this, clearly. We women are pragmatic about such things; we call upon whoever we think might answer us, with no nonsense about whether it is your god or mine. I have even been known to invoke one of Heklatis' Akkadian goddesses now and again."

The Thet priest brightened at that. "It could be," he said, with some deliberation, "that with the number of sacrifices from Tian altars growing fewer, and those from the Sanctuary altars growing more numerous, they might be inclined to *actually* remove their favor from Tia and bestow it here. The impression we are trying to create may become the actuality."

"That, too, was my thought," Nofret said briskly, as Kaleth smiled slightly and Ari looked very thoughtful indeed.

"Even if the Jousters had needed the temple, under the circumstances I would have said to take it," Ari said gravely, speaking up for the first time this evening. "Let us give all the gods their due, Tian and Altan together. If they look with favor upon us, so much the better for us all."

And so, the hatching of the dragonets, that had caused so much concern about eroding resources, proved to be the source of a great improvement in the lives of everyone in Sanctuary *and* of the Bedu as well. The Bedu made their painless raids—the only injuries were to a couple of too eager youngsters who fell from their swift desert-bred horses and broke a bone or two. They moved the herds to secret oases, and for their pains got ten percent of the beasts. Only as many of the sacrificial animals as were needed were brought, moved by night to Sanctuary, to give up their blood on the altar, fulfilling their destinies. And their flesh fed not only the dragonets, but the full-grown dragons *and* the people of Sanctuary. There was not the overabundance of meat there had been in Mefis—that would have been a criminal waste, since there was, as yet, no way to store it in great quantity; cold rooms, it seemed, took more effort than heating the pens. And unlike in Mefis and in Alta, where there were so many sacrifices in a day that there was always some wastage, every littlest scrap was used. But the overall improvement in diet made people feel less as if they were undergoing great hardship and sacrifice to live in Sanctuary. And another added benefit—so many hides available meant that not only was there an abundance of leather for sandals and belts, blacksmith aprons and other domestic needs, there was plenty for shields and new saddles and harnesses, and even chariot covers. For the first time, a handful of craftsmen from both Tia and Alta began to make the swift-moving chariots used for both war and hunting, to train Bedu horses to pull them, and to allow the charioteers from Lord Ya-tiren's household to train others.

And not too very long after the last of the eggs in the hatching pen cracked and gave up a handsome little blue dragonet, Coresan's clutch began to hatch.

"Should I help?" Nofret asked anxiously, as Coresan prowled around and around the rocking egg.

"No," Aket-ten said immediately. "Keep away from her. She's on edge, and while she's all right with us being within sight, even I can't tell what she'll do if you try to get any nearer."

"Within sight" was something of a misnomer. In fact, they were up on the cliff above the nest. Aket-ten and Re-eth-ke had come in first, realized immediately that the first of the eggs was hatching, and cut off Ava-tre, Kiron, and Nofret, waving them up to the cliff. Kiron was more than willing to follow her lead in this. He had never seen a dragon with hatching eggs before, and according to Ari, they got positively bloodthirsty until all the hatchlings were safely out and fed. He had said that they *should* all hatch nearly at once; dragons didn't start incubation until all the eggs were laid, so that there wasn't much more than a day or two between the oldest and the youngest.

One of the five eggs Coresan had laid was clearly infertile; she had pushed it off to one side, out of the nest. The others were moving, one violently. And it sounded like there was tapping coming from all of them.

Suddenly Coresan stopped prowling, and practically leaped on the egg that had been moving the most. Trapping it between her foreclaws, she tilted her head to the side, and—

Kiron watched avidly. He knew what must be coming. Dragon egg shells were thicker than the walls of water jars and a great deal less fragile; they had to be, to contain the developing dragon safely. But that meant they were hard. He, Ari, and every other human that had ever helped an egg to hatch had been forced to use hammers to help the baby inside crack the shell. But no one knew how dragons assisted their young. Not even Ari, who had studied dragons nesting in caves to keep the hatching young out of the rains, and had been unable as a consequence to get close enough to see the crucial moment.

He, Nofret, and Aket-ten would be the first humans to witness the event, and it would solve a great mystery, for dragon teeth were hardly formed in a way that would let them be used like hammers or chisels, and no one had ever seen a dragon pick up anything in its foreclaws to use like a tool.

Coresan tilted her head to the side, listening intently to the baby within. Then she bent to the egg, and licked a spot on the top. Then she waited a moment, and with the tips of her very front fangs, began scraping at the same spot. Then she stopped, licked, waited, and scraped again. After the third time, Kiron realized that the shell where she had licked was flaking away.

"Something in her saliva must be eating at the shell!" he exclaimed. "Or making it more brittle!"

And now that all made perfect sense. He already knew that a dragon's droppings would burn the skin of anyone foolish enough to touch them without gloves, so it stood to reason that there might be something caustic or acidic in the dragon's saliva. No wonder they could gulp down bones without harm, and without the bone bits appearing fundamentally intact out the other end!

"I hope we aren't traumatizing the little ones we're helping to hatch with all the banging," Nofret replied, her brows furrowing with sudden worry.

Aket-ten laughed. "What would be worse, the banging of the hammers, or that scrape-scrape-scrape?" she asked. "It certainly isn't *quieter*. I don't think we're hurting anything."

"They respond to the tapping," Kiron assured her. "Aket-ten is right, I don't think tapping or scraping makes any real difference; either sound tells the little one inside the egg where it needs to work to get out."

As abruptly as she had begun, Coresan stopped, and let go of the egg. It balanced on its end for a moment, then rolled over on its side, and with a shudder, a roughly triangular piece popped off, and the very end of a snout shoved through the hole.

They were too far away to actually see more than that, and then only because the deep red snout was such a strong contrast to the mottled-cream-and-sand-colored egg, but Kiron remembered very well what that moment had been like for Avatre. After the first tremendous effort of cracking the shell, she had simply rested quietly within in it for a few moments, taking her first breaths and gathering her strength to finish the job. Her then-tiny nostrils had flared with each panting breath, and at that moment he had wanted to tear the shell apart to free her.

But he hadn't, because hatching babies of any sort were in a state of transition. It was quite possible to harm them irrevocably by rushing things. Every farmer's child knew that.

Coresan now came back to the egg, and began to lick

it again, starting from the broken, and presumably weakened spot, and working her way back from that point. The egg and the baby inside it remained quiescent for a short time, then the rocking began again. Coresan confined herself to licking this time, occasionally stopping to make muttering noises at the baby. Whether these were meant to be reassurances or encouragement, Kiron couldn't tell for sure.

But within a much shorter time than he remembered, the egg cracked open and lay in two halves on the sand, and the dragonet sprawled out inelegantly, a tangle of ungainly wings and limbs, panting with exhaustion.

Now Coresan began frantically licking the baby all over—to clean it? Certainly the dragonet was clean and dry in a much shorter time than Avatre had been under Kiron's inexpert care. Her ministrations had the effect of moving it away from the shell, which she batted out of the nest with her tail. She licked and nudged until the little one was in a much more comfortable-looking position, curled up with his wings tucked in around him, in the sun to soak up the heat.

Then, and only then, did she begin looking around—and then looked straight up at them.

And snorted.

It did not take having Aket-ten's god-touched Gift of Silent Speech with animals to read Coresan's look at that moment. It said, as clearly as could be, "*What* are you doing up there with my food, when I need it down *here* with my baby?"

And Nofret did not need any urging to scramble up into the saddle. Kiron had already decided that if Coresan showed willingness to permit Nofret close, it should be she, and not he, who delivered that first meal to mother and offspring. Coresan accepted all of them, but it was time for Nofret to attain a special level of trust, if she was going to be able to get near the babies. He and Avatre had practiced the concept of taking someone *other* than him on her back off within a reasonable distance; now, he waved at Avatre in the proper signal, pointed at Coresan, and called, "Take her down, girl!"

Nofret couldn't control or guide Avatre yet, but she didn't have to. As she clung to the saddle, Avatre did a "gentle" launch, leaping up and out with wings spread, rather than diving off the cliff to snap open her wings at the last possible moment. And with Coresan watching and fidgeting with impatience, she spiraled down to the ground near—but not too near—the nest.

The meat had been divided up into portions manageable by one slender woman; as Kiron and Aket-ten watched, with Aket-ten in Re-eth-ke's saddle, ready to fly in and force Coresan off if the mother dragon turned aggressive, Nofret untied the first of the bundles and dragged it over to Coresan as the dragon rocked from side to side. Tail lashing with impatience, Coresan actually left the nest to come and take it from her before she had gotten halfway there!

Nofret had the presence of mind to drop the meat

and back up a pace or three before Coresan reached her. But she showed no fear, and Coresan showed no aggression. There was a moment of eyes meeting, then both of them turned and retraced their steps, Nofret to get another load, Coresan to take the food to her weary infant.

Aket-ten merely nodded, but of course, she would have known if Coresan was feeling anything but hunger and impatience to get the food. Kiron, however, felt a burden of concern lift from his shoulders.

One less thing to worry about.

Now that he could relax, it was fascinating for Kiron to watch as Coresan tore off the tiniest of bits with her front teeth and offered them to the baby, who sniffed, opened his mouth—it was a "he" by the incipient "horns"—and gulped it down. Coresan continued feeding him, as Nofret returned with her second burden. The female dragon paid no attention to the human at all, as Nofret brought the meat right up to the edge of the nest and left it there, the nearest she had ever come to the eggs before this moment. It appeared that their plan was working; Nofret had risen to a new level of acceptance.

Then again, all of Coresan's attention was on this, her first baby (or at least, the first one she knew of) and she had no time for anything else.

Nofret was at the edge with the last of the meat bundles when Coresan finally finished stuffing the youngster and looked up. Kiron held his breath again, but

Coresan only blinked benevolently at her benefactor, and got slowly to her feet, stretching as she did so, then paced over to Nofret in a leisurely manner. Nofret stood her ground.

Kiron held his breath. Aket-ten looked entirely relaxed, but Coresan's reputation back in Mefis had been that she was unpredictable.

"Unpredictable" was not what they needed right now.

Coresan looked back over her shoulder at her sleeping baby, then dropped her head, picked up a shoulder of beef, and took it back to the little one, where she proceeded to feed herself.

Only then did Nofret turn and go back to Avatre, climb into the saddle, and wait for Kiron's whistled signal to tell Avatre to return.

It was only when Nofret got up onto the cliff with them that Kiron saw she was sweating and trembling, and any rebuke he had been planning on giving her about taking chances died on his tongue.

She slid out of Avatre's saddle and her knees buckled; Kiron and Aket-ten both caught her and helped her to sit on the ground.

"I didn't know she was going to do those things until she started toward me, and then it was too late," Nofret said, shivering with reaction. "Coming to meet me was bad enough, but then stalking right over and taking the meat practically from under my hand—I thought I was going to die right then and there! And once she started moving, I knew I didn't dare back away, or I might become prey—"

"I'm glad you remembered that," Kiron said, awkwardly patting her shoulder. "You did very well! And you were right to meet her eyes."

"You did *wonderfully!*" Aket-ten exclaimed. "And we won't tell Ari any details. You've done it, Nofret— she's accepted you as a feeder, if not a nest tender. Yet."

"Yet?" Kiron responded instantly, with astonishment. "You think Coresan is actually going to accept Nofret as a nest tender?"

"She's already thinking about it," said Aket-ten, with a nod toward the feeding dragon. "Or—well, not *thinking* about it, it's just that she's been on the nest herself for a long time without a break, and she's starting to feel impatient. She wants to fly, she wants to stretch her wings, she wants to hunt for herself and the babies, and all of that is lying under the nest tending and getting stronger every time she looks at Nofret. So when the *go* feelings are stronger than the *stay* feelings, if Nofret is there, I think Coresan will just leave, as if Nofret was another female dragon or her mate."

"Would that mean—" Nofret's color was coming back. "—would I be able to get right in with the babies?"

"She just *might* push you in with them," Kiron said thoughtfully. "It's what she'd do with another dragon, Ari says. Younger siblings with no nest of their own, or older daughters are often used to tend the nests for mothers whose mates are inexperienced and don't know to help tend the nest. It depends on how much like another dragon she thinks you are."

"One step at a time!" Aket-ten interrupted. "It's enough that Coresan is letting her bring the meat right up to the edge of the nest! And—oh, look!"

She pointed down at the nest, where another egg, this one slightly larger than the first, had begun the violent rocking that had signaled the beginning of real hatching for the first egg. Coresan abandoned her meal and, with a nudge to make sure her first offspring was properly positioned, went to aid the second.

"We're going hunting," Kiron told Aket-ten. "Unless you want to—"

"Oh, no, I'd much rather watch!" Aket-ten said, with undisguised enjoyment. "If Coresan finishes what Nofret brought her, I'll fly her down with the next load myself."

Satisfied that his partner had things well in hand, Kiron leaped into Avatre's saddle, and gave her the signal to fly. Avatre was only too happy to oblige. He had the feeling she found all this baby tending and baby watching to be utterly boring and pointless.

"It's all right, girl; this will be over before too long," he called to her as they angled out over the desert in search of prey. "Then things—"

He stopped himself before he could finish that with

"—can go back to normal again" because it wasn't likely that they ever would. Or could. And he wasn't going to make a promise he would only have to break, especially not to Avatre, whether or not she understood it.

"—things will let us move Nofret and her new dragonet back to Sanctuary," he said instead. Because at least that was a promise he had some likelihood of keeping.

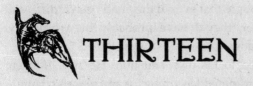

THIRTEEN

"THIS is driving me mad, you know," Ari said, in a completely conversational tone, as he and Kiron stared down into Coresan's ravine. Coresan was dozing on one side of the nest, Nofret was sitting on the other side, and the dragonets were tumbling all over each other in between them, in a clumsy, awkward tangle of wings and limbs. They looked like a moving pile of jewelry.

Kiron was getting very, very tired of hearing Ari fret over Nofret's safety. Nofret herself wasn't putting up with it, which was probably why Ari was fretting at Kiron instead of his Royal Wife. After a fortnight of this, Kiron was at the end of his patience, too. And, truth to tell, Kiron was rather jealous; there had been so much public pressure for the two of them to become an official couple that even if they had been indifferent to each other, they'd have probably been officially married by now.

As opposed to his own situation. He and Aket-ten were both considered too young for any serious commitments, and even if they had been older, well—they still had duties and responsibilities that didn't leave a lot of room for anything *but* those duties and responsibilities.

There wasn't any special public ceremony to make a couple man and wife, not even for two people who were functioning as rulers, even if they didn't have thrones or crowns. But there was no doubt that Ari's courtship of Nofret had succeeded, seeing as they were sharing a sleeping chamber . . . even if Kiron hadn't already known they had privately gone before both Kaleth and the High Priest of Thet to make their union official.

And Kiron was jealous. But also apprehensive. It was one thing to want Aket-ten so badly his loins ached—but it was quite another to pair off like Ari and Nofret had. There were consequences to that, above and beyond the obvious, consequences he wasn't at all sure he was ready to deal with. For instance, Lord Ya-tiren might decide that her husband ought to be trying to curb some of Aket-ten's more outrageous escapades, and not her father. In fact, Lord Ya-tiren might even insist on some similar condition before he would bestow his approval on the match.

Kiron was quite certain such a thing was entirely beyond *his* abilities. Aket-ten was going to do exactly as she always had, and no one was going to be able to stop her once she made up her mind about it.

He was also not so secure in his position as wing-leader that he thought he dared to tip the balance among them by turning an unofficial and private relationship into a public one. Aket-ten was part of the wing, after all, and if they were husband and wife, the others might reasonably expect there was favoritism going on.

And there were other consequences, too; and lots of them. Those were nothing more than the tip of what might be a very, very large rock under the sand dune. Consequences like—as Aket-ten had said herself—babies. Whatever mysterious means there were that women in Alta and Tia used to regulate such a thing, they evidently weren't available here in Sanctuary yet, if the rash of big bellies among Lord Ya-tiren's household and the Tian priestesses was anything to go by.

Still—on the other hand—there was a wing full of handsome young men that Aket-ten flew with every day. True, Lord Ya-tiren had given his consent, but all of them were better matches for her than a former serf who had never been anything more than a simple farmer's son. Granted, the nobles weren't lords of anything right now, but they had the blood and—

And he could make *himself* crazy with thoughts like that in a very short time.

So between one thing and another, he was coming to the end of his patience with Ari's fretting.

"Nofret says she's fine. Aket-ten says Coresan has accepted her as another dragon," he snapped. "There is never a time when someone with a dragon isn't in the air around here to make sure nothing can get at her or Coresan—not that I think anything *could* show up here that Coresan couldn't or wouldn't handle on her own. Enough, Ari, she knows what she's doing, we know what we're doing, so give us all a little credit for caution and good sense, will you?"

Ari looked taken aback by Kiron's tone. "I just— worry," he said.

"Well, it's stupid to worry for no reason." Kiron set his chin. "If you have to worry, worry about something we've got reasons to worry about. There's plenty of *those.*"

Ari said nothing, but he had the grace to look chastised. And he did stop fretting, at least for the rest of that afternoon, which proceeded as it always did. They hunted, going out in turn, while Aket-ten went back to Sanctuary and brought back sacrificed animals— sheep, today; it was Hamun's turn to be sacrificed to, and in the interest of encouraging harmony, the priests of both Alta and Tia presided over and attended the sacrifices for both sets of gods.

In the interest of harmony. . . .

Kaleth had some ideas on that score. *"If both sets of priests preside now, well, it won't be long before they're agreeing on a fixed set of rites, and the two sets of gods merge into one."* It certainly seemed to be working.

If only other problems could be solved so easily.

As the sun-disk neared the horizon, Ari collected Nofret—Kashet was still the biggest, strongest dragon in the wing, and it was much easier for him to carry double. Maybe snapping at Ari had done some good; at least outwardly he didn't act as anxious when he got Nofret, and she seemed more relaxed as they all headed back home, flying high to get the advantage of the cooler air.

Odd, though, how quickly he, at least, had gotten used to the desert. The heat just didn't seem to bother him as much anymore.

He had no idea how prophetic those words about "worrying over things we have reason to worry about" would be.

Because as they arrived back at Sanctuary and started dropping down toward the buildings, they could see that the place was like an overturned beehive, with people milling about and forming little knots of tense conversation. One of Lord Khumun's men was waiting for them as they approached their pens, standing on top of the dividing wall, waving frantically at them.

That's not good. . . .

"Council chamber," was all he shouted up at them, eyes shielded against the wind of the dragon's wing-beats as it kicked up sand. "It's an emergency!"

"You go!" Aket-ten called over to him and Ari and Nofret. "Land there, and send the dragons back! I'll take care of them and rejoin you when I'm done!"

Kiron didn't have to be told twice; he signaled to Avatre to abort her landing; with a grunt of effort, she rowed for height, and after a moment of confusion and hesitation as he resolved the conflict between habit and Ari's new direction, Kashet followed her.

They landed in the street outside the council chamber—the building now serving only the dual purpose of being the place for meetings and Kaleth and Marit's home, rather than as a full temple as well. Ari and Nofret were out of the saddle and on the ground as soon as the dragons furled their wings, and running through the doorway before Kiron had even thrown his leg over Avatre's back. He slid down her shoulder, then turned and slapped Avatre on the foreleg, and called "Home!" and she shoved off from the ground without hesitation. He felt a momentary burst of pride at that; it had taken a long time to train her to follow an order without him on her back, but it was more than worth the effort at times like this one. Kashet, however, looked momentarily confused.

Kiron whistled and got the big male's attention. "Kashet," he said firmly, and making the "up" gesture with both hands. "Fly! Pen!" Kashet didn't know the word "home"—which to Avatre meant two things; both Sanctuary itself, and any pen in which she had spent more than a couple of nights. But he did know "pen," and "fly" as separate concepts—he just didn't know what "fly" meant if Ari wasn't on his back.

Kiron had done a lot more training to make Avatre autonomous from the beginning than Ari had ever done with Kashet. He'd had to; on their trek to Alta, he'd needed to be able to direct Avatre in hunting from some other place than in her saddle, because sometimes he needed to drive the game into Avatre's waiting talons. Kashet, on the other hand, had never had to meet that challenge. The dragon looked at him with his head to one side, as if he was hearing some strange sound he didn't recognize at all.

"Pen," Kiron repeated, putting as much emphasis as he could on the simple word. Kashet knew what it meant, and he'd just seen Avatre fly off in that direction—surely he could reason out that he was meant to go there, too. . . .

Kashet blew out his breath in a puff, then turned away, but instead of flying as Avatre had, he stalked off through the streets afoot. People scrambled to get out of his way, not with any sign of fear, but only because the streets of Sanctuary were very narrow, and there wasn't really room for a dragon and even a small person to pass side by side in them. He was going in the right direction.

Maybe he remembers walking all those corridors in the Jousters' Compound, Kiron thought, *He was used to walking in the Compound, rather than flying. Well, as long as it gets him there on his own, he can walk or fly as he chooses!*

He turned to enter the chamber himself, reasonably sure that Kashet would get himself to where he belonged, because even if he got confused, by now one of the other Jousters would have heard he was stalking through the streets and come to guide him back. Or else Aket-ten would send someone to get him.

Or both, Kiron thought, as he slipped in through the doorway, and started to edge around the walls to get to his spot among the other councilors.

He saw that there was a woman in the gown of a priestess—a compromise between the tightly-pleated mist linen of the Tian priestesses, and the loosely-draped, heavier linen of the Altans, this was mist linen for coolness and comfort, but without pleating, and held in place by twin shoulder pins and a belt. Most other women of Sanctuary wore purely Altan gowns, since most women here *were* Altans.

". . . and every one of them has confirmed it," the speaker was Tir-ama-ten, the Priestess of Beshet of the Far-Seeing eye. She looked very unhappy. "I do not know how it is that those whose Gift is to see forward did not warn us about this!"

"Because, Great Lady, their gaze was confused and befogged," Kaleth said soothingly. "As my gaze has been increasingly confused and befogged. We have known this was happening, as the Magi make the future more uncertain. There is no responsibility to be laid on you or on them; rather, allow me to thank you for always having the eyes of one of your Far-Seeing

Priestesses keep watch over the Winged Ones of Alta. Your duty is to the people of Tia, not of Alta, and yet you have been bending your eyes to my folk. If you had not, we would never have known they were besieged until it was too late."

"Besieged?" Kiron said—though it was not really a question. "The Magi, of course."

"And every armed man of their private guard they can put around the Temple of the Twins," Kaleth confirmed. "I think they would have used the army to break down the doors, except that they knew the army would not obey them in such a task."

"I wonder how they get even their private guard to attack priests," Lord Khumun said, looking grim. "To raise hands against the servants of the gods—"

"They grow bold, these Magi," said Pta-hetop the Tian Thet priest. "First they move to take our acolytes, and now your priests. I wonder that they do not use your army."

"I do not think they could gain obedience from the army to move against the servants of the gods," Haraket said. "Oh, yes, it has happened in the past— the far past—of our land, but only when the priests themselves were corrupt, so corrupt that the people wept beneath their heels."

"I think you are right," Kaleth nodded. "We had two warnings it was happening today; one from the acolytes of Beshet, the other a cry for help that I heard from those trapped within the temple."

"According to my acolytes, the siege began this morning. Somehow enough of the Winged Ones mustered strength and will to bar the temple doors against the Magi," said Tir-ama-ten, her face a study in anger, though the gods being so insulted were not technically her own. "When the Magi could not get at the Winged Ones, they immediately mounted an armed siege. But it is a curious sort of siege; they mount guard around the temple and let no man in or out, but otherwise, do nothing."

"I think they do not dare—yet," Heklatis said, with a nod of his grizzled head. "The Winged Ones are much beloved of the people. The Magi may be saying that the Winged Ones are in danger, and that they are being guarded for their own protection."

"It may be so. Fortunately, the temple might have been designed to withstand such a siege," Kaleth replied, making a soothing motion with his hand. "And before my contact with him was blocked, the Winged One who called to me told me that the temple itself is well-provisioned and has its own well of pure water. The great danger is that the Magi will decide to use the Eye on them."

Kiron shuddered, and Nofret made a little strangled sound in the back of her throat. Kiron was just as glad Aket-ten wasn't here to have heard that. She had a great many friends in that temple. He remembered only too well seeing the Eye lash down out of the

Magi's Tower. It had been a fearsome sight that had left nothing but earth turned to glass behind it.

"I don't think they will yet," Ari said, thoughtfully. "If they do, they'll lose the very thing they are anxious to have back—and they will earn themselves the hatred of the people. Fear is one thing; it is useful to them, but hatred? Hatred is dangerous. Hatred turns fear into anger, and anger turns inaction into action. No, I think they'll wait for a few days at least, to see if they can force the Winged Ones out with hunger or thirst. And when that doesn't work, they'll try some sort of magic first, I think. Maybe try to enspell them from outside and make them walk out, or at least open the doors. Then, perhaps, they will try to get a traitor inside, to open the doors from within. Mind you, I don't think they would hesitate for a moment to kill your Winged Ones if they can't use them anymore. But I believe they will hope to find some other way, not the Eye, and that will take time."

I hope you're right, Kiron thought apprehensively.

"That is my judgment, too," Kaleth agreed. "So we have a window of time during which we can get the Winged Ones *out* of their trap." He looked straight at Kiron.

Kiron felt his eyes widening as he realized that Kaleth intended him and his Jousters to rescue the Winged Ones. "There are only ten of us!" he objected. "We can't carry more than a single passenger, *perhaps* two, if they are children! That would take—"

"—days," Ari interrupted, with a nod to Kaleth. "Or rather, nights, because I am in no mood to have that fire-sword you lot call an Eye burning me out of the sky. Kiron says he thinks it can't work without sunlight, so there's another reason besides stealth to fly in darkness. We couldn't be better set up for this. We're in the sickle moon, and it's waning toward the three nights of dark; we'll have full moon in a fortnight, and I'm willing to try flying in a full moon. We'll just have to be careful."

"*Even more* careful," Kiron countered. "But—flying by night, even under a full moon? It's never been done! The dragons are asleep as soon as the sun goes down!" He tried, and failed, to imagine flying in the darkness. It would be worse than flying in a storm, because no matter how high you went, you wouldn't be able to *see* anything. How could you know where you were? Even at the full of the moon, how could you tell what was below you, or even how near it was?

"So there's no reason not to try, because the Magi won't be expecting it," Kaleth countered serenely. "We don't need to get them *far*, just out of the city proper, and then our human smugglers can take it from there."

"We can take them to my sister Re-keron's estate," Lord Ya-tiren said instantly. "She has been one of our agents from the first. I can have word to her by the time the moon begins to wax. She can hide some and scatter the rest, so that they come to Sanctuary by ones and twos. No one will trouble her; she is known to take dangerously ill patients, and if she bruits it about that she has those with a pox—"

"But we need more than that!" Kiron said, throttling down his emotions as best he could. Not that he didn't want to help the Winged Ones escape, but he wanted to have a reasonable chance of getting everyone out alive! "We need something to distract the Magi *and* their men from the temple, or we will never get more than a few Winged Ones away!" His stomach clenched, as he thought of trying to maneuver Avatre down to a landing when he couldn't even guess where the ground was. "The only way we can get them is off the roof, and the only way we can do that is if we have light up there to see where to land. We need something so distracting no one will notice lights on the roof—" He shook his head. "I never thought I would ever say this, but we need something like an earthshake—"

Kaleth went white, and Marit put her hand on his arm.

He straightened, eyes wide, pupils dilated, and Kiron felt a touch of chill on the back of his neck

"What do you see?" Marit asked, urgently.

He stared straight ahead. "Fire—" he whispered. "Fire and smoke in the city, and fire from the sky, and then—then the earth crying out—"

He went rigid, sitting bolt upright, with his arms stretched rigidly along his thighs, and the chamber fell silent. The hair stood up on Kiron's arms, his entire body went cold, and he had *seen* this before. Kaleth was in the grip of a vision, but not the "ordinary" sort granted by the powers of a priest or a Winged One. This was a vision sent straight from the hands of the gods, and their presence hung heavily in this room—now he was no longer Kaleth, once Prince of Alta. Now he was Kaleth, who spoke for the gods themselves.

"Train your dragons, Wingleader," Kaleth said, his voice echoing hollowly, as though he spoke in a room much larger than this one. "Train them to trust you to be their eyes in the darkness. And make your ways of escape, Altan Lord, and ready your refuge. Watch well, Tian Priests, for only you will know when the time has come to act. This one will speak with the Winged Ones this night, and none shall prevent his voice, nor theirs, from being heard. Unhallowed fire will come from the sky, and the earth shall cry out after, and that will be your moment. So prepare to use it, and use it well, for there will not be another chance." Kaleth's face had a kind of inner light to it, as if it was a lamp made of alabaster, and his eyes looked into places no human was meant to see.

Kiron stole a glance at the Tians, who had never seen Kaleth speak as the Mouth of the Gods before. From their widened eyes and startled expressions, they knew very well what they were seeing and hearing. And they were also astonished beyond measure.

Has it been that long since one of theirs had that power? he wondered.

Well, it didn't matter, for a moment later, that inward light faded, and Kaleth somehow—diminished—and became himself again. And, with it, that paralysis compounded of awe and a touch of terror eased, and it was possible to move.

Move, the Tian priests certainly did. Pta-hetop threw himself on his face, and the rest of the Tian priests followed suit before he was halfway to the floor.

"Oh, do get up," Kaleth said mildly, rubbing his eyes and looking down at them. "Worship the gods, not their instrument. Do you honor the scalpel—or the surgeon? The hammer or the jewelsmith? The pen or the scribe? It is no great virtue of mine that makes me the tool of something greater than I."

"Your humility is—" Pta-hetop began.

"—justified," Kaleth said firmly. "I am a man, I have a gift, but it belongs to the gods and they may take it from me if they choose, just as they gave it to me. Now get up, so that I can tell you what they showed me. I hate speaking to the backs of heads."

Slowly, and with some reluctance, the priests rose and resumed their places, although they still regarded Kaleth with trepidation and awe. Well, Kiron couldn't blame them. He'd seen Kaleth serve as the Mouth several times now, and it never failed to make *him* want to fall on his face.

"At some point before the Winged Ones run too short of supplies, the people of Alta are going to take note of the fact that literally nothing is going into or out of the Temple of the Twins," Kaleth said, as Marit held his hand. He was looking rather white about the lips, which was normal after he'd been granted a vision or used as the Mouth, and in this case, he'd been served with both. "I think it will be on or about the time of the full moon, but my vision didn't give me too many details of that sort. They're going to mob the temple to demand that the Winged Ones be let out. Finally, the Magi are going to loose the Eye on them."

"No!" That cry of anguish and protest was wrung from several throats, Kiron's among them, when Kaleth held up his hand.

"Don't worry. They haven't yet completely gone mad—they'll be creeping the fire along at less than a walking pace. They'll mean to frighten the mob away, not to really kill anyone." Kaleth frowned. "I don't think it's out of kindness, though. I think it's for some other reason. Maybe they're afraid if they use the Eye openly on people who only want to protect their Winged Ones, the people will turn on *them*. Or maybe they think if they indiscriminately or openly kill too many with the Eye, people will flee the city in such numbers that there will be no one left to serve them. I don't think even the army would remain if they overstepped this time."

"They'll use the Eye—" Heklatis repeated, and snapped his fingers. "By the gods! I just put things together! Using the Eye will trigger an earthshake, won't it? And that's our distraction!"

Kaleth nodded, looking sick but resolute. "Yes, it will. As it has from the beginning; most of us never noticed it because they used the Eye so seldom. I don't know why it invokes an earthshake, but it disturbs something beneath the surface of the earth, and the more they use it, the worse the shake. By moving the beam of the Eye slowly, they will be using it for quite a long time, and the earthshake that follows, which will come right after sunset, will be very bad indeed."

"Very bad?" Heklatis sucked on his lower lip. "Length of shake proportionate to time of use, chasing a mob—it's going to be worse than anything we've seen in *our* lifetimes."

"Yes," Kaleth replied, and shook his head. "Terrifying, and even the Magi will be afraid. There will be fires all over the city, a great deal of chaos, and the guards watching the temple will, for the most part, flee. And that will be the distraction you need, Kiron. For that night, and the next three, there will be no one watching the temple; instead, the Magi will order the doors blocked or sealed shut, certain that the people will have too many problems of their own to think about releasing the Winged Ones, and equally certain that the temple will also have its share of deaths and injury. They will trust to the Eye and the earthshake to drive the Winged Ones out and into their hands."

Kiron felt nausea in the back of his throat; he had endured the aftermath of one earthshake that had wrought terrible destruction in Alta City. He didn't want to think about what this would do to a city already afraid and demoralized. "I would rather not have such an opportunity at that cost," he replied.

But Kaleth shook his head. "It is none of our doing, or of the gods'," he said firmly. "The Magi have already put all of this in motion, and it will happen whether we use the opportunity or not. *They* have chosen to besiege the Winged Ones, the people *will* come to protest, and *they* will use the Eye, triggering the shake."

"Then we must make use of it, and take the bitter herb and make a medicine of it," Ari said, standing up. "We have a plan. Let us put *that* into motion."

Train your dragons to trust you to be their eyes in the darkness.

Easier said than done. And without Aket-ten, it would have been impossible.

First, the dragons did *not* want to be kept from their warm sands when the sun went down. They whined and complained and rebelled as much as if they had been asked to fly in the rain. If Aket-ten had not been able to tell them it was a needed thing—though she could not explain to them in ways they would understand why it was needed—it would not have been possible to keep them from their pens and well-earned sleep.

Second, they truly, passionately, fearfully did not want to fly once the sun was down, even when it was only dusk, and not true dark.

Because, according to Aket-ten, they could not see a quarter of what their humans could see once the brightest light was gone. As they lined up in the last light of the day, heads down and tails lashing, their apprehension was so thick Kiron could practically taste it.

"It is the opposite of cats," she said, putting a comforting hand on the quivering shoulder of Re-eth-ke, whose objections to doing this unnatural thing were as strong as any other dragon's, despite Aket-ten's constant reassurances in her mind. "They may be able to see a mouse from the clouds by day, but they cannot see an elephant at fifty paces once the darkness comes."

Kiron and Baken racked their brains to try and devise some training that would lead the dragons to trust in their riders, and in the end, it came down to breaking all of flying down to the simplest of parts.

First, and hardest—landing in the dark. If they could manage to give their beasts the confidence that they could do this, that they *could* trust their riders to be their eyes, everything else would follow.

They all began by taking their dragons up just as the sun set. Now, this was actually an advantage. The dragons could still see, and they were very anxious to be down again—

So, as soon as the sun-disk dropped completely below the horizon, they all *allowed* their dragons to descend. Slowly. Very, very slowly.

Which the dragons were all perfectly fine with—they were having trouble seeing, and were paying, as a consequence, exquisite attention to every tiny nuance of signal that their riders gave them.

Then Kiron made them take off again, as the dragon boys, now freed by the coming of dark from tending their dragonets, lit the fires they would use to land by.

This time, it was dusk, not sunset, and not all of them would rise. Kiron had figured as much; if they wouldn't, he'd told the others not to force them; eventually, it would come. They might not be able to clearly see the rest of the wing taking off, but they could hear it, and instinct would urge them to do the same.

Avatre answered to his order; a measure of her trust in him was that she whined and whimpered but did not hesitate, though her wingbeats were heavy and reluctant. He put her to flying in a slow circle with the fires below at its center. When he peered through the dusk and counted, he found he had been joined in the air by Aket-ten and Re-eth-ke, Ari and Kashet, and Kalen and Se-atmen. Ari's Kashet was still visibly blue, even in the dusk; Re-eth-ke, however, was hardly more than a shadow with silver edges. And brown-and-gold Se-atmen was merely warm shades of gray. That made something else occur to him; it was going to be difficult, if not impossible, to tell each other apart. They would have to have everything perfectly coordinated once darkness fell, and stick strictly to the plan.

But he could feel Avatre's panic under his legs, in her trembling muscles and the way she darted her head around, trying to see the other dragons that she could *hear*. And he knew that she wouldn't rise a third time tonight; she was terrified of a collision in the dark, and rightly so.

Of all of them, Kashet was probably the most panicked, because he was the most set in his ways, the least used to being asked to do the unusual. Only the love he had for Ari had driven him into the sky in the first place. "Ari!" he called into the growing darkness. "You down first!"

Kashet was a wind and a shadow below them, as he spiraled down toward the four fires, for those, at least, he *could* see. And he didn't make a graceful landing— it was certainly the clumsiest he'd made since he learned to fly properly—but there were no sounds of disaster, and in the flickering firelight below, Kiron made out the dragon shadow scuttling out of the square, clearing it for the next pair.

"Kalen!" he called, but Se-atmen, having seen, however dimly, one dragon make a safe landing, was already on his way down.

"You first," Aket-ten called to him. "Re-eth-ke will stay as long as I need her to once the sky isn't crowded anymore."

He didn't intend to ask twice, for Avatre was straining her head toward the ground, whining anxiously, and he let her follow her instincts and the firelight, in a tight spiral down toward the light. But he could feel how much she trusted him and his eyes in the way she angled her flight to every shift in his weight, and the way she began her backwing instantly when he tugged on the reins. Her landing was much more graceful than Kashet's had been, nearly as good as a daylight landing would have been. He jumped from her back and quickly led her out of the square of light, and none too soon, for not even Aket-ten could hold Re-eth-ke back when she knew she was going to be allowed to land.

He didn't wait to watch it; Avatre was straining toward her pen, and he wanted her to have the reward of good work as immediately as possible. She followed his lead through the streets and corridors open to the sky that he had ordered left dark, with no torches or lanterns as were usually in place. The dragons *had* to learn to place all their trust in what their riders "told" them, and this was a good, safe way for them to continue the night's lesson. Avatre knew her pen as soon as they stepped across the threshold, and with a cry, she waded out into the sand without waiting for him to unsaddle her.

And it just didn't seem fair to make her get out again.

So he removed her equipment right where she stood, even though he hadn't had to work so hard since the first time he'd unharnessed Kashet. Then he left her to work herself into her wallow, and she was asleep before he'd finished putting the equipment on its racks.

He joined the others by prearrangement in Lord Yatiren's kitchen, where they were all enjoying well-earned jars of beer.

"They hated it," Orest called, spotting him as he came in. "They were terrified. If it hadn't been for Aket-ten, we'd never have gotten them up."

"But they did it anyway," Kiron pointed out. "And four of them actually took off again in the dark and landed a second time. I wish we could try this blindfolded and increase our training time, but we also need them to learn to use what little they *can* see. Ari, I am amazed Kaleth went up for you on the second try."

"Not half as amazed as I am," Ari replied, gulping down half his jar at a single go. "I think I was almost as frightened as he was. I thought he was going to fly right into you, and so did he."

"We need more room," Gan said decisively, shaking his head to get the hair out of his eyes. "Separate fires. They won't be as frightened if they can't hear other dragons flying so closely above them. That was why Khaleph wouldn't rise; he heard the others and dug his talons in and wouldn't move, and I know he was afraid of a collision. So more fires."

"Or torches," said Oset-re. "Four torches ought to give plenty of light."

Good answer! "We'll do it," Kiron said instantly. "Absolutely. If it will make them feel more confident, we'll do anything we have to."

"Yes," Huras said slowly. "I think we will. I think we *can* do this." He looked around at all of them, that Altan baker's son who had never been more than two streets away from his home before he'd become a Jouster and a rider of one of the first full clutch of dragons to be raised from the egg in Alta. "I thought you were mad, you and Kaleth together—but after tonight—yes. We *can* do this."

"Yes, we can," Ari replied, not quite slamming his empty jar on the table. "Yes, by the gods, we can. We have to; there's no question. And we *will*."

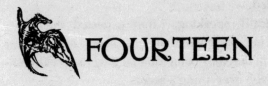

FOURTEEN

TEN dragons rose into the hot, late-afternoon sky, heading into the west, and climbing steeply for as much height as they could get. The higher they were, the less likely it would be that someone on the ground could see riders on the dragons. If anyone—other than the Bedu—saw them, Kiron wanted the watcher to think they were wild. Every bit of this scheme was fraught with peril, and every moment of it contained some potential for mischance. If it went off unthinkably well, no one would know how the Winged Ones escaped. If it all fell to pieces, either the dragons would refuse to fly, or be unable to rescue everyone, or the Winged Ones would refuse to take to the skies, or someone would find out in advance how they were to get out, and where their refuge was, and seize them as they landed.

Realistically speaking, Kiron expected their outcome to fall somewhere in between. There wasn't much more that they could do that they hadn't already done to keep everything a secret.

Aket-ten's Aunt Re had already spread the word that she had taken patients with the pox into her care, and to bolster that tale, several artfully made-up "patients"—in reality, more covert escapees from the city—had been brought by donkey cart to her estate.

Interestingly, no one was as yet making any attempt to stop people from leaving the city, so long as they were perfectly ordinary sorts. These were not perfectly ordinary sorts; they were lesser nobles, and had already been turned back once, probably because they had tried to leave with everything portable they owned piled up on carts behind them. This time they had smuggled their portable goods out ahead, and themselves out as Re-keron's patients, rather than trying to leave with all their goods and gear at once. And probably someone would steal some of those possessions on the way, but that was the price they would have to pay to get any of it out. They should count themselves lucky, or so Kiron thought, to get out with more than their skins and the clothing they stood up in.

There was no way of telling if the Magi would have allowed them to leave had they simply walked out on their own two feet without taking all their belongings—or if the Magi didn't care about the goods, but had no intention of allowing any of the city's elite to leave. Forewarned by his children and Kaleth, Lord Ya-tiren had taken the precaution of moving people and goods in small quantities over a period of two fortnights, then had made a great show of taking the household, as he often did, to his riverside estate. He had encountered no opposition, but when it was discovered that he was not to be found, perhaps the Magi had decided that there would be no more such defections.

The nobles who had been turned back had quickly found one of Lord Khumun's covert agents, who had seen them as the ideal candidates for the initial move of the greater plan of rescue. He had suggested the disguise as pox victims; they had no idea that they were just one more item in a much larger plan.

They had arrived at Re-keron's home several days ago and were already gone, but Re-keron was keeping up the fiction that she was still tending them. As predicted, no one had ventured anywhere near the boundary of the estate as marked by the plague marker stones. It was by no means the first time Re-keron had taken in such people. She had a reputation for being able to make amazing cures, and an equal reputation for eccentricity that made people go to her only as a last resort.

There were some things not even the Magi could

compel a man to face, and the pox was one of them. No one had bothered to follow the donkey carts, and no one was going to go past the plague marker stones until Re-keron herself took them away.

Re-keron's son trained horses to pull chariots. He had a huge, bare-earth training ground hemmed in on all four sides by a wall for that purpose. That was where the dragons would be landing, just after dark. There were supposed to be fire pots all around the perimeter, and to every third one, some salts of copper had been added to make the flames green and blue. It should be easy to spot, even in the darkness, from the air. Aket-ten had flown there and back several times to get the timing right so that they would arrive after darkness fell.

It was a good plan. Kiron only hoped that it would work exactly as they had mapped it out. There were a great many things that were out of their hands. They couldn't predict exactly when the earthshake would strike, for instance, nor how much damage it would do. They couldn't know how visible they would be when they landed on the roof of the temple.

And no one knew if the earthshake would be felt as far as Re-keron's estate or if the dragons would be so frightened by it that they would refuse to make the first flight out that night. Aket-ten had tried to explain it to them, but this was something that was going to happen in some nebulous "future," and dragons were not very good at understanding things like "the future."

At least Avatre was no longer afraid to fly after darkness fell. She didn't *like* it, and he didn't blame her, but she wasn't afraid, and she was willing to trust him to keep her safe. In fact, of all the dragons, the only one still showing some fear of flying by night was Kashet—once again, perhaps, because he was the oldest and the least used to changing his ways. But for Ari, he would do anything, and he was certainly proving that now. They were flying right outside of what Kashet considered to be "safe" territory, known lands, and they were doing it at sunset. Soon enough, it would be dark.

It had been Nofret's turn to fret tonight. Ari could not be spared from this mission. Kashet and Kashet alone was big enough to take some of the heaviest of the Winged Ones. Nofret had not made a scene, but she had been white-lipped and wide-eyed, and her farewell embrace was as fervent as even Ari could have wished.

"I cannot come this time," she had said, as they drew apart, "but the next time, I will have my dragon, and I will *never* leave your side!"

Kiron's shoulders were tight with apprehension, but he tried not to communicate that to Avatre. He actually had to fly without looking in the direction they were going, for the setting sun was straight ahead, and they were flying into it. Instead, he kept his eyes on the ground, judging their height by the landmarks they passed over.

Shadows stretched long blue fingers over sands turning ruddy with the light from the setting sun. It was easy to make out every dune, every wind ripple, by the shadows they cast. From time to time, he spotted one of the Bedu on a camel, smaller than an ant, standing a motionless guard atop a dune or a ridge. They were there to keep watch over the desert, looking for spies along their path.

But they had an advantage that the Magi did not. They had the gods with them. Kiron kept reminding himself of that.

Thanks to Kaleth and the Tians, the Magi could no more use *their* powers to spy on Sanctuary—or even find it—than Kaleth could use his to spy on their counsels. They might guess that it existed, but they could not know where, nor could they know how many people had fled to it.

And they could have no idea that there were still dragons that answered to the hand of man. And *that* was their best weapon at the moment. It was a secret that would probably not survive the rescue of the Winged Ones, but for now, the one direction that the Magi would *not* look for interference coming from was "up."

The two most dangerous parts of this mission were the physical landings and take offs, and being able to remain hidden at Aunt Re's for the three days they thought it would take to get everyone out.

At least the one thing they would not lack was food for the dragons—or for themselves, for that matter. Rekeron's estate was very wealthy, so much so that she did not charge for her ministrations; she could afford to be a Healer as a hobby. It was that wealth, and her reputation as a doer of good works, as well as the distance from the capital, that had so far kept her safe from the Magi.

The shadows below were blending into one another, with only the tops of things still gilded with the last light. It was possible to look at the sun now; it was a flattened ball on the horizon, red as a pomegranate. Desert was giving way to marginal land, and Kiron could only hope that anyone who saw them would think them a string of swamp dragons going back to their nests along the Red and Black Daughters of Great Mother River.

The last of the sun tipped below the horizon as they flew over the first signs of arable land, and Kiron saluted the god in his heart, asking in a brief prayer for his blessing. Overhead, the stars on the robe of Nofet, the Goddess of Night, began to shine.

Oh, sweet and gentle one, you who are the keeper of the shadows, make your shadows to hide us from your enemies and ours! he prayed, as the sky darkened. *Hold your hand above us; let the night demons go to haunt those who have sent so many needlessly to their deaths—and shelter us from all those who would do harm to us.*

This was the next tricky part of the journey; they had to find the Black Daughter before the last light faded, so that they could follow it to Re-keron's estate. Kiron took a quick glimpse over his shoulder, and with great relief, saw that the nearly-full moon was already above the horizon. So at least, once they actually found the river, they'd be able to see it by the moonlight on the water.

As the sky turned black and filled with Nofet's Jewels, he felt a moment of panic—looking for the Black Daughter, and still not seeing it—

And then, at last, a glint of moonlight on the water, and there it was. With what was almost a sob of relief, he turned Avatre to follow it downstream, toward the sea, toward Alta once again—

The others followed him, like a skein of geese. No fear now that anyone would spot them from below—or know what they saw, if by chance they did catch a glimpse of a shadow crossing the moon.

As they winged their way across the star-strewn sky, their dragons' wings making the pattern of three beats and a glide, a feeling that all of this was a dream came over him. It was certainly unnatural. He should not be flying by night. No dragon ever flew by night before. From below came an entirely different set of sounds from those that came up during the day; the song of the nightingale, the barking of dogs, a snatch of song from a hut as they passed over it, and in the distance, the bellow of a river horse. The scent of the river came up to his nostrils, thick, heavy, and very wet; a complicated aroma of mud and weeds, *latas* and lily, fish and decay. Overpowering for a moment; he had completely forgotten that scent in the relative absence of scent in the desert. It filled him with sudden memories of his first days and nights in Alta, his first days and nights of freedom. . . .

It had taken so long to get to Alta City once he had crossed into the lands that Alta claimed! But then, Avatre had been young, and not nearly so strong as she was now. And they were not going to Alta City; Aunt Re's estate was one of the farthest from the city on this river.

It had taken him most of three days to get to the city. It would take them most of the night to get to Aunt Re's Great House. That was a long time to be flying without thermals to help, but the dragons were all fit and well fed, and thoroughly rested. There would never be a better time for this.

The first lights appeared below, marking the homes of farmers, fisher folk, the occasional Great House. Each time, Avatre looked longingly toward them and whined, but obeyed when Kiron gave her the signal to fly on. This was something they had not been able to train for, but apparently the general habit of obedience was enough.

He would have liked to call to the others, but voices

carried in the darkness, and voices out of the sky would certainly alert people below. Even if they thought it was ghosts or demons, they might be tempted to peek. So they were maintaining strict silence until they landed.

It was a curious thing—he would have thought, if there was any such thing as ghosts or night-prowling demons to be seen, they would have been visible from above. Yet there was nothing, or rather, nothing out of the ordinary, though once he did get a glimpse of the astonishing sight of a herd of river horses on land. He would not have thought their ponderous bulk could have been sustained out of the water.

The moon passed, slowly and with all the regal deliberation of the goddess that she was, from east to west. The dragons flew on, but Kiron sensed Avatre growing weary, putting more effort into her wing-beats, and he pummeled his brain to try and remember how long Aket-ten had said it would be before they saw Aunt Re's fires.

And just when he was starting to really worry—he saw them.

A welcome sight they were, too—several furlongs away from the river itself, a blazing rectangle of yellow and blue-green, to his dark-accustomed eyes the center of the training ground looked as bright as day. And there was no holding Avatre back either; she spotted it, and put on a burst of energy to reach it. Like it or not, she *was* going to land there!

He glanced behind at the eight other shadows ranged out in a V-shape from either of Avatre's wings, and saw that their dragons, too, had spotted the fires and come to a similar decision, for they had stopped the pattern of three beats and a glide and were plowing through the air with will and determination.

It was a very good thing that the training ground was as large as the old Landing Court of the Jousters' Compound in Tia because there was no holding back any of them. Avatre landed first, but only by the smallest of margins. The rest came in anyhow, picking a spot by virtue of the fact that no one else was in it. In a way, the landing was an anticlimax; while it wasn't done neatly, it was completed with no injuries or collisions.

Only when all of them were down, and the dragons' wings were furled and the riders out of the saddles, did anyone emerge from the gate at the end of the training ground. And then, it was not some*one*, but an entire procession of people, headed by a very formidable-looking woman in a fine, if plain, wig and an equally fine, if plain, linen gown. No jewels adorned Aunt Re, but she didn't need them to denote her authority. Her erect carriage, her challenging gaze, and her rather formidable prow of a nose marked her as someone to be reckoned with.

But she smiled as Aket-ten ran toward her and flung her arms around her neck, and gestured to some of her servants to extinguish the fire pots.

"Where is the wingleader?" she called.

"Stay," he told Avatre, and approached Aket-ten's aunt, giving her a bow of respect when he came within a few paces of her.

"Well done, boy," she said warmly. "That was no easy journey."

"It was the easiest part of what we are to do," he said somberly, and she nodded in agreement.

"My people have brought meat for your dragons; do you wish to remain with them, or would you care to eat in the dining chamber?" she asked.

Kiron ran his hand through his hair, and made a rueful face. "I think we had *rather* eat in the dining chamber, but had *better* remain with our dragons," he replied. "They're going to be uneasy enough as it is, and they don't like to be parted from us."

He had halfway expected her to be offended, but to his surprise, she broke into an enormous smile. "Well said!" she exclaimed, clapping her hands together. "I like a man who thinks of his beast's and servant's comfort before his own! I raised my sons that way, and I cannot count the number of times one of them has declined a feast to sit with an ill or birthing animal, and rightly, too!" She turned to Aket-ten. "You've chosen well, niece, you may keep him."

Kiron felt himself growing warm, and even though most of the fire pots had been extinguished, he saw Aket-ten blushing. No wonder Aunt Re had a reputation for being eccentric! And no wonder the Magi had not challenged her! He rather pitied them if they tried.

But she paid no attention to their reactions; instead, she turned to her servants and gestured, and they began bringing, first wheelbarrows full of meat, then the makings for sleeping pallets, while off to one side, a few more patiently stood, laden with platters of food.

The dragons, already exhausted, wolfed down their meat with weary determination to get as much into their bellies as they could before they had to lie down. Each of them chose a place to curl up on hard-packed earth that still held some of the sun's warmth in it; most of them chose places close together, with only Avatre and Kashet choosing to be a little aloof. Interestingly, Aunt Re's servants showed no fear of the dragons as they moved about, helping the equally weary riders spread pallets on the ground next to their beasts, then coming to offer them food from the platters.

And as Kiron made his selections, he felt as if the first part of their ordeal had been well-rewarded, for he hadn't seen food like this since they had left Alta. Fresh fruit, dripping with juice, milk as well as beer to drink, cheese, duck, fish—oh, fish! He would have felt ashamed to help himself so greedily to the fish, except that he saw out of the corner of his eye that even elegant, aristocratic Gan was digging into the fish with the glee of a sweet-starved child and with as little regard for manners.

Aunt Re observed them all with a maternal smile on her face. "It does my heart good to see healthy boys enjoying food," she said, ostensibly to Aket-ten, but loud enough for them all to hear. "The gods put good food on this earth for us to appreciate it, and it is blasphemous to do otherwise. And as you can see, I follow that creed!" Then she laughed, and patted her ample middle.

Aket-ten grinned around a mouthful of palm fruit. "Aunt Re, I don't think any of us would disagree with you."

"And which of these young men is the Queen-in-waiting's Consort?" she asked, and not waiting for an answer, picked out Ari with her keen eyes. "Ah, there you are! Come here, boy, if you would."

Ari wisely did as he was told, rising from his cross-legged position on the pallet spread next to Kashet (already dozing) and coming to stand before Aunt Re like a soldier about to be evaluated by his commander. She looked up at him with her arms crossed over her chest, and nodded.

"I like you, Tian," she said. "You'll do. It's about time we got someone with some spine in his bloodline on a throne. You see to it that this nonsense is ended once and for all, and crush those vipers calling themselves Magi under your heel."

And with that, she looked over the rest of them. "Get what sleep you can," she said. "When the sun rises, and it gets too hot for humans, you can either move under the canopies I'll have brought or come inside. My people will bring you more food for yourselves and your beasts; all you have to do is ask for it."

She patted Ari's arm. "Back to your dragon, before he misses you."

And with that, she turned and led her procession of servants back out of the training ground, leaving behind a few lit torches, filled water jars and dippers, and the semichaotic sprawl of dragons and riders.

Aket-ten saw to Re-eth-ke—who, having been here before, had settled down as soon as she was stuffed full and now was sleeping blissfully—and flopped down beside Kiron.

"Why wasn't that woman on one of the Twin Thrones?" he demanded, half laughing, half seriously.

"Because she didn't want to be?" Aket-ten grinned. "Aunt Re, so far as I can tell, has never had any patience with what she calls 'trivialities.' That's probably why the family put her out here in the first place. According to Father, it was a minor estate when she was sent here mostly to keep her from outraging anyone she talked to. She took over the management of it, made it into a very wealthy estate, married her Overseer, had six sons, and all of it without asking anyone's permission. Father adores her."

"You'd either adore her or hate her." He nibbled his lip. "I think I adore her, too. Has she any magic?"

Aket-ten shook her head. "Not a bit. All of her Healing is done with herb and knife, and she's very, very good. When her husband died, she just decided one day that she was going to learn Healing, brought in several Healers to teach her, and just—absorbed it all the way dry ground absorbs rain."

"But why Healing?" he persisted.

"I don't know. She only told me that no other man could ever fill her life the way We-ra-te did, so she wasn't going to try to find another husband, that the estate was pretty much running itself and what little it needed ought to be her eldest son's purview anyway, so she needed something that would fill her thoughts and her time, if not her life." Aket-ten shrugged. "If you were going to ask me, I'd say it was probably something she'd wanted to do before she was sent here, and wasn't allowed."

"She's a wonder," Kiron said, looking at the gate through which she had exited.

"She's every bit of that." Aket-ten yawned. "Now I want to sleep. If that earthshake comes tomorrow, we'll need all the rest we can get."

Kiron nodded, looked around, and saw that pretty much everyone else had come to the same conclusion. Ari was already asleep, with his hand on Kashet's foreleg. The others had curled up in various other positions of contact with their dragons, each taking comfort from the other in this strange place. Aket-ten bent and softly kissed his forehead before taking herself to her own pallet, and he found the most comfortable position for himself, with his back against Avatre's belly.

Sleep was a long time in coming, as he played over in his mind all the possible variations the rescue could have, and tried to think of others that hadn't yet occurred to him. But eventually, sleep did come, and took all further thoughts and plans away.

 FIFTEEN

THE dragons slept like so many statues, and for a while, so did their riders—until the sun rose a bit too far and it was too hot for a human to take, even those used to the heat of the desert. As the riders woke, one by one, the dragons roused just enough to eat, but went back to sleep immediately. Kiron worried about turning their night and day all round about for them, but there really wasn't a choice, not if they were going to have any hope at all of rescuing the Winged Ones. Still, as he stumbled with the rest to the shelter of the canopies Aunt Re's servants had erected, stomach a bit queasy, thoughts fogged, and head aching, he wondered—if the humans felt this unsettled, how did the dragons feel?

He fell asleep again almost as soon as he'd had a drink and gotten into the shade, as had the rest. The rest! They were flat as dried-up lizards on their low Altan couches, made to stand as near to the ground and the cooler air near the floor as possible without actually being on the floor. It probably would have been cooler inside, but none of them wanted to leave the dragons.

He woke again, feeling much more clear-headed, to the sound of quiet voices, and levered himself off the couch to see that it was mid- to late afternoon, and Aunt Re was deep in conversation with Ari. Oset-re was cleaning his harness. Gan, Pe-atep, and Orest were feeding their dragons; only Kalen, Huras, and Aket-ten still slept. His mind felt immensely clearer, and the dragons looked quite their normal selves. In fact, Avatre caught the slight movement he made in looking up and raised her head to snort at him in that demanding fashion that told him she wanted food and she wanted it *now*. The others were being fed, and here he was asleep!

Aunt Re glanced over at the imperious scarlet beauty and chuckled. He knuckled the last sleep out of his eyes and got up to obey her, nudging the couches of Aket-ten and Huras as he passed to stir them up. Kalen was already blinking, looking as ruffled as an owl awakened during the day.

It was all so peaceful, it was easy to forget the situation that brought them here, the crisis that was building within an easy flight of this place, the war, the Magi, and everything else.

He asked one of the waiting servants to bring him meat for Avatre, and trundled the waiting barrow to her with a pang of regret. This was a very temporary respite in a terrible conflict, and he found himself longing for this peace as much as starving little Vetch had longed for food. Avatre bent her head to the barrow of meat and, rather than gulping down the chunks as he had expected she would, ate them daintily as she had in Alta; slowly, as if savoring the fleeting moment herself and trying to make it last.

By the time she was done, the rest had all finished feeding, even Re-eth-ke; none of the others was willing to linger over a meal, however tasty. And as the servants filled the horse troughs so that the dragons could get a drink, they all, even Avatre, kept their heads up, looking about warily, as if expecting something. Even when they were all led to the water, they would not all drink at the same time, but took it in turns to keep watch for something only they could sense.

And Kiron wondered—had the Magi employed the Eye, as Kaleth had said they would? Could the dragons sense the horror scorching down out of the Tower out there? Kaleth's vision had shown it happening late some afternoon, but there was no telling *which* afternoon it would be; they had picked the most likely, but it could come tomorrow, or the day after that, or yet another day. And part of him wanted desperately to put the hour off, but the rest of him wanted just as desperately to get it all over with.

Whatever was causing them to be wary, the dragons didn't settle down completely once they'd drunk. Not even a rubdown and a brisk oiling made them give over that constant looking around for *something* that no one else could sense. Aket-ten could only say, "They're uneasy, they're on edge, and they don't know why," which was obvious enough even to anyone without the ability to speak with them.

The boat of the sun sank to the horizon, and still they would not settle, even though their instincts were surely telling them it was getting on time to sleep. The servants reported that none of the other animals around the estate were keyed up—with the single exception of Aunt Re's pet cheetah, who was prowling the confines of her special chamber with the same wary urgency with which the dragons were prowling the training grounds.

And just as the sun-disk sank out of sight—everything suddenly went very, very quiet. Too quiet. Not a goose honked, not a bird sang, not even a single insect buzzed or rattled. The hair suddenly rose on the back of Kiron's neck, and he felt cold all over, and instinctively looked around for something to clutch. The dragons went rigid.

Then—it came.

That moment of silence warned them, and they had

all braced themselves, but it was still gut-wrenching. When the ground below one moves, the body automatically reacts, sharply, and with the most acute of terror.

And this was no ordinary shake, for it went on for what seemed like an eternity. It was not *bad* as such things went; in fact, it was no worse than many such that Kiron had felt before the Magi began employing the Eye on a regular basis. But it went on, and on, and on, while humans and animals alike screamed with atavistic fear, while birds exploded up into the darkening sky, calling alarm at the tops of their lungs, and the dragons ramped and snorted and hissed, clustering close until their heads and long necks formed a bizarre, ever-weaving bouquet. Under the crash of things falling over, pottery breaking, cries and howls and screams was another sound, deep, that rattled the chest and the gut. It was worse than the worst thunder he had ever heard, a moaning of earth and stone providing the drumming of this dance of disaster. The voice of the earthshake was like the groan of an earth wounded near to death.

But only Khaleph lifted off, and even then, not for long, only for a moment, and he set down again in spite of the fact that the ground was still heaving.

Nearly all of them had dropped to their knees, not because it was hard to keep their footing, but because the terror that welled up inside them made it impossible to stand. Only Ari and Aunt Re remained on their feet, and Kiron could not imagine how they were coping with abject fear that made his insides turn to water and his muscles to dough. They *felt* it; he could see it on their faces. Yet they were holding against it.

The shake continued to go on and on for *far* too long, until he could scarcely think or see, hardly draw a breath for the terror that tightened his chest.

Then, as abruptly as it had begun, it stopped, leaving behind only the cacophony of birds, the terrified whinnying of horses from the stables and paddocks beside the training ground, and the hissing and whining of the dragons. Kiron picked himself up and went to Avatre to calm her; around the courtyard, the rest were doing the same. Out of the corner of his eye he saw Aunt Re going to her servants, one after the other, helping them up, giving them a maternal pat here, a bit of a shake there, a shove to get them moving again.

". . . knew it was coming," she said briskly, as she moved into his range of hearing. "Now we need to find out the damage! Come on, come on, we don't want to find river horses trying to take shelter in the duck pond, now, do we?"

Even as he was calming Avatre, he had to admire her; she was like a general mustering the courage of her troops.

"I'm glad she's on our side," he said to Aket-ten, who had quickly gotten Re-eth-ke under control, and was now working her way around the other dragons, bestowing calm with a touch, a silent "word," or both.

She gave him a shaky smile, her teeth flashing whitely in the growing darkness, but said nothing.

By this time, the birds had settled again, and though there was anxious complaining from the trees around the house, there was no more shrieking. Those that could still see in the half light had flown off, the rest had no choice but to settle down. Someone was getting to the horses, too; they were calming.

We have to go, he realized, still numb with the aftershock. *This is it. We have to go, and soon.*

It wasn't long before Aunt Re had her servants out of the training ground and back in again, bringing back those fire pots. They placed the pots exactly as they had for the dragons' arrival, and Kiron was grateful; Aunt Re must have understood it would be impossible to get the dragons up into the air without light now.

He only hoped it would be possible to get them up into the air *with* light.

With hands that still shook more than a little he saddled and harnessed Avatre while the servants placed and lit the fire pots, lighting up the training ground with a welcome golden glow. Light seemed to make everything safer; this made no sense at all, of course, because an overturned fire pot was more danger than the earthshake, but there was no reasoning with feelings.

The dragons certainly felt that way, though given how little they could see in the dark, their reaction was perfectly understandable. The question was, after that shake, could he possibly induce them to leave this "safe" haven of light?

Well, there was only one way to find out, and this time, Aket-ten would have to lead the way. If she could get Re-eth-ke up, the rest would surely follow.

He whistled the signal to mount; a little raggedly, they all got into their saddles. He looked over to Aket-ten, met her dark, serious gaze, and nodded. It was up to her now. From here on, she would lead the way, and it would all be done by the numbers.

"Re-eth-ke!" she called, her voice sounding a little high and shrill. "Up!"

And as if she could not shake the dust of the treacherous earth from her talons swiftly enough, Re-eth-ke leaped into the deepening blue of the sky.

He didn't have to do more than lift his reins to signal Avatre, she was up like a shot, and she must have been taking comfort in a routine they had practiced until it was second nature.

Perhaps, like the birds, she felt that safety was in the air, not the ground.

As she labored higher, her sides heaving under his legs and growing warmer with exertion with every wingbeat, he glanced behind, to see that Khaleph was already airborne as well, and Wastet leaping upward with wings outstretched.

Beneath them, in Aunt Re's compound, there was ordered activity. He could not see much damage, although things like cracked walls would not be visible until daylight. But servants were going here and there, gathering children together for comfort, moving pallets out into open spaces for safety if there were aftershakes, seeing that beasts were secure, tending to the few—remarkably few, he was relieved to see—injured. Outside her estate, however, as the full moon crested the horizon and spread her cold light over the fields, the case was otherwise. People ran here and there with torches, without really seeming to know where they needed to go. He saw collapsed farmhouses, broken walls, cattle, goats, and pigs running loose. There were fires, too, and shouts and weeping came up to them on the night air.

It made him angry that because there was a greater need for them in Alta City, they could not stop to help *here*. He could only hope that Aunt Re had already considered that, and when her estate was secure, would send her people out to help her neighbors.

Meanwhile, the river beckoned, a long, flat silver ribbon in the moonlight, and their guide to their goal. But it was not the serene river it had been last night; there was a taste of mud and ancient muck in the air. The animals voiced their own outrage; river horses bellowed their anger from among the pools and backwaters, and crocodiles roared and thrashed as they fought with each other or caught—well, he only hoped they were catching some luckless farmer's terrified stock, and not the farmer's children, or the farmer himself.

The closer they came to the Outer Canal and the

Seventh Ring, the worse the damage, and the greater the chaos, and now it was physically painful to see from the air what he had not been able to see the night of his first experience of earthshake. There were fires everywhere, and not just shouts and weeping, but real screaming coming up from below. He could see places where buildings had canted over and fallen sideways, or where they were sunk up to the roofline, as if the ground had turned to water beneath them.

And that shook him. There had been nothing like *that* before. . . .

What had they done?

Not us, he reminded himself desperately. *We didn't do this. We didn't trigger it, we didn't ask for the riot that made the Magi use the Eye. All we did was take advantage of what the gods showed us the people would do, and the Magi would do, and what would come of it—it wasn't our fault. And we couldn't have stopped it.*

But his insides were not convinced.

The shake must have been terrible indeed to have reached this far. Up until now, the worst damage had been confined within the first three rings. And what could have made the ground behave in that strange fashion, to swallow up whole buildings?

Ahead of him, the dark, silver-gilt shadow that was Re-eth-ke flew steadily onward. Behind him trailed the rest of the wing, or at least the rest of it up to Orest and Wastet. A new concern; how many of them had made it into the air?

They passed the Sixth Ring; the Fifth. Then, at the Fourth Ring, though there were still fires, was still shouting and crying and chaos, there was, unaccountably, less of it.

And at the Third Ring, there was order again, and he could have shouted with relief. Not surprising; this *was* where the military were housed and trained. But still, to look down and see people dealing with the aftermath of the earthshake with the same calm as Aunt Re's people made him feel considerably less guilty.

Then Second Ring, and again, there did not seem to be the same amount of chaos and catastrophe as in the Outer Rings, although there certainly was more than enough—and it suddenly dawned on him *why*. So much damage had been wrought here already by the shakes before they had left, as well as the ones after, that almost everything that could be knocked down had been, and many people were probably sleeping in the open at night out of hopeless resignation.

For some reason, that realization transmuted his feelings from guilt into anger, and if he could have gotten his hands around the throat of a Magus just then, he'd have throttled any one of them without a second thought.

This was what they had brought the great city-state of Alta to! This state of helpless apathy, this fear that drained even the ability to properly *feel* fear, this crawling wretchedness not even a slave would envy! *You worms!* he thought angrily up at Royal Hill. *You*

vermin! You scorpions, that eat your own young! How dare
you do this—may the gods help me to bring you down for
it—

But ahead of them, among the many buildings that
were damaged, or afire, or ominously dark and silent,
stood one he knew well. The Temple of the Twins. And
though its ornamental pools were cracked and empty,
and some of its statues and columns toppled, the
building itself stood strong.

And visible only from above, there was a carefully
laid-out square of torches on the roof.

As they drew nearer, he could see people up there,
too, and after all that devastation below, his heart rose
a little to see that the plan they had made in faith was
being carried out in fact.

Now it all depended on the dragons; if they would
remember and stick to the drill, even though the drill
had taken place amid calm, and without all the
screaming, the fires, and the upset from the shake.

They had paced out the dimensions of the temple,
they had plotted it and the grounds around it on the
earth in a pattern of stones. And now, as Kiron
watched, Re-eth-ke banked slightly to take herself and
Aket-ten down to that lighted rooftop—not nearly as
well-lit as Aunt Re's training ground, but it would
have to do, because it was all they had. And as Re-eth-
ke banked, he took Avatre to one corner of that rough
square they had paced out, marked by a clump of date
palms, a square whose dimensions were large enough

that eight or nine dragons could fly the perimeter in the darkness and not be afraid of collisions

By the numbers— he reminded himself, and began to count under his breath.

By the numbers—because they would not necessarily be able to *see* when each of them landed and took off again.

The first count of thirty took him to the second corner of the square; he risked a glance at the rooftop as Avatre made a sharp left-hand bank, and thought he saw Re-eth-ke was safely down. The next count took him to the third corner, and he searched the sky at his own height for the dark-winged shadows of the others.

Yes! One, two—he counted up to eight, and let out a strangled cheer, that would surely be lost in the noise below. They had all followed from Aunt Re's estate! It was working!

One more count of thirty, and a glance at the roof showed it empty of anything but people; Avatre made her turn as neatly as if they were practicing over Sanctuary, a long, shallow glide down over the square of torches, a thunder of wings and a wind that made the flames stream sideways as she came in to a halt, the moment of fumbling hesitation beneath him as she felt for a secure talonhold, and then—

Then she was down.

She barely had time to pull in her wings, and *he* didn't get time to draw a breath before someone with a pale blur of a face wrapped in a dark cloak shoved two smaller objects wrapped in equally dark cloth at him.

Children; Nestlings, probably, not even old enough to be Fledglings, and their inert limpness made him go stiff with rage. But he wasted no time on speech; he couldn't hold them *and* fly, so he belted them to himself before and behind the saddle with the straps they handed up to him silently. Below this place, weeping and cries of pain; here, only silence, as if he was being served by shadows and ghosts. And once they were secure, he gave Avatre the signal, and they were away.

Avatre seemed to have picked up on some of his emotion, however, for he could feel a new energy in her flight as they sped away into the darkness, deliberately going higher to take them above the flying square of dragons. As they neared Aunt Re's estate, he thought he caught sight of Aket-ten and Re-eth-ke coming back, and once again he gave a little exclamation of triumph; this was the second sticking point— having come back to the safe haven, could the dragons be persuaded into the air again? Re-eth-ke, at least, could be.

They landed, and eager hands reached for the children, swarming over Avatre like cleaner birds over a river horse. She seemed to have grasped the serious nature of what they were doing now; she stood as patiently as anyone could have wished while strangers crowded her and treated her like nothing more than a living cart while getting the children unstrapped. Then, at last, they were free again, and Avatre took to the sky without a moment of hesitation.

As they made height, he definitely caught sight of Kashet coming in, though he could not tell what kind of burden he and Ari carried. And then he passed the others, one at a time, really knowing who they were only by their order; Wastet and Orest, Deoth and Pe-atep, Apetma and Oset-re, Khaleph and Gan, Bethlan and Menet-ka, and last of all, the steadiest and strongest of the lot after Kashet and Avatre, big Tathu-lan and Huras.

Now—if they would all make the second trip, and not refuse—and if no one saw them, or realized what they were seeing if they did—

Only when he had formed up the second square did he know for certain that the plan was working in its entirety, and Avatre seemed to have been set afire by the urgency of what they were doing. She came in with the speed and snap she had when she was making a kill when hungry; she stood like a rock as the next to be rescued was helped onto her back. This time, though it was another pair of children, these must have been Fledglings, and they were able to cling to him and not be bound to him like inert bundles, though they *were* secured with straps. Avatre was in the air almost before the last of the Winged Ones was out of the way, and the two children gasped as she rowed for height.

Halfway to Aunt Re's the one behind him tugged at his tunic. "Jouster?" came a thin, pathetic little whisper. "Are you taking us away from the Magi?"

"Far away," he called back, over the steady, strong flapping of Avatre's wings. "Far, far away, where the sand of the desert will hide you, and the swords of the Bedu will guard you, and they will never, ever find you again."

Both children burst into tears of pure release, reaching for one another's hands on either side of him, and it was all he could do to keep from joining them. Instead, he pointed out the white egrets in the tops of the trees they flew over, a pair of fighting river horses, the reflection of the moon on the river, the pattern of the stars—anything except the places where people were still trying to save themselves and their property below. His distraction must have been effective; they listened and watched, and most importantly, stopped crying.

They began again as soon as he handed them over to Aunt Re's people, but at that point they were no longer his concern, and he had to concentrate on the next trip.

And the next.

And the next.

Avatre had never flown so strongly, but by the fourth trip, they had lost Deoth to exhaustion—not to unwillingness, because he tried to take off, but Pe-atep was too wise to let him. Apetma simply dropped, so tired she simply couldn't rise. By the fifth, Se-atmen,

Wastet, and Bethlan were out, too, and on the sixth, poor Khaleph and Tathulan were so tired their wings were trembling. That left only Kiron and Avatre, Ari and Kashet, and Aket-ten and Re-eth-ke for the seventh and final trip of the night. Kashet had carried double every time; probably Aket-ten's lighter weight was what had made it possible for Re-eth-ke to carry on to the end. But she was lagging on that final leg, and as they actually flew into the gray of predawn, halfway back to Aunt Re's compound, Kashet and Avatre caught up with her. Ari and Kiron exchanged a glance, and Kashet pulled into the lead, allowing Re-eth-ke and Avatre to fall back into the wake-position off his left and right wings. It was easier flying there; he could see Re-eth-ke's breathing ease a little.

With plenty of light to see by, they all landed together, too, letting down their exhausted passengers into the hands of equally exhausted servants, who bustled them off before the Jousters were even out of their saddles. The rest of the dragons and their riders were already dead asleep, and from the look of them, not even another earthshake would wake them.

But Kiron found himself being helped in unsaddling Avatre by a handsome, muscular young man with the powerful upper torso of a charioteer, who had also come wheeling up a heaped-high barrow of meat that Avatre began wolfing down without waiting to be unharnessed.

"You've gotten out eighteen Nestlings," he said

without preamble, raising his voice enough so that Ari and Aket-ten could hear. "That was the first trip. You got out twice that many Fledglings on the second and third trips, another six Fledglings and three Winged Ones on the fourth, six Winged Ones on the fifth trip, five on the sixth, and three on the seventh trip, which is three more trips than anyone ever thought you'd make in their wildest dreams."

Kiron tried to add the total up in his mind, and felt the numbers slipping through his mind like the yolk from a broken egg. "Um. Sixty—ah—"

"Seventy-seven," the young man corrected him. "One more night, and you'll have all the Winged Ones out. If you want to try for three nights, you can probably evacuate the servants that are left, too."

Kiron looked over at Ari, and rubbed a gritty hand over his forehead.

"I think we should," Ari said firmly. "The dragons are clearly willing, and I don't want to leave anyone to suffer back there."

There was something intensely bitter and angry in Ari's tone as he said that—something that cast Kiron back in time to a moment when he had heard Ari cry out, *I do not make war on children!* It rocked him back on his heels, and he stared at Ari wide-eyed.

Ari stared back. "There are some things," he said, "that no man can countenance."

Someone told him something. Maybe more than one someone. Well, Ari was the only one with a dragon

strong enough to carry the largest of the adults. Once
the youngest had been gotten out, surely the next to go
would have been the very oldest. No one had been
draining the Winged Ones for several days now, which
meant some of them would have started to recover
their powers. They *had* to have recovered their wits, or
they would never have been able to barricade themselves in the temple.

If one of them recognized Ari for what he was—and
it would take a Winged One no more than an un-
guarded touch to do that—then they would have
known that their rescuer was also the titular King of
Sanctuary.

*So of course they told him something. They probably told
him everything they could before they were set down. He's
the King. He has to know.*

It was one thing to be told in abstract that the Magi
were draining the god-touched, damaging them,
sometimes killing them. Kiron suspected that it was
quite another thing to be told what that was like, *by*
someone who had experienced it, day after day, for the
last year.

Well, that was a good thing. If Ari had any doubts
about what he should do, they were gone now.

But Kiron was very, very glad that he was not the
one who'd had to hear those tales. Truth be told, he already knew more than was comfortable.

"Mother is sending the strongest of them off today,"
the young man continued—that clue telling Kiron that

his helper was the horse-training son of Aunt Re, which explained his family resemblance. "But they will be very, very glad to hear that you intend to evacuate the entire temple. I'll go tell them now."

"Do that," Ari said, and managed a wan smile. "And meanwhile, I think we had better emulate our wingmates."

Avatre was already doing just that, dropping down where she stood after swallowing a last mouthful of meat. With a groan, Kashet did the same. Re-eth-ke looked about and went to curl up beside Tathulan, then changed her mind and put her back up against Avatre, who didn't even stir.

Ari raised an eyebrow at Kiron, who was too tired to even blush.

More servants brought them meat, onions, and soured milk wrapped up in flatbread, and jars of beer, that they ate and drank while pallets were spread beside their dragons. Then, like their dragons, they dropped down to sleep, and did not awaken until their dragons' hunger roused everyone.

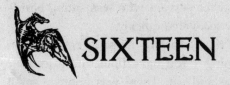 **SIXTEEN**

HE had thought they had slept like the dead yesterday. That was nothing, compared with today. Even an earthshake didn't wake them, for they did get a minor rumble, and neither he nor any of the others was aware there had been one until they clawed their way up out of slumber. He didn't even remember stumbling his way to a couch in the shade when the sun grew too hot; he only knew he had gone to sleep beside Avatre and woke, once again on the couch, and not even the same one as the last time.

But when he woke, it was with a rush, and he woke all at once, out of a dream of flying Winged Ones off the roof of the temple, burning with a desire to get more of them away before the Magi understood what was happening.

He didn't sit up with a yell, though he might as well have. He startled the servant who was sitting beside him. But the boy recovered quickly.

"It is not yet time, master," he said, before Kiron could say anything. "You have time to see to your dragon, to bathe and eat. There was another small shake after dawn. Did you feel it?"

He shook his head, but his attention was caught by a single word. Bathe! At the sound of that word, Kiron itched all over; not that there wasn't water enough to bathe at Sanctuary, but it seemed wrong to use so precious a thing for bathing. They all *did*, of course, but it seemed wrong. Now, the hot spring at Coresan's nest was another matter entirely—but he hadn't had a bath there since two days before this journey.

But this was Alta, where water was abundant, so after he saw Avatre fed, he allowed the servant to take him off to the baths, both hot and cold. And once reclothed in a common tunic of the sort Aunt Re gave her upper servants, which was enough like what the Jousters wore these days that it made no difference, he helped himself from the food left out for all of them and made a hasty meal. Aket-ten was the last of the riders to wake, and he didn't blame her for sleeping so long; she had been doing two jobs at once—guiding her own dragon, and keeping track of all of the rest of them.

She woke just as quickly as he had when she finally did break through her slumbers, and was just as impatient to be gone as the rest of them. She surely imparted that impatience to the dragons, all ten of them, for the moment she came awake, they began to fidget and look skyward. And at that moment, Kiron would have given all that he had or ever hoped to have for one flight—just one!—with all the wings that Alta had once had. With that many dragons, they could have left *now*, to arrive just after sunset, and it wouldn't matter who saw them. The Magi couldn't use the Eye at night, and they would have been able to pull out every last person all at once.

But dragons had no mystical ability to go back or forward in time, so the wing he had was all he was going to get. And as soon as Aket-ten had rejoined them, hair plastered flat to her skull from her bath, he called a meeting.

"Last night was the easy one," he told them, and at Orest's indignant stare, shook his head. "Yes, I know, from just the point of view of uncertainty about whether we'd get the dragons up at all, it was the hard one. But in terms of getting people out, it was the easy one." He tilted his head to the side, then lifted his head and looked each of them in the eyes. "Think about it; we had it all our own way last night. The Magi were busy making sure of their own safety, and didn't give a toss about anyone else. We got out the children, the old, and the sick, all of them lightweight, all of them tractable."

"Or unconscious," Gan said soberly, raking his fingers through his hair to help it dry. "You have a good point, though; easy to fly, and they didn't make a fuss, or scream, or anything."

"Tonight, we get the able-bodied and the heaviest, but there's more to it than that," he replied. "The people we will take out tonight are the senior Winged Ones, ruling priests, important priestesses. They're used to giving orders and having them obeyed."

"What possible orders could they give?" Pe-atep asked, incredulously. " 'Fly faster'? As if we could?"

Oset-re made a face and shook his head. "They're Great Lords and Ladies in their own right. Who knows what they'll demand when we are airborne?"

Kiron silently applauded Oset-re for seeing at once where the danger was. He was very aware of Aunt Re standing off to one side, listening, but not commenting. "We are very young men, all looking rather like servants—and one young woman with what is, by their standards, a minor power, who should by all rights rank just about Fledgling status. They won't think when they see us. If they aren't too sick and tired to do anything but hang on, there is no telling what they might try to order us to do."

"Fly lower!" squeaked Gan in an imperious-old-lady voice, swatting at Pe-atep. Aunt Re hid a smile behind her hand.

He nodded. Now he had to remind them of what they were and that they had to disobey. "Or higher. Certainly faster or slower. And while you might be able to fob them off by telling them the dragons can't do that, there's other things they might want you to do. *Stop*, because I must get this or that treasure or sacred object. Land *there* to tell my mother I'm safe—" he shrugged. "There's no telling. But they might well become real nuisances, some of them, when they're in the air. They've been powerless a long time. They'll want to command something, if only us."

"Trouble." Orest shook his head. "You don't think they'll go so far as to fight us, do you?"

For that, he had to look to Aket-ten and Orest.

Aket-ten shook her head. "I think they'll still be torn between the excitement of escape and the fear of being captured. But they might start to shout, and—voices coming from the sky might not be a good idea."

"Try telling them no matter what they want, it's Lord Khumun's orders," Orest offered. "Most of them know they can half-bully Father, but nobody's ever gotten around Lord Khumun, not even a Winged One."

Well, if it came to that, Lord Khumun was going to end up with an earful when they finally all got to Sanctuary.

Lord Khumun can take care of himself, he decided.

"I just want you to keep those things in mind," he went on. "First, heavier passengers. Second, passengers who want to make demands. And three—" he paused. "We don't know what the Magi have done in our absence, nor what they might do after darkness falls. *Maybe* they'll still be too concerned with their own safety and comfort after so big a shake that they won't keep a magical eye on the temple. But I don't think we can count on that. Do you?"

One by one, the others shook their heads. Overhead, vultures circled on the thermals their dragons would be using, if only they could, dared, fly by day. At least darkness would hide them in part. Until they came in to pick up the first escapees. Until they came into the light.

"So tonight we run the risk of being seen." He chewed on his lower lip. "I don't think there's anything we can really do about that—not being overlooked by magic, anyway."

"Uh—" Aket-ten flushed, and held up a fistful of leather thongs. "I think these might help."

He peered at them, frowning. There were little faience medallions hanging from them. They looked familiar.

"Pashet's teeth!" exclaimed Oset-re with delight. "Heklatis' amulets!" He jumped to his feet, pulled Aket-ten up, whirled her around like a child, and kissed her on the top of the head before letting her drop back down again, flushed and laughing.

"Here," she said, passing them out. "I collected them after we came to Sanctuary; you lot kept losing them or leaving them lying around, and there's no point in discarding something magic, even if you don't need it at the time. I thought they might be useful again. Heklatis knows I have them and I told him I was taking them along. He said it was a good thing, otherwise he'd have had to make a new batch and send them along, and I saved him the work."

Kiron accepted the amulet with a rueful shrug; once in the safety of Sanctuary, he'd been one of the worst at forgetting to keep track of his amulet. Heklatis had made them to interfere with the Magi's scrying, or seeing-at-a-distance, back when they were all in the Jousters' Compound together. But although the protection had been priceless while they were scheming to destroy the *tala* and escape right under the Magi's noses, they had seemed of little utility out in the middle of the trackless desert, where the distance *and* Kaleth's god-assisted protections kept them from being overlooked by means of magic.

But Aket-ten never forgot anything, it seemed.

"All right, then," he said, pulling the thong over his head. "We can keep them from seeing us with magic, but we can't stop someone from spotting us just by looking up. So we have to assume they will have eyes in the city, especially eyes keeping watch on the temple, and those eyes will report whatever they see. Even if it's dragons where no dragons should be."

Oset-re snorted, and behind him, her neck arched so that her head was right above his, coppery Apetma snorted so exactly like him that, serious as the situation was, it startled a laugh out of all of them.

"*Especially* dragons where no dragons should be, you mean," Oset-re said. "No, you're right. Those miserable crocodiles wouldn't spare a man to help a single person on the Outer Rings, but once *they're* certain of being comfortable and safe, they'll put spies back on the temple." He thrust out his jaw belligerently. "All the more reason to get out as many tonight as we can. We know what to do now."

"Which is, above all else, to not let your dragons fly past their strength." Kiron glared at him. "You can't afford to go to ground between here and the temple. *But*—it did come to me that if a dragon were to stop at round three or four, but regain enough strength to join the final round—I think it would be important enough to let him, or her, do so. But you *must* judge your dragon's strength to the last wingbeat. Failure on the return leg—" He shook his head. "—landing in the dark, or in the river, with the crocodiles and the river horses so excited and upset by the earthshake—"

Most of them had seen men hurt or killed in a river horse hunt. All had seen the injuries men got from the seemingly soft and passive beasts. And a crocodile, or worse yet, a swarm of them—they'd take a man and a dragon to pieces in moments. Swamp dragons could hold their own against both river horse and crocodile, but these were desert dragons, and utterly unsuited to such foes.

"No, we can't afford that," Kalen agreed. "And I've got a horrible truth for you. There are a lot more Winged Ones than there are Jousters. We cannot go into this certain that we will get them all out; we must *try*, but we might not be able to. If someone has to be left behind, it had better not be a Jouster."

Aket-ten made a little cry of protest, but Ari nodded, and so did Kiron. "An ugly truth, too, and that is what, as your wingleader, I am *ordering* you to do, if it comes to that," he said, making his voice as hard as he could manage. "There are ten of us, and already we have saved six times that number of Winged Ones. I can't replace one of you. I can probably replace a Winged One. Agreed?"

Aket-ten's face crumpled and she looked utterly miserable, but glancing at Ari gave her no reprieve, so reluctantly, she nodded.

"With luck, it won't come up," he said, injecting a little cheer into his tone. "Haras give us strength and luck, we'll succeed despite their ill will. Can anybody think of anything else?"

No one could, so at that point, it was just a matter of waiting.

Just! If there was anything harder than waiting, he certainly didn't know what it was.

The first passenger was an imperious old woman, with a voice so exactly like Gan's imitation that he had to catch himself to keep from laughing aloud. "Fly faster!" she demanded in his ear—at least she was making an effort to keep her commands quiet.

"Dragon's flying as fast as she can, Great Lady," he replied, taking a moment to remind himself who these people were, and how much respect they were due. And he heard the fear under the arrogance; perhaps the arrogance was born of fear. He wanted that respect in his voice before he answered her. "None of them are used to carrying double."

The old woman mulled that over for a bit, then poked him in the ribs with a bony finger. "Then land beside Te-aten-ka's apothecary shop on Fourth Ring. I need—"

"I'm sorry, Great Lady, but no landing until we get to Re-keron's estate in the country," he interrupted. "Lord Khumun's orders. Even if I knew where the place was, which I don't, and even if it's still standing when we got there, which it probably isn't. What Lady Re-keron doesn't have you'll have to do without until you can find a way to get it."

She bristled, forgetting her fear in the shock of being thwarted by a mere boy. He could *feel* her back behind him, bristling up with indignation like a hedgehog. "Now see here, young man, I will not—"

"Great Lady, I'm afraid you must," he interrupted again. "What you don't have, you will have to do without, and anyone you wished to speak with to assure them of your safety will have to go unwarned. Avatre is not like a chariot; if you seize the reins, you will only confuse and upset her, and if you upset her, she may well decide you are too much trouble to carry."

Astonished silence followed that revelation, "But—"

she began again, this time with more uncertainty in her voice.

"Great Lady, can you swim?" Kiron interrupted again. "Because if Avatre decides to rid herself of you, there is very little I can do about it, but at least we will be above the Great Mother River's daughter most of the way."

Behind him, he sensed that the old woman was opening and closing her mouth silently, like a fish pulled up on the bank. Well, she could do whatever she wanted, as far as he was concerned, as long as she made no noise.

Her shock kept her silent the rest of the way; when he handed her down to her waiting attendants, she looked up as if she was about to say something, but didn't get a chance to before they rushed her away.

The next trip, the man they put up behind him was silent and looked exhausted. He said not a word until they landed, and then it was only a whispered "thank you," as he dismounted.

The third trip, however, and the passenger being a tall, cadaverous looking man with haunted eyes, the ones who helped him strap himself to Kiron looked faintly familiar. Enough so that he glanced back in puzzlement as Avatre took off.

"Think you know them, do you?" the Winged One said in his ear. "You probably do. They were two of your little friend Aket-ten's teachers."

But they weren't wearing the medallions of the Winged Ones, his mind protested.

He didn't say it aloud, but he had forgotten, for a moment, that with these people, he didn't have to say something aloud to be heard. "They aren't Winged anymore," the bitter man said, in a tone of venomous anger.

Not Winged? But—that wasn't possible, surely, you were either Winged or not—

"They fought the Magi. The Magi didn't like that, so they kept the ones who fought instead of letting them come back to the temple to rest, and used them until they burned them out. Unfortunately for them, they didn't die of it." Not only hatred but fear, and the kind of anger that gripped Kiron like the talons of a vulture. "*Then*, the Magi brought them back as a lesson to the rest of us. They're no more god-touched now than you are."

"At least they're alive," Kiron offered, feeling it was a weak solace, but still—they *were* alive when all those acolytes in Tia weren't. They might not be Winged anymore but thousands of people weren't Winged—

"I wouldn't call it living," the bitter man said, acid etching every word. "A man can live without a hand, a foot, even an eye, but what happens when you take part of what he *is*? He's better off dead! I'd say that, and they'd say the same!"

Kiron had no good response for that. There was no good response for that. All he could do was to guide

Avatre through the night, and wonder what, if anything, the angry man thought he could do about it.

"I'm sorry" seemed a bit inadequate, but it was all
he had.

The man didn't say anything more until they
reached the estate and landed. Then, once he was
down on the ground, he gave Kiron a searching gaze.

"You're a good lad," he said. "Just do what you came
to do as best you can, and don't take more on yourself
than you can be responsible for."

And with that he staggered away, limping heavily
and leaning on the arm of an attendant, and if there
had been time, Kiron would have hurried after him to
demand a meaning for such cryptic remarks.

But there wasn't, and he didn't, and Avatre was already off the ground as he wrenched his gaze back to
the direction of Alta City.

When he picked up the seventh passenger of the
night, there were people bringing heavy coils of rope
up to the top of the building.

And as he took off with the man—he and Ari were
getting the men, of course, since their dragons were
the oldest and biggest—the Winged One kept looking
back. Kiron followed his gaze and saw that the rope
had been tied off to some ornamental stone-work, and
someone was just slipping over the edge to climb
down.

"That's a relief," his passenger said, turning back to

face forward. "I'm glad to see someone talked sense into them."

"Talked sense into who?" Kiron asked.

"Some of the servants—young ones, who actually have the strength to go down a rope like a monkey." The man sighed. "With two thirds of us gone, there's no need for all of the servants, and there's no telling what *They're* up to, spying on us, I've no doubt. If they discover that some of us are gone, they'll try and break the siege, and we've been telling the servants that there's no odds one way or another on whether you'll be able to get them out before the Magi and their guards turn up. Someone must have talked them around to going out over the wall."

"It's what I'd do," Kiron agreed, "If I wasn't needed."

"They aren't, and if the Magi guess what's happening, they're likely to get—" the man paused choosing his words carefully, "—vindictive."

Vindictive.

Kiron didn't like the sound of that. "Would they turn the Eye on the temple?" he asked, feeling his stomach sink with dread.

But the answer he got reassured him. "They can't. Once they use it, they have to recharge it for days before it's fit to be used again. But it would be better for no one to be here when the temple is broken into."

That was surely an understatement.

When they landed in the beginning light of dawn,

the man went off with Re's servants without saying a thing more—but then, Kiron was so tired, he probably couldn't have asked his questions coherently anyway.

So for the third night, he fell asleep in the curve of Avatre's belly, more exhausted than he would ever have thought possible.

For the third afternoon, he woke in a rush, this time out of a confused dream of flying, fire, and death. He lay there for a moment while his heart pounded with anxiety, and forced it to calm.

After all, it was only a dream. And it was a dream of things he'd gone through many times before this, and would do so many times in the future. He wasn't a Winged One, to have dreams of portent.

In fact, right now, he was altogether glad that was the case. It would have been much too heavy a burden to carry.

And this time, there was someone from among the rescued of last night waiting for him when he gathered all of them for their meeting, a lady with more of the air of a Queen about her than Nofret.

Someone Aket-ten clearly knew very well. "Wing-leader Kiron, I make you known to Winged One Ma-an-ed-jat," she said, with utmost formality. "She is the High Priestess of all of the Winged Ones of Alta."

Kiron bowed about as much as he did to Lord Khu-mun. The lady lifted a sardonic brow, but gave him a little smile of approval. "Not afraid, I see."

He shrugged. "Fear of you would serve no purpose, and we need to keep our wits about us. How many Winged Ones are left to be rescued?"

"No more than a handful," the High Priestess said. "You'll have them out on your first trip. The rest are all servants and—" she hesitated, then said, "—servants and friends. But I came to tell you that the Magi suspect something. I am Far-Sighted, and I have been bending my will to see what I may see this day. They've brought their private guards there now, and it looks as if they're planning to break down the doors."

Before Kiron could say anything, Oset-re laughed, although it did not sound as if what he was about to say was something he considered humorous. "Much good may it do them. My last man said you people have moved everything movable and packed the antechamber behind every door solid. They can break the doors, but they won't get in until they clear the place."

The woman nodded. "But our time is short," she told them all. "That is what I came to say, and to thank you, and to tell you that I know that not only will you and your dragons do their best, I also know that no one anywhere would put as much of themselves into this as you have."

She bowed—deeply—to all of them, then turned and left the training ground without a backward glance.

Huras broke the silence, laughing shakily. "I feel as

if I have just had Lady Iris appear, pat my head, and tell me I have been a good boy and to finish cleaning my room and run along now," he said, which made them all laugh.

"The ways of gods are strange, and the ways of their servants even stranger," Ari said briskly.

"She's exhausted," Aket-ten said doubtfully, looking after the woman. "I've never seen her so thin and drained-looking."

"So the sooner we finish this thing, the sooner she'll have no people back in that temple to worry about," Kiron replied, putting a bit of a whip-crack into his words. "You heard the Winged One. Let's get into the saddle and into the air. Either the Magi will spot us, or they won't, and in either case this is the last night, and we'll be gone before they can do anything about it."

"From your mouth to the ear of Haras," Menet-ka said, earning himself a swat from Oset-re.

"Haras helps those who help themselves," Kiron reminded them. "Into the sky, Jousters! We'll be seeing our own beds again by midmorning!"

Which reminder was enough to put fire into the most tired of them, after all.

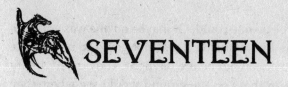 # SEVENTEEN

BUT as they approached the temple this time, it was clear that something was very different. There was a lot of light on the horizon, and a red glow in the sky. It looked like a fire—

As they got nearer, what had looked like a building on fire resolved itself into a scene of purposeful activity. Armed men with torches swarmed the grounds, and there were bonfires burning under the walls, the light reflected in the pale stone from bottom to top. Smoke rose into the air in clouds, making his nose itch.

No one would be escaping over the walls by ropes tonight.

His heart sank a little. He could only hope that anyone willing to get out that way had, last night.

How many were left? No one had given him a number.

Maybe no one could. Or maybe no one was going to, to spare him knowing it was not going to be possible to get them all out before daylight. They dared not fly by day, or those on the ground would see where they went, leading the Magi straight to Aunt Re.

The dragons didn't like the smoke and the fires, but they were bred for cavorting in and around sulfurous springs. The smoke was going to bother their riders a lot more than it would trouble them. It was a still night, and the smoke rose into the air and hung there like low clouds; though it made his eyes burn, it might not be a bad thing; they might be able to use it to hide behind. There was one thing; the extra light would make it easier for the dragons to see where they were going.

He kept Avatre high as they came in behind Aketten, forming the square well into those clouds of smoke. He glanced behind to see if the next rider caught the hint and was gratified to see that the others were following his lead.

At least there will be more light to land by.

Re-eth-ke descended into the smoke to the square defined by torches on the roof of the Temple. There were a lot of torches up there now, more than there had been last night. More than enough for all those men on the ground to notice.

Well, it's not as if it's going to make any difference.

Incredibly, no one on the ground saw the dragon landing on the roof. But then, Re-eth-ke was a flickering shadow in the smoke, indigo with a confusing touch of silver. When she rose again with her double burden, she was still barely visible among the shifting shadows in the smoke, and there was no outcry.

Not so for Avatre.

As she fanned her wings to land, he heard the cries from below, and ducked instinctively as arrows whistled through the night sky. As his helpers handed his next passenger up behind him, and tied them together with rope, he saw that they all had improvised wicker shields strapped to their backs. A moment later, he understood why, as a clatter of spent arrows bounced off the shields or the rooftop. One or two had a little more energy and stuck in the shields.

His young female passenger shook with fear; no older than Aket-ten, surely, and just as surely had never personally seen a shot fired in anger, much less had one directed at her. Those who helped tie her in place were made of sterner stuff.

"Clever story they're putting out about you," said one of those men he'd thought he'd recognized last night. "Evidently you're Tians, come to steal us away."

"Really?" He gave the rope a good hard tug to test it, and coughed as he breathed in a little too much smoke. "I don't suppose they've got an explanation as to why you're tying yourselves onto our dragons."

"Not yet," came the reply, and a sardonic sneer. "But

I expect they'll think of something soon. They're shooting to kill us, you know. I overheard the Captain of Tens giving the orders. We're better off dead than in your hands, according to him."

A muffled wail behind his back made it very clear what his passenger thought of all this.

"Then we'll just have to be where the arrows aren't," he said, keeping his tone confident. The helpers stepped away, and he sent Avatre up.

His passenger alternated distraught sobs with coughs the entire way back; he tried to get some answers out of her, but she replied with nothing but weeping. He tried not to be too irritated with her, but it was difficult; he desperately wanted to know how many people were left in that temple, and she was about as sensible as a terrified hare and just as articulate.

As he approached the temple the second time, he saw that there were archers not only on the ground, but on the roofs of nearby buildings, trying to keep up a steady barrage of arrows. Most fell short, but there were enough that were reaching the roof of the temple that he felt a thrill of alarm. But when he landed this time, instead of the clattering of falling shafts, or worse, the sound of arrows striking nearby, there was nothing, and he wondered why—

Wondered, until he heard the swish of arrows through air again and a thudding—but it was a thudding sound that was far off to the right, literally as far away as it was possible to get and still be on the rooftop. He looked to that side, and to his utter astonishment, saw a roll of straw matting standing on the edge of the roof, bristling with arrows, with more thudding into it with each moment.

"Magic," said one of the helpers, following his glance. "Your current passenger's idea." He patted the middle-aged woman's plump arm, and she smiled wanly. "Seems she's been dabbling in Magus work; learned it from some Akkadian friend of hers. Now that straw roll somehow sucks all the arrows toward it. Damned useful, but now it's time for you to get her out of here."

Avatre launched herself skyward before he could reply; she didn't want to be on that roof any more than he did. His passenger looked down at the besiegers as they passed overhead, and shivered.

"It's a very difficult thing, seeing all those people and knowing they want to kill you," she said forlornly, as they passed into darker, cleaner air and out over the canal.

"It's what every soldier sees, when he looks at the enemy," he offered, hoping to make her feel a little better, or at least, less vulnerable.

"You're right, of course," she said. "But it's still a hard thing. No one ever wanted to kill *me* before."

He thought about how cherished, how respected, admired, even loved the Winged Ones had been, and felt a certain sympathy for her distress.

"You've been very sheltered," he said reluctantly.

She said nothing for a while. Then, "Too sheltered," she replied, sounding a little less sorry for herself. "If we had been paying attention, instead of isolating ourselves in our own little world, we would have noticed that rot beginning. What's happening now is partly our own fault. There were signs . . . when the Magi singled out certain Nestlings for extra training that somehow made them lose their powers, or sent them on errands during which there were . . . accidents. But when the Magi proposed making the storms stronger, it seemed like such a good idea at the time—"

"It might go back farther than that," he pointed out, as Avatre sneezed, then pumped her wings to get a little more height. "Back to when they first made the Eye."

"Oh, yes. The Eye." He felt her shiver. "How could we ever have thought that was a good idea? It's not like building walls; walls can't be turned against your own people. We should have known then that they were on no one's side but their own."

Yes, you should have, he thought. *For people who were supposedly Far-Sighted, you certainly kept looking in the wrong places.*

His passenger didn't know how many people were left in the temple, but when he returned for another trip, he saw something going on below that made him think they had even less time than he'd assumed.

The besiegers were building piles of wood against the doors. And he thought about what the man on the roof had said; *"Better dead than in your hands."*

The doors were wood, not stone; set fires against them and the doors would burn through, the fire moving into the building through all that closely-packed furniture and debris. How long would the fires burn before they reached the roof? The rooms below were crammed full of all manner of flammable furnishings to prevent the besiegers from breaking in once the doors were broken down. Fire would block the exits as soon as the doors burned through. There would be no escape that way.

There was a crowd gathering on the edge of the temple grounds, watching. Would they do anything if they saw the Magi's men were going to burn out the Winged Ones? Or were they, by this point, too afraid? Had the use of the Eye destroyed any spirit of rebellion that still lay within them? He was rather afraid that it had.

He landed, and took aboard his first physically injured passenger, a middle-aged man with a heavily bandaged head who seemed dizzy and partly disoriented. "When he saw what they were doing down there, he went to the edge of the roof and tried to reason with them," said the man Kiron thought had once been a Winged One, and whose name he still didn't know. "Somebody got him with a stone from a sling. Don't let him fall asleep."

"No fear of that," Kiron replied, as the man climbed up behind him, clumsily. "It's not exactly a smooth ride."

"They're coming!" called someone who was watching at the edge of the roof under cover of an improvised shield.

"Get out of here!" the man barked at Kiron, slapping at Avatre's shoulder, startling her into rearing away from him, then leaping skyward, before he could ask *who* or *what* was coming.

Not that it mattered; he saw what it was as soon as Avatre cleared the rooftop. "They" were more of the Magi's men, and they were firing the wood stacked up against the doors of the Temple.

Time had just run out.

He wanted to turn back and take on another passenger, but Avatre was not having any of that idea, and at any rate, she was burdened with as much as she could bear right now. So Kiron and his passenger flapped off into the darkness, both of them looking over their shoulders in white-lipped silence, until the temple, with its rising fires, was out of sight.

In fact, it was a rougher ride than before, as Avatre dodged and snapped at arrows as she rose, and continued to fly evasively even when there were no missiles speeding toward them. His passenger hung on grimly, arms wrapped around Kiron's chest, sucking in his breath in pain whenever Avatre jolted sideways.

Despite his orders to everyone else, he urged Avatre

to greater speed. This was only the fourth trip. How many more would they be able to manage before fire consumed the temple? One? Two at most? There was no point in saving her strength now. . . .

Mercifully, his passenger was silent except for the occasional whimper of pain. Kiron wondered what he had been to the Winged Ones, since he was not wearing their emblem, but evidently felt enough authority to try to reason with the Magi's men. Was he the Overseer of the Temple Servants? Merely someone of rank caught in the temple when the siege started?

The flight took far, far longer than he wanted it to, even though Avatre had caught his urgency and was flying faster than she'd ever dared do in darkness before. He landed Avatre hard, and hurried to untie himself from his passenger, but because of the man's head injury, the helpers had tied him on far more securely than the last, and the knots resisted his clawing fingers. Orest landed while he was still trying to get the ropes undone—

—and then, with the edges of his passenger's cloak still smoldering, Ari landed—and behind him, in a cluster, all the rest. Including Aket-ten.

And no one had a passenger except Orest and Ari.

He felt a sick numbness wash over him as his hands went cold. He caught Ari's eyes as Ari handed down a middle-aged woman who was still coughing, and Ari shook his head.

His mind wouldn't encompass it. Surely the fires

couldn't have moved that fast! Surely there was time for another round of rescues—

But Aket-ten was weeping silently, tears making black tracks through the soot and ash on her face.

"I don't understand it," Gan said, his voice flat and expressionless. "It all burned like everything was soaked in oil. Even the stone was burning! It makes no sense!"

"Some mischief of the Magi, I've no doubt," replied Aunt Re grimly, as two of her servants cut the last man free from Kiron and handed him down. "Some way to make stone burn like wood, and wood like oil-soaked papyrus." She said nothing more then, only went to Aket-ten, who slid down from Re-eth-ke's back and into her aunt's comforting arms.

Kiron felt cold all over. He thought about the men he'd last seen on that rooftop, about the servants that might have been still waiting just below, and wanted to vomit. He glanced up in the direction of the city, and saw an ugly red glare on the horizon.

When he looked back down again, one of Re's servants was handing him a bundle: a waterskin and food. "What—" he began.

The High Priestess moved out of the shadows like a ghost, startling him. "New orders, Wingleader," she said gravely. "Orders sent through me to you, from the Mouth of the Gods who is called Kaleth. There is no reason to stay, and your presence will bring danger to Re-keron as the Magi seek for your dragons. Come home, he says. We will scatter, and come to Sanctuary safe."

Kiron swallowed down his nausea and looked at the others. "Can you all make the flight?" he asked.

One by one, they nodded as Re's servants handed them identical bundles to his. Even Aket-ten looked up, face smeared with tears and soot, and nodded. And he felt, at that moment, a terrible, aching need for the desert, for a place that was clean, where people did not put each other to the flame because they could not be controlled.

And where other people did not stand by and watch them do so. He had thought the Tians were cruel. What the Magi had turned his own people into was something far worse—people who now were so afraid for themselves that they had lost every vestige of morality.

"Right," he said harshly. "Let's get out of here."

And that was what haunted him, the entire flight back. The priestess had called it a "rot." If so, it was a rot that killed the conscience, and maybe the soul along with it. Those people had watched the Magi drag the Winged Ones away, day after day, and had done nothing. They had watched the Magi's men lay siege to the temple for weeks, and had done nothing. The mob that had finally gathered to protest had done very little, and had scattered quickly when the Eye was used. And it *should* have been possible to save the

Winged Ones; why had the army not rebelled at their treatment? No point in saying they were under orders either; since when was it right to follow orders you knew were immoral?

And tonight, they had watched while the Magi's men prepared to burn the temple to the ground, and had done nothing.

And it had all begun long before this. Hadn't they been spending these last moons simply looking the other way while friends and relations were denounced and hauled away? Hadn't many of them been willing to make accusations of their own to prove their "loyalty" and turn suspicious eyes away from themselves?

And why? Because they were too attached to possessions, to the city itself, to flee? Because it was easy to look away when the Magi were only hurting the foreigners, or the nobles, or the people in the next Ring that you didn't know, and because when you looked the other way once, it was easy to keep doing so?

Or because it was easier to believe the lies that the Magi told? Easier not to think for one's own self? Easier to accept at face value everything that was told to you?

It gnawed at him all the way back, and when he and Avatre finally landed in the gray light of dawn, he felt as if he could not sleep until he had cleaned his body of the stench of burning. He went down into the cavern, and took a rare bath, scrubbing himself until his skin felt raw to be rid of the smell.

He went to find Aket-ten, but she was nowhere to be seen. Maybe that was just as well. He wasn't sure he could offer her any kind of comfort, when she had just seen a place where she knew people burning to the ground.

When he staggered off to his bed, Avatre was already asleep, and as he gazed on her, he felt a moment of envy to see her, so calm and peaceful, with no nightmares to trouble her sleep.

They certainly troubled his, that night, and for many nights to come.

And yet, sooner than he would have thought, things got back to normal, or mostly normal.

Perhaps it was because he had not actually seen the temple burning. Only Ari had endured that particular sight, and maybe his experience in fighting had hardened him somewhat to such things. Maybe it was because, once the last of the Winged Ones arrived, there was another shrine made to the memories and spirits of those who had been lost.

Maybe it was nothing more than time—time which was, of a certainty, filled.

It would have been far worse had Aket-ten actually witnessed the horror of the burning temple, but the others had turned her back at the halfway point, and all she knew was that it had burned, and those who were left, with it. She sought Kiron out the night after their return to Sanctuary, and spent all of it weeping herself sick in his arms. It was a very long night; perhaps the longest in his life, save only one. He would have spared her that distress if he could have.

And yet, this was the face of war from which she had been sheltered. Death, and not death in battle, but terrible, useless, needless death, the deaths of those you knew, cared about—even loved.

War was no longer an abstract to her. And, in fact, neither was death.

After that, though he was sure it preyed on her mind as nothing in her life ever had before, not even her own fear, she never said another word about it.

She drooped despondently about for a while, and that was worse than if she had wept and raged and railed against the Magi. And he was tempted—oh, how tempted!—to weigh his pain against hers; the miserable deaths of father, mother, sisters against the deaths of her friends.

But he didn't. You couldn't weigh pain as if it was the Feather of Truth. He knew that now, something he had not known before Toreth's murder. One pain couldn't outweigh another; no pain could balance out another. In the end, all pain stood alone.

And that wasn't something he could tell her either. It was something she would have to learn herself.

Eventually, she regained her spirits as the Winged Ones trickled in a few at a time, and she was able to gain some sort of consolation with them. This was one place in her life where Kiron felt absolutely helpless to give her exactly the kind of consolation she needed. He didn't know these people; they hadn't been his friends. He could only mourn them in the abstract— and it wasn't as if he didn't already have enough deaths in his life to mourn.

And it wasn't as if their days didn't have plenty to fill them.

Not only were the dragonets hatched out in Sanctuary growing rapidly and requiring preliminary training, but Coresan's family was doing so as well, and he had a whole new problem to deal with.

Nofret was besotted. It was all anyone could do to get her to tear herself away from the dragonets every evening, and she was beside herself with impatience to get out to them in the morning. Kiron wouldn't have credited it. He would have thought that while she would feel some affection for them, she wouldn't have felt that bond that every other Jouster with a hand-raised dragon did.

But there was not a shadow of a doubt; she obsessed over those dragonets just as if she was their own mother. In particular, she was attracted to a gorgeous little creature of Thurian purple shading to deep scarlet that she named "The-on"; the smallest of the lot, but still larger than the smallest dragonet back in Sanctuary, for once again, Coresan had thrown an outstanding clutch. And this little female was just as attracted to Nofret as Nofret was to her. Every day, she ventured nearer and nearer to her human watcher, always with one eye on her mother, who would snort warningly whenever her offspring drew too near to the human. But every day, what Coresan considered "too near" grew less, until one day while Coresan was dozing and all of them were worn out from playing, the dragonet waddled over to Nofret, dropped her head in Nofret's lap, and fell immediately asleep.

Nofret froze, not daring to touch; Aket-ten and Kiron tensed, Kiron signaling Avatre to be ready to dive in to the rescue if need be. Coresan raised her head, gave Nofret a penetrating look, and dropped her head back down to her own foreclaws, closing her eyes.

After that, Coresan allowed Nofret to touch, clean, and play with all four babies, and even to feed them. In fact, the older and more clamorous the babies got, the more she seemed to welcome the help. Aket-ten reported that Coresan was coming to think of Nofret as another dragon; a very peculiarly shaped, tragically dwarfed, and inadequately scaled dragon, but a dragon, nevertheless.

Even Ari began to relax when he saw how Coresan acted around Nofret. The peculiar thing was, even as Coresan acted as if Nofret was a dragon, she continued to make threat postures whenever any other humans ventured too near. Aket-ten couldn't explain it.

"Nofret is a dragon, and we aren't, not in Coresan's mind," was all she could say. "Maybe it's because we always dropped food from a height, and Nofret was the first to bring it to her on the ground. Maybe it's because Nofret doesn't look like a Jouster."

"Then if Coresan lays again and we can find her and the clutch, we have to replicate everything we did this time," he said firmly. Aket-ten nodded.

There was no change in either the situation in Alta or in Tia, and Kiron was content to leave all such weighty matters in the minds and hands of those his senior in experience and wisdom. Often enough, as he lay staring into the dark at night, he thought of the uncertain future and he felt, with Orest, that he would rather, far rather, not think of it at all. That he would rather be told what to do.

But that was the path that had led here in the first place—people giving over thinking to others, and doing what they were told, believing what they were told to believe, even when it went against their own good sense and all reason.

Still, he was glad enough to have something else to occupy his mind, however temporarily.

As the days passed, the babies began to exercise their wings, pumping them vigorously and making little hops into the air. Those back in Sanctuary were learning to bear saddle and rider, and exercising against weight. Coresan's offspring, however, were not to be meddled with. They would be fledging soon—

"—and I have no idea how we're going to get Theon to follow me," Nofret said, as Kiron and Avatre flew her out to Coresan's nest the morning after the first of the Sanctuary dragonets had made his First Flight. "I know Coresan's getting restless. Are they like cats, where they move their nest periodically?"

"Not so far as I know," he said truthfully. "I wish I could tell you more, but all I know is how the hand-raised ones act."

"Well, I'm afraid she's trying to move the nest, and if the little ones follow her, we might never find them again," she fretted.

As they swooped in to land, it looked as if Nofret's fears might be well-founded. Coresan was pacing, fanning her wings, then pacing again, peering up at the sky whenever she snapped her wings open. The babies were imitating her, and they usually were not awake at this hour.

Aket-ten landed Re-eth-ke beside Avatre on the canyon floor, as Nofret hurried over to Coresan and the dragonets with the first lot of meat. Coresan took it—

Then, uncharacteristically, began to eat it herself, leaving it to Nofret to feed the little ones.

Aket-ten watched them with her eyes narrowed and a speculative look on her face.

"What?" Kiron demanded.

"I don't—know," she said slowly. "There is something very odd going on." She continued to stare. "I'm trying to encourage the little ones to stay with Nofret if Coresan flies."

Coresan finished her first portion, and looked straight at Kiron, rather than Nofret. And snorted, in that old imperious fashion he had come to know. He didn't need Aket-ten's interpretation to take down another portion of meat and drag it over to her. She seized it, and began tearing chunks off of it, one eye on him, and one on the sky.

It took a third and a fourth to satisfy her, and not once in all that time did she feed any of her babies, not even when they came to her, nudged her portion, and begged pitiably. After a while, the beggar would go right back to Nofret, who was infinitely more reliable, if rather too slow. . . .

Then, when the fourth helping was a memory, Coresan stood up, raised her head and stared at Nofret for a very long moment, as if measuring her for something.

Nofret stopped feeding the dragonets, feeling the eyes of their mother on her, and turned.

She swallowed hard—and visibly. Coresan had Nofret fixed in an unwinking gaze, and Kiron didn't blame Nofret for a sudden surge of unease. He started to loosen his knife in its sheath, but Aket-ten stopped him with a gesture.

"It's not what you think," she whispered.

Just then, Nofret began to slowly back away from the dragonets. It wasn't the first time that Coresan had leveled a challenging stare at her, and always, once Nofret began to move away from them, Coresan stopped challenging.

Not this time.

This time, Coresan took the two enormous strides needed to reach Nofret, bent her head down before anyone could react, and shoved Nofret in the gut with her nose, tumbling her back into the midst of the dragonet pack.

And then she turned, spread her wings wide, and with a few lumbering steps threw herself into the air. Within moments, she was a dot in the sky. In another, she was gone.

"She's gone!" Aket-ten said with astonishment.

Kiron shrugged. "Off to hunt, I suppose," he said. This wasn't the first time she'd gone off to do so; the only real difference was that this time she had very graphically put Nofret in charge of the babies.

"No, I mean she's *gone*," said Aket-ten. "She's gone for good! I felt what she meant in my mind. She left Nofret in charge, and now she's gone for good and she's not coming back!"

Nofret hauled herself to her feet, pulling on dragonet necks and shoulders to get there. "She might have been a bit more polite about it!" she said indignantly. And then, as Kiron stared at her, she blinked. "What do you mean, she's gone for good and left me in charge?"

It took a while for the implications of that to sink in, but when they finally did, Kiron found himself at a loss for words.

"Oh," was all he could manage. "Ah—how are we going to get them back to Sanctuary?"

In the end, there was no good way to get them back to Sanctuary. They weren't fledged yet; they couldn't fly on their own. They certainly couldn't walk. You couldn't tie them to a camel. They were too big for even Kashet to carry, and at any rate, no one wanted to terrify them by bundling them into a carry net to be flown back. So the only answer was for Nofret to spend the night with them.

Perhaps more than one night with them, but he wasn't going to suggest *that* just now.

Ari was *not* happy about that, but what could he do? They accepted Re-eth-ke and Re-eth-ke was willing to curl up with them, though they were wary about Avatre, so Aket-ten stayed with her, which Kiron was no happier about than Ari was.

But in the morning, three of the dragon boys who had not gotten an egg were flown in by himself, Ari, and Gan, to join Nofret in her baby tending.

A night without their mother had made them a lot more accepting, and having someone willing to feed them without having to take turns competing with a sibling cemented the acceptance of these strangers. They were not shy at all after about midmorning, and at least that meant that Nofret did not have to spend another night with them; the boys could do that, taking it in turns to play night guard.

By the next day, an additional night guard of actual former soldiers from Tia had managed to make the journey over the sands by camel. And at that point, there seemed no reason why this batch of dragonets needed to leave.

And, since no one else seemed inclined to bring it up, Kiron did, in council.

He waxed a great deal more eloquent on the subject than he had expected to be. No reason why some of those strange cliff dwellings couldn't be made habitable either. Granted, no one had mentioned that the abandoned city *should* be inhabited again right now, but if Sanctuary was going to be the city of priests, then the new city would have to be made ready for everyone else at some point. Why not now? The repairs and improvements could be made gradually, if they began now. Wouldn't it be better to have them underway, if an emergency came up?

"After all, if Sanctuary is attacked, we're going to need somewhere more defensible to send the children to," Kiron pointed out, as Kaleth hid a smile. Ari threw up his hands.

"You won't rest until you've got your dragon city, will you?" he said crossly. "All right. Have it your way. But when The-on fledges, Nofret is bringing her back *here*."

The-on did fledge shortly thereafter, and Nofret did lead her back to Sanctuary, riding behind Kiron while The-on lumbered clumsily along behind, whining piteously and looking absolutely exhausted when they all came in to land. But the other three dragonets and their putative riders stayed—and so did the guards. And, too, some of the Altans who found the desert *too* dry elected to try the new city, and found it to their liking. As more refugees arrived, some stayed at Sanctuary, but some moved on to Dragon Court (as the new city was dubbed), finding that Sanctuary was just a little too full of Winged Ones and priests and priestly magic to be altogether comfortable for ordinary mortals. When all of the new dragons were fledged, all (except The-on) moved to Dragon Court for their initial training; there was more room there, for one thing, and Baken was perfectly capable of taking them up to the point where they needed to form wings.

And at that point, Kalen and Pe-atep moved there as well, wingleaders of the new Black and Yellow Wings, to take over the training from Baken. Kiron actually felt a little relief at that; there was something about having all of the dragons quartered in one place that made him nervous. Having them divided like this meant a greater margin of safety for them all. They met for joint training in the air over the desert, halfway between the two strongholds. Day by day, the dragonets grew into their size and strength and coordination.

Day by day, the older dragons grew in skill. There were new maneuvers to learn; now that they no longer needed to evade other Jousters, their strategy must be directed against men on the ground, and as they were few and vulnerable, they must choose their targets carefully. . . .

And that was how matters stood, the day that another messenger came from Alta, bloody and battered, with word that the Magi had finally stepped over the boundary of sanity.

They had decided that yet another group required being brought to heel.

This time, it was the Healers that they had put under siege.

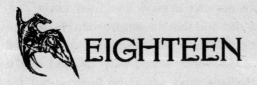 EIGHTEEN

"AND the people are doing what?" Kaleth demanded of the messenger, who shrugged wearily.

"The people are doing nothing. The Healers have been trying to foment discontent ever since the burning of the temple," he replied. "The Magi finally took notice. They say—" He paused, and his brow wrinkled in exhausted thought. "They say that the Healers hear much—and a great deal of truth—from those who are in pain or otherwise vulnerable. They say the Healers must speak for the good of Alta. They demand that the Healers are to turn over to them any who have spoken against the Magi, and also all those who Heal by touch, rather than by herb or knife."

"All those who Heal by touch. . . ." Nofret's lip

lifted. "It seems they have decided to drain even Alta's most precious resource to serve their own needs."

"And they demand that the sanctity of a Healer's silence be broken." Marit was absolutely white-lipped with anger. Odd. Kiron would have thought that it would be Heklatis who would be furious, but the Akkadian only looked sad and resigned.

"It is said—" the messenger began, then stopped.

"It is said, *what?*" Ari demanded sharply.

"It is said that the Magi are looking—older. Older than they have in years, though who knows what their true ages are." He shrugged. "I have not seen them, so I cannot be sure."

Ari looked to Lord Khumun. "How goes the war?"

"My spies tell me that it has stalled on the edge of the marshlands," Lord Khumun replied. "The Tians are reluctant to go into the true marshlands, and the Altans are reluctant to come out of them."

"So the Magi are not battening on the deaths that they had hoped for." Ari looked to the messenger and then to Kaleth. "Mouth of the Gods, I think it begins."

There was silence, and Kaleth bowed his head. Kiron held his breath.

"It begins," Kaleth said, from behind the curtain of his hair. "And only the gods know how it will end. I have seen the beginning; I cannot thread my way through the maze that will follow this bad beginning."

Ari nodded, as if he had expected exactly this answer. "Then it is for mortals to decide. And one thing I do know; we cannot let the Healers stand alone. Agreed?"

Heklatis' eyes lit, as if he had not expected that answer. Kaleth, however, raised his head again, and regarded Ari with a wry smile—as if he had.

Time was not on their side, they needed to act quickly, and the means of getting messages to the Healers were very limited. There was, in fact, only one sure way, and reluctant as he was to use it, at least the time of year was in their favor. The rains had just begun, and the Magi would not be able to use the Eye even during daylight hours if there was no sun.

Which was a good thing, since the way to get a message to the Healers was to drop it on them from the sky. While the best time to drop such a message was at night, it could not be too late at night, or it might be lost. Furthermore, with the Magi now aware that there were dragons and Jousters still in the world, and acting as the heart of the rebellion, they would be watching the skies.

There was a great deal of sky between Sanctuary and Alta. And of all the dragons that were capable of such a journey, there were really only two of colors that would blend in with the storm clouds. Bethlan was one, and Kiron had no issues with Menet-ka taking the task. But the other was Re-eth-ke, and Aketten's reaction when she discovered that Kiron had assigned Menet-ka without even considering her was . . . emphatic.

In fact, she stormed into Avatre's pen as if she was taking a citadel, and with nearly as much noise.

"I can't *believe* you simply assumed Menet-ka was the only person fit to take this job without even considering me!" she shouted, as she shoved her way past her brother, who was lingering in the doorway, listening, while Kiron went over the plan with Menet-ka. "You must be insane! I'm the smallest Jouster, I'll be less of a burden to my dragon—"

"Menet-ka is not much larger than you, Bethlan is bigger than Re-eth-ke, and both of them have more experience flying in the rain than Re-eth-ke does," Kiron countered, as she stood there with her fists on her hips, glaring.

"Not as much in storms!" she shouted back.

"He won't be flying in a storm!" Kiron replied. "And Bethlan is steadier in bad weather than Re-eth-ke!"

"Who says?" she demanded furiously.

"*I* say, and I'm the wingleader!" he replied, his own anger rising to meet hers halfway.

"Oh, *fine.* Use that as an argument." She crossed her arms over her chest and glared at him. "Abandon logic altogether and fall back on 'I'm the wingleader.' Never mind that I have more communication with my dragon than he has with his, or that I have more experience flying high *and* in storms *and* long distances, or that I'm lighter, or that silver and blue-black blends into clouds better than indigo and purple. Ignore all that. Ignore the fact that if you're going to do something risky, it's better to have two people doing it to double your chances of getting through. And completely forget about the fact that it looks as if you're cosseting me because I'm a girl. . . ."

There were tears in her voice when she said that last, and he couldn't meet her accusing gaze, because he *was* trying to protect her, and it was entirely true that the only reason he had dismissed the idea of her going was because she was who and what she was—his beloved, and yes, "a girl."

"How can I expect to deserve equal treatment if you won't give me equal responsibility?" she asked tearfully when he still wouldn't look at her.

"She has a point, Kiron," Orest said, not at all helpfully.

He clenched his jaw so hard it hurt. He wanted to tell Orest to mind his own business, but that would mean he would have to pull wingleader rank again, and that ploy was growing weaker by the moment.

"Don't you think you ought to give her the chance?" Orest continued, even less helpfully. "It's only fair."

He glared at Orest and decided to bring up family instead. "Lord Ya-tiren wouldn't thank me for putting her in danger. Neither would Lady Iris-aten."

He'd hoped invoking both parents would get Aketten to reconsider. Unfortunately, she was made of sterner stuff than he'd thought.

"I'll get his consent," she said, clenching her own jaw. "When he gives his consent to anything, Mother simply steps aside and lets it happen. If I get his consent, will you assign this to me?"

Dear gods. Well, at least Lord Ya-tiren won't be able to put the blame on me for sending his daughter into danger. He'll know it was all her own idea. "And Lord Khumun's," he replied, transferring his glare to her.

She traded him glare for glare. "*And* Lord Khumun's," she agreed. She sounded confident. He only hoped that confidence would be shattered.

"If both of them give their consent, then you can go," he said, sure that even if she could convince her father, Lord Khumun would never agree.

Lord Khumun agreed.

So did Lord Ya-tiren, although he was not at all *happy* about it, which left Kiron without any reason to forbid her. He even went to Heklatis to beg something that would make her feel too ill to fly; the Healer stared at him as if he thought Kiron had gone mad, and simply answered, "Are you daft? It would be worth my life, because you *know* she'd know I'd done it. No. Absolutely, positively, no."

And Kaleth was no help either; he simply shrugged, opined that no one could hope to stop Aket-ten from doing anything she really wanted to do, and repeated that he could not "see" past the Magi interference, not into the city, and not into the future.

So, despite his misgivings, despite the nebulous feeling of dread in the bottom of his stomach, there was nothing Kiron could say or do, reasonably, to keep her from going. All he could do was to make her swear to be cautious.

She and Menet-ka were going to drop sandbags with messages in them into the inner courts of the Healers, messages detailing what the Jousters already knew, and advising them that when there was a huge distraction, the Healers should escape by whatever means they could.

The distraction was already well in hand. Heklatis knew the formulation of some vile concoction called "Akkadian Fire," a substance that stuck to anything it splashed on and burned and couldn't be put out with water. He was making pots of the evil stuff; they would all come in with a load of pots and a brazier apiece, drop in coals, and drop the pots. Half of them would unload their burdens on the men besieging the Healers, but the other half would unload over the Tower of Wisdom, the Magi's stronghold. When they found their home burning down around their ears, Kiron doubted very much that any of them would think about the Healers.

That was the hope anyway.

As for the besiegers, this Akkadian Fire stuck to flesh as well as wood and stone, and the higher the Jousters were, the more it would splash about when it hit. A nasty trick . . . but anyone who had stood by while the Temple of the Twins and those left inside it burned, de-served whatever he got, to Kiron's way of thinking.

The Healers likely would not agree, but that was why Lord Khumun wasn't going to *tell* them what the distraction was going to be.

Well, *some* of the Healers wouldn't agree . . . Heklatis, after all, was a Healer, and he was the one who would be making up those fire pots.

"Don't take any risks," he told Menet-ka and Aket-ten, for the hundredth time. "Don't let yourselves be seen. Just drop your messages and get out of there. The best revenge we can have is to get the Healers out underneath their noses, like we got ourselves and the Winged Ones out."

They both nodded, Menet-ka earnestly, Aket-ten with impatience and rebellion in her eyes. He saw it, and it made him sick with dread, but what could he do? He had given his word, and she already resented that she'd been forced to prove she had the right to a place among the Jousters and an equal share in the danger they all faced. All he could do was to urge the utmost caution.

"This is probably even part of an elaborate trap," he went on, knowing he was grasping at straws, but hoping against hope that something would get through to her. "You know how much the Magi hated the Jousters, and that was before we pulled the Winged Ones out under their noses. Now, they must really loathe us, and they would probably do anything to capture any of us."

Unfortunately, Menet-ka chose to take this as evidence that Kiron was letting his concerns and fears get the better of him. "I doubt it's gone that far," the Jouster said with a weak laugh. "Oh, I'm sure you're right about the Magi hating us, but they have no reason to think we would come to the rescue of the Healers."

Kiron didn't agree with that in the least, but there was no point in arguing. "Just remember what they did to the Winged Ones," he repeated, and stepped back.

Aket-ten was only waiting for that, it seemed, because she was in the air and flying toward Alta the moment he was clear of Re-eth-ke's wings. Menet-ka gave him a sympathetic look, and then sent Bethlan into the sky after her. And all he could do was to watch after them.

"She feels as if she *has* to do this, Kiron," said Nofret quietly in his ear. "She feels guilty that she didn't manage to save all of the Winged Ones; she thinks if she'd just been brave enough, or fast enough, or— something, the gods only know what—she'd have been able to get them all out. You can't argue with that sort of guilt; it doesn't answer to logic."

"Well, if she wants me to treat her as if she's a logical person, she ought to behave like one," he replied, irritation momentarily overcoming his feeling of sick dread.

Nofret gave him a crooked smile, and patted his arm. "This is logical," she pointed out. "No one is going to take her seriously if she doesn't do everything one of the boys is doing."

And what, after all, could he say? The Far-sighted Priestesses saw nothing—well, they actually could not see anything anyway, for the Magi had now effectively blocked their ability to See inside the Seventh Ring. But they had no intuitions of anything going wrong. Kaleth saw nothing, and the gods had not spoken through him to warn them. By all logic, he was over-reacting, being overprotective of Aket-ten.

And yet, he was certain, so completely certain down deep in his soul that this was going to end in disaster that he avoided everyone else for the rest of the evening, and all but hid in Avatre's pen. She seemed to be just as uneasy as he was—

But that could just be because she's picking up my un-happiness, he reminded himself, and tried to soothe her even if he could not himself be soothed.

And he resolved not to sleep. They were supposed to return before dawn, and he was going to be awake—

Despite his best efforts, he dozed off, sitting in Avatre's sand, some time after the middle of the night. And it was a cry of wordless anguish coming from above that woke him.

It woke him out of nightmare into nightmare.

And he knew. He knew, without being told, what that haunting cry on the wind meant. The nameless dread he had been laboring under turned to the certainty of disaster, and as he struggled to clear the fog of sleep from his eyes and stagger upright, he felt, not an anguish matching the wails now coming from the landing field, but a kind of numbness.

It was as if someone had just cut off his arm, and he hadn't yet felt it. It was going to hurt; he *knew* it was going to hurt. But at the moment, he could only stare at the bleeding stump in a mingling of despair and disbelief. . . .

Except that instead of a bleeding stump of a limb, he knew that it was Aket-ten who had been amputated out of his life. He knew when he *felt* what had happened, it would be worse than any physical wound.

With leaden feet, he forced himself to go to Bethlan's pen. There, they were all gathered, all those who were still awake and eager to hear how the message drop had gone. And he did not say a word, could not manage a single syllable, as he listened to Menet-ka stammer out the tale, while someone else unsaddled Bethlan. Both of them looked terrible. Menet-ka must have pushed Bethlan to new speeds to get here as quickly as he had.

"There was fog," he said, exhaustion dulling his eyes and blurring his voice, as he leaned heavily against the wall. "We hadn't expected fog. We couldn't tell where we were. Except that we could see a ring of torches and bonfires, and *I* figured that was where the soldiers that the Magi had set to watch had put up a line of guards. I thought we should just drop our messages in the center of all of that and hope that some of them landed in courtyards instead of on the roof. But she wouldn't hear of it, and before I could say or do anything, she took Re-eth-ke down. And that was when the fog just—cleared away. It practically melted out of sight; she wasn't more than halfway down when it was all gone, and by then, it was too late to pull up."

"It was magic, then?" Gan managed, his eyes gone round and horrified.

"A trap," said Ari flatly, and closed his eyes. "Curse it all, Kiron was right. At least half of this business with going after the Healers was a trap meant to take Jousters. They set a trap for you, Menet-ka. They knew we'd send Jousters if they did to another group what they'd done to the Winged Ones, at least to scout, and they set it all up as a trap and used the Healers as bait."

I was right, he thought dully, with no sense of triumph. He had never wished to have been wrong more.

"They used war javelins and throwing sticks, they didn't use bows and arrows," Menet-ka said trying to control the quaver in his voice. "And they weren't wasting time trying to hit the rider *or* me; they aimed for Re-eth-ke."

"They hit her?" Orest gulped, and Kiron choked back a sob.

Menet-ka nodded miserably. "I couldn't see how many hit or where; enough anyway, that she just—just crumpled her wings and fell out of the sky. They were both screaming and screaming—it was horrible, hearing them scream like that."

He could see it; in his mind's eye, he could see it. The javelins filling the air, the dragon folding up in pain. He could almost hear Aket-ten's scream of fear and anguish. . . .

"She hit the ground with Aket-ten still in the saddle, and she absorbed most of the impact," Menet-ka continued, unconsciously pulling at his own hair with his right hand. "But I knew she hadn't been *that* high, just skimming the rooftops—I pulled Bethlan around, and I saw Aket-ten moving, and I tried to get down to her—"

What? After all that, he expected to hear that she'd broken her neck in the fall!

She was alive—but she was also a Winged One.

He felt himself shuddering. *By now she might be wishing she'd died in the fall.*

"You mean Aket-ten's alive!" Gan shouted incredulously. "She's all right! We can go back, we can rescue her!"

But Menet-ka shook his head, bleakly, and voiced the same thoughts that were running through Kiron's head. "The soldiers were just all over her before I could even get Bethlan's head around. They've got her, Gan—the *Magi* have her. And you know what they almost did to her before! The soldiers spotted me and started shooting, and I couldn't hold Bethlan; she was scared, scared by seeing Re-eth-ke drop out of the sky and hearing both Re-eth-ke and Aket-ten screaming, scared of the arrows, I couldn't hold her—" Kiron heard the emotion, the thought behind the words. *I failed her.*

I should tell him it's not his fault— But he couldn't. He couldn't bring himself to tell Menet-ka what he himself did not feel. It *was* Menet-ka's fault, and his. He should have trusted the presentiment of disaster. Menet-ka should have kept her from going down into the fog; should have insisted on turning back the moment they saw the fog.

Menet-ka looked up, past the others, and saw him. The others followed Menet-ka's gaze, and an echoing silence fell, one those silences in which, no matter how it is broken, it just sounds wroing.

He stared at them, stared at their stricken expressions, at the guilt in Menet-ka's eyes, at the pain in Ari's face. Stared, and finally, because there was nothing he could say to any of them that would not simply have brought more pain, he turned away.

He stumbled blindly back to Avatre's pen, falling into walls and bruising his shoulders, as his eyes burned and he held back his tears by main force of will. He couldn't weep until he got some privacy. But once he was back in Avatre's pen, he threw himself down onto the sand next to her, and howled his grief to the stars.

They left him alone. Not even Heklatis came near him. And that suited him just fine, because he didn't want their pain, he wanted only his own; he didn't want their apologies, he wanted to nurse his anger against everyone who hadn't listened to him and had encouraged her in this madness. But even the anger wasn't enough to overcome his own guilt or his anguish, and he wept into Avatre's neck until he had no more tears to weep. He pillowed his face against her cheek, moaning like a dying animal under his breath, clinging to Avatre's neck as the only place of safety in the world, as the sun rose, and burned its way across the heavens, and sank again. Someone brought Avatre food; he wasn't sure who. They had to bring the meat right into her sand pit, for she wouldn't come out to them.

In fact, Avatre refused to leave him, even long enough to eat. So long as he was clinging to her neck, she showed no signs of budging. So whoever fed her brought her food to her, and she ate it with one eye on Kiron, her tail coiled protectively around him.

Which was how Kaleth found him, at some point before sunset.

He heard the footsteps and looked up dully. "What?" he asked, not really caring to hear the answer, and hoping that Kaleth would respond to the rudeness by going away.

But Kaleth didn't go away. Instead, he squatted down in the sand next to both of them.

"Don't give up. She's alive, and she's not even hurt," he said. "We've been able to see that much. They're saving her for something—"

"They've killed her dragon," Kiron interrupted, harshly. "They shot Re-eth-ke right out from under her. They don't *have* to do anything to her to destroy her now! Don't you understand that?"

Kaleth sat back on his heels, and watched him measuringly. "We aren't even seeing a fraction of what is going on," he replied, with an urgency that penetrated even Kiron's grief. "Listen to me—they won't hurt her, not right now. They're keeping her for some purpose—and that gives us a chance; we can get her away. She's tough. She knows we won't give up on her, and she knows we'll do anything we can think of to rescue her. She'll stay strong as long as there's any chance at all. And we will find a way—"

His heart leaped, and he seized Kaleth's shoulders and shook him. "You've Seen it?" he gasped, hope making him choke on his own words. "You've Seen us rescuing her?"

And his heart plummeted again, as Kaleth shook his head. "Nothing so sure—nothing so definite," he admitted. "But—"

"Then stop toying with me!" He shoved Kaleth away. "Don't give me hope and snatch it away again!"

"Now *listen* to me, damn you!" Kaleth burst out, grabbing *his* shoulders and forcing him to look into Kaleth's eyes. "In all of the futures I've seen that end in Sanctuary prospering, *Aket-ten is there!*" He gave Kiron a little shake. "Why would I lie to you? That was why I wasn't concerned, why I thought, since she felt so resentful about being protected, I should just encourage you to let her do this thing!" He shook Kiron again hard, twice. "I cannot See the way to those futures, but I have *Seen* it, and I know that once we have all the facts, what is happening will make sense and we will find a way to rescue her!"

He looked into those deep, black eyes, could not look away, and found his heart rising again, just a little. Kaleth believed this. Kaleth had not been wrong yet. . . .

"Be patient!" Kaleth said, with a bit less force. "I don't know how this will be, but—the only futures I have seen that do not have her in them are futures we do not wish to live in anyway."

He closed his eyes for a moment, and tried not to think of the other implications of that statement—that the fact that Aket-ten had been taken meant that losing her had doomed them all. . . .

"Wait," said Kaleth. "Hold to hope. That is all I can tell you right now."

He stood up, and although Kiron would have done the same under ordinary circumstances, all he could do was to sag back against Avatre's shoulder and stare. "You ask a great deal," he managed. "And you promise very little."

"That is so I do not play you false," said Kaleth somberly. "Now—I go to consult with the Tian priestesses, the Thet priests, the Winged Ones, and Heklatis. And, shortly, what we know, you will know."

With that, he turned and left Avatre's pen.

Avatre blew into his hair and whined. He looked up at her numbly and realized that she must be hungry. Whoever had brought her meat, it had only been for the morning meal. The fact that she had put off her hunger while he needed comfort almost made him burst into tears again.

But weeping wouldn't get her fed, and she had been patient long enough.

He got to his feet, and headed for the cold room and some of the stored meat that was there.

If he did not yet have hope—he would try not to sink into despair. Not yet anyway.

After all, even if there was nothing else for him, there was always revenge.

 **NINETEEN**

SOMEHOW he stumbled through taking care of Avatre; Pe-atep tried to get him to eat and drink something. He managed the drink, but his throat closed when he tried to swallow food, and he ended up giving it to one of the dragon boys. After Kaleth and Pe-atep left him, he sank back into leaden despair. Easy enough to say "hold to hope," but there didn't seem to be any hope to hold onto.

If anything, knowing that Aket-ten was probably alive made it all worse. He kept thinking of the bleak despair in that former Winged One's eyes, and wondering how long it would take before the Magi burned her out. Or, with Re-eth-ke gone, would she even care anymore? He remembered only too sharply how, faced with losing Avatre, he had intended to die rather than lose her. Aket-ten had been immeasurably closer to Re-eth-ke than that. He couldn't even begin to imagine how she must be feeling now.

He curled himself up against Avatre's warm side, as she crooned over him with anxiety. He closed his sore eyes, mostly because they hurt, rather than with any expectation of falling asleep.

I'll just rest here for a moment, he thought, insofar as he could still think at all—

And then, the next thing he knew, Huras was shaking him awake, and it was black night.

"Wha—" he said confusedly.

"Kaleth wants you," the big fellow announced. "Now."

He got awkwardly to his feet, stiff and sore from sleeping in such a tortured position. "What is it?" he asked, still sleep-fogged.

Huras shook his head. "I don't know," he confessed. "But messengers came in not long ago, and then half the Tian priests came running over. I think something really unexpected and big has happened. I'm supposed to get the others."

He helped Kiron to his feet, and then disappeared, leaving Kiron to make his own way.

When he got to the audience chamber, the place was lit, and Kaleth, Lord Khumun, and Ari were all bent over a map that was spread out on the floor of the chamber because it was too long for a table. "—so they're coming here and here," Kaleth was saying, tapping the end of a long stick on some place on the map.

Kaleth looked up at Kiron's entrance. "Good, you're here. *Now* we have all the pieces. Everything just erupted; there was no warning. All at once, we're looking at a full-scale invasion of Alta. The war we've had up until now is nothing to the war that we're about to see."

"The Tian army is on the move," said Ari, studying the map with a frown in his face. "They're actually invading Altan lands right this moment; they've crossed the last border and they're into the delta."

"And I think I know what the Magi are saving Aketten for," Kaleth said, bluntly, looking up at him as he winced. "Look here, what season is this?"

"Rains," Kiron replied, wondering why that should be relevant—except that the season of rains was a miserable time to be invading the delta. Normally, the Tian army remained on simple border guard during this season. If they were invading now, they must have a compelling reason to think they needed to.

Or—perhaps the advisers believed there was a compelling reason to mount their invasion in the face of constant rain and rising waters.

"And the Magi can't use the Eye when it's dark, or there's cloud cover," Kaleth said, his mouth set in a grim line. "The Magi now posing as advisers to the Great King of Tia know that. They were waiting for the rains. They must have been."

Kiron nodded, interest fading fast. What did he care what the Tian Magi did or did not decide to do? What could this invasion possibly matter? How could it change anything?

"It looks like real war between the two sets of Magi," Kaleth told him. "I don't know what happened that the ones with the Tians got exiled from Alta, but it looks as if it isn't just that they're battening on the war dead that keeps them there, and it certainly doesn't look as if they're cooperating with the Altan Magi. They seem to want it all, and they've now got the army to get it for them."

"But—if the Magi are really fighting each other—" Could this be the key to getting Aket-ten free?

"We forgot one thing," said Ari, as Kiron nodded. "And so did the Tian Magi. The Magi have been—and are—weather workers."

Kiron shook his head. "Which means what, exactly? They haven't the power anymore to send a storm down on the Tian forces—"

"No," Kaleth agreed grimly. "But if they use Aket-ten, *they have the power to clear the storm over Alta City.* At least, for a little while."

He blinked, and suddenly it all made sense. "The Tians were waiting for the rains to invade!" he exclaimed. "But the Altans were waiting for them to invade and get as far as where the Eye would reach before clearing the storm!"

It all made perfect sense. Horrible, perfect sense.

Once the Altan Magi knew that their exiles had attained positions of power in Tia, they must have known what would happen, that their exiles would challenge them. But the Altans had the advantage; they knew what the exiles knew, so they could predict what the exiles would do.

Kaleth nodded. "I told you it would all become clear when we put the pieces together. They planned this all along, as soon as they knew the Magi that had been ousted had gotten established in Tia. They *knew* the Tian Magi would know the Eye didn't work without sun, and that the rains would be the only safe time to invade." He shook his head. "The exiles are playing right into their hands. It wouldn't surprise me to learn that they've pulled back some of the Altan army to tempt them. Certainly by the time we found out about this and went to look, the Altans had already fallen back to here—and here—"

Kiron nodded; it made altogether too much sense to him, too.

"Look here—" Lord Khumun pointed to where squares of stone were playing the part of the Tian forces on the map. "This is what Gan and Huras reported to me when I sent them to scout, and the Tians are definitely being funneled."

"But how does this have anything to do with Aket-ten?" he demanded desperately. "How can this possibly connect to her?"

"It's the timing; Aket-ten is captured, and then by

midafternoon, the Tians are making their way across Altan lands," said Lord Khumun. "It's too much to be a coincidence, not when a fast courier could have gotten to those in command of the Altan forces by early afternoon, telling them the time has come to start the trap. If the Tians had been waiting for an opportunity to open up, the Magi just gave it to them on a platter."

He shook his head; not that he disbelieved them, because it made entirely too much sense, but what would the Magi have done if they hadn't gotten their hands on Aket-ten?

"They probably planned this a long time ago," Kaleth mused aloud. "Then they lost the Winged Ones. They must have been frantic, trying to figure out how to get the power they needed to clear the skies and use the Eye."

"Frantic enough to be willing to try draining a Healer by touch," Ari said, with a nod. "And knowing they could lure some of us there by putting the Healers under siege is probably why they didn't just lure a few of the Healers by touch out and have their men seize some of them. When they discovered who the Jouster was that they had captured, they must have been beside themselves with glee."

Kiron gritted his teeth. He could well imagine it, especially the couple of Magi that had personally given Aket-ten trouble in the past. "Or because the Healers aren't going anywhere alone anymore, not after some of them have been drained by stealth in the past."

"They only have to clear the clouds for a little while," Kaleth went on. "For that, given how strong Aket-ten is, and that she hasn't been drained over and over—well, they probably only need her to give them open skies for as long as they want. They're going to allow the Tian army to close in, then close the jaws of the trap on them and wipe them out with the Eye."

"And then—then they can take Tia at their leisure," Lord Khumun said somberly. "Aket-ten is their key. Small wonder they want to use her now, before the Tian Magi know they have her. And the Tians' greed has made them play right into the Altan Magi's hands."

"We have to get to her before—" he couldn't finish the sentence; he choked on the words. "But—where?"

"Ah. That part I know," Kaleth said, much to his relief. "The Tian priests came to me with the news of the invasion, then, when I sent Jousters to scout, turned their attention back to the Magi of Alta. The Tian Far-Sighted Priestesses didn't see *much,* but one of them did see the single piece of information that was crucial—one of those who sees the future got a brief glimpse of Aket-ten in what I suspect must be the Tower of Wisdom, in a chamber with some mechanism holding an enormous piece of crystal. We believe, the Haras priests and I, that in that future moment they were preparing to clear the sky, then somehow tie her power into the Eye."

All in an instant, his mind went from grief-clouded

and leaden to alert and sharp as a shard of obsidian. Hope! Now he had it; now he could think again.

"We'll have to divide the wing," he said, thinking aloud. "Five need to go after the Tian forces; I'm sure the Magi calling themselves advisers will be with the army, and we can't risk *them* getting away." He paused. "That should be you, Orest, Menet-ka, and Gan under Kalen, I think. Get both Menet-ka and Orest away from the rescue attempt, so they don't feel as if they need to kill themselves in the rescue or have the opportunity to try something without thinking first."

"Good," Ari said, nodding. "And the rest—except for you, that is—under Pe-atep to run a feint, while you go for the actual rescue, I presume?"

He rubbed his eyes with one hand, and felt something inside him falter. "I—that's what I want, but it might be better if you were the rescuer, because I'm afraid *I* might try something stupid—"

"You won't," Ari said flatly. "And of the two of us, you are the most likely to be able to get into that Tower. Avatre will do anything you ask; I do not have that level of cooperation from Kashet. No, you'll keep your head, and you do the rescue attempt while we run a feint, let them think we're trying to rescue Healers."

"All right, then." He closed his eyes a moment to think. "You're right in thinking our best chance is to rescue her out of the Tower; I wouldn't have the faintest idea where they'd be keeping her before then.

We'll have to come in above the clouds for the surprise to work in our favor, and it will have to be at night."

"Kashet would never do that," Ari said firmly. "He went in where there was light, but he will refuse to land in the dark. And on the top of the Tower? Impossible."

Kiron nodded. "Kaleth, have you any idea when this business in the Tower is going to happen? Aside from tomorrow, that is?"

Kaleth shook his head regretfully, then brightened. "But—the priests say this kind of magic takes time, so they'll probably begin as soon as the sun is up."

"Which means I should be in place that night." He pondered that for a moment. "Avatre can't take a full night of cold on the bare top of the Tower. And I can't get into the Tower from the ground." He thought for a moment more. "I need to talk to someone who knows magic. I need to talk—"

"To a Thet priest," said a deep voice from the door. "And here is one."

One of the tallest and most heavily muscled men Kiron had ever seen outside of the army or the Jousters stood in the door.

"Be-ka-re at your service," he said soberly. "The High Priest tells me you have need of magic. Tell me what you need, and I will tell you if any of us can do this."

"A way to keep Avatre warm all night at the top of a tower," Kiron said instantly. "And I need a way to know, from above the clouds, that the Magi's Tower is right below me." *Now* he had something he could do.

These were simple things, and yet—so crucial, and so impossible to achieve without magic.

Be-ka-re pursed his lips, then looked up at the ceiling. Kiron waited; he got the impression that the priest was thinking hard and rapidly.

Finally, the reward for his patience.

"I think," Be-ka-re said, "we can do this."

As the last light faded, Kiron and Avatre circled above the clouds over Alta City. No one could see him from here; the only problem, of course, was that he couldn't see anything. And he needed to wait until darkness fell, while people's eyes were still making the adjustment from light to dark, and a shadow could fall from the clouds and have less chance of being seen.

In his hand was a disk made of glass, and on that disk was a glowing spot that moved as he moved. When the spot was in the center of the disk, it meant he was directly over the Tower.

So small a thing, and it would not last for long. By midnight, its power would be exhausted. But by midnight he would be on the Tower, and would not need it. Without it, he would have to come in beneath the clouds and approach the Tower from a distance, drastically increasing the chance of being seen. With it, he could drop down from directly above.

The Tower, it seemed, sent out magic. The little

glowing spot was a reflection of that magic. The disk was not, as the use of the Far-Seeing Eye was, an active thing that could be blocked. It was more like a mirror, a passive thing showing only what another Magus might see merely by looking in the right way.

"Magi and those of us priests who also know the ways of magic can see this," Be-ka-re had told him. "I merely give you a way to see what I can see."

The last of the sun tipped below the clouds, which turned blood-red below him. He hoped it wasn't an omen; Avatre continued to circle at his direction, though she was growing uneasy, as her frequent glances down showed him. She knew it would be dark soon, and she didn't like to land in the dark any more than any other dragon did. But other than her glances downward, she did nothing; she trusted him.

When the last red of sunset had left the sky, and stars had begun to appear in the east, he centered the glowing spot on the disk, and sent Avatre plunging down through the clouds. She could not have been more willing; she pulled in her wings and dove, trusting to him to be her eyes. As the drop sent his heart racing and his stomach clenched, there was also a moment of eye-stinging awe that she *did* trust him so much.

It was nothing like the wild plunges he and Aket-ten had made when they seeded the winds with the plant disease that rendered *tala* useless. There didn't seem to be any lightning anywhere around, and if there was wind, it was too little to take note of. What there was a great deal of, however, was rain. Avatre was forced to moderate her fall, spreading her wings and turning the plunge into a tight spiral downward.

He was soaked within moments of passing into the clouds, as if someone had emptied an entire bath over him. And the farther they dropped, the worse it got until, as they broke through the bottom of the clouds, he had begun to wonder if he was going to find himself swimming to the Tower.

This was the central island of Alta City, the place where the elite of the elite lived. Here, too, stood the temples to the most important gods, the Royal Palace, and, of course, the Tower of Wisdom, the tallest building on the island, and the symbol of the power of the Magi.

Though even in the semidarkness the damage wrought by Eye and earthshake on the rings was obvious, there was no obvious sign of any such damage here on the center island. There were no buildings in ruins, no burned-out places—

But Kiron didn't have much time to look either; he and Avatre were coming straight down to the top of the Tower to avoid being seen, and the faster he got her down, the better.

And, of course, Avatre was all but blind in this light, depending on him to tell her what to do in time for her to do it.

At the height of a single-storied house above the top

of the Tower, he signaled her to backwing and start to land. She responded instantly, fanning her wings furiously and tucking her hindquarters under, then stretching out with her back legs as she felt for the surface she trusted would soon be there. This was the moment they were most likely to be seen—or heard, as her wings pumped, creating a kind of thunder.

He felt it when a single talon touched that surface; she backwinged a little harder, and he felt her hindquarters stretching, then as she got her weight onto the surface, he felt her legs take it. She folded her wings and settled onto the Tower top with hardly more than a whisper of sound.

Kiron sagged against her neck for a moment in relief. She'd never done this in the full dark before, and yet she had trusted him, trusted him even though they had no more communication than shifting weight, hand signals on her neck, and whispered voice.

He told her fervently what a clever dragon she was, then slipped off her back and onto the wet sandstone of the Tower. He saw with relief that there was a knee-high parapet running all around the edge. So Avatre would not be immediately visible.

Of course, when dawn came, there was the little problem of a scarlet dragon perching on the top of the pale stone of the Tower of Knowledge. Not all of her was going to fit behind that parapet.

But first, she needed to be fed.

There were two bundles of food for her, in baskets

on either side of her flanks. Not butchered meat; this was all whole small animals, things she could, and would, swallow whole. There would be no blood and no mess.

He emptied one pannier in front of her, and she gulped down everything while he untied the other and put it aside. He'd feed it to her in the morning, before he went—inside.

He quickly untied the bundle he'd brought from behind the saddle and shook it out as she finished the last of her meal.

It was, to all outward signs, a simple huge square of canvas, like one of the awnings that used to keep rain off the pens, or a sail of the sort you would find on any vessel moving up and down the Great Mother River and her daughters. But the moment he shook it out, this expanse of canvas began to radiate the same heat as a flat rock on a pleasant summer day.

The same heating spell that kept the sands of the dragons' pens hot kept this piece of fabric just as warm—courtesy of the Thet priests. This was how Avatre would be able to endure the cold and rain of the night. He shook it out over Avatre and made sure that she was entirely covered, before climbing in under it with her.

His clothing quickly began to steam; this was every bit as hot as the sands. Avatre was already relaxing.

It's a pity this is so complicated a bit of magic, he thought, trying to keep his mind on something other than the fact that Aket-ten was somewhere below. *Well, perhaps someday . . . someday when there are more of us. And no Magi.*

The canvas had another use besides keeping Avatre warm all night. It was nearly the same color as the sandstone; if Avatre kept her head down and her tail tucked in, chances were no one would see her from directly below. And it wasn't likely anyone across the canal would look at the Tower long enough to notice a lump on the top of it.

At least, no one would see her until he needed her to be seen.

And Aket-ten was somewhere below. Hurt, perhaps. Kaleth said that she hadn't been hurt, but how could he be sure? Frightened, she was surely frightened, and mourning her dragon. Praying that help would somehow come before it was too late.

I'm here! he thought, hard, wondering if she could somehow pick it up. *We'll get you out, just hold on. . . .*

It was very comfortable under the folds of that cloth. The canvas was waterproof enough that his clothing was drying out. The Thet priests said that the Magi wouldn't sense this magic, even though it was so close to them, because the thing in the Tower was so magical already. The sail would be like a lit lantern under the desert sun at noon; you wouldn't see the flame unless you were looking for it, and even then you would have to be practically on top of it.

How scared is she? How hurt is she? Have they already

done anything to her? Was she in a bare, cold cell some-where down below, chilled, aching, maybe hungry?

What had they been doing to her? He didn't really want to think about it. . . .

He went over his plan in his mind. Before dawn he would have to get into place, moving while there was just enough light to see by, but not so much that any-one would be around to spot him. He hoped. There was a lot of hope involved in this. An awful lot of hope.

Avatre was already asleep. He could feel her breath-ing; she was very comfortable under this sail. And with the rain drumming on it, it was like the old days, back when he was just beginning the new wing of dragons, with rain drumming on the canopy that kept the water out of the hot sand.

Back when Toreth was alive. Before Aket-ten be-came one of them.

If they've hurt her. . . .

His stomach knotted, and not just with anxiety over Aket-ten.

He wished he was doing something other than just waiting.

Fear crept slowly over him, chilling his heart; he tried to drive it away by throwing himself into his planning.

There wasn't a lot of room inside the tower; he would probably not have to face more than two peo-ple, the Magus and whoever he brought to help him. A guard, probably. He would have to get rid of both of them. . . .

Be honest. I'm going to have to kill them.

This was going to be hard. He'd never killed anyone face-to-face before, and he might have to. Would have to. Almost a certainty.

Actually, he hadn't ever killed anyone—not that he was certain of. In that last fight when the *tala* ran out, he and the others had mostly just tried to make the Tian dragons angry, so they'd throw their riders. Or at least, get the dragons so agitated that they'd fight their Jousters, force them to make their beasts go to ground just so the Jouster could get off before the dragon *could* throw them. He'd wanted people dead, but he'd never done the deed with his own hands. He felt very conscious of the long knife at his hip. He was going to have to use that knife. . . .

That, he tried not to think about. He just drilled himself in what he had to do next when dawn came, dozing off, then waking, to go over it all again. He willed himself to see every step, over and over, until, as the rain slackened just a little and the first hint of dawn lightened the sky, he shook off the last of his sleepiness and went to work.

And it felt like he had done it a hundred times before.

First, he unloaded the second pannier in front of Avatre; she wasn't awake enough to be hungry yet, but when she was, her breakfast would be waiting right there for her and she wouldn't have to move from under the comfortable canvas to eat it. And then, she could go right back to sleep again. She probably would.

He fastened his rope to Avatre's saddle, pulled on it to make sure it was going to hold. Avatre opened one eye sleepily.

"Stay," he whispered to her. "Hold."

Not at all loath to do just that, she closed her eye again, and went back to drowsing.

He slipped over the parapet at the corner, where the rope wouldn't dangle in front of the window, getting soaked in the process, and walked his way down the wall until he got to a window. He'd been afraid it might be a narrow squeeze, but there was plenty of room for the windows were enormous, far bigger than he had thought, and there was nothing in the way of shutters or bars on them.

Then again, why should there be shutters or bars? Who would be up here? Who would want to break into the stronghold of the Magi?

Um, that would be me.

He clambered in through the window, flipped the rope out of the way so it wouldn't show if anyone looked out, and waited right in the opening in the darkness. He had to wait for his eyes to adjust, and he wanted to avoid betraying his presence to someone who was paying attention by dripping all over the floor and leaving patches of water there.

The room in this tower was half full of something mechanical, and it was not what he had expected. He'd thought vaguely of statues of strange gods, of a room thick with incense, of—well, now he couldn't put a name to what he'd expected.

It stood in the middle of a "magic circle" of inlaid brass in the middle of the room. He knew it was a magic circle because he had watched the Thet priests lay out something similar when they made the canvas for Avatre—in chalk on the floor, not in permanent brass inlaid in the floor. But the construction itself looked like one of Heklatis' little mechanical toys. Except that it wasn't so very "little."

The mechanism itself was also made of brass. From the look of things, it could be swiveled and pointed in just about any direction.

The heart of the thing was the biggest crystal he had ever seen. Shaped like two pyramids clapped together, an enormous, perfect octahedron, he had never seen anything like it. It was flawless, clear, and half again as tall as he was. For a long moment, all he could do was to stare at it in wonder. He hadn't known quite what to expect, but whatever it had been, his imagination had not been able to anticipate *this*.

Though why it should be called an "Eye," he couldn't think.

He shook off his amazement, and began looking for a place to hide. He might be here a long time.

There weren't a lot of hiding places here; he finally

found a kind of storage area, a three-sided cupboard in the corner between the windows opposite the place where he had come in. When he pulled the door open, it looked as if it hadn't been opened in years. If there had ever been shelves in there, they were gone now. There were dusty bottles and jars on the floor, some of which inexplicably made his skin crawl. He shoved them aside and squeezed himself in, watching the room through the crack in the door. And it made him wonder, what had this place been used for, before it had been made into the home for the Eye? The Tower was older than the Eye. Probably the reason that the cupboard was still here was only because it was too much trouble to pull it out.

So far, so good.

Back to the hard part.

Waiting.

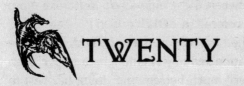 **TWENTY**

THERE were two possibilities for what would happen next. Either the Magi would bring Aket-ten here before the rest of the wing began their attack, or they would do so because the wing had begun their attack. He thought he was ready in either case.

It turned out to be the former rather than the latter.

He heard them coming long before he saw them. The hollow tower amplified every little sound from below.

A door opening and slamming shut, then footsteps, then voices.

A harsh, angry voice. "Get her under control, curse you! OW!"

"My lord specified that she is not to be damaged." A second voice. Much calmer and deeper than the first.

"Not being damaged doesn't—OW!—mean you can't secure her—OW!—legs—OW! Seft take you, bitch! But not before I'm—OW!"

Kiron clutched the side of the cupboard, overcome by mingled elation and rage. Elation, because Aket-ten was clearly very much herself, and doing her best to inflict as much damage on her captor as she could. And rage—he wanted to fly down those stairs and slaughter both the men he could hear on the spot. Or the Magus, at least.

"If my Lord would just permit me to knock the girl unconscious—" Perfectly calm, and matter-of-fact. Which only made Kiron's blood heat as he clenched his fists. Not just the Magus, then. He'd kill both of them.

"No! I need her awake and aware and undamaged in any—OW!—way!"

The first speaker was obviously the Magus. The other—probably a guard or a servant. From the sound of things, Aket-ten was concentrating on taking out her anger on the Magus.

"The stair is too steep to risk carrying a struggling girl up it, and carry her is what I shall be forced to do. So my lord will have to permit her the freedom of her legs, and bear with the consequences. Unless my lord is going to insist on my carrying her and is willing to take the chance of both of us falling and breaking our respective necks?"

The long pause that followed the statement, and the

sense that the Magus was actually considering the option, made Kiron wince in spite of the fact that he wanted to pound both of them into the floor. Whoever this Magus was, he hadn't won himself any friends with that pause. "No, no of course not," said the Magus, a little too late. "But—OW!"

"If my lord would at least walk a few paces ahead, so that the girl cannot reach him—" Now the voice sounded wary as well as impatient, and Kiron wasn't at all surprised. The Magi were not known for their forbearance toward their servants. And if anything went wrong, it would be the servant who was blamed for it.

He wished he could see them. What kind of servant was this? A guard? Or someone less able to put up a fight if—when—Kiron attacked? It didn't take being a guard or a soldier to talk about hitting a bound and gagged girl on the head.

He'd like to think that no real soldier would think of such a thing—but he knew better. From the Tian Jousters who had hauled helpless Altan peasants (including women and children) into the air and dropped them, to the Altan soldiers who had put the Temple of the Twins under siege, there was rot in both armies, and the only way to stop it was to stop the war that had made atrocity acceptable and rewarded the officers who ordered it or looked the other way while it happened.

"Seft take you! Just get her up these stairs, and I don't care how you do it!" the voice snarled.

He's not gaining any goodwill from the servants today, that's for sure.

"My lord is surely aware that even if I do not carry her, the girl could succeed in pushing me down the stairs or tripping me if her feet are left free. Is this truly what my lord wishes?"

The Magus paused, for too long, leaving the impression that he *was* considering the option of risking his servant's life and limb.

You're not going higher in his estimation, you bastard.

"Just get that halter on her neck and get her up here!" There was the sound of one set of footsteps moving a bit faster up the stairs, while the other two plodded along behind. "Walk in front of her and drag her if you have to! Come *on!* Get her moving, you lack-wit!"

After that, there was only the sound of footsteps; evidently, Aket-ten wisely elected not to resist anymore. Kiron held his breath as they made their way up the staircase. The big question was what the nature of the man helping the Magus would be. And how big he was.

Stay hidden, he warned himself. *If you rush out without thinking, they can take you. If you wait until you can catch them both by surprise, you can take them. At some point fairly soon, the others will begin their attack, and it will attract a lot of attention. If you haven't found an opening before then, that will be the time.*

But he didn't want to wait, not at all. His stomach was in a knot, every muscle was alive with the need to fight, and he practically vibrated with tension. He wanted to get out there and *hurt* them, the moment they appeared—

But he wasn't exactly trained or armed for a real fight, not the kind that was going to happen here. He didn't have a sword, because he didn't know how to use one. He had a club, and a knife, and his wits. Not so bad against a Magus, but suicide against a trained soldier.

From his vantage point behind the crack in the door, Kiron saw the gleam of a light in the opening in the floor through which the staircase rose. Moments later, the Magus himself, carrying a lantern, emerged through the opening.

He wasn't one of the Magi that Kiron knew, but his clothing, a fine long robe of purple linen and short cloak of the same material, a belt of gold plates, and a matching collar, marked him as someone important. Otherwise, he looked perfectly ordinary, not the sort of man that Kiron would look twice at, if they passed each other in the street. Middle-aged, thinning hair cropped at chin-level, clean-shaven, with the kind of visage that Orest called a "face-shaped face" with nothing to distinguish it from a thousand like it.

It struck him, as he looked at the perfectly average, beardless face, neither young nor old-looking, perhaps a little plumper than he should be, but nothing that could be called "fat," that it was wrong that evil should look so banal. For evil this man was; he might or might not be *personally* responsible for the murder of dozens, the deaths of thousands, but he was involved, he knew about it, and he had willingly agreed to it, had probably participated in some fashion.

He had definitely participated in draining the Winged Ones, and their inability to see into the future as a consequence had killed and hurt people all over Alta during the earthshakes they could no longer predict.

So how was it that someone who had done all of this looked like a prosperous merchant about to make a great deal? There was a smug, self-satisfied smirk on the man's face that made Kiron want to punch it.

But the next man rising out of the stair prevented him from doing any such thing.

Definitely a professional soldier, or at least, a professional bodyguard. The man was big, well-muscled, and Kiron was nowhere near a match for him.

But he was also angry. Kiron read that in his posture and his lack of expression. He might feign a servile nature, but he hated this Magus, and given half a chance and the certain knowledge that he could not be blamed for what followed, he would desert his "lord" in a heartbeat.

Trailing behind him, with a kind of collar and leash around her neck, gagged, with her hands tied in front of her, was Aket-ten.

Once again, he had to restrain himself to keep from rushing out.

If the bodyguard was angry, she was furious. Her eyes above the gag flashed with rage. Her posture was rigid, her whole manner proclaiming that, the moment she got a chance, she was going to do *something* to the man that he would regret for the rest of his days.

And that if she had anything to say about it, those days would be very short indeed,

That made him weak-kneed with relief. If she had been cowed, intimidated, beaten down, he would not have been able to keep himself from running in to rescue her immediately. And if she had been sunk deep in depression and mourning for Re-eth-ke, it would be a lot harder to get her motivated to get her out. She was ready to fight for her life and her freedom and that meant she was an ally and a potential accomplice, not a potential burden.

"Tie her over there," the Magus said, pointing to a spot Kiron couldn't see. "Look there—see the ring in the wall. Get her wrists tied up to that, then go, get out of here. I won't need your so-called services any more."

"If my lord is quite certain," said the man.

"Yes, I am *quite* certain!" the Magus snapped. "I do not need your halfhearted and incompetent help, and what is more, you'll only be a hindrance once I begin working magic."

"Very well, my lord," the man said, hiding both

anger and satisfaction under a bland façade. "It will be as you wish."

He took Aket-ten to the other side of the Eye, where Kiron couldn't see them. When he moved back into Kiron's narrow field of vision, he was alone.

"Go on, get out of here," the Magus snarled, as he moved around to the same side of the device and out of sight. "Go! I don't need you anymore."

"Very well, my lord." The guard bowed just enough to keep from being reprimanded, then followed his orders to the letter, leaving by the stair so quickly that if the Magus had been paying attention, he *would* have been more than just reprimanded.

But the Magus was busy with the device. Kiron knew that it was the device he was meddling with, and not Aket-ten, because the huge crystal began moving, very slowly rotating. And the Magus was muttering something, too low for Kiron to hear what it was.

The entire atmosphere of the room changed. Kiron felt his hair starting to stand on end, and not just metaphorically, but physically, the way it did sometimes during midnight *kamiseens* or when he was flying in the dangerous tempests of the season of rains, when lightning played in the storm.

There was a low hum coming from the Eye, like the droning of bees about to swarm. The Magus moved into his field of vision again, sketching signs in the air with his hands, still muttering under his breath.

The Eye rotated a little faster. It still wasn't going at

any great speed; a desert tortoise was a hundred times faster than it, but the fact that it was moving without anyone touching it was disturbing.

Aket-ten made a noise around her gag. If it had been a scream, or anything that sounded like a cry for help, Kiron would have been out there in an instant. It wasn't; it sounded like an insult. The Magus ignored it, and Aket-ten. Whatever he wanted her for, she wasn't a priority right now.

The room began to brighten. At first, for a confused moment, Kiron thought it was because the light was coming from the Eye. Then he realized that the light was coming from the wrong direction—not from the Eye, but roughly from the east.

He's cleared the sky above the Tower. Now he has light to work with.

The Eye rotated a little faster, the hum deepened and strengthened, and now Kiron felt not only his hair standing on end, but a gut-deep reaction that made his knees feel weak. This was—*wrong*—wrong in a way he couldn't put a name to, but could only feel.

No, it was more than that, worse than that. This was something that had once been right and good, and had been twisted out of all recognition; something deep inside him recognized that evil for what it was, and wanted only to run.

Never in all his life had he felt this deep, soul-shaking fear. Khefti-the-Fat had only threatened his body. The Tian soldiers had only taken his father. The

Tian Jousters would only have taken his heart, had they taken Avatre. This thing—this thing would eat everything that he was, ever had been, or ever would be and leave behind an empty shell that might live, speak, talk, but would be less than an *ashabti*-figure of flesh instead of clay—and worst of all, the most horrible of all, he would *know* what had happened, know what he had lost, and know he would never get it back. All pleasure, all joy, all creativity would be sucked out of him, leaving nothing but an interminable gray and unvarying existence.

No wonder those former Winged Ones had done so little to save themselves. Death was preferable to that death-in-life of emptiness.

Aket-ten screamed, her shriek muffled by her gag, but giving voice to exactly the same terror that he was feeling.

He clutched the frame of the cupboard to keep himself upright, and concentrated all his will on not giving in to the terror.

And then, the Eye began to move faster, the pitch of that steady hum rose a little, and the terrible fear faded. It didn't disappear, but it faded enough so that it was bearable.

What—was—that?

He shook his head a little to clear it. His stomach was still churning, and he was so drenched with sweat he was surprised the Magus couldn't smell him. What had caused that overwhelming fear?

Why hadn't the Magus been affected?

Now he could hear Aket-ten, choking on the gag, weeping hysterically and moaning. The Magus came into his field of vision, tilting his head to the side, and wearing an expression of pleased avidity.

"So sorry to upset you, girl," he said, sounding gleeful rather than sorry. "But I needed to test you. The more power you have, the more strongly you react to the Eye as it spins up to full speed. By your reaction, I would say that you have *quite* a lot of power. Far more than we suspected."

Kiron took a very slow, deep breath, as anger chased out the last remnants of terror. And in the brief moment when terror was gone, but anger had not yet flooded him with unreason, he knew he would have to keep that rage under complete control.

And he also knew that he could.

A slave, a serf, lives with endurance and patience. He learns it because he has no other choice; he must learn to be patient or die. Orest would have attacked the Magus the moment he appeared with Aket-ten in tow. Any of the others would have burst out of hiding in rage or terror by now. Even Ari probably would not have managed to control himself.

So maybe he was the right person to be here. . . .

Keep gloating, you bastard, he thought, behind the white-hot rage invoked by the sound of Aket-ten weeping. *Keep right on. When the Feather of Truth is weighed against your heart . . . I would not care to be you.*

And I swear you are going to meet the Judges a great deal sooner than you think.

"Now, I will just bring the Eye fully to life," the Magus went on blithely. "Would you like to hear what your destined fate is?"

Aket-ten's sobs choked off. Kiron couldn't tell if it was because her own fear had turned to anger, or if it was because she was too terrified to weep. He hoped it was the former. He was controlling himself so tightly that every muscle felt as tight as a bowstring.

The Magus laughed. "Oh, do glare at me, girl. Really, you should feel flattered and honored. Your power will be going to serve Alta *far* more effectively than that trivial ability of yours to speak with animals ever could. Or—well, it goes to serve the Magi, but soon enough our welfare and that of Alta will be one and the same, so it hardly matters. First—" He made a few more passes in the air, and this time Kiron's eyes nearly bulged out of his head as he saw the fingers leaving trails of glow in the air where they had passed, forming, for just one moment, signs and glyphs. "—first, I will bring the Eye up to full speed. I have already used some of your power, oh, about half of it, to clear the storm out of the skies over the Tower, so that the Eye has some sunlight to work with. I will use the rest of your power to *keep* the sky over the Tower clear forever, no matter what the season, by making a link between the earth and air energies, using the Eye itself as the physical aspect of that link. Never again will the rains prevent us from using the Eye to punish those who defy and endanger us. Just think! As long as the sun shines, the Eye will always be usable by daylight after this! Then, when I am finished with you—well, by then that pesky Tian army under the command of our renegades will be at the Fourth Ring, and I will proceed to use the Eye to remove them all from our consideration. Do you understand now what your trivial sacrifice is—"

The Magus stopped in midsentence, and stared out the window somewhere behind Aket-ten. "—what in the—"

Kiron strained his ears, and thought he heard faint and far-off crashes, screams.

"Curse them all to Seft!" the Magus exclaimed angrily. "Wretched dragons! I *knew* we should have exterminated them all while we had the chance!"

They've begun! Kiron thought, with a lift of his heart. The others had begun the attack on the forces surrounding the Temple of All Gods, using the jars of Akkadian Fire. They could not have chosen a better moment to mount their distraction.

"Well, we'll just have to speed this up so I can exterminate them *now*," the Magus muttered under his breath. "Burn the vermin out of the sky—about time—should have been done years ago." He made a few more passes, and this time the glowing lines he left in the air hung there and stayed. And then, as the Eye spun faster and faster, it, too, began to emit light, until a glowing blur hung in its place.

"And now, girl, it's time for you to fulfill your destiny," the Magus said, and turned his back on Kiron's hiding place.

Knowing he would never get a better chance, Kiron grabbed his dagger, and flung open the door. It crashed into the wall as he leaped for the Magus's back.

Only a last-moment dodge by his opponent saved the Magus from the fate he had meted out to others.

The Magus twisted cleverly out of the way, then whirled and grappled with him, trying to seize control of the dagger he held. At that moment, he realized something else. For someone as portly and out-of-shape as the Magus looked, he was still heavier and stronger than Kiron.

Kiron was angry; the Magus would not hesitate for a moment to kill.

Immobilize him—

The Magus wrenched free of him, leaving his cloak in Kiron's hands. Kiron flung it aside, and the Magus went for him again, all of his attention on the knife in Kiron's hand.

Behind them, the Eye was glowing white-hot, too bright to look at directly, spinning so fast that the hum had become a howl.

The Magus grabbed with both hands for his knife hand, intent on getting the weapon away from him, and suddenly Kiron had a flash of inspiration.

He let the Magus have the knife, just let it go as soon as the Magus got his hands on the hilt. And in the moment of confusion, while the Magus stared at the weapon he was now in control of, Kiron pulled the club he was carrying out of the waistband of his kilt, and cracked it down, *hard,* on the offending wrist.

With a screech of pain, the Magus dropped the knife from fingers that suddenly didn't want to work anymore.

On the backswing, Kiron connected with his temple with a solid *thunk* that nearly knocked the Magus over.

The Magus staggered sideways, rotated on his heel, stumbled blindly toward the Eye and—

And crossed the brass circle inlaid in the floor.

And that was when every plan Kiron had made went right out the metaphorical window.

The Magus went rigidly upright, and began to scream, as his body began to—

Well, Kiron could only think "unravel" because as Kiron stared in horrified disbelief, it looked as if invisible fingers were tearing him apart, bit by bit, except the bits didn't bleed. All the bits were sucked into the glowing vortex that the Eye had become as they were torn off. It started at his hands and feet, and as his feet vanished, he just hung in the air, as if suspended on a hook, like a discarded garment.

The screaming went on and on, as the unraveling went on, and the Eye glowed brighter and brighter with every little bit of the Magus that it sucked into itself. And part of Kiron wanted to stand and watch in stunned amazement—

But the part of him that was in control scooped up the knife from the floor, and ran to where Aket-ten was standing with her back against the wall, her hands over her head, tied at the wrist to a brass ring embedded in the wall. As he sawed through the leather thongs biting into her wrist, the screaming mercifully stopped.

But the Eye continued to spin—

There was a feeling of intense pressure as he cut through the last of the thongs, and then, a kind of dull *whuff,* as if something very heavy, but soft, had been dropped in the middle of the room.

As he untied the gag holding a ball of rags in her mouth, Aket-ten's eyes went wider than he'd ever seen before. And when he turned to look, he understood.

The Eye was awake, and evidently had a mind of its own about what should be done now. That beam of light, thicker than his thigh, and too bright to look at, lanced out of the window, and was burning its way across the buildings of the Central Island. Flames rose beneath the Tower, and the sounds of screams and a terrible heat and the smell of scorched rock surrounded him.

The Eye had already incinerated the Royal Palace by the time he turned, had decimated the buildings around it, and was cutting a swathe across the Island toward the canal. When it reached the edge of the canal and kept going, water bubbled and exploded in steam where it passed.

"How do you stop this thing?" he yelled at Aket-ten over the discordant howl the thing was putting out.

"I don't know!" she shouted back.

And just as if the situation they were in wasn't bad enough, he felt the stone of the Tower beneath him tremble, and his stomach lurched with that all-too-familiar, sickening sensation that marked an earthshake.

No time for argument. He grabbed Aket-ten's wrist and ran for the window—not, thank heavens, the one the Eye was aiming its light-weapon out of.

He thrust his arm out of it, and groped for the rope. It wasn't there.

His stomach lurched again, this time with fear. *Oh, no—where's Avatre? Did she fly off? Did the Eye frighten her? Great Hamun, is she anywhere nearby?*

Panicked now, he whistled, praying she was near and could hear him, because if she wasn't—

And Avatre swooped down out of the sky, just as the Tower shook and swayed under his feet again, and out of the window he could *see* the ripple of the earthshake move across the land and water, as if someone had shaken out a rug.

It flung them toward the window as Aket-ten shrieked at the top of her lungs; it tossed Aket-ten over the sill, while he shouted for Avatre and the dragon tried desperately to maneuver closer.

"Kiron!" Aket-ten screamed—the rest was undecipherable.

"Hold on!" he screamed back. He hung on with one

hand to the windowframe, precariously sprawled over the windowsill; Aket-ten had been pitched right out of the window and only his grip on her wrist kept her from plummeting to her death below.

A second jolt rocked the Tower and broke his grip on the stone, and he felt himself rolling over the windowsill and out the window, completely unable to stop himself, pulled by Aket-ten's weight.

Avatre twisted herself over sideways in some impossible maneuver his eyes refused to accept just as he began to fall, and somehow she got herself halfway under him, with Aket-ten still hanging desperately onto his left hand, and he sprawled over the saddle, holding on desperately with his right. As the beam of the Eye began to go everywhere with the rocking of the Tower, Avatre lurched over in the air and kited sideways, trying to compensate for their weight, trying to get down to the ground before they fell—

No— Aket-ten's hand slipped a little out of his grip, as she continued to scream at the top of her lungs, her eyes fixed on his and full of terror. Sweat poured down his arm, making his hand, and hers, slippery. He tried to pull her up to where she could grab a harness strap or something, but though his arm screamed with the effort, he couldn't raise her at all. She flailed, trying to catch his hand with her free hand, but couldn't seem to get a grip.

No! Her hand slipped a little more, despite the fact that they were both holding on as hard as they could.

Now instead of holding to her wrist, he only had hold of her hand. And his fingers were loosening. . . .

NO! He felt it—she was still slipping, as the tower collapsed behind them in a tumble and roar of stone and dust, as the earth continued to shake, as Avatre fanned her wings and tilted over sideways, desperately trying to keep them from falling—

She screamed, he screamed—

And then, lumbering clumsily out of the dust cloud, canted to one side, an indigo-and-silver miracle.

Mouth gaping open with effort, Re-eth-ke tucked herself under Aket-ten just as her fingers slipped out of his.

And caught her, as they had all practiced with sandbags, sliding her head under the falling human and forcing the victim to slide down her neck to her shoulders. It was perfect. It was beautiful. He shouted aloud with elation.

Aket-ten sprawled athwart her dragon's neck and shoulders, and as Re-eth-ke sank lower with every wingbeat, she clung on desperately without saddle or reins to help her.

There was a wound in the dragon's shoulder that had been stitched shut, and holes in the webbing of her wing. Still she bravely fought to get her rider to the ground safely—which, in her mind, quite clearly meant away from the Central Island, *across the canal.*

Across the canal, where a line of fire divided the half-ruined Temple of All Gods from the armed force that had been besieging it (and which now was fleeing to a man). Well, staggering away, because the earth was still convulsing, and mounting wreckage made every step hazardous.

Re-eth-ke landed heavily in an open courtyard, with Avatre right behind her. Half a dozen Healers came running into the center of the courtyard to take Aket-ten from Re-eth-ke's back, but she slid off by herself, and flung herself into Kiron's arms as he jumped down from Avatre's saddle to meet her.

Ah, gods! I have you, I have you safe at last!

"I knew you'd come!" she sobbed, as she clung to him, her wet cheek pressed into his chest. "I knew you'd come! I knew it!" She was trembling all over, his brave Aket-ten, but so was he.

As he held her, it dawned on him now just *why* she had been so aggressive and ready to fight, rather than sunk in mourning. She had known, of course, that Re-eth-ke was alive, something none of the rest of them had any way of knowing, and that had bolstered her courage and her spirits. She had what he did not, the bond of mind-to-mind communication with her dragon, so she had known all along how hurt Re-eth-ke was, that her injuries were being tended to (which they obviously had been), and what was happening to her. Very probably, it had been the Healers themselves who had gone out to bring the wounded dragon into the shelter of their temple when the guards had taken Aket-ten away.

And the moment that the injured dragon had sensed that Aket-ten was in deadly danger and afraid, she came, as fast as her damaged body would carry her. Given how slowly she was flying, she had probably begun looking for release from the moment that the Magus worked that magic that had so frightened them both.

But now, she needed human reassurance as well.

For that matter, so did he. He had come close, so close to losing her. He wrapped his arms around her and held her; his heart seemed to swell until it occupied his whole chest, and all he could think was how he never wanted to let her go. "I'd come for you no matter where you were," he murmured into her hair. "I always will."

Another earthshake rocked the courtyard, throwing them against each other. The dragons flattened out their necks and whined, looking anxiously from side to side, and as the shaking went on, something odd, some inner prompting, made him look up and across the canal to the central island—

—the central island. Which was sinking. Or least, the *buildings* were sinking. Even as he watched, bracing himself against the trembling of the earth, arms holding tight to Aket-ten, a great plume of mixed sand and water erupted from the place where the Tower had stood, and the remains of the Temple of Hamun vanished from sight.

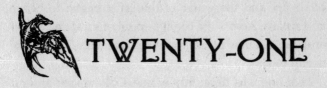# TWENTY-ONE

WHEN the shake stopped, Kiron reached out to seize one of the Healers without letting go of Aket-ten. "Where are—" he began.

"The rest of the Jousters have already taken some of our people to safety," the Healer replied, even though she was shaking with reaction. "They said they are coming back—"

"We cannot count on them returning soon enough, nor often enough to get you all out," he interrupted her. "You have to get off this ring, maybe out of Alta altogether. The shocks are getting worse and—" He let go of her arm and gestured at the Central Island, at buildings half-sunk or completely vanished. "—Look. I don't know *why* this is happening, but it is, and it isn't—"

Another shake began, he and Aket-ten held each other up, and the water of the canal began to heave and splash. Across the canal a spout of sand and water erupted in a new place, and what was left of the Palace began to sink.

This one was definitely worse. Colonnades around the garden went over, one after another, and several people were knocked off their feet. And the Temple of All Gods had been *made* to withstand shakes.

"This isn't right!" the woman cried, when the shake was over, from where she was kneeling on the ground. "They're getting stronger!"

"And longer. We have to get you out of here." He thought, hard. "On the water is safest. Have you boats?"

She nodded, relief suffusing her round features. "Enough for everyone, I think, since so many of us have already escaped. And people who know how to row them." Without waiting for direction, she got to her feet and moved purposefully in the direction of the Healers clustered around Re-eth-ke.

One of them shortly came over to him. "We can get out by water," he said soberly, "But there are hundreds, thousands of people on this ring." And he looked at Kiron expectantly.

Kiron blinked, realizing that this man, this Healer—who was by no means an inexperienced man by his age—was looking to him for an answer.

And one came to him. "Aket-ten and I can get where

no one else can, and see what no one else can—from above. And the people of Alta know Jousters, and probably trust Jousters more than anyone else right now."

Aket-ten wiped her eyes with the back of her hand and gently shoved at him to get him to loosen his arms. She stood away from him a little bit, and sniffed, but raised her chin. "I am Aket-ten, Winged One, Daughter of Lord Ya-tiren. People will listen to me. We will guide folk off this ring, and off the next, until they are safely away from danger. But Alta is dead, and there is no saving it."

The Healer dropped his head, and when he raised it again, Kiron saw the marks of grief on his face. "You say no more than what we have thought these many moons, Winged One. But it is an ill moment, hearing it spoken aloud."

"Someone must say it, or we will all perish."

The speaker was an old woman, hair entirely white, falling in the "royal" hairstyle of hundreds of tiny plaits, each ending in a gold bead. She stood very erect, and her eyes, dark and shadowed, looked directly into Kiron's. He had never seen her, but he knew who she was, the Eldest, the Chief Healer of the Temple of All Gods. "We must save what we can. We will take the boats and make for the harbor—"

"No!" That was still another Healer, a rough-looking old fellow with a fair number of scars. "Not so, Eldest. I know the sea, and the sea does strange things in shakes; it can withdraw for leagues, then come rushing back and overwhelm all in its path. No, we must take the boats and make our way through the canals inland, to one of the Daughters, and thence up the Great Mother River if we must."

"I bow to your experience, Te-ren-hatem," she said, after a moment. "But there is one thing we *must* do; it is more important to Heal that dragon now than anything else, no matter how much it costs our Healers by touch."

The man looked at her aghast. "But Eldest, it is but an animal, and there are many, many injured and more to come!"

"You Healers by touch can Heal a few, perhaps even a dozen, before you are exhausted," the old woman said, with a look that dared him to challenge her. "But unless you spend that same strength to heal that dragon, *she* will not last past noon. And then, where will all those *thousands* be who will need the guidance of her Jouster?" As the man's face fell, she softened her tone. "I know it is hard hearing this, Te," she said softly. "But you know as well as I that Healing is, and always has been, a balancing game, weighing out resources against the greatest good. In the best of times, that balancing never needs to come into play, but this is the worst of times, and we must do what must be done. The greatest good, right now, is to heal that poor, faithful animal, so that she can serve all of Alta that survives."

He bowed. "Yes, Eldest," he said softly. "I will get the others."

As he moved off, the Healer turned back to Kiron and Aket-ten. "And as for you—heed me, children. The same advice—nay, orders!—apply to you. Save the ones you can. Save the *most* that you can. There will be people trapped, hurt, begging for help that you cannot aid. You must leave them, leave them behind, leave them to others, but leave them. If there is a later, you may come back, but if you linger over one, when you could have saved many in that same time, you will have done the wrong thing."

He gritted his teeth; he hated hearing that, but he knew it was true, and he silenced Aket-ten's protest with a squeeze of his hand on hers. "Hard truths are still truths. Eldest, thank you. I will get aloft; I know that when Re-eth-ke is fit to fly, Aket-ten will do likewise, and as we see the others returning, I will send them to do the same." He squeezed Aket-ten's hand again, just as another shake began.

This time all three of them instinctively reached for each other and braced one another through the shake. "They are getting worse," the Eldest Healer said, when the dreadful rumbling and crashing had subsided— and across the canal, yet another building (or what was left of one) had vanished.

"Then I must go." He bent and kissed Aket-ten. "You and I must separate, to cover the widest area. If the sea does what that Healer thinks it will—you must go to the harbor and warn them first, for you *are* the daughter of Ya-tiren, and you know how to command."

Her head came up, though her lower lip trembled a little. "I will do that," she said, without hesitation. "Then I shall return and work the First Ring and so forth."

"Good." He did not say, *I know you will be fine*, or *I am counting on you*, because he did not need to say any such thing. This was Wingleader to Jouster. He would treat her as she wanted to be treated, not as his beloved whom he wished to protect, nor the noble daughter, but as any of the other members of his wing.

She could not manage a smile, but she gave a solemn nod. He sketched a salute, and sprinted for Avatre. *She* was only too happy to be in the air, even if that air was full of dust and thick with the smoke of many fires.

He began working his way along the canal, for that was where there were likely to be boats. His appearance was marked by shouts and cries for help, some of which made him want to break down and weep with frustration over how little he could actually do. But he hardened himself, and limited himself to sending people to where he had seen undamaged boats, despite pleas for other aid. "There are only two of us Jousters right now; we have to find and warn others. Make for the river," he told them, over and over again. "The sea is not to be trusted in a shake! Get as far away as you can, until you can no longer feel the shaking."

"The Magi?" he was asked, by virtually every party he encountered. "What has happened to the Magi?"

"They are dead," he always responded, because even if it wasn't entirely true, no Magus would be safe in these lands for generations to come. "As are the Great Kings and Queens, and most who dwelled on Central Island. The gods have deserted them, even the evil gods that they once served. Alta is dying and there is no saving her. Ocean and marsh alike are taking her back with each new shake; it is the gods' own will, and you cannot fight the gods. Now fly! Fly, lest you die with her!"

And at that point, since most of them owned no more than what they stood up in or had saved from the wreckage of their homes, they did not argue with him, they picked up their belongings, aided the wounded, and made for the boats.

Strangely enough—at least, until he thought about it—was that no one begged him to carry them away. That was what he had most dreaded, especially if it came from someone who was injured.

But they didn't. In fact, they kept a cautious distance from him when he landed. And then, after a few frantic reactions to sudden moves from Avatre he realized that they were used, not to tame dragons, but the wild-caught ones.

The wild-caught ones were still dangerous to anyone not a Jouster or a dragon boy. Someone visibly injured might well be considered a possible menu item . . . and the injured were well aware of that and made a great effort to appear perfectly fine. It might have been funny, if it hadn't been so tragic.

The only times when he did stop and pick someone up were when he found children wandering alone, or—more tragically—infants with dead parents. Then he stopped, caught them up, and carried them to the next group with children or infants. He never gave the impromptu guardians a chance to object either. "We are all Altans," he would say bluntly. "We will care for our own. Tend to this little one."

No one refused. Maybe they were afraid to. In any event, when he checked back with groups with which he had left children, they were caring for the foundlings as well as their own. In a couple of cases, he found a woman in the party cradling the child possessively, and he wondered, had he united a bereft mother with a replacement for the child she had lost?

Ari was the first to return. Kiron spotted him coming in from the south, and went to meet him. By then, Aket-ten was in the air, had presumably dealt with the people at the harbor, and was working the interior of the First Ring, guiding people through the maze of broken buildings and toppled statues to the one causeway still intact—a floating footbridge made of raft sections lashed together, a replacement for a causeway that had collapsed in an earlier shake.

He didn't even need to say anything, he just pointed at Re-eth-ke hovering in the middle distance, and Ari practically went limp with relief. He straightened immediately, though. "We saw Re-eth-ke rise from the Healers' Court!" he called. "I thought I was having a vision at first. But Seft's own chaos was breaking loose, so we landed and each took a sick or wounded Healer out."

"It's getting w—" Kiron began, when another shake interrupted him.

By now, there wasn't much left of the Central Island, and with this shake, buildings were beginning to sink on First Ring as well. Ari took in the damage with widened eyes.

"By Hamun's horns!" he exclaimed. "What is happening here?"

"We're evacuating the city, sending them south, getting as many into boats as we can," Kiron called. "The rest—we're finding safe paths to that causeway and guiding them from the air, and I don't know why things are sinking. Maybe it's a different sort of shake than we've ever had before. I want you to intercept the others and tell them that's what they're to do. Then *you* go to the others, the ones with the Tian army, Great King. The Magi here are dead or running, the Queens and most of the nobles, if they were on Central Island, are dead, too. You are Great King and commander of the Armies of Alta, which are about to close in on the Tian forces. The greater need for you is there, not here."

He'd thought about that, as well, in the time since he and Aket-ten had begun this evacuation. There was no doubt of it in his mind; under the heading of "greatest good," Ari could help to save a few thousand, of which most could save themselves so long as they knew where a clear path was, *or* he could take his place as the ruler of Alta, and save—perhaps—hundreds of thousands.

And, Ari being Ari and very far from stupid, saw that for himself right away. So he just saluted, with no sense of irony or mocking at all, and turned Kashet's head south without another word.

Oset-re was the next back, and he took immediately to working directly across First Ring from where Aketten was. By the time Huras arrived, they had most of First Ring cleared, or at least, as much as it was going to be cleared without help to extricate people who were trapped past bare hands getting them out. Those who hadn't already gotten across the causeway at least knew where the clear path to it was. Aket-ten had gotten the brilliant notion of having the survivors splash paint, or mud, or use anything else that would make a mark on the way, to show where the safe route was. That sped up the evacuation of those behind the first out immeasurably.

The Second Ring had begun to evacuate itself, warned by the collapse of Central Island and the First Ring, and by those escaping across the causeway. Boats were already fleeing, and people streaming across the two floating-raft causeways linking the Second Ring to the Third.

And on the Third Ring—now there was help. The Third Ring was home to the army. There were fewer buildings as such; fewer places for people to get trapped in wreckage. But even more important, the soldiers of Alta were used to helping in the wake of shakes, and now they, under the direction of their officers, were organizing the evacuation as refugees poured over the causeways.

It was to these officers that Kiron now gave a different piece of news.

"The False Kings are dead," he said grimly, "and their foolish or deluded Queens with them. But Alta has a Great Queen and a King; Queen Nofret-te-en, once betrothed of Toreth-aket. She was wedded by the Mouth of the Gods, Kaleth-aket, to Ari-en-anethet, rider of the dragon Kashet; he who was chosen to be Great King by birth, marriage to the Lady Nofret, and the will of the gods. And," he would add with a significant lift of an eyebrow, "He is no friend of the Magi."

Of course, this was news to them, but it was clearly welcome news. It put heart in them, gave impetus to their effort.

But the one thing they asked that he couldn't answer was, "How far are we to evacuate?"

To which he could only answer "Judge by what you would do yourself. How far would *you*?"

Because he wanted to say that the Third Ring was far enough . . . but as another shake hit, and he got up into the air, he saw that half of First Ring was gone, the same sand-and-water geysers were spouting on Second, and buildings there were sinking.

"The shakes are getting worse," said one grizzled Captain of Hundreds grimly, when it was over. "It's not natural. You get a big shake, then you get your smaller after-shakes. You don't get shakes that are bigger with each one that hits! It's all the fault of those cursed Magi!"

Kiron nodded. By now, his half of the wing was back; Aket-ten, Kiron himself, Huras, Oset-re and Pe-atep had divided Third Ring into quarters. Aket-ten, Huras, Oset-re and Pe-atep were working the sections, while Kiron made contact with the officers. Some of those officers had, to his immense relief, sent rescue parties back to Second Ring to try and dig out the trapped.

Though, truth be told, there were fewer of those than he would have thought. The shakes that Altans had been living with since the Magi began using the Eye had knocked down most dubious structures a year or more ago, and living with so many shakes had taught most Altans how to survive them.

But now that the officers and fighters had shaken off their brief paralysis of being without orders or a leader to give those orders, it was looking as though the Jousters were redundant here.

Which meant it was time for the wing to reunite.

As the army moved its rescue and evacuation efforts

to Fourth Ring, and the other four finished their segments of Third, he rounded them up, and signaled them to land. "We're done!" he called, and got nods of agreement from all four.

"Seventh Ring and Ari?" Huras called back, looking much more at ease than he had in—well, months. By this, Kiron deduced he'd found his family intact, and they were already making their way to safer ground.

"Have you—" he began, then hesitated. "Are your families—"

"Mine's in a boat," Huras replied, with satisfaction.

"What there is of my family should be across the causeway to Third Ring by now," Pe-atep told him, and shrugged.

"Our city manor is deserted," Oset-re said. "But it was shut up in an orderly fashion. I assume the family went to the estate in River Horse Nome, and the servants and slaves left behind have gotten out."

"Right. Then Ari needs us. Time to go be the Great King's wing."

"Time to find those so-called advisers, you mean," Aket-ten said grimly, as he signaled Avatre to take off.

True enough, he thought, *but what will we do with them when we find them?*

He did not doubt that they were with the Tian army. The Tian King would be leading his forces, and he would insist on his three closest advisers being with him. No King, whether he be Tian, Altan, or skin-wearing barbarian, left the leading of his army at such a decisive moment to his generals. Such a duty was part of being King, and unless the King was very old, or sick, or had a coregent to wear the War Crown for him, it was expected. Where the King went, the advisers went also.

We aren't Thet priests, to defend ourselves against magic. . . .

Then, of course, there was an entirely separate issue in Ari meeting with the Tian King—the King who had personally given him the Gold of Honor, not once, but several times. Impossible that he would not recognize Ari. What he would do about it was anybody's guess.

And then to find out—if he didn't already know— that Ari was a hitherto-unacknowledged, and possibly unknown nephew. . . .

But that was not Kiron's problem, it was Ari's. Kiron's problem was to get the rest of the wing to wherever Ari was—

Then he realized that would be easier than he thought.

"Aket-ten!" he shouted, as they moved south across the Fifth Canal (which was now dotted with boats). "Ask Re-eth-ke where the others are!"

He suspected that the dragons would have some innate sense of where the rest of their kind might be, especially if they were nestmates, and it seemed he was right. Aket-ten pointed, and they all changed direction in accordance with her guidance, as another shake made the water of the canal slosh in its basin.

So intent was he on assessing the damage to the rings below them that it wasn't until they were crossing the Seventh Ring (wide enough that entire farming estates were set up there) and approaching the eighth and final canal, that he realized he should have known all along where the Tian army would be.

Because the Tian army was just starting across the only "bridge" that could accommodate them all, the so-called "Grand Causeway" of the Eighth Canal. It was huge, wide enough for forty men to march side by side. Of course, it had to be that big, after all, the *Altan* army had to use it to get out of Alta City. It was also the only way for a large force to cross the Eighth Canal without going hundreds of leagues north.

The advisers—and Kiron could see them, in three war chariots behind the King's chariot—knew that this was a potential ambush point, and they knew that the Eye could reach this far. But there was no sign of the Altan army, and the advisers must be certain that on an overcast and rainy day like this one, the Eye could not be used.

There was no need to look for Ari, though. Planted right in the middle of the causeway, just before it connected with the land of the Seventh Ring, were Ari and Kashet. Lined up behind them, Orest and blue Wastet, Menet-ka and indigo Bethlan, Gan and green Khaleph, and Kalen on brown Se-atmen.

The Tians might have expected an ambush. They didn't expect this.

The Tian King, mindful of the fact that the massive number of troops behind him took time to react to anything, had already slowed his chariot to a crawl as they approached Ari. Ari was wearing his blue War Crown rather than a Jousting helmet, and that would keep the Tian King from recognizing him until they got very close, but it couldn't be long now. And just how did Ari intend to stop the Tian army with five Jousters?

This isn't what I'd have done, Kiron thought, as he urged Avatre to more speed; Ari was going to need all of them to back him if he had any hope of pulling off a bluff. *I'd have come in and plucked those advisers off their chariots and dropped them. Then I'd have gone into negotiation. . . .*

But he wasn't the Great King. Ari was. And Ari was the one making the decisions.

Then, some instinct, something caught out of the corner of his eye, or a distant rumble made him turn his gaze briefly back the way they had come. So *he* was the one who saw the thing that was going to render all of Ari's plans null, the ripples in the land, like ocean waves, racing toward Eighth Canal and the causeway. . . .

He shouted in alarm, and pointed back at the onrushing earthshake; the others looked, and stared, dumbfounded. Knowing that Ari couldn't hear him, he shouted at the Jouster anyway. When that wave hit the causeway—

Perhaps Ari couldn't hear him, but Kashet most certainly could sense *something.*

With a startled bark of alarm, and with no warning to his rider, Kashet launched himself into the air, followed shortly thereafter by the other four.

The Tian King and his advisers had just about enough time to register that there was something else wrong, when the shake-wave hit where they were standing.

For hundreds of years, this causeway had stood firm, proof against the worst that man or nature could throw at it. Today, it met something it could not stand firm against.

As Avatre threw up her head, snorting with alarm, the causeway disintegrated in an explosion of churning water, sand spouts, flying stones and brick, and thrashing horses. The last few soldiers just setting foot on the causeway had enough time to fling themselves backward to save themselves. The rest were flung into the water of the Eighth Canal. Whether or not they could swim was irrelevant; very little was going to survive being dropped into the midst of a collapsing causeway.

The Great Tian King and his advisers did not even have time to understand what was happening before they were gone.

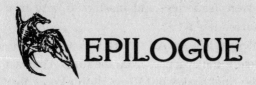# EPILOGUE

ROUGHLY half of the Tian army was left after the causeway collapsed, but most of the senior officers of the army were gone, and the rest were having no luck in convincing the common foot soldiers that the collapse had been anything other than the hand of the gods raised against the Tians.

Ari was in no way discouraging this attitude. When he landed again, wearing the very Tian Blue War Crown, and declaring his lineage, most of the army was perfectly willing to declare for him, and the rest were perfectly willing to keep their mouths shut about their opinions.

Especially after the Altan army that had been lying in ambush closed in behind them. They were trapped between the canal and an overwhelming opposing force; they were leaderless and masterless, and to a man, they surrendered.

With ruthless efficiency, Ari set the Tian army to creating shelters for the evacuees from the rings. That last shake *was* the final shake, but Kiron didn't know that for two days, because he had gotten an idea, and as soon as Ari was firmly in charge, he took the entire wing back to Sanctuary. But not to stay.

The dragons remained only for a good long night's rest, and then came flying back—but this time, carrying double burdens.

Kaleth, in full priestly regalia, was up behind Kiron. Nofret flew on her own dragon, which was just old enough and strong enough to keep up—and she was begowned in mist linen and a small fortune in ancient jewelry, wearing something enough like the Iris Crown of the Great Queens as made no difference. The rest of them carried Tian senior priests, except for Aket-ten, who had the Eldest Winged One.

By this time, it looked as if the inevitable conflict between Tians and Altans was about ready to explode, though the presence of the Eldest Healer and her seniors, and several High Priests from major Altan temples was mitigating things so far as the Altans were concerned.

Kaleth dismounted first; the Tians probably had never seen a living Mouth of the Gods before, but there was no mistaking the aura that hung about him.

He'd had that *look* from the moment that Kiron had come to get him and the Tian priests, but now it was so powerful that even those who were not particularly sensitive to such things were staring at him open-mouthed.

There was also no mistaking the fact that the most senior of all priests of Tia were deferring to him with profound humility.

The crowd cleared a path for them as they marched—with as much grace as middle-aged men and women who have just endured a long and somewhat uncomfortable trip can muster—toward Ari. Meanwhile Nofret landed on her own, putting her dragon down right beside Kashet, but remaining in her saddle.

As they reached Ari, Kiron was halfway expecting some sort of portentous announcement, a "Hail, Great King of Tia and Alta" sort of thing.

Instead, Kaleth paused for a beat or two, then with great deliberation, gave Ari the Bow of Equals, which the others echoed, and which Ari returned.

"We come at your summons, Great King," Kaleth said simply. "How may we serve you?"

There it was; the implied blessing, not only of the gods of Alta, but of Tia as well. There was a stirring throughout the ranks as word of what had happened was passed from man to man.

At that point, Nofret dismounted from her dragon and joined him. He reached out to her, and the two stood side by side, a somewhat foreign sight to the Tians, but a comforting and familiar sight to the Altans.

Ari's reply was equally simple.

"Help us build a kingdom from these two shattered lands," he told them, more than loudly enough to be heard.

"Then, Great King, perhaps we could begin with a double crowning," said the High Priest of Haras, and so, with a lack of pomp and ceremony that was somehow more impressive than all the chants and processions, all the clouds of incense and weighty speeches possible, it was done.

It was at that point that Kiron signaled to the rest of the wing, and with a lifted chin, suggested they take themselves elsewhere. Lord Khumun and Lord Yatiren would be coming in a more conventional fashion along with whatever others of rank wished to appear, and Ari and Nofret had the all the support they needed for right now.

They took themselves to a sand blow from which all the water had drained, and which had absorbed sunlight and was now satisfactorily, by draconic standards, hot. The dragons promptly made themselves wallows, and Kiron looked with longing at a patch of lush grass shaded by date palms nearby.

Gan yawned. "I could sleep for a week!" he exclaimed.

"Me, too," Orest agreed, as Aket-ten and Kiron exchanged a glance and hastily looked away. But Orest—observant, for once—caught it.

"Oh, here," he said gruffly, giving his sister a shove so that she stumbled and ended up in Kiron's arms. "Stop mooning at each other. You thought you'd never see each other again, and now everything has turned out fine! Or—well, fine for us! Act like flesh-and-blood people for a change and *do* something about it!"

Kiron felt himself flushing and grinning at the same time. "I don't know," he said to Aket-ten. "Should we really give him the satisfaction of following his advice?"

"Yes," she said decisively. "It's the first time he's ever given good advice on anything. We'd better take advantage of it while it lasts!"

She put her arms around him, and he held her while the others sauntered pointedly away. This was not going to be easy. In fact, they were going to have a long, hard slog to get to that attractive future Kaleth had promised. Two enemies were being united into a single people, and that alone was going to make for a thousand problems.

But for now, there was a little peace, and someone to savor it with.

"You're right," he said to the pair of merry brown eyes turned up to look into his. "We should. Good advice from your brother is too rare to squander."

"Hmm," she replied, and raised one eyebrow. "Shall we let this lot of sluggards loll about while we go take a flight?"

A flight—a flight where they were not hunting, not scouting, not doing anything but fly, together. As if responding to their very thoughts, Avatre and Re-eth-ke heaved up out of the sand wallow and came trotting over to them, making eager little noises.

"I think," he replied, with his heart already soaring into that free, blue sky as he looked down into those eyes, "that would be perfect."

MERCEDES LACKEY

The Novels of Valdemar

To Order Call: 1-800-788-6262

Mercedes Lackey
& Larry Dixon

The Novels of Valdemar

"Lackey and Dixon always offer a well-told tale"
—*Booklist*

DARIAN'S TALE

THE MAGE WARS

To Order Call: 1-800-788-6262

DAW 26

Kristen Britain

GREEN RIDER

As Karigan G'ladheon, on the run from school, makes her way through the deep forest, a galloping horse plunges out of the brush, its rider impaled by two black arrows. With his dying breath, he tells her he is a Green Rider, one of the king's special messengers. Giving her his green coat with its symbolic brooch of office, he makes Karigan swear to deliver the message he was carrying. Pursued by unknown assassins, following a path only the horse seems to know, Karigan finds herself thrust into in a world of danger and complex magic....   0-88677-858-1

FIRST RIDER'S CALL

With evil forces once again at large in the kingdom and with the messenger service depleted and weakened, can Karigan reach through the walls of time to get help from the First Rider, a woman dead for a millennium?   0-7564-0209-3

To Order Call: 1-800-788-6262

C.S. Friedman

The Coldfire Trilogy

"A feast for those who like their fantasies dark, and as
emotionally heady as a rich red wine." —*Locus*

Centuries after being stranded on the planet
Erna, humans have achieved an uneasy stale-
mate with the fae, a terrifying natural force with
the power to prey upon people s minds. Damien
Vryce, the warrior priest, and Gerald Tarrant, the
undead sorcerer must join together in an uneasy
alliance confront a power that threatens the very
essence of the human spirit, in a battle which
could cost them not only their lives, but the soul
of all mankind.

BLACK SUN RISING	0-88677-527-2
WHEN TRUE NIGHT FALLS	0-88677-615-5
CROWN OF SHADOWS	0-88677-717-8

To Order Call: 1-800-788-6262

DAW 18